"*The City of Shadows: A Romance of Morocco* returns to print Charles Beadle's first novel (originally published in 1911), which vividly portrays the 1908 Battle of Marrakech that led to the defeat of Morocco's Sultan Aziz. The story is embedded in real history that brings the times, place, and politics to life ... These characters and elements will attract readers who may hold little prior familiarity with the politics of Moroccan culture, but who will find plenty of insights and attractions woven into the Moroccan backdrop and events....

Editor Rob Couteau provides numerous footnotes that reference background history. This also is unusual for a novel, but proves perfect as a reference for historical fiction readers interested in the background supporting these events.

Librarians and readers looking for novels of North African history that bring these times alive through characters that make important decisions that affect the world around them will relish the opportunity to see Morocco through the eyes of a man and woman who risk much to achieve their vision of happiness.

The City of Shadows's blend of high adventure, risk-taking, and immersion in Moroccan affairs is cemented by characters whose lives and concerns are realistic and thoroughly engrossing."

– **Diane Donovan, *Midwest Book Review*, February 2026**.

CHARLES BEADLE was a world traveler who was born at sea in 1881. When he was eighteen years old he expatriated from England and spent over a decade exploring South Africa, Rhodesia, Zambia, Uganda, the Congo, Mozambique, Borneo, and Morocco. In his mid-twenties he organized an expedition to Fez and traveled there disguised as a dancing girl to interview the sultan of Morocco. In the 1910s he lived in Montmartre, where he befriended his neighbor Beatrice Hastings, the mistress of Modigliani and translator of Max Jacob. Modigliani later portrayed Beadle in a drawing titled *Le Pèlerin* ("The Pilgrim"), which may have been a reference to Beadle's first banned book, *A Passionate Pilgrimage*. During World War I he traveled to the United States, where he published stories in *Adventure* and in the *International*, a cultural journal edited by Aleister Crowley. He returned to the City of Light in the fall of 1919, where he lived throughout most of the 1920s, eventually moving to the French Riviera.

In 1938 Jack Kahane's Obelisk Press published Beadle's last novel, *Dark Refuge*: an unrecognized modern masterpiece that quickly fell into obscurity. It contains thinly disguised portraits of Modigliani, Max Jacob, Beatrice Hastings, Léopold Zborowski, and various other figures who haunted the Parisian demimonde of this period. Beadle's brazen portrayal of drug fueled pansexual orgies prevented the chronicle from being distributed in the Anglo-Saxon world despite its literary merit and lyrical beauty.

In 1941 Faber and Faber published *Artist Quarter*, a nonfiction work pseudonymously coauthored by Beadle with Douglas Goldring, which is still considered to be the urtext of Modigliani biography.

Although the time and place of his death remained a mystery until 2025, we now know that Beadle spent his final years in Nice, where he died on 27 January 1957.

ROB COUTEAU is a Brooklyn-born author and visual artist. His publications have been praised in *Evergreen Review*, *Publishers Weekly*, *New Art Examiner*, *Midwest Book Review*, and *Witty Partition*. In 1985 he won the North American Essay Award, sponsored by the American Humanist Association. His work has been cited in books such as *Ghetto Images in Twentieth-Century American Literature* by Tyrone Simpson, *Gabriel Garcia Marquez's 'Love in the Time of Cholera'* by Thomas Fahy, *Conversations with Ray Bradbury* edited by Steven Aggelis, and David Cohen's *Forgotten Millions*, a book about the homeless. His interviews include conversations with Pulitzer Prize-winning author Justin Kaplan, *Last Exit to Brooklyn* novelist Hubert Selby, Simon & Schuster editor Michael Korda, LSD discoverer Albert Hofmann, Picasso's model and muse Sylvette David, sci-fi author Ray Bradbury, film star and bibliophile Neil Pearson, and historian Philip Willan, author *Puppetmasters: The Political Use of Terrorism in Italy*. Couteau has appeared as a guest on Bob Barrett's *The Best of Our Knowledge* (WAMC), Len Osanic's *Black Op Radio*, and on Monocle 24 in Europe. In 2023 he published *Intimate Souvenirs*, a memoir featuring an Introduction by Robert Roper, author of *Nabokov in America: On the Road to Lolita* and *Now the Drum of War: Walt Whitman and His Brothers in the Civil War*. Since 2020 he has devoted himself to republishing annotated texts of important but forgotten authors such as Stanley Marks, Charles Beadle, and Francis Carco.

The City of Shadows

A Romance of Morocco

Portrait of Charles Beadle, courtesy of Beadle's great-niece Patricia and her daughter Liz. An inscription on the back identifies it as a Christmas gift from "your loving son." Circa 1899.

The City of Shadows

A Romance of Morocco

Charles Beadle

Edited with Annotations and
an Afterword by Rob Couteau

DOMINANTSTAR

The text provided here is copied from a hardcover edition of *The City of Shadows: A Romance of Morocco*, originally published in 1911 by Everett & Co., Ltd. in London and dedicated to Olive Grimaldi, a fashion artist whose work appeared in numerous periodicals of the time, including *Pall Mall* magazine (which featured Beadle's "A Talk with the New Sultan of Morocco"). In this newly revised edition, British spelling has been Americanized and grammatical errors have been corrected. Textual changes involving anything more complex (such as inserting missing words or phrases) are indicated by brackets. Variant spelling of surnames is retained in the section that reproduces newspaper articles and in memos from the British Foreign Office. Since Moroccan Arabic (Darija) is not standardized in writing, latinization tends to follow practical phonetic rules. Although I've maintained most of Beadle's (largely phonetic) renderings of Arabic and Darija, modernized spellings in Latin transliteration are provided via footnotes.

Special thanks to all those who helped to make this possible, including Khadija Bendahou, John Locke, Liz Marsden, and Geoffrey Pocock.

Cover: Rob Couteau. *Portrait of a Moroccan woman.* 20 September 2016. India ink on Stonehenge Natural paper. 30 x 23 inches (76 x 58 cm). Collection Li Hong Shan, China.

Contents

This newly revised edition of *The City of Shadows*
is dedicated to a modern-day Moroccan Princess,

Khadija Bendahou

Map of Morocco showing regional and international boundaries.

CHAPTER I

"Al-lah — Ak-ba-ah!"[1]

In the brilliant afternoon sunshine, the distant call to prayer floated over the end of the wooden jetty above the laughing ripple of the waters and the murmurous song of the surf, eerie and plaintive.

On the wooden steps lounged half a score of Arab watermen, lazily discussing, in their peculiar patois of Arabic and Spanish, the approach of a rowboat. In the stern sheets[2] sat a passenger, a fair-bearded man, bronzed with the sun of many climes. He gloomily smoked a cigar, staring moodily about him with the despondent abstraction of a disconsolate Hamlet. In front of him lay the old Moorish town climbing from the water edge up the hillside, a jumbled mass of white roofs, patches of blue of the Jewish houses, lesser splashes of green, and the old gray embattled walls wriggling like a snake through the brilliant color scheme. Out in the bay, a gorgeous blue with the foaming white surf breaking lazily on the long strip of sand curving out in the haze of distant hills, lay French torpedo craft, cruisers and an ancient wooden Spanish frigate, all lifting easily to the gentle swell running through the straits. And closer in shore was anchored the red-and-black funnelled *Gibel Musa* in which Paul Towers had traveled from Gibraltar; about her a noisy throng of rowing boats and lighters.

---

[1] Allahu Akbar: "God is the greatest." In the original text, Beadle renders this (phonetically) as "Al-lah — Ak-ba-ah."
[2] Stern sheets: the space in the stern of an open boat not occupied by the seats extending athwart a boat.

As the cry of the Muedhin[3] broke the lazy murmur, Towers glanced up with a faint suggestion of welcome recognition of an old friend. The boat glided to the jetty, and amid an excited altercation he mounted the steps, irritably pushing aside the clamorous offers of assistance. A gray-hooded figure, that had remained placidly leaning upon the rail, stepped forward.

"You come along me, Mister. I take you 'otel Savoy?"

Towers stared contemptuously at the native tout.

"You come along me, ole chap," urged the other confidentially. "Me best man. Me show you plenty dancing girl, ole chap."

"Well — all right. See after these trunks of mine. Yes, in that boat."

"Yessir, orlright. You go long Custom House. Me see you, orlright."

Towers stood for a moment smoking gloomily, and flinging the half-smoked cigar away with a feverish action, sauntered slowly along the wooden jetty, between trolley rails towards the whitewashed arches and sheds of the Moorish Custom House.

A trolley of luggage rattling along the rail behind disturbed him from a lazy view of the scene. Upon the top of the trolley, with the air of a potentate enthroned in his state carriage, rode the weedy bearded guide, his red Fez cap jauntily on one side, the hood of his blue djellaba[4] hanging carelessly over a shoulder.

"You ride, ole chap," he suggested, affably waving a cigarette. "These dawgs push us — whaat?"

The queer accent, suggestive of a caricature of a Balliol affectation,[5] sounded weirdly uncanny.

---

[3] Muedhin: an older or variant spelling of *Mu'adhdhin*, the caller to prayer in Islam. Also spelled *muezzin* in modern English.

[4] Djellaba: jallāba. A long loose-fitting robe with a pointed hood.

[5] A "Balliol affectation" refers to the culture of Balliol College at Oxford. A mannerism that is not genuine but is intended to impress others, especially

"Look here," observed Towers with annoyance. "A little bit less of that 'ole chap,' d'you understand?"

"Orlright; you my frien', ole chap!" returned the other imperturbably. "You and me get along orlright, whaat?"

"What's your name?" inquired Towers.

"Name? Me 'Rabbit,' ole chap."

"Rabbit? Don't play the fool — "

"Ana Mohammed Rabat ben Bussulham,"[6] with great dignity; then relaxing to his ordinary manner, "but me Rabbit, ole chap. All my friends call me Rabbit. Rabbit known Rock; Rabbit known Algeciras;[7] Rabbit known — "

"Where's the Customs man, in there?"

Towers advanced under a horseshoe arch towards a venerable bespectacled Moor clad in filmy white, who sat cross-legged before a glaring yellow French desk. Said he:

---

a pretentious, artificial behavior that attempts to reflect the elite intellectual image of the college.

[6] "Ana": "I am." Thus, "I am Mohammed Rabat ben Bussulham." Rabat, aka "Rabbit," was an actual local guide who was probably known to Beadle. "A reliable guide was essential for any trip inland. The best one in Tangiers was known simply as 'Rabbit,' because of the peculiar shape of his ears and nose." Douglas Porch, *The Conquest of Morocco: A History* (New York: Farrar, Straus and Giroux, 2024), e-book edition, p. 34. Rabat / Rabbit is also prominently featured in two of Beadle's adventure stories, "Rabbit: Philosopher," a "novelette" published in the 18 January 1919 issue of *Adventure*; and "Through Rabat's Eyes," a three-part serial featured in *Argosy*, 2-16 August 1919. For more on Rabat see my Afterword, below.

[7] A reference to the Algeciras Convention: an agreement reached in 1906 that attempted to resolve the First Moroccan Crisis between France and Germany, which opened Morocco to international trade. Beadle held a dim view of the agreement, regarding it as "a contradictory act providing for the development of Morocco in one clause and annulling any effect in the next." See Charles Beadle, "What Has Happened to Muley Hafid," *The Sphere*, 3 July 1909, p. 14. Reproduced in full in this edition, below.

"Salkhair, ya Sidi!"[8]

The Moor peered at him gravely over the top of his spectacles, and responded:

"Salkhair!"

"La bas alik?"[9] queried Towers, in the orthodox manner.

"La bas! Keef entsa?"[10]

After the lengthy formal exchange of greeting Towers gave the necessary declaration and explanations in fluent Arabic. He was interrupted by a gasp of astonishment from behind, where stood the estimable Rabbit, full of righteous indignation.

"You — you spik my Arabie?"[11] he gasped, as if Towers had stolen something of his very own.

"You spik — Oh!" His feelings overcame his linguistic capabilities, for he saw so much baksheesh[12] and other perquisites fading before his eyes.

Towers continued the argument with the Moorish official, and by aid of judicious tipping, evaded the nuisance of having his boxes overhauled, after which he and his guide made their way up the steep, slippery cobbled street, the luggage upon donkeys behind them.

Rabbit, fearful no doubt of making another faux pas, only once referred to the subject, lavishing all his native eloquence upon the donkeys and their attendants. Said he reproachfully:

"Why you not tell me spik my Arabie? And you my friend!" sorrowfully.

Upon arrival at the hotel, Rabbit, having disgustedly watched his employer pay the donkeymen their proper money, stalked

---

[8] Salkhair, ya Sidi!: "Good afternoon, sir." More properly rendered as "Masalkhair, ya Sidi!" (Or, informally, as "Msal'khair, ya Sidi!")

[9] La bas alik: "How are you?"

[10] La bas! Keef entsa: "Good! How are you?"

[11] You spik my Arabie: You speak my Arabic.

[12] Baksheesh: from Persian bakhshīsh, "gift, tip, present."

to the room and commenced to unpack the trunks. Towers pitched him half-a-dollar Spanish, and told him to go.

Rabbit gazed at the coin, grimaced, and said:

"You no want me, ole chap? Me show — "

"Go!" said Towers in Arabic.

"Well," expostulated the other, "what you goin' to do? You get drunk, eh? Me know one Scotchman, he come here often, he get drunk — oh, *very* drunk — and give me plenty dollar. That Scotchman *dear* frien' o' mine! You no get drunk?" regretfully.

"No, confound you!"

"Well," — in pained surprise — "What you come here for?"

"Does no one come here for anything else?" inquired Towers.

"You know Ro'ley, from Rock? Lefften'nt Ro'ley you know?" persuasively. "He *dear* frien' o' mine. He come here get drunk — oh, very drunk — offen! and cons'quently — conskquent — "

"Look here, you ugly devil," said Towers, half smiling. "If you libel men like that, you'll get into trouble. Clear' out!"

"You no want me for servant? I say, ole chap, me show you da — "

"Get out!" exclaimed Towers, angry with the man as the cause, and with himself for having permitted the ghost of a smile. Seizing him by the folds of the djellaba, he propelled him roughly through the doorway.

"You liver dambad, ole chap!" came the conciliatory voice from the other side of the door.

"Confound the brute," muttered Towers, with a scowl.

He sat down in a chair, staring out across the bay, thinking over the past; the future was on the knees of the gods.

Paul Towers was the son of General Towers, of Indian fame, and had been educated to follow in his father's footsteps. He had duly received a commission, and had seen some seven years' service abroad. The father had been of an imperious temperament, and the only son had inherited a full share intensified perhaps by being the child of his mother, a haughty, wayward scion of an illustrious Irish house. The individuality and high spirit of the youngster had brought him endless trouble in the Service, with the result that he had quarreled hopelessly with superior officers. At length the powers that be had intimated that if Captain Towers were to send in his papers, they would not be refused; so he came home and, as it happened, in time to attend his father's funeral. For a while he wandered aimlessly along social paths, endeavoring to bury his disappointments, and at length found consolation by falling in love. Irene Trevelyan was the daughter of a naval family with a distinguished record, and she, in her pride, refused to marry a man who had done nothing. This answer, strangely enough, intensified his love and respect for her, and moreover awakened the slumbering fires of ambition. Within a month he had found an opportunity. A Head of Department, upon having his digestive doze disturbed to receive the enthusiastic young man, remembered his previous career and bethought himself of a post that demanded a keen, intelligent and daring man to fill it. The great man had in the past known and appreciated Paul's character, and with a vague idea of making amends, gave him the refusal. The work was of a political nature requiring great tact, secrecy, and in the face of almost overwhelming odds, with the proviso that if he failed or was discovered, the Government would, for obvious reasons, be compelled to deny all knowledge of him; but on the other hand, were his mission successful, then honor and great awards awaited him. Paul accepted without hesitation. The woman of his choice congratulated him, consented to a private engagement, and swore she would wait forever. Paul departed in high spirits. Months afterwards in the desert his caravan was attacked and massacred and himself made a prisoner. For two years he suffered privation, which nearly killed him, but at length escaped to return with his mission accomplished and to find the woman married to another. Paul had been madly infatuated with her, and during his imprisonment amongst the Arabs he had, with the natural enthusiasm of a young lover, clothed her in all the ideal virtues that occurred to him; placed her upon a lofty pedestal until she became more than human — a goddess, whom he worshipped.

The idol was broken; the joy of life and success turned to bitter ashes.[13] He met her one night at dinner. She congratulated him upon his return from the grave, chattered on conventional topics, and turned to her partner. Paul had never been so brilliant as he was that evening; by the next he left by the Continental Express, throwing all the future to the four winds of Heaven. He neither knew nor cared what became of him, he only felt that if he stayed in England he would go mad or make a fool of himself. He spent a wild week in Paris[14] trying to forget, and traveled on by stages to Spain intending to catch an eastward bound boat from Gibraltar to — anywhere. Upon arrival he found that there was no boat due for four days, chafed at the delay, and came across the Straits to kill time.

As he sat in the window brooding over the past he idly wondered what life held for him. He refused to attempt any solution or to make any decision, telling himself, savagely, that he was in the hands of Fate with a vague idea that he was in some way revenging himself upon the woman, wholly oblivious to the childish principle of cutting one's nose to spite one's face. Paul was gradually drifting into the danger of the jilted love becoming an obsession; already he felt the desire to

---

[13] The relationship between the unobtainable *ideal* and the frangible *idol* is explored in several of Beadle's works of fiction, including the novels *A Passionate Pilgrimage* (1915) and *Witch-Doctors* (1922). The idol also prominently appears in his adventure stories "The Idol of 'It'" (1918) and "The Breaker of Idols" (1919). Beadle's last (and greatest) novel, *Dark Refuge* (1938), features a hashish idol that serves as a major device in the tale. The story ends with the phrase: "and I was blinking at the middle eye of the alabaster idol, Ganesha, in the flickering light of the guttering candle stub."

[14] Possibly a reference to Beadle's first trip to Paris.

sit still and brood, becoming irritable if anyone or any circumstance detained him from this morbid pastime.

At length he rose reluctantly, bathed, and went down to dinner.

He selected a small table in order to be by his beloved self. As dinner progressed he idly took stock of his neighbors. At one large table were a party of obvious American tourists. At another a group of three: a tall, nearly bald, middle-aged, dissipated-looking man with a weak mouth; the center man fair-haired, with predatory nose and chin; the other a small, dark tubby little man. The center man drew Paul's scrutiny. He observed the long, hatchet face, small closely set eyes, yellow moustache, with more than ordinary interest, and wondered who and what the fellow might be. Several other diners — the place was nearly empty — failed to amuse him; his eyes involuntarily returned to hatchet-face, as he mentally nicknamed him.

At length he finished the ill-cooked dinner, called for coffee and cigarettes to the Moorish waiter, pranked[15] in a weird compound of Turkish and European uniform, and sauntered out on to the plaza. For a while he felt content to inhale cigarettes, sip coffee and gaze at the starlit sea. The waiter's garb vaguely suggested Cairo to his mind and he mentally decided to return to Gibraltar in time to catch the mail boat for Alexandria.

"Goo' evenin', ole chap!"

Paul started irritably. A big pair of yellow boots and cloth gaiters below the baggy Turkish trousers, tarboosh[16] on one side, and djellaba all askew, showing European coat underneath, together with the sharp black eyes set in a pasty

---

[15] Pranked: to dress or to adorn gaily or showily.
[16] Tarboosh: ṭarbūsh. A flat-topped red felt hat with a tassel, traditionally worn in Morocco and the Ottoman world, sometimes referred to as a *fez*.

brown face fringed with pathetic whiskers, huge ears, and a gash for a mouth formed the apotheosis of the ludicrous.

"What d'you want? Go away! I don't want you."

The man exhaled smoke and grinned extensively.

"No, ole chap, me want you."

There was an air of finality in the statement.

"Confound you, you're a most extraordinary brute!" said Paul surveying him. "You look like nothing on earth — yes, you do, though; the Prophet of the Utterly Absurd!"

"Prophet! prophet!" exclaimed the other, scratching his shaven skull. "Ah! Mahommed?"

"No! you don't look like Mahommed — at least, I don't suppose so, but what're you doing here?"

"Me? Me come take you along dan — "

"I'm not coming along."

"What you goin' do?" with huge expostulatory hands. "Get drunk?"

"Confound you, you seem obsessed with that idea. Why don't you look after the tourists here?"

"Me not want tourist — me want my frien' — you! Me show you real Moorish dancing lady — not Jewish — real Moorish — only dance me an' my frien's. You come along, ole chap!"

"No, I'm going for a walk."

"Orlright, ole chap," very cheerfully; "me come walk, too!"

"Oh, go away and leave me in peace."

"No! you come along me."

"Be quiet; here go away and smoke."

"Tanks," accepting proffered cigar with alacrity. "Awfly good o' you, ole chap!"

Paul completely failed to repress a broad smile.

"Where on earth did you get that expression?"

"Me learn Englees in school."

"You didn't learn that in school?"

"Wha-at? Awfly good o' you, ole chap? My frien' Jack — Lefften'nt Ro'ley, y'know — he always say that. Now, you come along me, ole chap."

"You're an extraordinary brute" observed Paul again, and then relapsed into gloom as if suddenly remembering that laughter was a crime. As a matter of fact, Rabbit seemed designed by a kindly Fate to give Paul the only tonic he really needed, laughter and forgetfulness.

"Come on, ole chap," remarked the unconscious disciple of Billiken,[17] puffing with gusto at the cigar "You come along."

Paul at length, telling himself that he could not get rid of the man short of physical violence, arose, and together the oddly assorted pair sauntered off into the night, Rabbit keeping up a fire of quaintly expressed information.

"Well," observed Paul, as they crossed the crowded Soko Chiko[18] with cafés upon all sides; "I'm going to have a drink," and sat himself at a small table under an awning.

Rather to his annoyance his companion drew up a chair also remarking affably:

"Whaat you drink, ole chap? Whiskey soda, whaat?"

For a moment Paul hesitated, glancing about the café, which he observed was crowded with Europeans, Moors and negroes.

Whilst the waiter went to fetch the drinks he caught sight of hatchet-face at an adjacent table.

"Who is that?" he asked the loquacious Rabbit.

"That? That master of liddle dawg."

"Master of *what?*"

"That his name," Rabbit repeated it in Arabic. "All people call him that because he always have liddle dawg. See?"

---

[17] Billiken: A charm doll, patented in 1908 and sold to the Billiken Company of Chicago.

[18] Soko Chiko: Soko Chico, a historic marketplace in Tangier.

Paul looked again and saw upon a chair alongside the man a small mongrel dog, nearer akin to a dachshund than any known breed.

"Yes, ole chap," went on Rabbit, "he always have liddle dawg. He ride horse, mule, camel — always liddle dawg in front in liddle house."

"What nationality is he? English?"

"English? He speak Spanish. Spanish man he say Spanish man; French man, he say French man; German man, he say German man; English man, he say he English man; me not know."

"What an extraordinary brute! What does he do?"

"Do?" Rabbit had a trick of invariably repeating the last word of a sentence. "Do? He do every people."

"What on earth do you mean?" queried Paul laughing without restraint.

"Mean? Why, ole chap, he — he do — you know 'do'? — make plenty dollar from every people."

"Oh, I see, a bad man, eh?"

"Plenty bad — *ibn Iblees!*"[19]

Paul laughed.

"Son of the devil is he — very interesting!"

"Now you come see dancing girl, ole chap," commanded Rabbit, having finished his whiskey soda.

"No; I don't want to see dancing girls. I know; they're all the same. I've seen too many in Cairo."

"Cairo? Where Cairo?"

"El Masr."[20]

"Ah! el Masr — you know el Masr — good, eh? But you come now. This girl awfly good."

---

[19] Ibn Iblees: literally, "son of Satan."
[20] El Masr: al-Misr or Egypt, in Arabic.

Paul assented reluctantly, and together they made their way through a labyrinth of narrow pitch-dark evil-smelling streets up the hill to the inner wall encircling the Moorish quarter of the town. Rabbit, still puffing away at his cigar, followed the outside of the wall, diving through black arches and along between very high walls, the glittering stars showing above as from the bottom of a well. At length he halted before an iron-studded door flush with the wall and hammered with his stick. After a lengthy pause a muffled voice spoke on the inside, Rabbit replied, and they were admitted into a narrow, dark passage.

As Paul stumbled along after Rabbit he heard the familiar wail of oriental instruments. Passing between dirty curtains hung in an arch, Paul found himself in a fair-sized room, crowded with Moors in white and blue robes; Berbers in gray and brown robes, festooned with tiny gaudy rosettes, camel-hair rope twisted in place of a turban, long black locks of hair protruding through or behind; all seated on stools or chairs at dirty little tables, drinking coffee or sweet mint tea out of glasses. At the far end upon a rough platform squatted three young girls; and in one corner huddled the band composed mainly of Spanish violins, played after the manner of a 'cello, and a zither. The musicians, two filthy Jews in greasy black robes, one young, the other old with rheumy eyes, two hideous hawk-nosed fleshy Jewesses and a rouged emaciated boy, were at the moment resting and drinking at the expense of some patron. The flaring American lamp swinging overhead cast a yellow glare upon the dancers, mere children, clad in tattered Moorish finery of diaphanous texture.

The reek of the fetid atmosphere and the sordidness of the environment were not new to Paul, who reprimanded Rabbit sharply for bringing him so far to see such a poor show; but the guide only grinned, maintaining that Zolika,[21] the Moorish belle in the center, was "awf'ly good." Paul ordered coffee, intending to pay and leave.

As they waited the band commenced with a discordant crash. Zolika, the youngest and only dancer with any claim to good looks, rose wearily and stepping to the middle of the stage, commenced the rhythmic sway and posture of the customary dance. But presently the violins changed the meter to a soft languorous wail and Zolika for the first time showed some interest in her work. Swaying from side to side she gestured languidly with her arms to the measure; then slowly, almost imperceptibly, the music increased in rapidity, working up in a mild crescendo and breaking suddenly as the dancer posed to allow a shuddering quiver to run down her body. Again and again the music crept softly up to pause for the quivering girl. Presently the time and key changed; a new note of sensual passion. Faster and faster flew the notes and more rapid grew the movements of the girl, her eyes growing brighter as the spirit of the wild sensuous sounds entered into her. Her posturing became more and more suggestive, abandoned. She seemed possessed by the spirit of unholy passion. Her excitement was caught by the perspiring, reeking orchestra who sawed at their instruments in a frenzy. The audience, forgetting to chatter, gazed spellbound, the excitement mounting the blood in their swarthy faces and bringing out all the carnal desire in their eyes. Even Paul, the placid Englishman, was influenced by the hypnotic suggestion and felt the blood stir fiercely through his veins.

Without warning, just as it seemed as if the frenzied girl would break a blood vessel, the music ceased with dramatic suddenness; the dancer collapsed upon the stage panting and

---

[21] Zolika: More commonly spelled "Zulekha."

sobbing, the audience gasped with relief, and the next instant burst into a storm of applause.

For the moment Paul had been dragged back to the primeval man, but a wave of civilized insularity surged back over him creating a momentary feeling of shame — really because others had shared the sight. The next instant worldwide experience and commonsense restored the normal equilibrium.

Yet, as the girl, lightly springing from the stage, tripped towards him and, dropping on her knees, extended her forehead, he felt a touch of self-consciousness. Naturally all eyes were turned upon him as with slightly heightened color he drew a half-sovereign from his vest pocket and placed it on the smooth dusky forehead, adding a word of praise in Arabic.

"Barakolofik! Barakolofik!"[22] she exclaimed delightedly as she flew back to her place.

"Awfly good — awfly good girl, whaat?" announced Rabbit condescendingly.

"Yes, quite above the ordinary," admitted Paul, his eye wandering round the room. "Hullo, there's Sid-el-keleeb![23] Wonder when he came in?"

"Came in? Him come in when girl dance — everyone very busy, whaat?"

The master of the little dog to whom they referred was sitting on the opposite side of the café alone, with the inevitable dog in his lap.

The orchestra was resting as Paul rose to leave, but a quick movement behind and an exclamation from Rabbit caused him to wheel about. A tall, hawk-nosed mountaineer, big black locks of hair peeping from under his hood giving a gypsy semblance, was standing up pointing and gesticulating towards the only other European — the man with the little dog. He spoke

---

[22] Barakolofik: Barak Allāh fīk. Literally, "May God's blessing be upon you."
[23] Sid-el-keleeb: Sīd al-Kalb, lord or master of the dog.

excitedly in the Shluh tongue,[24] which neither Paul nor Rabbit understood.

Suddenly he sprang forward whipping a long dagger from underneath his homespun robes. As quick as thought Paul picked up a wooden stool, hurled it and, striking the man full on the near shoulder, knocked the weapon flying. In an instant the room was in uproar, men shouted, women squealed. The dog yelped dismally as his master roughly bundled him behind, picking up a table with which to defend himself. Paul, with a bound, oversetting chairs and tables, ranged himself beside him. For a moment the Berber and his tribal friends jabbered together excitedly amid the babel of the rest of the room, shouting to each other and at the Europeans.

The affray was brought to a crisis by a united attack from the friends of the injured man, with drawn daggers. Paul, who saw the rush coming, flung a light stool at the hanging lamp, and picking up another table club fashion, shouted to the other to fight their way to the door. The lamp had fallen with a crash amid an increased uproar, flared up for a moment on the ground, and was fortunately trodden out by the mob. Paul and his fellow hit out right and left, quickly clearing a ring as the light was extinguished. They commenced to move, shoulder to shoulder, towards the door, still striking blindly in the darkness. Shouts, yells, guttural curses rose from the mass, all struggling to escape through the narrow passage. Paul heard his companion cry:

"Ach, mein lieber, mein lieber! Blut mit Eisen!"[25] — and turn back, groping and calling to his dog in the darkness.

---

[24] The Shluh tongue: a Berber language of the Shluh people of southern Morocco.
[25] Ach, mein lieber, mein lieber! Blut mit Eisen: "Oh, my dear, my dear! Blood with iron!"

Paul halted a moment, feeling inclined to curse the fool and his dog as at any moment they might get a knife between their ribs. He felt a hand touch his arm; he raised the table to strike. A woman's voice cried in Arabic:

"Aji[26] — come, follow me! They will kill thee."

He shouted in English to the other man who had, judging by the sounds, found his beloved animal.

The girl reached for Paul's hand and commenced to lead him; he grabbed the other man's arm. Together they stumbled through the darkness. He felt her clambering on to the platform and presently they passed through a small door. He suddenly remembered Rabbit and paused on the threshold to shout for him.

"Skut![27] be quiet," the girl cried, and thinking that Rabbit would be quite capable of taking care of himself, he followed, to emerge into a starlit courtyard. The slim childish figure of Zolika looked like a wraith in the dim light as he paused to thank her. He wanted her to accept reward for her prompt services, but she vehemently refused; and Paul, knowing the Arab character, did not insist. The man, a spare small figure, over whom the trouble had commenced, had stood apart engaged in soothing the dog, which apparently he placed above everybody.

He turned abruptly as Paul ceased speaking; said he, with an elaborate bow, still hugging the dog:

"Permit me, sir, to tender my sincere thanks for your timely aid. You saved my life and I thank you for it."

Paul was puzzled. He remembered the exclamation in German, and yet the speech, although rather formal and precise, was in perfect English without trace of accent.

---

[26] Aji: "Come."

[27] Skut: correctly translated here as "be quiet" (also, "shut up").

"Not at all," he replied; "I only did what anybody would have done. Whom have I — ?"

"de Bouche — Baron de Bouche."[28]

"Thanks, my name's Towers — Paul Towers. Er — quite romantic introduction, isn't it? This little girl's done far more than I. Listen! You can hear the row going on still."

He became conscious of a pair of large luminous eyes intently watching him in the starlight. He turned to her:

"Come little one, if thou wilt not take from me, mayhap thy sisters — "

She shook her head impatiently.

"They lie in yonder room," she said contemptuously.

"Well," said Paul, feeling embarrassed under the battery of her eyes. "We will leave — "

"Nay; I am my lord's slave!"

She spoke passionately, clinging to him. The Baron laughed.

"Nay, little one, that is not to be," replied Paul.

"Well, if you won't, I will," said the Baron with a laugh, and ceasing to caress his pet he advanced towards Zolika. Paul frowned with annoyance, he scarce knew why. It was nothing to him; she was only an ordinary dancing girl. But Zolika settled the matter by eluding the amorous Baron, and disappearing like a frail ghost into the house.

The sounds of excited voices floated from the street.

"Hullo, ole chap; you orlright, whaat?"

"Where the dickens have you been?" queried Paul, wheeling on the placid Rabbit.

"Been? Me follow you when light distinguished."

"Extinguished, you solemn ass! But you couldn't see us in the dark?"

"Dark? No, but me know him door. Him awfly good, eh, whaat?"

---

28 Bouche = mouth, in French.

"Him? Ashkoon?"[29]

"Zolika, him dancing girl."

"Oh! well, how're we going to get out of this hole? D'you know this place, Baron?"

"Only the usual entrance," replied the Baron, fondling the dog. "This is not my usual pastime," he added with a chuckle.

"No, I suppose not," said Paul smiling, "but Rabbit — "

"Orlright, ole chap, you follow Rabbit."

They followed his lead through the house and emerged at the back; in front stretched a clear open common.

"By the way, Baron," said Paul tentatively, as they made their way back to the hotel; "if it's not a rude question, what upset our friend from the Gharb (North)?"[30]

The Baron chuckled sardonically. "Need you ask? Inquire of M'sieur Dumas père!"[31]

And Paul scowled at the stars, remembering.

The combination of circumstances which consisted of Rabbit, the dancing girl and the fracas lifted Paul away from himself and his morbid brooding for the first time since the woman in whose hand he had rashly chosen to place his happiness had jilted him. The excitement of the evening induced sleep to place her gentle fingers upon his eyelids almost as soon as he stretched himself on the bed. But he awoke in the still early hours of the morning to hear the mournful bray of a donkey confiding his woes to the stars echoed and answered by others through the stillness of the city. There seemed an epidemic of asinine trouble in the air, and Paul giving up the idea of further sleep, moved out on to the balcony. A newly risen moon bathed the city in soft mellow light, white roofs and walls appearing

---

[29] Ashkoon: 'Ashkūn. Who is this?

[30] Actually, *gharb* means "west."

[31] M'sieur Dumas père: a reference to Alexandre Dumas, the French novelist, playwright, and author of *The Count of Monte Cristo*.

filmy and ghostlike against the dense shadows of streets and angles. Again the sobbing lamentation of an ass broke the perfect stillness and witchery of the languorous glamour.

Paul's thoughts reviewed the events of the previous evening. The eccentric Rabbit amused him. At one time he had possessed and cultivated the ludicrous side of things, but he had not reached that stage when a man can even take a jilted love affair as a humorous subject. Paul had accepted that too seriously, and since, all the laughter had been stifled. It was still there, although he told himself that he could never smile again. Until the previous evening, hardly a glimmer of a smile had softened his features. But Rabbit was really too absurd. Paul smiled at the stars as he thought of him. That was a distinct gain. Paul was beginning to show signs of convalescence, although he sternly denied it to himself.

The wild, barbaric grace of the dance girl had forced his admiration for the beauty of natural art; but Zolika did not enter into his scheme of things as an individual at all; merely as the concrete instrument of the abstract poetry of passion; hence he refrained from any cynicism regarding her. Since the great event he had met all women with distrust and bitter cynicism, illogically, but so naturally, condemning every woman on the altar of one disappointment. It was childish, but very human; it is only in matters that do not really matter that one can have any hope of approaching logical reason.

The Baron de Bouche interested him immensely. Here was a personality, a character. Paul tried to determine the man's nationality, and decided that he must be a German. Paul felt strongly attracted towards the Baron, although he intuitively sensed that the man was utterly unscrupulous. Rabbit's crude condemnation as a man who would "'do' every people" was probably right. Then a vague feeling of prescience disturbed Paul; that uncanny sense that something was going to happen.

Perhaps it was an answer from Fate to his constantly reiterated statement regarding the future; "it is on the knees of the gods."

As he gazed out into the night, he shivered involuntarily. The next instant a new sound broke the silence: a prolonged musical cry, eerie in its perfect simplicity, rising to a higher note, and quavering away in plaintive cadence:

"Al-lah — Ak-ba-ah!"

A Mueddhin from the mosque tower calling the faithful to prayer. Again the cry floated over the sleeping city, losing itself in the heights. Paul had heard the cry many thousands of times from the gilded minarets of Cairo, and from a humble goat-skin tent in the illimitable desert, but always it seemed to vibrate through him with that eerie effect.

"Al-lah — Ak-ba-ah!"

God is great. Paul repeated the phrase in thought. God, Nature, the Creator, that Great Architect of the Universe was great. How wonderful was everything! He looked down at the murmuring sea, up at the brilliant heavens and at himself; then he laughed. How seriously he had taken himself and his puny affairs! The very universe had seemed upheaved to his restricted view, life had not been worth living, all mankind was evil; and why? Because he had been slighted by another mortal as insignificant as himself; he, the child, wished to kick the world to pieces because he could not have the toy he had set his heart upon!

"Al-lah — Ak-ba-ah!"

Paul laughed., threw back his head and laughed.

"What a fool I am!" he exclaimed aloud to the moon. "I'm going to bed."

And as Paul turned from the window the first pale flush of dawn appeared across the arc of the heavens bidding Hecate grow faint with rapturous welcome of another day.

"Al-lah — Ak-ba-ah!"

CHAPTER II

Paul, after a dip in open sea, sat down to breakfast feeling a new man. The gloomy, careworn look had left his eyes; he felt again the wonderful joie de vivre, the natural right of a healthy man.

With the second egg the Baron walked in and sat himself at Paul's table. Later, Paul casually inquired who the Baron's companions were.

"The tall, bald-headed one," said the Baron, "is Prince Ferdinand — of the Guadella family; and the fat man — Marquis de Ferreira; the first, as you will know, claims a neighboring throne, and the other is rightful heir to a Principality. Both very decent chaps indeed. Er — if you permit the question — are you a soldier?"

"Well, yes; that is, I have been in the Service."

"Ah! I thought I was not mistaken. You have, presumably, come here for your health?"

The Baron looked up under his eyebrows with a significant twinkle.

Paul laughed. "Well, er — yes, I suppose so."

"Ah! So *many* people come here for their health, do they not?"

"Well, I really don't know. I haven't been here before."

"No?"

There was open disbelief in the query.

"No; and, moreover, I'm leaving tomorrow for Cairo."

"Ah! You know Cairo well?"

"Oh, yes; and Egypt."

"Ah! Have you been much in the interior?"

"Yes," said Paul smiling; "rather more than I wished — at the time."

"Ah, yes; you were a prisoner amongst the tribes, were you not?"

"Eh?" exclaimed Paul, raising his eyebrows. "Pardon me, but may I ask how you knew?"

"Oh, certainly; I recognized your name. You see I'm greatly interested in all Arabian questions. I am very glad to have met you — very glad indeed."

For a moment Paul had been startled; but a moment's reflection told him that the Baron could not have failed to have heard of the incident from bazaar chatter in any part of Egypt at the time; and .anyhow it did not matter, the mission was accomplished.

For a while they ate in silence, until the Baron, pushing away his plate, drew forth a cigarette.

"No objection? Thanks! I suppose," he said between puffs, lolling back on two legs of the chair; "I suppose — you're quite free now?"

"I'm afraid I don't follow you," said Paul guardedly.

"Well — I'll speak openly. Cigarette? — I have a scheme on just now in which I require a man of your stamp, and if you are not bound to anything else — well, you won't go to Cairo. This will, I know, appeal to you. Finished? Well come out into the lounge — there's no one there and we can talk freely."

Now, thought Paul, as they strolled out, the "Something" is going to happen.

"I have been resident in this country for some years," resumed the Baron, as soon as they were comfortably seated; "and having studied the political and commercial state I have developed this scheme, and, moreover, have set such in motion, which will, without a shadow of doubt, place me in the position of an uncrowned king of an enormous territory and over five millions of people."

He paused, fixing Paul with steady eyes. Paul nodded.

"What it is I will explain later. You know the present political position here?"

"Well, not exactly," said Paul, frowning at the touch of the past. "You see I haven't paid much attention to — to anything just lately except — er — private affairs. I know that, as usual, there's revolutionary trouble of some sort going on — "

"Exactly."

"— and — that's about all."

"Good. Now the present Sultan, Abd-el-Rahman,[32] has got into the French toils, he's hopelessly in debt to them; the masses accuse him of having deserted the Faith and have revolted, as you know. The half-brother, Abd-el-Kader, has raised his standard in the south, backed by El Hammo,[33] the great Berber chief. As you probably know, there are the two great factions: Moors, the descendants of the Arabian conquerors, and the Berbers, the aborigines of the country. The latter are the fighting power, the former the religiopolitical power. El Hammo, by reason of his Berber origin, is debarred any chance of claiming the throne, so in default he supports El Kader, practically his nominee. El Hammo is enormously wealthy whereas El Kader has nothing. El Kader is now about to leave Marrakech but he has only a small following at present, from lack of funds; the support of the people merely means sufficient hard cash. El Hammo is upon his way to join him with money. But — they have practically no arms or ammunition, whereas the other man has an army of sorts and arms. Moreover, any military

---

[32] In 1908 "the present Sultan" was actually Sultan Abd al-Aziz (1878 – 1943), not the forenamed Abd-el-Rahman. On 19 August 1908, during the Battle of Marrakesh, Aziz will be defeated by his brother, the Pretender Sultan, Moulay Abd al-Hafid (c. 1875/80 – 1937), all of which is dramatized in *The City of Shadows*. The triumphant Sultan, Moulay Hafid, is represented in the novel as "Abd-el-Kader." Perhaps Beadle was forced to change their names in order to avoid legal problems and threats to his life, should he ever decide to return to Morocco.

[33] "El Hammo, the great Berber chief": Si Mohammed ben Hammou (aka Tibibit; d. 1886), qaid of Telouet. Father of Thami el Glaoui (1879 – 1956), the wealthy and corrupt Pasha of Marrakesh (1909 – 1911; 1912 – 1956), whose cooperation with the French led the common people to regard him as a traitor.

equipment that he lacks will be supplied by the French. It is to their interest to keep him on the throne — under their control — and to crush the new Pretender."

Paul nodded. "And you intend to supply the necessary arms?" he suggested.

"Exactly. More, in fact; but before I reveal the whole plot I want your decision."

"Whether I will come in with you?"

"Exactly."

"On what terms?"

The Baron laughed. "The scheme is so vast. How can I tell at this stage? My wish for you is because you speak the language, you are accustomed to the tribes and you understand military affairs. But I — I am also a soldier; I have held commissions in the Danish, Dutch, French — *Légion étrangère* — and Spanish armies. Pah! you will be my second in command. There are others — but you will see. I have at my back twenty million marks. Now what do you say?"

"It is very generous of you, Baron — very generous, but how do you know that I am *the* man?"

The Baron shrugged his shoulders. "I fancy so — enough! Come, I leave you for ten minutes to make up your mind."

The Baron rose and departed in the direction of his room.

Paul sat and smoked hard, thinking. It was a mad scheme, and he knew none of the details. The only momentary consideration concerned the position it might place him in with the Government in case it failed, and he should want other employment.

Yet he felt that it had all been ordained by Fate, and he felt the personal magnetism of the Baron. Before that strange individual had reached the far corner of the corridor Paul had decided. Then his thoughts flew to the necessity of arranging his private affairs.

The Baron returned with the dog in his arms. "Well?" he queried, caressing the animal and sucking a black cheroot.

Paul nodded silently.

"Ah, good! I knew you would. That is your formal assent, eh?"

"Yes."

"My congratulations, then!"

He held out one hand which Paul took.

"Now, mein lieber," he said to the dog, "what think you of the new recruit?"

A mixed sneeze and a bark answered him.

"There! he approves!" exclaimed his master. "Your future success is assured, Towers. Kismet approves."

"Kismet?" echoed Paul in astonishment.

"Yes; that is mein lieber's name. He is Kismet!"

The idea of this absurd caricature of a dog as the personification of Fate[34] tickled Paul into a roar of laughter.

Kismet's master — paradoxical phrase! — frowned.

"I'm sorry," apologized Paul, endeavoring to restrain his mirth.

"Kismet is, I assure you, a serious matter," remarked the other with a hint of resentment in his voice.

"Yes, I agree with you, Baron," returned Paul, smiling afresh at the double entente, "but may I ask where you fou — how Kis — how he came into your possession?"

"Certainly," said the Baron gravely, "I dying of thirst in the desert. The Arabs had poisoned the only water available, and I, in my pain, called on Fate to save me. I became unconscious and awoke to find Kismet here licking my face. He led me to sweet water. How he came I never knew. Hence his name. But now we will discuss business."

---

[34] Kismet: a personified power or force that determines the course of future events. Fate, destiny. From the Arabic *qisma*, "portion" or "lot."

For the next two hours the Baron explained the details of the scheme, the gist of which was that it would be financed partly by the German Government for political reasons, and partly by American speculators. The Baron represented the German interest, and one Cyrus Tarkas and his wife the American side. The two high-born companions of the Baron were also in the scheme. They, the Baron and Paul, were to leave for the interior immediately to join the new claimant, and make terms with him, whilst the Tarkas returned to America to arrange for the running of the arms upon receipt of a wire from the Baron that all was well. The Baron reckoned that, after having settled the affairs in the northern portion of the country, and established Abd-el-Kader on the throne under their influence, in return for full mineral and agricultural rights, to turn attention to the vast province of Sus[35] in the south, which, under the regime of a local Pope, had never acknowledged the sovereign power of the nominal Sultan. By aid of a well-equipped army, this rich country was to be conquered; and the rival Pontiff brought under the nominal yoke of the orthodox Sultan, but really under the Baron as the Viceroy of this potentate. It was the latter dream which enthralled the cosmopolitan adventurer. He thought in continents, and the dream of a vast African Empire under his sway intoxicated him. Once upon this dream of Empire, enthusiasm swept over him. His eyes grew steely bright, he gesticulated freely as he propounded the scheme, entering into the most minute details that, as he said, the scheme had been the one object of his life for seven years. Paul became magnetized with the same enthusiasm, waking the flames of ambition phoenix-like from the ashes frozen by disappointed love.

---

[35] Sus: the Sous region of Morocco, also rendered as Sus, Suss, Souss, or Sousse.

There were, the Baron also explained, others in the field; concession mongers, who, if successful in ruining their immediate venture would of necessity destroy their ultimate dream of a Saharan Eldorado.

"Lebaudy was not mad!"[36] declared the Baron. "He was a fool — ah, Herr Gott, what a fool! He failed because of the sycophantic blood-suckers who surrounded him. The Sahara a desert! Herr Gott, what a desert! But you know, you know."

For the rest of the forenoon and all the afternoon they discussed the scheme in all its aspects, wandering now and again into the realms of personal experiences, of which the Baron had a rich store, from dueling on the Continent to native fighting in Borneo and Sumatra, where he had been in the Dutch service.

Returning from a stroll in the dusk, they dressed, and sauntered to the Soko Chiko to while away an hour before dinner, at which Paul was to meet the other conspirators. As they sat at a small marble-topped table amid the crowded café, Paul, with the flood of information and experiences of his new companion digesting in his mind, observed afresh the small spare figure opposite him. The lean hard face, almost defying an estimate of age, and his quick bird-like movements were strongly individual; although there was no bulk to emphasize a commanding figure, yet rapid decision and command oozed at every pore; an awkward customer to handle, thought Paul.

The busy life of the Soko, where the East and the West intermingled, ebbed and flowed. A group of three hideous ragged Moorish beggars crouched against the wall of a bank chanting in chorus an appeal to their patron saint: "Ya Mulai

---

[36] Jacques Lebaudy (1868 – 1919), an eccentric and wealthy Frenchman, who hoped to create a new nation: the Empire of the Sahara.

Idrees. Oh, Lord Idrees!"[37] Across the cobbled center clattered a crowd of donkeys and mules laden with goods; stout richly clad Moors upon equally rotund mules; a dirty low-class Spaniard peddling peanuts from an old tin bath on wheels with a mast and a funnel rigged up to represent a ship; the huddled blanketed forms of women selling bread; now and again the bright colors of an Algerian or French soldier, the yellow head shawl of a Jewess; and Europeans in incongruous broadcloth and bowler hats being jostled and harried amid this motley maelstrom of humanity.

"Hullo," exclaimed the Baron, "there's young Carl Büttner," indicating a European clad in tennis clothes, racket in hand. "He's here over a little affair at Munich; killed his man, you know. And the fellow just behind him — they're together I think — is Gensdorp — little fracas in Paris — knife went too deep, or something of that sort. Cherchez la femme in both cases. A-ah, M'sieur Dumas!"

Paul laughed. "Interesting people!" said he, "any more of that stamp here?"

"Ah, yes! I told you that people only came here for their health, so? Well! — ah, there is another fine character. Yes, the man with the beard. He did not always wear a beard. Ah, no! You remember perhaps the bank fraud in London two months ago?"

"Something about it," said Paul vaguely.

"Well, to the tune of fifteen thousand — a mere bagatelle! — but that is the man — Arthur Gedde."

"How do you know?"

---

[37] Idris I (Moulay Idris; aka Idris the Elder; 740? – 791): a descendant of Muhammad, born in Mecca, and founder of the Idrisid dynasty. Idris ruled from 788 until his death in 791. Moulay (also spelled Mulay or Mūlāy): a Moroccan honorific title, derived from *mawlāy*, literally "my lord" or "my master."

"I have to learn many things; but that is the man — for certain. They all come here. Only four months ago Pinkerton's people arrested a Chicago swindler right here in the Soko."

"But won't somebody give this fellow away?"

The Baron shrugged his shoulders.

"Why? It is not my business nor your business, nor these people's, unless they are paid for it. Everything everywhere is a matter of fluss (money),[38] only here, more so. Come! it is nearly eight."

As they turned away into a lampless street a dark shadow flitted out of the darkness.

"Goo' night, ole chap," it said.

Paul halted. "Oh, it's Rabbit, is it? Where have you been all day? I was going to pay you."

Rabbit pushed the hood back from his face.

"That orlright, ole chap," waving a hand away. "You pay every month."

"But I haven't engaged you! I'm going away — soon."

"Orlright, me come too. Where you go now?"

"You're a cool hand," said Paul smiling; "you seem to have adopted me!"

"'Dopted me?" repeated Rabbit, catching at a new word. "'Dopted — 'dopted — "

"*Adopted.*"

"A-a-dopted? Yes; me aadopted you."

"But you don't even know where I'm going!"

---

[38] Fluss: an Anglicized spelling of the German *fluss*. Literally, a large flowing body of water, but also used figuratively to mean an uninterrupted current, as in "the flow of time." Here *fluss* is used to imply a flow of cash or currency: a financial flow. But *fluss* may also be a variant of the Arabic *flous*, a colloquial term for money, employed across North Africa and the Middle East.

"No, me come "— simply and definitely. "You go with your friend, whaat? Goo'-night!" and turning, moved off with his peculiar cross between a Moorish shuffle and an English stride.

"That man your servant?" inquired the Baron as they climbed the dark cobbled streets.

"I suppose so; he seems to have engaged himself, and he amuses me. Fantastic brute!"

"H'm."

"You don't like him?"

"Oh, he is as the rest, but better than a Jew — Blut und Eisen![39] how I hate Jews!" He spoke with sudden intensity.

"Oh, they are as the rest of the world," said Paul tolerantly, "good and bad."

"Ugh! For me, I loathe them."

The Baron grunted and trudged along in silence.

At length, after passing along the open Marshan,[40] they halted at a gate, were presently admitted, and led through extensive gardens to a charming villa, from the verandah of which the white foam of the sea could be seen and heard breaking on the rocks at the base of the cliff. At the sound of their footsteps on the gravel path a tall figure appeared in the lighted hall: a shock of black hair hung over the man's clean-shaven face, a very loose dinner jacket, extremely baggy trousers; and a floppy French bow tied at a low collar above a soft shirt, gave a distinct flavor of the Quartier Latin.

"Gee! Guessed it were yew, Baron," he ejaculated with a suggestion of a banjo accompaniment. "Who's your friend, anyway?"

"A new recruit to the Cause — Mr. Paul Towers — Mr. Cyrus Tarkas!"

---

[39] "Blut und Eisen!": "Blood and iron!"

[40] Marshan: a prominent esplanade on a hill west of Tangier's medina, overlooking the Atlantic and Strait of Gibraltar.

Paul shook hands, feeling the other's dark eyes summing him up. The healthy firm grip of a light sinewy hand made him intuitively like the man.

"Say! Guess yew're the merchant the Baron cottoned to at the dancing house? Come right in, Colonel! This is my wife!"

A handsome dark-haired woman had appeared in the doorway.

"How do?" said she, smiling, extending a hand. "Cy never gets a grip on names!"

"Towers," answered Paul; "Paul Towers."

"Say," interrupted Tarkas, who had exchanged a few private words with the Baron. "Come right in! The Dook and the Markiss 're shouting for grub."

Further introductions completed, dinner proceeded with conventional conversation. They all removed out into an arbor of the garden afterwards to discuss coffee and liqueurs; then the subject of the plot was broached and discussed. The longer Paul observed the two scions of royalty, the less he approved of their presence in the scheme. The Prince seemed to him a mere invertebrate, vapid idler, and the stout little man shifty and thoroughly unreliable. The Tarkas, on the other hand, were undoubtedly a thoroughly capable, brisk, and clever couple. They all seemed to yield, without question, to the leadership of the Baron. The Tarkas were very keen for the scheme to develop and apparently had their side already cut and dried. Paul, when the others were otherwise engaged, candidly told the Baron his views; and, rather to his surprise, the Baron concurred, adding that it did not matter, as he did not intend that the two in question should do more than they were doing at the moment, which was obviously nothing, except to swallow vast quantities of cognac. This puzzled Paul considerably; as the Baron was no fool, he would not have brought them in without reason, therefore they must have some hold over him. Paul remembered Rabbit's sweeping statement and also felt, as he sat, the feeling of physical aversion to the Baron which mingled with the attractive magnetism of the man.

As they sat under the stars in the light of Moorish candle lanterns, a shrill scream rang out from the depths of the garden. The Baron continued talking without apparently noticing, but as the shrieks continued, Paul could not refrain from remarking the fact.

"Oh, only some slave of Bu Draa's. His gardens adjoin these, you know," replied the Baron, slightly annoyed at an interruption over so ordinary an incident.

The Baron had, it appeared, received a message from a native agent in the following of El Kader: the Pretender had left Marrakech intending to gather followers en route to Fez; if once Fez were taken and the confirmation of the Ullema[41] — Holy College — obtained, El Kader, in the religious eyes of the people, would be Sultan; but he was in the need of arms with which to give battle to the forces of the nominal Sultan at the coast. The Baron proposed that he and Paul should leave immediately and endeavor to force their way through the country to him and make terms, whilst the Tarkas left for America in readiness to run a cargo of arms. It was nearly midnight before all the necessary details were arranged, and then, with his customary enthusiasm, the Baron, standing upon a chair, bade them fill up their glasses and drink to the venture and the new Sultan, Abd-el-Kader.

The witchery of the starlight night, the oriental sense of mystery pervading the quiet gardens, and the romance of the venture with an empire the goal, seized and swayed Paul as he

---

[41] Ullema: Ulema. The body of mullahs or religious scholars that guide the Muslim community.

voiced the toast of the Baron: "Vive l'Abd-el-Kader! A bas le Sultan!"[42]

The echo of the shout mocked them from the recesses of the garden. A tinkle of glasses, the distant sighing seethe of ocean, and then, far away over the ancient city behind them, came the long drawn mystic call:

"Al-lah — Ak-ba-ah!"

The eerie sensation of the presence of unthought-of forces at work ran through Paul; he felt as if the hand of Fate touched him on the shoulder.

"Gee!" twanged Tarkas, breaking rudely in upon Paul's sense of the mystic East. "Gee! Guess we're goin' to hustle right through now! Shake these bully boys' some, sure!"

"Inshallah! (If God wills!)" said the Baron solemnly. "Kismet! Listen: the voice of Fate!"

"Al-lah — Ak-ba-ah"

---

[42] Vive l'Abd-el-Kader! A bas le Sultan!: "Long live the Abd-el-Kader! Down with the Sultan!"

CHAPTER III

Four weeks later, the rays of the sun rising above the mountaintop alighted upon a small cavalcade climbing up the steep and stony track to the pass of El Fahs. Behind them rose the ragged, tumbled mass of the foothills, and beyond as they breasted the summit, a glorious expanse of wild, rugged country, purple, blue and white patches of wild flowers carpeting the green-clad slopes and valleys; and still farther to the right the mist-laden smiling sea.

A little in front of the main body rode a red-bearded Moor, a long native gun across his scarlet saddle which, together with the blue silham,[43] red cap and black long-maned stallion, formed a picturesque splash of color. At about thirty yards in his rear came two more riders clad in the loose native garments, both wearing the hood over the turban, the near side one, a tall bearded man, in whom it would have been difficult to recognize Paul Towers. By his side, upon a fast-pacing mule, rode the Baron, a stubbly beard upon his jowl; and strapped upon the pommel of his red-flannelled saddle a box containing a funny, ill-shaped little dog — Kismet — who seemed quite comfortable and happy in his strange abode. Immediately behind them rode Rabbit, placid and ugly as usual, with other servants upon mules carrying panniers containing food and native camp equipment.

Paul had been very surprised to see the Baron's absurd pet upon his saddle bow when they had met at the rendezvous some miles outside the town. Great care and much bribery had been necessary in order to escape the vigilance of Moorish and French-Algerian guards, who guarded all exits from the town. However, this had been managed and they had ridden straight

---

[43] Silham: also spelled *selham* or *salham*. A cloak worn by men, typically over a djellaba, featuring an oversized pointed hood or "qob."

on with a view to putting as great a distance between the Sultan's loyal subjects and themselves as possible. The hill tribes through whose country they were passing held allegiance to no one unless compelled to at the end of a gun; mountain tribesmen preferred to pass their time in raiding, for choice a wealthy Moor or European, if not, then amongst themselves for the joy of fighting and loot. An armed force would only excite suspicion; hence the small party, by which the Baron hoped to pass unobserved, or at any rate to appear as if they were not worth holding to ransom.

Paul, in the excitement of the first few days, had had little time to brood over the past. His thoughts flew back as they rode silently hour after hour, and he discovered that the sense of loss and bitter disappointment was dulled; as if, in fact, all his previous life was but disconnected and half-forgotten dreams. He was subject to that strange psychological phenomenon in which a new phase of life seems alone to be alive, the past nebulous, indistinct. He had not the remotest idea of what the outcome of this wildcat scheme would be, merely rejoicing in the sense of dangerous adventure, just as he had felt his pulse beat the quicker when starting upon his previous expedition; although then he felt his love hanging as a weight about his neck and now there was no responsibility — he was as free as air and therefore happier.[44] Paul had not succeeded in pinning the Baron to any definite statement regarding his own position; sometimes he had talked enthusiastically, but vaguely, of Paul as the military governor of the nebulous empire, at others of a governorship, of what or where he did not say. However, Paul had not pressed him, foreseeing that any promises or agreements, other than stated shares resulting from cash transactions, were of necessity unreliable and foolish. He felt

---

[44] A lovelorn period in Beadle's early life is described in detail in his largely autobiographical novel, *A Passionate Pilgrimage* (1915).

attracted by the adventure purely as an adventure, and left the future in the hands of Fate. He had had a little passage of arms[45] with the Baron over the "Rabbit." At first he had not entertained the idea of taking Rabbit with him, pointing out that he was a town guide, and therefore probably useless on such an expedition; but Rabbit had placidly ignored all objections and made Paul laugh by his quaint definite statement: "Orlright, ole chap — me come look after you when you get drunk, whaat?" The Baron demurred a little, but Paul, having given his consent, insisted; at any rate, he had said, Rabbit will be of more use than Kismet, at which the Baron had frowned and walked away. He could appreciate a joke on every subject under the sun, except his beloved pet which he seemed to regard as a fetish.

As they neared the first slope beyond the pass some mounted tribesmen appeared on an adjacent hillside.

"I say, ole chap," said Rabbit, drawing alongside Paul with a jingle of pots and pans in the panniers. "You see El Fahs," pointing with a cigarette. "Dey watch us. Tonight come for you, and cons'quently — er — cons'quently — "

"Rubbish," said Paul. "What's put that idea into your head?"

"Head? You know Raisuli,[46] eh? Well, these his people — Inshallah! We will see what will come out of him!"

---

[45] "Passage of arms": a skirmish, conflict, dispute, or fight.

[46] Raisuli: Moulay Ahmed er Raisuni (aka Raisuli; 1871 – 1925), a sharif and leader of the Jebala tribal confederacy. He died after being captured and imprisoned by his rival, Abd el Krim (1882/83 – 1963), president of the Republic of the Rif (the mountainous region in northern Morocco, along the Mediterranean coast). In 1904, Raisuni kidnapped Ion Perdicaris (a Greek-American expatriate) and Perdicaris' stepson Cromwell Varley, prompting American President Theodore Roosevelt to send a squadron of warships to Tangier. In 1907 Raisuni kidnapped British army officer Sir Harry Maclean, demanding a ransom of £20,000 from the British government (the equivalent of £2,720,000 in 2023).

Something "came out of him" quicker than Rabbit had predicted. As he finished speaking the Moor in advance drew his horse back on his haunches, and a shot rang out from a cluster of rocks nearby as he wheeled about and galloped back to them. As they too drew up, a dozen mounted men, in gray djellabaas and camel-hair rope turbans, galloped recklessly from round a curve of the hillside towards them. When within twenty yards the strangers pulled up abruptly with a clatter of hooves and shouted a greeting, to which Absalom replied. They all carried their guns at the ready, and their abnormally restive horses edged closer whilst the leader, a big brown-bearded fellow, exchanged the lengthy salutations with Absalom.

"Look out!" whispered Paul, "they mean mischief."

"Hast seen a black bull running loose upon the mountainside," queried the leader.

"Nay," answered Absalom, keeping a wary eye upon his interlocutor who was intently scrutinizing the Baron. "Nay; we have not. Hast lost a black bull?"

"No matter. Whither goest thou?"

"Sid Omar ben Ghalim, from Sidi Absalom, journeying to Sidi Hassan. Who art thou?" Gradually the other horsemen had encircled the little cavalcade. The leader's black eyes shifted from the Baron to Paul, as he suddenly dropped his reins to lift the long-beveled rifle. There was a crack of a revolver from the Baron; the rifle fell to the ground and the man reeled in his saddle with a broken wrist as his horse plunged affrighted; his companions shouted and fired straight into the group. Paul emptied his revolver in company with the Baron and Absalom. The air rang for a few moments with shouts of men, reports, and squeal of horses. Two of the assailants fell from their saddles, their animals cantered away, and the rest wheeling about, rode off at full gallop.

"That was a pretty shot, Baron," said Paul as they sat awaiting Absalom's examination of the fallen men.

"Cela va sans dire,"[47] grunted the Baron complacently, engaged in soothing his badly scared pet.

"One man is dead, O Pole," observed Absalom from the ground; "and the other is sorely wounded. The gun of the infidel bites hard," he muttered. "Yea, I would that I had one!"

"Pole" was the nearest attempt at enunciation of Paul that the Arab tongue could curl itself to pronounce.

Fortunately the brigands' aim had been harmless, even at so short a range. Rabbit's animal, at which they probably had not aimed, had a deep flesh wound, but not of serious hurt.

"Aliens!" said the Baron impatiently, "let us get on. We'll have these people and half their tribe down here."

"Well, I suppose we'd better bury the dead. Give the other some water, Rabbit!"

The Baron snorted impatiently. Said he:

"Come; we have no time to waste with these canailles," and prodding his mule, he moved on.

Paul waited whilst Rabbit and Absalom dragged the dead to one side and propped the wounded one in the shade of a shrub, leaving a water skin by his side, "O Pole," remarked Absalom as they jogged along; "the eyes of him-whose-father-was-the-offspring-of-swine perceived that the master-of-the-little-dog was a Nazarene,[48] therefore did he act so. Tell your friend to lower the veil that these dogs of the hills may not know him. For thyself," he added, with a broad smile, "thou art verily a true son of the Prophet."

And indeed Paul, with sunburnt skin and beard clipped in native fashion, looked every inch a dignified Moor of Fez.[49]

He passed the remark on to the Baron as he overtook him.

---

[47] Cela va sans dire:"That goes without saying."

[48] Nazarene (or N'srani): a term used by Muslims to refer to Christians or Westerners.

[49] Because certain natives of Fes are light-skinned.

"Yes," said he, "I knew. I had meant to drop a roll of the turban until my beard has fully grown. It was my fault; although I don't think they were after loot."

Rabbit, huddled on top of his beast of burden, smoked a cigarette, and eagerly examined the rifles and a silver dagger.

The other horsemen away upon the hillside had pulled up at the sound of firearms, apparently watched the fight, and were now brown specks in the distance, illustrating how very ordinary the little fracas was in the eyes of the natives.

For five hours they marched steadily, crossing a couple of rivers, gradually working round to the east, and leaving the chain of mountains on their left. They were now fairly safe from retaliation by their late enemies, as the tribes, in times of revolution when raid and plunder were the order of the day, seldom ventured into one another's territory unless in force, or in a swift raid at night. About noon they overtook a small camel caravan camped by the side of the road, from which they learned that another caravan bound for the coast had been looted the day previous.

Towards four in the afternoon Absalom pointed out a village perched on the crest of a hill at which it would be advisable to camp for the night. In piping times of peace, which seldom occurred in that portion of the country, it was customary for travelers to sleep under the protection of a village, the sheikh of which was responsible to the Sultan for the safety of his guests; but at this time they would necessarily be at their own risk: in fact, the village might, more than possibly, construe the occasion into a direct hint from the Prophet to profit by the good fortune sent by Allah in the shape of stray infidels. However, Absalom swore by many sacred things that the Sheikh had a heart as pure as a newly born lamb, and moreover, was a friend to the cause. The Sheikh in question proved to be an enormously stout pock-marked man with a big black beard, who at first demurred at sheltering a Nazarene, which, being interpreted, meant that the price would be increased exorbitantly. At length their native tent was pitched under the mud walls of the village.

Peasants in dirty, ragged, brown djellabaas herded cattle, sheep and goats within the village enclosure, where, among fowls and donkeys, the women of the village, exhibiting the nakedness of their faces before the world, ground barley, chopped wood, and performed other domestic work, whilst their lords and masters lounged upon mats, set upon dung heaps, sipping scalding mint tea. Two camels in a corner munched fodder, emitting their characteristic grunting gurgle of pleasure or annoyance amid a medley of sounds from cocks crowing, braying donkeys, shouts of men, and the weird rattle of the ubiquitous stork busy settling down for the night upon the rooftops. And in the air floated that peculiar odor characteristic of all the East — a combination of human, animal, and bird smell all pervaded with a flavor of hot spices, suggestive of curry powder. Upon the top of the mud wall a black-cloaked son of the mountains solemnly performed the religious calisthenics prescribed by Mohammed, face towards the east, turning his back on a glorious sunset.

The four wayfarers within their tent lounged upon a native carpet, conversing with the portly Sheikh, all sipping sweet mint tea provided by the host. He was very anxious to hear the latest news from the coast. Paul asked whether he was a supporter of Mulai Abd-el-Kader, to which he replied with the non-committal pious answer: Inshallah (if God wills!), adding that all Sultans were alike to the sons of the mountains. He was heartily amused at the recital of the affray in the morning, and knew well the leader, who it appeared was a virulent enemy of his, inasmuch that he held a dozen head of cattle of his to the good. The Sheikh and his men had attempted a raid upon the other's village a week since, but had met with a warm reception. They were expecting a return visit but opined that as the leader had suffered a broken wrist and lost two men, the call would probably be delayed; anyway it was as all things: Inshallah! A while since a Harka[50] (column) of the legitimate Sultan had commandeered nearly all their stock, which had not increased their love for the Makhzen (Government).[51]

Soon the sun set in a shower of golden-green glory; night was quickly upon them. At about nine in the evening hot dishes of stewed mutton and couscous — a pleasant tasting mess of semolina, sugar and fat — were sent out from the house of the Sheikh, which they ate in the Moorish fashion with their fingers. Both Paul and the Baron were accustomed to this method of feeding, and when at length they rolled over on their mats to sleep, the world seemed bright and good to both of them, as is usually the case when the belly is full.

Only the occasional grumblings of the camels and donkeys disturbed the peaceful starlight night. Towards the small hours masses of black cloud swept over from the mountains casting a dense shadow over the sleeping village. Just as the darkness was deepest the storks, perched asleep upon the housetops, suddenly commenced their rattling clatter, as of a police rattle, caused by rapid oscillations of the slender beak. The warning of the approach of strangers ceased for an instant to break out afresh among the other birds. The sentry, posted by the Sheikh a few yards from the tent door, huddled in his robes, woke up and peered round sleepily, but much smoking of kif[52] — hemp — had dulled his senses to all save dreams of Paradise.

---

[50] Harka: a military expedition, campaign, or raiding force organized by the sultan or a local governor.

[51] Makhzen: in Arabic *makhzen* translates to "warehouse" or "storehouse." But in the context of North African history, particularly that of Morocco, it refers to a central government or ruling elite: specifically, the political and administrative apparatus of the monarchy. It denotes the governing power structure, historically associated with the royal court, military, and bureaucracy.

[52] Kif (aka keef): a blend of low-potency cannabis leaf / flower and tobacco.

A donkey's loud lamentation next broke the silence, dying away to a choking sob; a camel voiced a liquid growl of dissatisfaction, and the clatter of the storks broke out again as shadowy forms stole up the rise. Slowly one shadow crept near the sentry. A knife glinted in the gloom, the man toppled over with a gasping sob and lay motionless. The shadows moved on more rapidly towards the tent. Once more the storks sounded their warning, and Absalom awaking peered sleepily out of the tent. With a yell he awoke the others, as the enemy, abandoning caution, shouted in answer and rushed the camp.

The Baron and Paul leapt to their feet, revolver in hand, as Absalom knocked the foremost raider down with a mighty sweep of his clubbed gun. At the same moment others tore up the sides of the tent, overturning it, and entangling the occupants in the folds, amid muttered curses and the yelps of Kismet. The alarm had been taken by the village from which proceeded uproar: shouts, screams, shots, dogs barking, donkeys braying.

The Baron disentangled himself to find everybody shouting at the top of his voice and that their assailants had vanished. The walls of the village were now manned with excited defenders ready to fire at anything. For a time confusion worse confounded. Absalom and Rabbit jabbered excitedly with the villagers whilst the Baron, roaring at everyone to be quiet, rescued the trembling dog from the ruins of the tent.

"Towers!" shouted the Baron in the darkness, nursing the dog; "where the devil are you? Towers! Blut und Eisen! Absalom, thou son of a shame, where is 'Pole'? Search, Rabat, eater of filth, for thy master!"

As the uproar died down, and they found no trace of Paul, the rhythmic thud of galloping hooves sounded faintly in the distance.

"Herr Gott!" exclaimed the Baron listening, ear to earth; "they have kidnapped him!"

That explained why the attack had ceased so unexpectedly. He cursed quietly to himself for a few minutes, and then endeavored to persuade the Sheikh, whose portly form was limned against the skyline on the top of the wall, to organize a rescue party, although he knew that such would be utterly futile, as the raiders had too long a start.

Absalom and Rabbit, cursing wrathfully to each other, erected the tent into which the Baron retired to nurse his pet and decide what had best be done.

"O Absalom," he said at length, "these sons of shame meant not to take him" — he chuckled — "they would have taken me!"

"True," replied Absalom. "They knew not that he was not a son of the Prophet, but ye, O Sid-el-Kelb, they knew as a Nazarene."

"Waali! [53]Waali!" moaned Rabbit to himself, "this accursed infidel hath brought the wrath of Allah upon my friend. Was he not of great height, a beard like unto the Prophet? Ah! such a man was my father — "

"Be quiet!" snarled the Baron, who did not like the impolite references to himself.

At daybreak the Baron, annoyed at the untoward event, decided to remain in camp whilst a messenger was sent to the village of the leader of the previous morning's attack, to whom he attributed, without hesitation, the authorship of the night raid. In all probability his captors, on discovering that they had kidnapped the wrong man, would merely hold him to ransom. The Baron did not imagine that any serious hurt was likely to happen to his late companion; at any rate, not whilst there was a chance of ransom, as the power of the dollar was great. Had they been successful in capturing him, he well knew that revenge for a broken wrist and the loss of two men would have

---

[53] Waali: wow.

insured an unpleasant sojourn even if another reckoning had not been paid. By hard riding both ways the messenger would be back by nightfall. The Baron hoped that the sum offered — two thousand dollars — would be sufficient; if the British Government were eventually persuaded to ransom Paul, the consequences to the scheme might be serious. He was distinctly annoyed at the possibility of interference with his plans, at the delay and the loss of a useful pawn in the game. The Baron allowed no personal feelings to sway him in the least; Paul and the others were merely necessary instruments. He decided that he would strike camp upon the following morning in any case; time was now valuable.

The day passed slowly, whilst to the chorus of village life were added the wails of the female relatives of the dead sentry. The old Sheikh was very vexed at the man's death; but solely on account, as he explained with many calls upon Allah and the Prophet, of the purchase of a horse which he had been about to complete with the deceased; now the animal had passed into the hands of a relative, a hard and greedy man, who demanded nearly double the price of the late owner. However, with luck, and if Allah willed it, the man might die soon!

Towards evening the Baron began to chafe at the delay, formulating fresh plans whereby he might continue to do without Paul's services; but it was very annoying, as one could trust no one in this country, and Paul had seemed a simple-minded gentleman whose word might be relied upon. "However, Inshallah!" said the Baron affectionately caressing Kismet. "'Tis thy doing, little one!" The Baron during his years of wandering in Mohammedan countries, seemed to have become imbued with the philosophical fatalism of the East.

The night wore on: with the first streaks of dawn the Baron emerged from the tent, waking Absalom with orders to load the mules.

"But what of thy friend?" objected Absalom. "The messenger hath not even returned!"

"Do as I bid thee," returned the Baron gruffly.

"Nay, by the beard of the Prophet," swore Rabbit, "I will not stir until news cometh from the mountains. — No, mister, me no go on. Me wait for my frien'"; he added in English.

"Who the devil asked you what you would do?" inquired the Baron wrathfully. "Thou son of a pig, thou dost not travel with me!"

As they quarreled the sound of galloping hooves reached their ears, and from over a rise of ground rode a figure on horseback holding in his arms a woman whose hair flew out in the wind.

CHAPTER IV

Dimly hearing Absalom's cry through his sleep, Paul had sprung to his feet, rightly surmising a surprise attack. As he groped for his revolver, which he wore beneath his robes, the tent collapsed, bringing him to the ground. Struggling furiously in the folds, expecting the sting of a knife or bullet every second, he felt his feet clutched and hauled by someone's hands. He lay passive, thinking that the Baron or Rabbit was aiding him. As his head emerged from under the canvas a cloak was roughly bundled round his face and arms, and he felt himself lifted from the ground, realizing that something was wrong. He fought and struggled to no purpose. He was borne swiftly over the ground. He could dimly hear the guttural voices of his captors. They seemed to carry him for a long distance, and once, giving a sudden frantic kick, he succeeded in wriggling from their hands on to the ground, but throwing themselves upon him, a knee in his throat nearly throttling him, they secured and bundled him roughly along.

Unexpectedly he found himself dumped on the ground; a host of men seemed to kneel upon his limbs and body. He thought they were about to cut his throat, but instead he felt ropes being hastily bound round and about him; then, with a heave, he was hoisted on to a packsaddle, bound there as one might a sack of flour, and the horse sprang into a gallop. The cloak, which still enveloped his head, half suffocated him, and the motion of the horse strained his back at every stride. Now his head pitched downward as the animal descended a hill, then the reverse when climbing the other side. Anon he felt the horse drop to a walk, and shortly afterwards cold water soaked his legs and body, nearly drowning him. Evidently a river, but not at the ford where he had crossed previously, because the water here was deep; the horse was swimming, he could tell by the gentle motion. Then up a steep bank and a steady walk for miles until another river. Paul came to the conclusion that his captors were the band who had attempted to assault them upon the high road. Were they merely taking him to their chief with the broken wrist for him to wreak his vengeance? Paul had a full and detailed knowledge of Arab methods of torture. If not, then it would undoubtedly be a case of ransom. Raisuli had succeeded in extracting ten thousand pounds sterling. Paul almost laughed at the idea of anyone paying such a sum for him. The British Government had signified their intention to refuse to supply speculative brigands with pocket money. The Baron would have to provide the necessary. There was surely ample to spare out of the twenty million marks he was so fond of talking about.

Then it suddenly occurred to Paul that perhaps the Baron too was a member of the party, accommodated with similar rough treatment. If so, what an ignominious end to the great Empire scheme! His thoughts wandered off to the past, Irene Trevelyan. Heavens! What a dream that all seemed now. He felt as if he had been tied to the horse traveling across country for years. With a queer twist of thought the ludicrous side appeared to him. He pictured himself as Mazeppa,[54] and smiled inwardly in spite of the discomfort and pain.

A rough hand suddenly wrenched away the cloak enveloping his head; he inhaled the fresh morning air with relief, and blinked in the daylight.

"Ah, thou dog of a Nazarene!" said a sallow, bearded face close to him, "art dead?"

"By the beard of the Prophet," laughed another, "truly we have forgotten the little dog of the master of the little dog!"

---

[54] Mazeppa: a reference to the Ukrainian historical figure Ivan Stepanovych Mazepa (1639 – 1709), whose life inspired several artistic creations, including music by Tchaikovsky; poetry by Byron, Pushkin, and Victor Hugo; and paintings by Géricault and Eugène Delacroix.

He guffawed with laughter at the play upon words. Paul gathered from this remark that the Baron also was a prisoner. His line of vision was too limited to see far. He screwed his neck as far as possible to look around him. Several horsemen were riding ahead of him upon a faint track carpeted with white flowers; above them towered the mountains.

"Here, N'srani," said the first speaker, thrusting a water skin towards Paul; and then remembering that the captive had not the use of his hands, pulled up both horses and tilted the neck of the gourd over Paul's mouth, saying curtly: "Drink."

Paul did drink, gratefully; although the water, swamping his face, nearly choked him. The coarse cloth of the cloak, none too savory, had worked into his mouth, leaving it dry and sore.

They resumed the march.

"Tell me, is another Nazarene also amongst us?" asked Paul.

"How can a dog live among lions?"

Then Paul reflected that the Baron was not a prisoner; and, moreover, that these men only knew of one European, instead of two, in his party.

"Whither go we?" inquired Paul.

"To Sidi Abdullah."

It was customary among the Arabs invariably to refer to a town or village by the name of its patron saint, of which every place has at least one; and as Paul did not know the country, the question was futile.

"What are you going to do with me?" he queried.

"Deliver thee into the hands of Omar ben Abdullah."

Again Paul was no wiser by the question.

"And what will Omar ben Abdullah do with me?"

"Nay, I know not. That is his will, not mine."

"Kill me?" suggested Paul.

"Inshallah!"

"Will he not then hold me to ransom?"

"Inshallah!"

Paul gave up the hopeless task of trying to extract information and stared about him One of the horsemen in the band dropped back. Paul thought he recognized the face.

"Wert thou not amongst those upon the road yesterday?" he inquired of him.

The man grinned.

"Eeyeh; Ana Larbi Gibilo!"[55]

Paul tried anew to elicit some information, but met with like results. He asked to have his arms released, but the request was studiously ignored.

What time he was thus borne along like so much broadcloth he tried to endure the inevitable without giving his wild captors the pleasure of listening to the futile complaint of a Christian in pain.

When the sun, scorching his unprotected face unmercifully, was yet an hour to its zenith, the party began to climb a rough stony mountain track until, rounding the hillside, a small walled town appeared nestling on the slope, sparkling white amongst the green of olive trees. Soon they had passed through the plantation under an arch of an ancient gate and up a narrow rocky street between old crumbling walls into a cool garden. Only four men, including the man who led Paul's horse, entered the garden, where, dismounting, they unbound their captive and searched him for weapons or money. The revolver was examined with guttural exclamations of delight. The finder, attempting to show off his knowledge to the others, jammed the extractor. Paul expected him to end up by accidentally shooting himself or his fellows, and refrained from offering advice, half hoping that he would. However, after turning it about and trying to look very wise, he stowed it away beneath his djellaba. They then squatted silently on each side of him, evidently awaiting someone's arrival.

---

[55] Eeyeh; Ana Larbi Gibilo: Yes; I am Larbi Gibilo.

Paul sat in the shade and painfully stretched his limbs, wondering what might be in store for him. After half an hour he became impatient, inquiring whether anybody was going to appear.

"Inshallah!" answered one of the guards.

"I am hungry," he said, "give me some food."

"Inshallah!"

Anyone with less than Paul's experience of the East would have straightway fallen into a temper. Paul resigned himself to the inevitable and, sprawling in the shade, fell asleep.

The sound of voices in conversation awakened him. The guards were still huddled in their robes beside him; amongst the trees stood two men observing him, one of whom he recognized as the leader of the road gang, the other a venerable graybeard. As Paul raised his head a startled exclamation broke from them.

"By my father's beard!" exclaimed the graybeard. "This is not the dog of a Nazarene I told thee! Ye sons of women of shame, ye dogs, ye sons of she asses, ye — "

He broke into a storm of invectives directed at the guards.

"True!" interrupted the broken-wristed one, "this is not the master of the little dog."

"Ya sidi,"[56] protested the raiders; "thou didst say, fetch the Nazarene who passeth by on the road to Sidi Absalom, and truly have we brought such an one!"

A noisy altercation ensued between the Sheikh and Paul's captors, from which Paul gathered that the Baron had in some way mortally insulted the Sheikh, who, learning that he would pass along the border of their country, had sent his son Abdullah ben Omar to avenge him, ending in the episode of the previous morning. After their defeat a further company had been dispatched to follow up the Baron's party to raid under

---

[56] Ya sidi: "Oh, my master"; or "Oh, sir."

cover of night, and at all risks, to bring back the hated European. Abdullah ben Omar and his party had not recognized Paul as a European, hence the failure of the second force to take any precautions in securing the right man.

At length the gray-bearded Omar ben Abdullah turned wrathfully away, ordering Paul to be safely imprisoned and fed.

He was led down the garden and roughly thrust into a dark cool chamber, the massive iron-studded door slammed and bolted. The room had one large heavily barred window and was devoid of furniture of any sort, even a mat. The window, he observed, looked out on to a street, contrary to the usual Moorish custom. Paul sat down in a corner hoping that food would be brought soon, and trying to determine what his fate would be. He began to feel the need of food, and the lowered vitality easily allowed his courage to ebb, the grim tentacles of despair to clutch at his heart. The vivid memory of his previous captivity amongst wild tribes came back to him; he decided that if a similar fate awaited him again, he would destroy himself somehow rather than endure the degradation of the mental and physical torture such an existence would entail. He had little hope that the old Sheikh would release him, although he was not the direct object of his vengeance; rather would he be inclined to glut his hatred upon him as one of the same accursed race. In Omar ben Abdullah's eyes he was an infidel and, therefore, a fit subject for ignominy and torture. Paul arose wearily and gazed out of the window at a blank, crumbling wall opposite. The shuffle of native slippers sounded; a negro slave appeared with a jar of water, some coarse barley bread, and a handful of dates; these he thrust through a hole in the wall which had escaped Paul's observation. He spoke to the man with the object of endeavoring to secure his friendship, but the other only grinned and shuffled away.

Paul hesitated a moment before tackling the food, the idea of poison running through his mind. Eventually, deciding that in all probability no such easy end awaited him, he devoured the food hungrily, and feeling more hopeful, stretched out on the hard floor and fell asleep.

Paul was awakened by a stinging blow upon the head. A roar of laughter rang in his ears. As he sat up confusedly, another stone struck him in the chest, which aroused another storm of merriment from a crowd of wild-looking tribesmen who were congregated in a turbulent throng without the window, staring in at the captive. Cries of "See the dog of a Nazarene! Watch the son of Shaitan![57] Kill the accursed infidel! Stir up the dog and make him dance!" rang out amid shaken sticks, scowls and laughter. Several other stones followed, raining about him as he struggled to his feet. For a moment a spasm of fear shook him, born of the knowledge of the terrible end that awaited him if these fanatical brutes were allowed to wreak their will upon him. One man much taller than his fellows, raising his arm to aim a mass of filth, drew Paul's attention. He instantly recognized him as the man who had attacked the Baron in the dancing café, Larbi Gibilo. So Paul was suffering as an unwilling deputy of the Baron! Paul cursed him as he sprang aside to avoid the shower of missiles. A bony-faced woman near the window succeeded in spitting upon him. The degradation angered Paul like the singe of a white-hot iron; he lost temporary control of himself, and rushing to the bars, like a furious caged animal, shouted and gibbered at them with rage, whilst they whooped, yelled and spat at him in delight. Another stone striking him upon the temple, brought the blood trickling down his face. He calmed himself by an effort, retiring to one side of the window out of sight, where huddled against the wall, he buried his face in his hands, nearly weeping with anger and humiliation. The crowd of persecutors continued to shout

---

[57] Shaitan: shayṭān. "Devil," "fiend," or "evil one."

and jeer for some time, shaking the bars with disappointment, because they could not see and insult the wretched Nazarene.

Then, over the shouts, cries, and rattle of stones, floated the afternoon call to prayer:

"Al-lah — Ak-b-ah!"

The musical bell notes seemed to mock Paul in his agony. He shook his fist, cursing the call, the religion, and everything connected with it.

The cry calmly, serenely oblivious of all petty personal affairs, seemed the apotheosis of destiny; the finality soothed Paul, helping him to summon all his philosophy to aid him. His stormy mood died, and setting his teeth firmly, he grimly determined to await whatever might be destined for him.

The fanatical crowd, tired at length of reviling a person who had the bad taste to hide himself, began to disperse, some squatting down in the road, their gray-hooded figures appearing like grim angels of Fate, awaiting the doom of the condemned one.

Slowly, wearily, the afternoon dragged on till sunset, when the negro again appeared with bread, fruit and water. The man stopped a while talking to the huddled watchers beneath the window, who at length, with curses of disappointment at some news elicited from the slave, slowly departed in dignified manner. The negro, having placed the food within the hole, paused and to Paul's amazement, divested himself of a long curved dagger and colored sash, which he handed without a word of explanation through the window bars. Paul took it, inquiring what was intended.

"Minshallah!"[58] (as Allah wills), replied the other grinning, and without further explanation, shuffled away.

---

[58] "Minshallah": a phonetic spelling of *Mashallah*, "what God has willed," which is employed to convey thanks, gratitude, or joy.

Paul stood holding the weapon in his hands, gazing at the silver scabbard and dudgeon[59] as if expecting to find instructions written thereon. He drew out the blade, testing it with his thumb; it was as sharp as a razor. Who had sent it? Surely not the negro! What was the object? A hint to take the happy dispatch and avoid a worse fate? Paul thanked the unknown giver, slung it under his robes, and turned to his frugal meal.

The thought that the dagger might assist him to escape made him turn his attention to the window bars as soon as night fell. After picking at the base of a bar, he discovered that each one had been built in the wall at least a foot each way. He returned to his seat by the opposite wall staring gloomily out at the starlight.

The night wore slowly on. Paul dozed and thought. At length, gazing moodily through the window, he noticed a shade, lighter than the surrounding gloom of the narrow street, move. He became conscious of a pair of eyes peering into his prison chamber. From the size and shape of the muffled figure, he concluded that it was some curious daughter of Eve pausing on her way to get a glimpse of the infidel, much as one might desire to peep at a strange and fierce wild animal. The woman moved softly up to the bars of the window, endeavoring to pierce the darkness. Then came a soft whisper:

"O Pole, art thou within?"

Paul started. What woman in this place could know his name? Yet the voice seemed vaguely familiar.

"Yea," he replied, without moving. "Who art thou?"

"Dost not know me?"

"Nay, how should I? What would ye with me?" The woman sighed gently, and whispered:

---

[59] Dudgeon (obsolete): a type of wood used for dagger hilts; a haft made of dudgeon.

"O Pole, dost not know Zolika?"

"Zolika! Good Heavens!"

Paul sprang to his feet, full of hope. A friend!

"Zolika!" cried he; "what dost thou in this place of jackals?"

"O Pole," she replied, dropping the veil, her pearly teeth glimmering in the darkness, "truly this is my home. Am I not a daughter of the mountains? Listen: without the gate of the merchants waits a noble horse for thee; here an instrument I have bought for thee in the street of Blacksmiths; make good thy escape and quickly!"

She thrust through the bars a rough file.

Thanking her, Paul set to work feverishly upon a bar of the window, talking the while as she sat patiently outside.

"Didst thou send the dagger?"

"Yea, even so!"

"Wherefore?"

"Because I feared these dogs — may the wrath of Allah strike them! — might desire to kill thee, O Pole."

"Didst thou bribe the slave?"

"Nay; he is the son of my mother's favorite slave, therefore he doth as I command."

"So. Tell me, O Zolika, who is Omar ben Abdullah, and what quarrel hath he with the master-of-the-little-dog."

"Truly, Omar ben Abdullah is my father, master of my mother. The master-of-the-little-dog took unto himself Fatma, the favorite daughter of a slave, whom Sidi Omar had marked as his own; therefore was his wrath as a storm in the mountains, and he swore by the beard of the Prophet that he would avenge the insult upon the cursed Nazarene. So it was."

"Cherchez la femme, Master Lothario!" muttered Paul grimly as he sawed away diligently.

"What sayest thou?"

"Naught, little one. And what would Sidi Omar do with me?"

"Nay, I know not. I know that he is exceeding wroth with those who took thee in error."

And so they chatted whilst Paul worked a file as he had never worked before, fearful that they might disturb him ere the iron bars were eaten through.

Suddenly, with a warning "Ssh!" Zolika flitted away in the darkness. Paul, concealing the tool beneath his djellaba, huddled against the wall feigning sleep.

A flickering light shone without, the sound of shuffling steps, and a hooded face appeared in the light of a candle lantern at the window.

"Hah!" commented the man, "the dog sleeps. Well he may, for the wrath of Sidi Omar is not like unto the milk from a woman's breast."

Muttering to himself, the man passed on and presently the gentle voice of Zolika spoke again assuring Paul that all was quiet once more.

At length the file had eaten a way round the solid bar, and Paul, after many futile attempts, succeeded in breaking the remainder. A few more powerful wrenches and the iron was twisted to one side. Then, working his arm and shoulder through the aperture, and placing the whole strength of his back and arms into a mighty heave, he buckled the two parallel bars sufficiently to permit of the passage of his body.

He stood free in the narrow street beside Zolika, who emitted a little gurgling laugh of pleasure and, without remark, swiftly led the way down the street. Paul, knowing that all town gates would be shut at night, wondered how she intended to find egress. At less than twenty yards away she halted at a small door in the wall and knocked softly. The door was opened immediately and, beckoning Paul to follow, she disappeared within. He obeyed without hesitation. A muffled figure of another woman stood by the threshold holding a lantern with which she curiously scanned Paul as he passed into the garden behind his late prison. Zolika led on without pausing to an open gate leading into another garden full of fruit trees. Paul cast a look up through the treetops, breathing a prayer of gratitude to the stars. After traversing a full quarter of a mile they came to a massive old wall, the city wall. Zolika drew Paul's attention to a series of holes forming rough steps between the time-worn slabs of rock of which the wall was built. These very steps, reflected Paul, could tell many romantic tales of intrigue [if] they could speak. Gravely handing her slippers to Paul, Zolika rapidly commenced to climb, looking like a great gray lizard. He quickly followed her to the top. The other side was a crumbling heap of masonry and rubbish down which they slid without difficulty. Another hundred yards through the olive plantation and he heard the clamping of horses. Tethered to different trees stood two powerful stallions, fully saddled.

"Come!" whispered Zolika, as Paul hesitated; "we must hasten. It is near to dawn."

"But who rides with me?"

"Zolika, ingrate!" said she, laughing into his face. "Come!"

Paul had expected a somewhat embarrassing farewell. That she should accompany him was quite unexpected; yet a moment's thought showed him his folly. He had little idea of the direction of the camp or Tanga,[60] and moreover, ignorant of the roads, would have lost invaluable time and perhaps been recaptured.

As the girl spoke she shed her outer muffling garments for greater freedom, standing in a white gossamer djellaba over a colored tunic and loose trousers; then, climbing with agility into the tree, lacking a mounting stone, she untied her animal and stepped across his back into the saddle.

---

[60] Tanga: Tangier.

Paul followed suit; as the Moorish stirrups are very high and the saddle girths worn loose, it is almost impossible to mount after the European style.

As they turned their horses' heads down the hill, Paul felt that peculiar eerie shiver; the next moment the cry rang forth:

"Al-lah — Ak-b-ah!"

The first call to prayer; two hours to sunrise.

This time the quavering notes lacked the sinister expression which had struck a note of fear in Paul's heart before. Rather they seemed to wake echoes of hope, though still conveying the sense of all-pervading destiny; that all tenors were futile unless so fated; not one jot or tittle to the right or left would a man's life waver, except as it is written: the apotheosis of "Mektub."[61]

"Al-lah — Ak-ba-a-ah!"

They walked their horses in silence for the first half hour, fearful that the sound of retreating hooves might arouse suspicion.

The live green odor of orchards, tempered by the mountain breeze, filled their nostrils. Paul inhaled the sweet, clean air hungrily, the air of freedom. Anon the sharp yelping bark of village dogs floated to them; a hill stream sung a night lullaby; owls hooted.

"Tell me, O Pole," said Zolika of a sudden; "what name hath the village where rests thy friend?"

Paul, racking his memory, could not remember if he had heard even.

"Nay, the name is not with me!" he replied at length. "Es-Sheikh is a gorbellied[62] man, of great height, a beard greater than mine, and marked by the eating sickness."

---

[61] Mektub: "It is written." A phrase that acknowledges the force of fate or destiny and conveys a belief that an event is predetermined and part of a larger, more meaningful plan.

[62] Gorbellied: a corpulent person with a protruding abdomen. A character known as "Gorbellied Godfrey" appears in an early sixteenth-century poem

Zolika laughed.

"Certes, it is Omar ben Abd-el-Kader. The village is well-known to me. Let us hasten!"

They broke into a canter for a mile or so. When walking their animals up a steep incline, Zolika suddenly pulled up.

"Listen!" she exclaimed.

Carried by the night wind came the faint thrum of hooves upon earth.

"They have discovered our escape," said Paul quietly. "Come, little one, we must hasten. These horses are fine and sound, of good blood. They will not overtake us. Come!"

And giving rein, they dashed away.

Erewhile as they galloped along a level stretch of downs, Zolika drew away to the east, saying:

"The village of Sidi Omar by the smooth way is far; as the stork flies it is near: let us take the rough road where the stream is fast and deep, for thy peril is great.

To Paul as he swerved to follow her, she, with her hair and white robes streaming, appeared like an aerial wraith upon the night wind. They rode on with the greatest possible speed, their horses sometimes compelled to slip and slide down rocky escarpments with the agility of a goat, of which feat only such mountain-trained animals were capable. Now and again, as they clattered past a village, the pariah dogs raised a chorus of inquiry. Soon the roar of the river came up to them. Paul hurriedly pulled off his djellaba in preparation for the struggle. Zolika led without hesitation along the top of the steep bank for a little way and then disappeared over the edge. Paul had to trust to his animal's sight and instinct to carry him down a goat track to the black swirling water beneath.

---

by John Skelton. Shakespeare later employed *gorbellied* as an adjective in the first part of *Henry IV* (1598): "Hang ye, gorbellied knaves, are ye undone?"

The opposite bank was not very far, but the river was running swift and deep: it looked an ugly crossing.

Zolika's horse hesitated a moment on the verge. She shouted a warning back to Paul and plunged in. The splash startled his animal, which, swerving from the narrow track half slid, half fell into the water beneath, almost on the top of the girl.

As the horse rose to the surface, Paul threw himself out of the saddle on the nearside, and hanging on with one hand, he endeavored to keep the animal's head up stream. The high banks on either side made the river surface as black as the pit of Tophet.[63] He could just discern a dull blot in the water a little ahead and above him, which indicated Zolika. The shortcut involuntarily taken by his beast had precipitated him into the river below her. The swirling of the waters roared in his ears; the far bank seemed flying above him. His horse was swimming well and gallantly. Paul calculated that he was about in mid-stream when the skyline formed by the bank began to run down to the water level. He hoped that it indicated shallows.

For a moment or two he had lost sight of Zolika. Then something came out of the darkness on top of him, a snorting kicking mass. In a flash Paul guessed that Zolika had lost control of her horse who had instantly turned his head downstream. For a moment he feared that the beast would maim either or both of them or his own animal. He changed the bridle hand and grabbed with the other at the girl's white robes, shouting to her to let her horse go. For a doubtful moment confusion, in which he nearly drowned; then somehow he managed to drag Zolika's body across his saddle and push the

---

[63] Tophet: a reference to the Pit of Tophet, as portrayed in the Old Testament. Tophet was located in the Valley of Hinnom (aka Gehenna), near Jerusalem. It became notorious as a site where the Canaanites and Israelites sacrificed children by fire to the god Moloch. Tophet came to symbolize divine wrath, judgment, and the horrific consequences of idolatry and moral corruption.

other beast's head away with his hand without losing control of his own horse.

Her animal passed to his fate behind and Paul, or his horse, struggled gamely on. As far as he could see and feel, he endeavored to keep the girl's head above water, but he did not know whether she was dead or alive. The horse's efforts gradually slackened, and Paul felt the motion change, the hooves touch bottom. Immediately the bank, fortunately low, was reached, he anxiously examined Zolika, and stretching her upon the sward he worked her arms forward and backward; at length her eyes opened.

For half an hour Zolika lay in his arms whilst the horse had a spell to recover from his gallant struggle. When they resumed their journey, Zolika rode behind Paul, pillion[64] fashion.

The first streaks of dawn tinted the eastern sky as they came down to the second river, which fortunately was a mere shallow stream, the headwaters. Upon the further bank Paul listened intently for any sound of the pursuers; but all was quiet. Evidently they had taken the long route or given up the chase. The struggle across the water had sapped Zolika's frail strength, and when endeavoring to climb to her place behind Paul, she collapsed; so he picked up the lithe form in his arms, supporting her upon the saddle bow. She whispered faintly that the village was now quite near. Soon he saw the storks wheeling above the village; heard the lowing of cattle and the barking of the dogs. Upon breasting the rise, he saw the camp under the village wall in the gathering light.

---

[64] Pillion: a pad or cushion positioned behind a man's saddle for a woman to ride on. When used in phrases such as "ride pillion" or "pillion fashion" (British usage), it means to ride as a passenger behind the driver.

CHAPTER V

"Good morning!" said the Baron.

As Paul dismounted, the Baron greeted him with characteristic placidity as if nothing out of the usual had happened; he raised his eyebrows upon recognizing Zolika, and smiled.

Rabbit stalked solemnly to take charge of Paul's horse, remarking cheerfully:

"Orlright, ole chap, whaat?"

Paul explained briefly how he had escaped, not referring in any way to the Baron's finger in the pie, whilst Zolika sat herself calmly upon a pile of luggage, watching the two Europeans.

After delaying, to give Paul and Zolika time to breakfast and a brief rest, the animals were packed and the journey recommenced.

The Baron suddenly commenced to chuckle to himself.

"The old Raid," said he with a sardonic laugh, "will not love either of us! I took Fatma, whilst you go one better by taking Zolika and a devilish fine animal!"

Paul frowned slightly. Said he:

"Maybe, Baron; but the circumstances are and *will* be different."

The Baron looked at Paul and laughed, muttering something to Kismet in front of him.

Zolika, the lighter weight, rode upon the new horse, having replaced her woman's blanket at the village. In it she wrapped herself in the orthodox fashion.

They rode on almost without incident the whole day; now and again parties of horsemen passed upon the road without comment beyond the customary greetings. The mountains were left behind, the road winding in and out amongst small conical hills and uplands, all covered by young barley, the fallow patches carpeted with flowers.

Now and again a mud-walled village, and once from the top of a ridge the white rooftops of Alcazar Kebir[65] glistening in the sun; beyond, the field of Ardath.[66] Anon, a crowd of peasants hoeing the rich loamy soil; a well around which a blindfolded donkey or camel paced his cycle of destiny. Once a party of tribesmen, all profusely armed, halted to converse with Absalom, whilst the Baron, with a fold of the turban concealing his half-grown beard, and the rest of the party, plodded on without hindrance. Absalom overtook them at the gallop with the news that El Hammo had joined Abd-el-Kader at Mekinez making a more rapid advance across country than the Baron had estimated.

At length the wearisome march came to an end; they camped towards five in the afternoon at another village, the Kaid[67] of which had been previously sounded by Absalom, riding ahead. Paul and Zolika, both tired out by their double journey, stretched themselves on the tent carpet, and slept until awakened for the Moorish supper with the Kaid. This man was an enthusiastic supporter of Mulai Abd-el-Kader, holding forth upon the iniquities of Mulai Abd-el-Rahman whom he accused of selling the country to the French. He waxed so eloquent that it was past midnight ere they escaped from interminable glasses of sweet mint tea to rest. The Baron, disturbed by the news from the interior, wished to make a dash straight through to Fez on the morrow; but Paul vetoed this by reminding him that the

---

[65] Alcazar Kebir: Ksar el-Kebir (aka Alcácer Quibir and al-Qasr al-Kabir), a city in northwestern Morocco.
[66] "The field of Ardath": the phonetically rendered "Ardath" may correspond to "Arbaoua," a rural locality located fourteen km south of Ksar el-Kebir, in the Rabat-Salé-Kenitra region.
[67] Kaid: qāʾid. An Arabic / Maghreb term, meaning a local commander, chief, or governor.

animals, particularly his latest acquisition, could never endure a thirty-hour march after their recent exertions. At length it was decided to rest all the following day and then to make a night and day ride.

During the day Paul had been greatly exercised regarding the future of Zolika. In conversation she would only smile into his face at every suggestion from Paul, and ejaculate:

"Inshallah!"

He felt that, owing his escape to her, he could not demand that she go away or turn her adrift in the middle of the country, although at the same time he foresaw that it would be impossible, besides inconvenient, to have the girl always in their caravan. Of course she was a wholly different proposition to an ordinary woman; in fact, she was almost as capable as a man, could cook and make herself generally useful. He suggested that perhaps she had friends or relations at Fez? She smiled: "In-shallah!"

Their tent on this occasion, at the invitation of the friendly Kaid, was pitched within the protecting village wall.

Stretched out upon the carpet, wrapped in their robes, they were soon all asleep, Kismet as usual, curled in a ball in the Baron's arms. Danger threatening to Kismet seemed the only thing capable of arousing the Baron from his placid tranquility.

But one recumbent figure appeared restless and incapable of slumber, Zolika. Twice during the night she half sat up, staring through the darkness at the figure next her, Paul. And once the head bent slowly, passionately kissing the hem of his robe, whilst he, all unconscious, slept dreamlessly.

During the day the Kaid tried to improve the shining hour by endeavoring to sell them a rawboned cream horse, to which he attributed, in the name of Allah and the Prophet, all the equine virtues known to man.

But, although they really needed another animal, they refused to deprive the owner of this wonderful beast, with incipient water on the knee, spavined, aged, and covered by open sores; the last, the Kaid volubly explained, were a considerable advantage for which extra money ought to be paid, as they kept the wretched beast awake, making him travel the faster! This was stated quite seriously; and it is so thought among the Moors who, on that account, keep open gall and saddle sores upon their mules and horses. On the fore shoulder of the beast in question was another example of the workings of the oriental mind: a series of gashes to permit of all disease in the subject's body escaping through these open wounds!

As the storks wheeled and glided through the air above their nests, against a matchless color scheme of a fiery golden, purple, soft green sunset, the small caravan wound away down the valley, accompanied by the enthusiastic Kaid still urging at intervals, the merits of the noble steed he bestrode. At length the head of the equine wonder was turned about, the owner departing amid profuse salaams.[68] Then, on into the gathering moonlit shadowland, up hill and down dale, across small streams and past villages, serenaded by village pariah dogs, through one illimitable treeless country of young barley. Once and again across a flat or along a fertile valley, the caravan cantered and trotted, the jingle of the sumpter[69] animals and the clatter of hooves alone breaking the night silence. Rabbit perched upon the folded tent, smoked innumerable cigarettes; Zolika, a mere shapeless bundle of white, ghostly in the moonlight; ahead Absalom on his long-tailed horse, gun across the saddle, limned against the stars as he breasted a hill; behind him, the Baron and Paul, for the most part silent. Plod, plod, canter, plod, the livelong night.

---

[68] Salaam: an obeisance performed by bowing low and placing the right palm on the forehead.
[69] Sumpter: a pack animal.

A halt was called at midnight for half an hour in a ravine where, lying amid the green barley, they allowed their animals a gorgeous snack. Then mounted again and on the road. The country now began to become more hilly, the moonlight playing queer optical illusions among the ravines and crags; abysmal chasms, fantastic grottoes and dissolving mountains. Towards dawn the clouds commenced to bank up in the east, producing magnificent effects of light and shade, as the coming day struggled against and conquered the sullen masses of dense shadows.

With the triumph of the sun they wearily climbed a long narrow gash in a chain of hills until, at the pass, a glorious panorama of wild and rugged country burst upon their view. Immediately in the foreground the bridle tracks wriggled like thin gray snakes amid a filmy white and yellow gloss of wild flowers, against the vivid green of the open champaign; in the middle distance the blue-green masses of jumbled hills; and in the background the majestic grandeur of the snow-capped Atlas, all tinted rose and purple in the rays of the rising sun.

Paul, a lover of wild nature, and Zolika, with the inherent instinct for color, involuntarily halted to admire the brushwork of the greatest Artist-Architect. Then, turning in the saddle, he beheld the reverse side: the tracks swallowed in the gloom of the ravine, beyond a rugged mass of hills fading into the depths of the shadows of receding night. It appeared as if he were balanced upon the knife edge of the world, or, as the simile occurred to him, standing in the Present looking into the gloomy Past with the hopeful glory of the Future to the front. Cheered by the fanciful thought, and accepting it as a good omen, he smiled at Zolika, and together they spurred on after the Baron, who, intent upon accomplishing practical dreams, had no time to spare upon landscapes.

As they plodded on through the valley beneath[,] the countryside began to awake for the day; cattle commenced to stream out to their pastures, peasants walked and rode along the highway, bound to their weekly open market near some other village; bands of horsemen appeared like clusters of gray ants upon the hillsides.

To the eye of the stranger all the country seemed fair and smiling, the people orderly: nothing to indicate that all authority, or the nominal semblance of such authority, had been withdrawn; that every man was practically a law unto himself and, did it seem good to him and his immediate fellows to make a raid, then forthwith they raided with enthusiasm and great joy. The people all wished in their hearts that internecine warfare, or again semblance of warfare, would continue forever, as the only benefit accruing to the peasant and the craftsman, from the piping times of peace and a strongly established Sultan, was the honor of being squeezed of every groat that they could earn (or steal); and moreover, the doubtful privilege of feudal military service to the local Kaid on behalf of the Sultan. Much dearer to the sons of the Prophet was the tribal raid, the seizure of the other's cattle and women. If those others succeeded in the like upon you, well "Inshallah!" another dash by night, a stab or two in the dark, and other dark-eyed houris and cattle to make the heart glad — Great is the mercy of Allah!

By high noon the party had crossed the wide reach of the Wad Seboo,[70] shallow and broad, and camped at a safe distance from the village, partook of a hasty dejeuner under the welcome shade of a stately fig tree.

The Baron, anxious for news, dispatched Absalom to the village to glean the latest rumor, which proved to be that Mulai Abd-el-Kader was camped in the Showya country, considerably to the west of Mekinez, thus directly contradicting the previous

---

[70] Wad Seboo: the Oued Sebou river, which carries the largest volume of water of any of Morocco's rivers. It flows through northern Morocco, passing near major cities such as Fes, Meknes, and Kenitra.

report. However, well knowing the absolute unreliability of news of any sort amongst the tribes, they determined to push on to the vicinity of Fez before accepting any report as authentic.

After a meal of luscious green figs and barley bread washed down by the inevitable green tea, they rested until about ten in the evening, when the moon arose, calculating to arrive in the Wad Fas valley[71] by sunrise. Then, in the wraith light of the moon, the party mounted and took to the road down the flat valley of the Wad Seboo. Canter and walk, walk and canter, up hill and down dale, a repetition of the previous night upon a couple of hours' sleep. Clip clop, down dale up hill, and the occasional chorus of village dogs, the vague shadowy stillness of the night. Once, a body of horse appeared upon the skyline, at which the little caravan halted; but the others, probably a raiding party, continued straight across, disappearing into the gloom of a valley. The motives of any man abroad at night were, for a certainty, not for the benefit of the community.

Little conversation of any kind throve on these night marches; each was occupied with his own thoughts, or trying to snatch a few minutes sleep in the saddles. The animals, accustomed to sudden calls upon their endurance, seemed to nurse their strength by instinct.

At length, as they passed a village upon the left, abreast of a walled town, filmy white against the gloom of an olive plantation, upon a hillside, Absalom drew up until the Baron and Paul overtook him to whisper: "See! one horn to the Wad Fas!"

The hour, seeming three by reason of the know-ledge, slowly passed and, as the faint flush of dawn appeared in the eastern sky, they halted at the junction of the small valley with the wide

---

[71] Oued Fes, a small river that flows into the Oued Sebou. The "Wad Fas valley" would refer to the valley formed by the Oued Fes.

plain of the Wad Fas, stretching from Fez to Mekinez,[72] the foothills of the mighty Atlas the further boundary. A consultation was held, whilst around them sped away the shadows of night, the countryside awaking in the distant lowing of cattle, crowing of cocks and barking of dogs. The roads would soon begin to fill with market people and other wayfarers, so that it was necessary to determine their movements. Absalom opined that the new claimant was away down in Showya, Paul thought Mekinez, the Baron convinced that he had already entered Fez, whilst Zolika, who also entered into their counsels, much to the amused indignation of Absalom, maintained that the Mulai Kader would be found between Fez and Mekinez. Eventually, they agreed to proceed towards Mekinez, and accordingly struck through the olive-planted foothills towards the southeast. The roads now began to fill again with peasants and mounted tribesmen.

As they rode along the track winding in and out amongst thickly cultivated hills, they suddenly came face to face with a band of Aissouwa[73] — corresponding to the Dervish of Egypt. In the front were borne a number of banners, green, blue, yellow, red, around which marched, sometimes capering, a crowd of the long-haired devotees, half naked, each and everyone violently rocking his head from side to side, chanting and singing as they marched. In each and every eye was the peculiar lackluster stare of the fanatic. In the rear other banners, and laymen fired with holy enthusiasm. It was a distinctly unfortunate meeting. Had Paul and his party seen them in time, a retreat would have been effected amongst the trees, but this was now impossible. The Baron hastily lowered a fold of his turban. If the procession passed without stopping, all would be

---

[72] Mekinez: Meknes, one of the four Imperial cities of Morocco.
[73] Aissouwa: Isawa. Members of a Muslim religious brotherhood, founded in Morocco about 1500.

well; on the other hand, if their identity as Europeans was discovered, serious trouble was certain.

They drew to the side of the road. To their mingled horror and disgust, the procession halted and a crazy white-haired man, capering and oscillating his head, sprang out of the crowd and made straight for the Baron. Now, it is the privilege of any Shareef[74] — Holy man who is adjudged a descendant of the Prophet — to demand or take anything he wishes from anybody. As a wealthy merchant or powerful official rides along, a Shareef may approach, roughly remove his cloak or dagger, but the great man will sit mute and suffer the saint to wreak his will. The Baron calmly eyed the gibbering devotee, who, apparently lost in ecstasy and unconscious of anybody on earth, made straight towards him, and with his clawlike hand, clutched the Baron's silham. He, well aware of the custom, raised the garment over his head, muttering a pious phrase in Arabic, to permit the sacred robber to retain it, but, unfortunately, the absence of the robe immediately revealed Kismet, who, with the cussedness of his namesake, sat up and barked shrilly. The fanatic, startled out of normal abstraction, paused. At the same moment the fold of the Baron's turban, loosened in disrobing the cloak, fell from his face. His hand darted up to replace it; but too late. Dropping the cloak, the man screeched, "N'srani! — (a Nazarene) — and his compatriots, taking up the cry, began to close round, screaming questions and curses.

The Baron, backing his animal, whispered "Run!" ramming home his sharp Moorish stirrups. The others, pausing to cover the Baron's retreat, closed in after him, Absalom digging the mule with his rifle barrel, as the band of fanatics, realizing that

---

[74] Shareef: variant spelling of *sharif*, a descendant of Muhammad through his daughter Fatima. Broadly: a person of noble ancestry or political preeminence in predominantly Islamic countries.

their victims were escaping, drew knives and shrieking in chorus, gave chase. Having the advantage of a sudden start and a flat road, the European party gained fifty yards in the first hundred, but they were handicapped by the comparatively slow pace of the Baron's mule. As they galloped round the corner of the hillside, they saw ahead of them the wide open plain of the Wad Fas and upon it an army of horsemen spread out, the track descending in an abrupt and stony escarpment which forbade a canter or gallop. Scrambling and slipping they were half down the hillside when the foremost of the howling mob overtook them. The first, a stalwart lay hill man carrying a naked dagger, sprang at the Baron. His revolver' spoke and the man dropped. Almost simultaneously three others attacked Paul, who was a little behind, defending the Baron's retreat. One seized his reins, as another springing behind, raised his dagger to stab. A sharp report and the man coughed and fell in a crumpled heap.

"Quits!" shouted the Baron above the noise of the melee.

Paul shot the man clutching at his reins and drove his horse on top of another. Absalom accounted for two more men. For a moment the onslaught of the shrieking horde was checked.

"Kill the Christian!"

"Down with the Infidel!"

"Kill, spare not, in the name of the Prophet!" Taking full advantage of the momentary lull, the party succeeded in reaching the bottom of the hill to be met by an excited throng of mounted tribesmen who had galloped towards the fracas.

Then the partisans of the Aissouwa, excited by the death of their comrades and egged on by the devotees, raced again to the attack, volleying stones. The Europeans, placed between two fires, formed, by mutual consent, back to back, Zolika in the center. Paul and the Baron realized that unless something unforeseen occurred the end was inevitable and prepared to sell their lives dearly. A chance stone struck Kismet, who, yelping shrilly, leapt out of his box on to the ground. Without a moment's hesitation the Baron threw himself from his mule and whilst Paul's revolver cracked over him, rescued his precious pet. The attackers, recognizing him as the hated N'srani, attempted a fresh rush, stopped by the last three shots of Paul's revolver. Then the Baron, holding the dog with one hand, sat upon a rock and coolly picked off a man with each of his remaining shots.

The mounted men had at first contented themselves with shouting curses and encouragement, but at the sight of their fallen countrymen, several emptied their long Moorish guns at the group, killing the Baron's mule, and wounding Rabbit's and Paul's horses. Another momentary lull occurred and then, with a fresh outburst of yells, a rush on all sides commenced. The Baron was reloading his revolver and Paul had wheeled round to fire into the rear attack when suddenly a fresh clamor was added. Seemingly from nowhere, a body of horse galloped furiously between the combatants, ranged around the little group, and charged back on their coreligionists.

Paul refrained from firing in amazement, and then, realizing that they wore the little red Fez caps of the Makhzenia[75] — civil guard — guessed that for some reason they had interfered to save the strangers from the fanatical hands of the mob. Evidently, the rabble of the tribesmen were influenced by the semblance of authority, for they fell back, still excitedly shouting curses, whilst the devotees capered and shouted in the background, far gone in frenzied madness.

The change had been almost magical. The charging mob, a sound of furious galloping, and they were surrounded by a wall of white-clad figures.

---

[75] "Makhzenia": derived from *makhzan* (or *makhzen*), the native Moroccan government.

From amidst the preservers, a black-bearded man in a gorgeous gilt-braided uniform and a tightly rolled spotless turban, wheeled his horse about and addressed the group:

"Who are ye? Whence came ye?"

Paul replied boldly: "We are two Nazarenes journeying to Mulai Abd-el-Kader — may Allah bless him!"

The other eyed him keenly.

"Art thou a Nazarene? Thy speech is that of El Masr." (Egypt.)

"Truly," replied Paul.

"Follow me," he commenced, "my master, the Sultan — may Allah — "

He paused as the ranks of his men broke to admit the passage of a tall, olive-complexioned man clad in spotless white, upon a white barb, by the side of which, a hand upon the crimson and gold saddle cloth, walked two negro slaves in white, huge silver sword scabbards dangling.

The grave dignity which enveloped him, the vivacious eyes, and the deference paid by the throng, caused Paul to surmise that it was Abd-el-Kader in person. The shouts of the mob died down, except for the wild chanting of the frenzied Aissouwa.

The Baron, also recognizing who the stranger was, stood up; he and Paul saluted together.

The man's eyes swept over the group; he checked his horse and nodded gravely in acknowledgment.

"Omar!" the voice was low and imperious.

"Naam, Sidi!"[76] replied their late interlocutor.

"Who are these people?"

"Ya Sidi," said the other; "they are two Nazarenes who say they journey to see thee. Of the others I know not."

Abd-el-Kader gazed straight at Paul upon his horse, and then at the Baron. His eyes rested for a fraction of a second upon Kismet, and the sides of the mouth, seen through the close

---

[76] Naam, Sidi: Yes, Sir.

clipped moustache and beard, quivered. He evidently had a sense of humor.

"Bring them with thee, O Omar," said he, and turning his horse, rode slowly away.

CHAPTER VI

Towards midday Abd-el-Kader and his multitudes approached a village where a camp would be pitched, an hour's journey from the city of Fez. In the far distance rode bodies, or rather mobs, of troops, after which came the long baggage caravan; and yet again in the rear straggled mobs of tribesmen and soldiery on foot and horseback, a few antiquated pieces of artillery, two Gatlings and a Maxim[77] on mules, and a vast crowd of camp followers, cattle, sheep and goats. Then a gap of a mile or more, after which rode Abd-el-Kader amid a crowd of counselors and supporters.

A tall, grim-visaged man, with a distinct suggestion of a Mongolian caste of feature, Paul learned was El Hammo, the great Berber lord of the Atlas, no less, who had met the new Pretender at Mekinez, bringing with him a vast horde of wild, shaggy mountain tribesmen. In the wake of these people rode Paul and his party with their escort, a target to curious eyes. The Baron, bereft of his mule, had been provided with another upon which rode he and Kismet. Behind and about this group rode and walked the officials and the Makhzenia — civil guard. In the far distance a column of white-robed and heavily veiled women mounted upon mules, in front and upon the flanks of which rode a powerful escort of soldiers whose chief duty was to prevent any common eye from resting upon their sacred charge — their royal master's harem. By their side, riding and walking, were the eunuchs and other palace attendants.

The whole of this host, white and gray, with color splashes of scarlet, yellow and blue, straggling across the verdant plain, carpeted with spring wild flowers of white and yellow, the silver-winding streak of the Wad Fas in the center, formed a

---

[77] Maxim: a Maxim machine gun.

scene of barbaric splendor — recalling the march of a Biblical king and his hosts.

A halt occurred of the multitude in the van. As the Imperial party drew near, the confusion and babel of unloading — (animals are seldom off saddled) — arose in the hot air.

From all the seething mass of men and animals, apparently in hopeless confusion, an unexpected method and order grew. Suddenly from the very center a large tent, having a gilded ball upon the apex, shot up, and, as upon a signal, a thousand other tents were simultaneously raised in a perfect wide circle around the center one, as if a fairy hand had raised a magic growth of mushrooms to illustrate an Euclidian problem.

Then around the gilded ball a high canvas fence was quickly erected, the wide space between this enclosure and the outer circle of tents cleared, save for the private sumpter animals, the convoy of women and attendants.

The new Sultan and suite arrived at a gap in the line of tents forming an entrance, where the courtiers with many salaams fell back whilst Abd-el-Kader rode on to his enclosure attended only by the slaves.

Kaid Omar, who seemed responsible for the wayfarers' safety and comfort, made them at ease in his tent, by the side of which their own was pitched. Upon brilliant colored carpets they lounged, chatting and drinking tea. Gradually the huge encampment settled down. By the sluggish river, where the tortoise flopped and swam a couple of hundred yards distant, soldiers, clad only in their sky-blue ragged knee trousers, bathed and washed clothes; women, muffled in blankets toiled from the adjacent hills, heavily laden with huge bundles of firewood or barley; smoke began to curl upwards from a hundred fires; animals picketed by forefoot and near hind neighed, squealed, and brayed, according to their kind; women with faces brazenly exposed, clad in brilliant hued garments, sat at tent doors, laughing, smoking, and playing the guinbri[78] to charm the rough, lusty mountaineer and soldier. Here, a barber at work shaving the skull of a soldier anxious to appear orthodox to enter the city on the morrow. Then three or four richly clad Kaids sitting in their tent, roughly decorated with a black and white dado pattern;[79] yonder a fervid tribesman in his brown djellaba trimmed with gaudy rosettes bowing and kneeling towards the East in prayer, and near him a mangy cur snuffling in a newly formed muck heap. All a moving kaleidoscope of rich color and sound in the rays of the setting sun.

Towards ten in the evening, after a sumptuous native dinner, a negro slave popped his black head round the tent curtain and simply announced: "Sidna[80] would speak with the Nazarenes."

Paul and the Baron arose to obey the Imperial summons as Kaid Omar and his friends present salaamed at the reference to the august person. As Paul stalked beside the Baron across the open towards the Imperial tent, he looked up at the quarter moon and remembering how his life had altered since the death of the last phase, wondered what destiny held for them in the man whom they were about to see.

Before the door of the tent a canvas verandah protruded under which sat cross-legged a shrouded white figure. As they stooped under the canvas flap, they recognized the Sultan. They saluted as he waved a hand towards two cushions in front of him. The Baron expressed the formal flowery salutations. Whilst the other's lips muttered the orthodox replies, his eyes were busy taking stock afresh of the two men before him. As soon as the Baron finished speaking, Abd-el-Kader disclosed a

---

[78] Guinbri: the *guembri* or *sintir* (aka the *gimbri* or *hejhouj*), a three-stringed lute, carved from a log and covered with a stretched camel skin.

[79] A black and white dado pattern: a decorative design used on walls, often created with tiles or paint, featuring alternating patterns of white and black.

[80] Sidna: "Our master."

naive anxiety, wholly discarding Oriental etiquette, by demanding the strangers' business. The Baron proceeded to explain, floundering now and again in the interpretation of different points, which the patois of the country was incapable of lucidly presenting, but which Paul having the tongue of the more pedantic Egyptian, was able to elucidate. The Sultan sat very quietly watching the speaker's face, nodding when he understood or turning to Paul for further enlightenment.

As the scheme, or the preliminary part, was unfolded, his eyes became brighter; he ejaculated at intervals in approbation, "Mezian!" "Mezian bizaff!"[81] (Good! Splendid!)

At the mention of money his eyes grew hard and keen. He interrupted, to have the sum repeated in Moorish and French equivalent.

From the camp without, the neighing of horses, braying of donkeys, dog barking, the hum of a large camp of men; and from within, the occasional hushed voice of a eunuch, or the silvery ripple of a woman's laugh. The stars and moon looked down cold and hard. It seemed to Paul that in some way everything should be with more pomp and ceremony, considering the issue that was at stake — the destiny of a kingdom, even perhaps of Europe, for who could say what might be the end? Three shrouded figures chatting in a tent beneath the stars, yet the destinies of the Roman Empire, or other great empires, had been settled under less auspicious circumstances.

The voice of Abd-el-Kader brought back Paul's wandering thoughts.

"From which country are ye? Englees?" There was a suggestion of hope in the last word. "Ya Sidi," replied the Baron, "I am of the Dutch — a country cousin to England, and

---

[81] Mezian bizaff: Mzyan bzaaf. "Very good," employed as a means of strongly complimenting something or someone.

Germany," he explained as the Sultan frowned perplexedly. "My friend is of the English."

"Thou art English?" looking at Paul with a pleased expression. "By Allah, thou art like unto a son of the Prophet," he added smiling.

"Yea, Ya Sidi, I have dwelt long in the land of the Prophet."

And at the other's question Paul told him briefly of his captivity.

Abd-el-Kader smiled approval.

"Truly thou speakest our tongue as one of us. Art thou a soldier? Even so; it is the hand of Allah that brings thee to me!"

Then with a rapid change of thought, he inquired: "Why hath England, who swore friendship with my father, turned her face away? Is it not that she bargains with France that she keep Egypt?"

"Even so," answered Paul diplomatically; "but we have a proverb — 'Ye know not what the morrow may bring forth.' Again, ye say: 'Doth not a man wear two faces, even according to the sun or the storm?'"

Abd-el-Kader nodded, smiling.

"Aye," said he, "the dogs sit around a bone, which neither dare swallow for fear that the others attack. But if the bone be wise, it will have luscious meat upon all sides, lest several, weary of watching, depart, and the bone is swallowed by those that are left."

His big vivacious eyes twinkled as he glanced from one to the other.

"Truly, Abd-el-Rahman hath permitted one dog to gnaw a piece of the bone, so that the bone cries out upon me. What number of guns have ye and where? Let no time be lost."

The Baron took up the conversational thread, again going into details regarding the landing of arms and ammunition.

At length Abd-el-Kader turned to Paul.

"I am in sore need for these my children to know the art of war, even as the Infidel fights, for they of Abd-el-Rahman are many, trained by Europeans, and many guns. Is it true, then, as I thought, that mine enemies say that I have declared the Jehad? Nay, but that is the talk of fools, for am I a goat to butt my head against a stone wall? If the bone stink in the nostrils of the dogs, then will they appoint the lesser dog to devour it. It is true that many of my children have spoken of the Jehad amongst themselves, and I have not denied it, for they are but children, and cannot see with the eyes of a wise man. Thinking thus, will they, in their blindness, flock to my standards, aiding the overthrow of my rival, but once that is accomplished then will I, their father and the true son of the Prophet, make for their good. The country is poor, for hath not El Rahman sorely oppressed the people that he may wallow in the luxuries of the Infidel? Things are now as they never were before, not since the days of the overthrow of Mulai Idrees.[82] Are there not two sons of cattle who also claim the holy inheritance? But I am the son of my father and the true preserver of the poor. Men accuse me of lusting after the same fruits as my brother, but they know me not. France, the smaller dog, hath long coveted this fair land, even as she coveted and took Algiers — the will of Allah! — but she shall not swallow the bone yet, for hath not the Emperor of the Germans sworn that the integrity of Morocco shall be respected? Hath not thy Bashador[83] of England sworn the like? — yet doth France snarl louder than any. Are the words of the Nazarene kings of water? The people of England have ever been true to their word. Are these not the words of Mulai Ismael who cried, saying: 'Am I a dog of an Englishman that I

---

[82] Idris was believed to be poisoned by the agents of the Abbasid caliph, Harun al-Rashid.
[83] Bashador: Ambassador.

should keep my word?'[84] Yet where is the spoken — aye, and written word which I will show thee anon — of thy English Queen? Truly, I know that the diplomacy of the Infidel is as the Oriental — words and actions at different ends. But will thy country uphold me?"

"Y a Sidi," replied Paul, "it is not for me to reply to these things, for ye know that the policy of a nation is ever changing; that a thing that hath seemed good and profitable may be outshone by greater things. This I know, that my country will not allow Germany to swallow thy country, for Germany is the young man entering upon man's estate, and the elder man fears to permit the younger too many footholds. With France she hath, as ye know, an understanding, but how long that will last Allah alone knows."

"Ya Sidi," interrupted the Baron, "all my friend says is true, but as I have told ye, the money which we have is that of German merchants, and trade is the power and strength of Germany as of England. A blind man hath no need to see in a dark night but he can feel the night winds."

As the Baron spoke, Paul for the first time became fully aware of the keen sense of patriotism. Before, he had regarded the whole scheme, even the vague plans of the nebulous empire, as a thing distinct and apart from a national view. Now he suddenly saw that the Baron was the advocate of a German Morocco, or at least of predominant German influence. The advantages likely to accrue to the Power holding such a

---

[84] The Moors were said to tell the truth and to keep "their word only if it was in their interest to do so: 'Do you think that I am a dog of a Christian that I should be bound by my word?' the Sultan Moulai Ismael is alleged to have told a European diplomat." Douglas Porch, *The Conquest of Morocco*, p. 28. Moulay Ismail Ibn Sharif was a Sultan of Morocco from 1672 to 1727. He was the seventh son of Moulay Sharif and was governor of the province of Fes and the north of Morocco from 1667 until the death of his half-brother, Sultan Moulay Rashid, in 1672.

position — not only the possession of a rich and fertile country, but a strategic position for coaling stations and a counter key to the Mediterranean — were incalculable.

All his patriotism awoke and he keenly desired to secure the plum for England.

Yet was the Baron really playing for Germany — or his own hand, prompting the German idea as a bait? Some Power must necessarily have predominant influence in Morocco. It once had been England, was now France, and after — ?

"Ye speak true words," Abd-el-Kader was saying. "Commerce is now the strength and hence would I have railways and the engines of the Infidels, that money may be squeezed from the sleeping lands. Yea, I know that by use of machines such as my countrymen use in Egypt, thrice as much grain and produce will these fat lands produce. Come!"

He arose and walked out into the open. As Paul followed him, he admired the commanding stature of the man, and the dignified, majestic mien.

"There," he exclaimed, sweeping with his right hand, "look ye upon a fairer country? These my people are as their forefathers before them from times before ye were," he proudly reminded his guests, although without offence. "Look, from Tstouan and Tanga to Agadir and Sus[85] is a fertile land flowing with milk and honey, and amid it all my children laugh and fight among themselves whilst the clash of arms is heard without."

He spoke quietly yet forcibly, his white teeth and eyeballs gleaming in the moonlight. "And yet they are but children! — Yonder lies El Fas from which I have good news. The townspeople open wide the gates to welcome me. Tried and oppressed were they by El Rahman who, shut within the palace with his gawds, fooled whilst the people starved. Yet there are

---

[85] Tétouan: former capital of the Spanish protectorate, located in northern Morocco.

others within who will not be pleased to greet me" — his eyes glinted cruelly, — "but it is late."

Accepting the hint of dismissal, they saluted, waiting apart until he had stooped beneath his tent door.

CHAPTER VII

The Sultan, together with the courtiers, the harem, and the army, marched late the next morning, leaving the camp to follow on.

The events of the previous night had acted as a stimulus to Paul. Before, although very keen and enthusiastic upon the scheme, he had not fully realized it as a fact; the interview of the previous evening had had a stimulating effect, bringing home to his mind the scheme as a concrete object. The change from the purposeless wander across France and Spain with life a burden to him to this maelstrom of active plot and counterplot had, for a while, a stultifying effect, leaving his mind in a state that, although it accepted ideas and thoughts, yet refused at the back to accept such as really and truly facts as it were. Now he had awakened from that phase, realizing the grim reality of it all. Before he had told himself that he was playing for an empire, which had aroused the dormant fire of ambition and had afforded him immense pleasure and relief, but that was as lager beer to old brandy in comparison with his state of mind as he rode along in the brilliant sunlight trying to digest the thousand and one ideas that his active brain prompted. He looked around at the masses of horse and foot; at the Baron lost, too, in mental empire building, with Kismet, ridiculous and contented in his box before his master; at the white shrouded figure of the Sultan ahead of him. Yes, it was all hard concrete fact. He had thrown in his lot with this man, and if he was successful, then what awaited him? His imagination suggested a dozen things at once. He saw himself the Cromer[86] of Morocco, the absolute autocrat of the Independent State of Sus,

---

[86] Evelyn Baring, 1st Earl of Cromer (1841 – 1917): the British consul-general in Egypt from 1883 to 1907. Known as an "empire-builder," he was later viewed as the personification of modern imperialism.

as Rajah Brooke had been in Borneo.[87] The latter, with the suggestion of unlimited power, fascinated, enthralled him. In a moment a vision was conjured up in which he sat upon a raised dais — not a throne, of course — just a dais around which thronged a multitude of white-robed courtiers and gold-laced figures of officials ready to obey his sovereign will. In the lift of a finger lay the power of life and death. It was intoxicating; the bare idea mounted like old wine to his head. He smiled grimly, majestically, to himself as he rode, unconsciously lifting his head higher in imperial dignity. Then his abstracted eyes caught upon Kismet and, focusing to this earthly range, he awoke from his daydreams. For a moment his late thoughts rather startled him. He looked at the little shaggy head of the dog, and smiled a normal smile. What a fool he was! There sat the absurd dog, a ludicrous symbol of destiny. Well, who knew what Fate might have in store for him? Napoleon, in his early day, could have barely imagined — he checked his errant thoughts half angrily. Ah! the Baron too: he had forgotten him. True, the Baron had brought him into the scheme, but then the Baron represented Germany, and, as an Englishman, he was compelled to uphold the national pride in land grabbing. Why, Cecil Rhodes[88] would never have been the great empire builder had he been checked by such little scruples.

In a second Paul saw himself at the least a second Rhodes. A thought flew generations ahead, showing him a statue of himself, the great empire builder who had painted another quarter of Africa a gaudy, staring red.

---

[87] James Brooke (1803/04 – 1868): British soldier who founded the Raj of Sarawak in Borneo. He ruled as the first White Rajah of Sarawak, from 1841 to 1868.

[88] Cecil Rhodes (1853 – 1902): known as the "empire builder" of British South Africa; prime minister of Cape Colony (1890 - 1896); and organizer of the diamond-mining company De Beers Consolidated Mines, the world's largest diamond producer.

"Towers! Towers!" the voice of the Baron came dimly to his ears as from a distance. "Are you deaf? I've spoken about half a dozen times. I was saying that the messenger ought to be in Tanga by tomorrow night, then Tarkas should get the wire in New York first thing in the morning. That again means his arrival at the coast in three weeks from now."

"Yes, of course," said Paul vaguely.

"We ought," went on the Baron caressing Kismet, "to whip Abd-el-Rahman's people within two months; then Abd-el-Kader is recognized Sultan and, Blut und Eisen, I am made! In two years I am Khedive of Sus,[89] Khedive du Sus," he repeated softly, very much in love with the phrase. Paul glanced at his eyes which had softened into that abstract look of one gazing at a long distance — probably into Sus, thought Paul with a sneer; then he felt ashamed. The Baron, too, was busy building empires, as he always had been for that matter, but Paul noticed the continual use of the first person singular, and resented it, inconsistently enough. A voice near him distracted his thoughts.

"N'srani! N'srani! Look thou, yonder is Fas Djeedidah![90] Mezian? Aye, Mezian bizaff!"

At the end of the narrowing valley plain, flanked by the foothills of the rugged Atlas on the east and the low olive-clad mounts on the west, the ground fell away into a rugged declivity.[91] On the slope a white host, two miles long, struggled

---

[89] Khedive of Sus: an Ottoman title meaning "Lord of Sus."

[90] Fas Djeedidah: Fes el-Jdid, or New Fes.

[91] Cf. Beadle's description of the same terrain in his photo-essay, "A Talk with the New Sultan of Morocco," *Pall Mall Magazine*, October 1908, p. 475: "I will spare my readers any details of the wretched journey stage by stage to Fez [....] But let us come to our destination, with its suburbs of olive gardens, and the Mehalla, or army corps, encamped along the valley stretching away in a southwesterly direction towards Mequinez." Mequinez (or Meknes) is located about 60 km west of Fes. A popular publication at the time, this same issue of *Pall Mall* features "The War in the Air," a story by

up the incline, marshaled by the grim gray walls, officered by mosque towers, green ball and flag crested; and led triumphant by the palace gardens at the summit, the Sultan's gilded mosque tower the banner of the general in the van, the whole seeming to swallow the sluggish river in a thousand greedy throats.

But Paul's first glimpse only revealed the tops of the minarets against a background of green hills; then the old embattled walls running round the city and out into the plain, enclosing the enormous gardens, green and cool, amid which gleamed the white housetops and the sloping red-tiled palace roofs. Without upon the plain a vast multitude, stretching from the silver river where it was swallowed under the garden walls, to the cactus hedges of the olive plantations on the hillsides to the north, amid which hundreds of brilliant-hued banners were flaunting. Away between the palace garden walls and the town gate a cleared space caught the eye, across which raced a score of mounted men. When they were, apparently, upon the top of the gate a puff of smoke shot out into the air, the horsemen pulled up abruptly and scattered as the report of firearms reached the ear. Again and again was the game — Powder Play — repeated.

A dull murmuring roar floated through the hot air, which, as they approached, resolved into a continuous shout:

"Allah ibarek F'amur Sidi!"[92] (God's blessing upon our lord.)

The answer, reiterated by the Kaid Meshwar riding in advance of Abd-el-Kader, was drowned in the volume of sound.

"God's blessing upon you! May you walk in the way of Allah, saith my lord."

---

the celebrated author H. G. Wells. Excerpts from Beadle's article were widely reproduced in the British press, even in Australia.

[92] Allah ibarek F'amur Sidi: Allah ybarek fi amr Sidi. "God bless your age / orders, sir." An expression of loyalty, used to address authority figures.

The envoys of Abd-el-Kader and El Hammo had done their work well, winning undoubtedly by extravagant promises interlarded with instructions from the Prophet and a little hard cash the support of the merchants and governors of Fez. The rabble, anxious for favors to come and swayed by the religious sanction of the Ullema — Holy College — thronged in thousands to welcome their new lord. Through this concourse of excited populace, Paul's party followed in the wake of the new Sultan, amid a pandemonium of brass bands, native instruments, chanting, cries and shouts, guns firing in the air, an old seven-pounder booming out an erratic royal salute from the inside of the palace grounds.

Slowly in the suffocating heat, dust and smell, they neared the Bab-el-Bushat.[93] The Sultan, in order to show himself to the enthusiastic populace, proceeded straight through the wide markets and walled squares down into the narrow dark streets, where one man can scarce ride in comfort, to the most sacred Mosque of Mulai Idrees,[94] the patron saint of Fez and all Morocco. Inside these crumbling embattled walls, built for archers and spearmen, not a single face, house, or window of an Infidel marred the sacred precincts.

As Paul rode beneath the old horseshoe arch of the Bab-el-Bushat, he tried to imagine the feelings of Alexander or Napoleon entering a city of conquest. Paul was not a conqueror in that sense but this old-world city was the goal of his present aim, and would probably be the arena where the preliminary rounds in the struggle for empire would be fought. Then, as he emerged into the sun after a prolonged halt in the packed gateway, he felt the eerie shiver as from a neighboring mosque

---

[93] Bab = "door." Bab-el-Bushat: the Bab Boujat or Bab Boujloud ("the gate of the carpet sellers"), an arched city gate leading into Fes el-Bali, or Old Fes.
[94] The mausoleum of Moulay Idriss I, composed of a mosque, shrine, school, and sanctuary.

tower, the Muedhin, oblivious to earthly pomp as the scythe of Time, cried: "Al-lah — Ak-ba-ah!"

This time there seemed to Paul a distinct note of triumph, as if welcoming him; still the strong sense of the call of Destiny, but withal favorable, encouraging.

"Al-lah — Ak-ba-ah!"

Paul glanced at the Baron who was keenly watching the seething throng about him, Kismet hidden beneath the folds of the silham. Paul felt a wave of personal antagonism sweep over him. There had always been some repelling force in the man, now that seemed intensified to a loathing. Then he realized that the waking of the lust of ambition was destroying his sense of fidelity, and grew angry with himself.

He observed that the soldiers composing their escort were roughly forcing a way through the dense throng in front whilst the main procession [was] turning to the right, pressing through the double arch of another gate through which he could see tremendously high walls lining a huge square thronged with a vast crowd salaaming to the Sultan as he rode slowly down the center.

"Whither go we?" he inquired of Kaid Omar, who happened to be beside him in the crush.

"To the house of a friend until word cometh from Sidna concerning ye."

Presently they emerged through an outer gate outside the walls of Fez once more, and traveling apace along an empty stony road, entered the town once more by the gate of the basket makers, winding in a maze of small narrow alleys. They came to a small sok[95] — marketplace — at the junction of these streets, and were held up whilst the whole of the procession passed upon its way to the lower town. Abd-el-Kader was halfway across the open space as they halted, and seeing them,

---

[95] Souk (aka *suq*): a stall in a marketplace.

nodded gravely. Paul noted the bright intelligent eyes flitting over the faces of the people, observing with experience the exact temper of the crowd of Fazi,[96] who, famous for their fair complexion, were equally notorious as being the most fickle of a changeable people. They who now shouted their loudest in praise of the new lord might, within a month or less, be crying equally lustily upon another side.

As Paul gazed around at the people, he became aware, as one does, of being the object of close scrutiny. During their progress through the city few eyes had detected the presence of Europeans, even though the Baron had discarded the turban mask. All were too intent upon the procession, much as an English crowd at any royal function.

Paul turned uneasily in his saddle, sweeping adjacent rooftops with a glance. Upon most were the figures of women, mere shapeless bundles of blanket wraps, peering at the passing show; but upon one roof, almost within two arms' length of him, his eye met and held a pair of bright, dark eyes peering intently over her haik.[97] Paul felt the look, to use a hackneyed expression, pierce his very soul. His eyes remained riveted, he forgot all his surroundings, only those eyes filled the universe, what time a delicious thrill shook him leaving his arteries throbbing violently at the temples. And as he looked and looked again, slowly the haik slid lower and lower, until the whole of the woman's face was revealed in its brain-maddening beauty. Under the gauzy hood Paul could see the glint of burnished copper, a high creamy brow above those limpid pools of eyes which seemed to burn him. The cupid bow of a mouth opened just the weeniest bit, permitting the glimmer of ivory teeth. Paul seemed hypnotized; dreams of empire, the

---

[96] Fazi: Fasi, a person from Fes.
[97] Haik (also spelled *hayk*): a large cloth worn by women, to cover their body and head when in public.

Sultan, the past and future obliterated, only those eyes set in an angel's face.

Never in all his life had Paul experienced a tittle of the sensation that shook him to his innermost being, as he gazed like to a man athirst drinking in new life. It seemed an eternity and a fraction of a second before the veil was slowly returned, covering all save those burning eyes.

Then, with an effort, Paul withdrew his eyes to come back to earth with that nauseating thud that distinguishes a nightmare.

He glanced around guiltily to find the Baron still interested in the crowd and the others similarly engaged; again his glance wandered round to meet and hold those eyes once more and revel in the glorious thrill that rioted through him at the contact.

For the remainder of the time until the streets were clear of the procession, Paul feasted his eyes in mute joy. He seemed to have known her always; that nothing had been or could be perfect without those eyes. Then, as they once more rode on after a last longing gaze, he came to his normal senses and laughed, calling himself a fool. "Woman!" thought he. "No, I've been made a fool of once, and never a woman will catch me again; besides I have an empire at stake, the. career of a man, not a squire of dames. Bah! the little fool, like all Oriental women, in love at first sight with any man. I might as well fall in love with Zolika."

And at the thought of Zolika the problem occurred regarding her immediate future. He knew that the girl was in love with him, and in accordance with her Oriental training, had offered herself to him body and soul; but to him she was merely a girl, a dancer, outside the scheme of things. Of course, he owed his life, at any rate his escape from captivity, to her, and would reward her in kind, and for this reason had permitted her to accompany the caravan. But she could not be always with him. Of course, Paul could have accepted her offer without incurring any binding responsibilities. Such was quite common in the

East, and West, too, for that matter. Paul was not aggressively virtuous by any means, but in this case the girl, beyond her dancing and fidelity, had no attraction for him.

With the lady of the eyes — but then, Paul laughed her to scorn as soon as he was out of reach of the battery of those orbs. However, he did not forget to inquire of Kaid Omar the name of the market by which they had been held up by the procession.

CHAPTER VIII

Since the memorable incident of the first interview with Abd-el-Kader, a mute but definite antagonism had sprung up between the Baron and Paul. The Baron, usually a very interesting raconteur of adventures in East and West, had become taciturn. He, apparently, with his large knowledge of the world and men, had immediately interpreted the struggle which had arisen in Paul's mind. He was always perfectly courteous, calm and agreeable, but devoted himself to his own thoughts and Kismet. When Paul, conquering for the moment the new antipathy, really jealousy, would endeavor to open the subject of the future of the scheme, the Baron would answer in monosyllables, or speak just the bare decision necessary to deal with any question that arose.

Paul felt really ashamed of himself for allowing his fidelity to waver at all, but, although he struggled hard to convince himself that he could and would remain true to his bargain, as his conscience dictated he should, yet he mounted the hobby horse of fancy and gave imagination the rein. He soared high above any petty scruples, rising to a Jesuitical atmosphere where the end justified any means.

And yet sometimes, as he would lie upon his bed, or stride up and down the courtyard, the wonderland of ambitious imagination would dissolve before the vision of two limpid orbs, which seemed to gaze at him in reproach. Then he would curse violently to himself, banish both the eyes and the dreams of empire, and returning to earth, would upbraid himself on the two counts of infidelity and fatuous idiocy, as he termed it. Yet as surely as the sun set, both the dreams and the vision of the eyes would haunt him in the watches of the night.

For a week they had remained the guests of Kaid Omar, during which they had not seen Abd-el-Kader who, occupied with the religious and state ceremonies concerned with the ratification by the Ullema of his claim to the Sultanate, and in the festivities of his marriage to the daughter of El Hammo — forming a political bond — had not had time to spare an audience. From time to time, however, he sent messages and presents with requests for them to go wherever they wished in company of the escort quartered with them.

This escort in question, although an honor accorded to ambassadors, was not without disadvantages, particularly to Paul who wished to explore the town, as he convinced himself. And, although still condemning his "fatuous idiocy," he maneuvered that on his return from several rides with the cavalcade clattering beside them, they returned via the first route through the little sok; but to Paul's angry disappointment, he failed to obtain a glimpse of the Lady of the Eyes. At length he was constrained, cursing Arab etiquette which forbade reference to a man's womenfolk, to inquire of Kaid Omar who the owner of the house and grounds might be.

The Shareef of Wazzan, he was told, and the knowledge that the old Shareef was a French protégée who had, years ago, married an English wife,[98] gave him food for thought.

---

[98] Wazzan: Ouazzane, a town and region in northern Morocco known as a spiritual center. The Sharif of Ouazzane was Sīdī al-Ḥājj 'Abd al-Salām (aka Sidi Mohammed, 1835 – 1891), "whose passion for things European inevitably drew him into the competition among the powers for influence in Morocco. The Englishwoman Emily Keene had come to Morocco as governess to the Greek-American Perdicaris family, who lived in some splendor in their villa Aidonia ('the Place of the Nightingales') near Tangiers. The sharif ... asked for her hand in 1873. In later years, Emily Keene told visitors to her home in Tangiers that hers had been a love match, that only a romantic impulse could have induced her to spend her life in an uncivilized and alien land. The truth was somewhat different. Negotiations over the marriage contract were long and difficult. Miss Keene wrested from the sharif a promise never to marry again, upon penalty of a large indemnity. When the sharif did finally take a second wife, a thirteen-year-old girl, Emily Keene was able to live very well off her caution money until her death in 1941." Douglas Porch, *The Conquest of Morocco*, pp. 42-43.

Then one morning their host announced that a house had been prepared for them by order of the Sultan, and that they were at liberty to remove there whenever they desired, adding, with traditional Arab hospitality, that his house was theirs forever if they so desired. However, they offered suitable excuses, and their small impedimenta, augmented by the Sultan's presents and supplies of clothes bought in Fez, were removed to the new residence, which they discovered to be a magnificently roomy house, profusely tiled after the Fezian manner,[99] with a fine marble fountain and spacious orange gardens. In every room was a jumble of heavy Turkish carpets, brass bedsteads, mirrors, and almost every conceivable article that could possibly be required.

During the sojourn at the house of Kaid Omar, Paul had seen little of Zolika who had, of course, retired to the women's quarters, but now the problem recurred regarding the status of Zolika in the new household.

As Paul stood in the middle of the courtyard, Zolika herself appeared and suggested a solution

"O Pole," said she, after the greetings, "what would my lord that I should do?"

"Nay, I know not, O Zolika. Even now am I seeking the will of Allah. What would'st thou?"

"Inshallah! I would be my lord's slave."

"Nay, Zolika; that cannot be."

Her slight figure crept nearer to him, and she placed one tiny hand upon his arm, pleading.

"Nay, O Pole, why should this thing not be? Thy will is my law, and when thou art aweary of me, one word from thee and I am gone."

Paul looked at her, and as he gazed a pair of great passionate eyes seemed to compel his glance from over her head. He

---

[99] The Fezian manner: the manners of the people from Fes.

turned away angry with himself, which Zolika, seeing, interpreted against herself.

"Woe is me!" she cried; "my lord is wroth with me. Waali! Waali! I am gone."

And throwing the haik about her face, she fled, the tears welling in her eyes.

"Zolika!" called Paul hastily.

She turned and came, looking up at him with the mute expression of a faithful dog that has been beaten unjustly and knows that his master knows.

"I am not wroth with thee, little one," said Paul contritely.

He stroked her uncovered hair and felt her tremble beneath his touch.

"Inshallah! What would'st thou?"

Then Paul inconsistently felt himself a cad. He said, after a pause:

"O Zolika, I would that thou leave me, for it is not the will of Allah that I should love thee. I owe thee much and would repay thee in — "

He stopped, seeing the reproachful anguish in the tear-dimmed eyes.

"Canst thou not stay in the City with friends?" he suggested.

Just then the Baron and Absalom entered from the gardens. The Baron, hugging Kismet, eyed the two with a cynical smile.

"Well, Towers," said he; "still quarrelling with the gifts of the Gods, eh?"

Paul frowned.

"As I said before," continued the Baron, stepping forward, "if you won't, I will!"

"You won't do anything of the sort," exclaimed Paul angrily.

The Baron raised his eyebrows.

"Don't be a fool, Towers! Zolika!" he spoke a callous inquiry in Arabic.

"Herr Gott, Towers, you are mad!" for Paul had stepped between the two threateningly. "Don't be a dog in the manger! She's only a cocotte from a café chantant."[100]

Then all the smoldering jealousy of the Baron and anger against himself for his infidelity blazed.

Paul deliberately struck the Baron with the open palm across the face.

Zolika screamed in affright, clinging to Paul; Absalom ejaculated a guttural Arabic oath. For a moment, as Paul stood over the Baron, the Baron's eyes blazed. Then they softened to a hard steely stare, as he said quite calmly:

"So! Over a cocotte you would wreck an Empire! It has been done before, I believe, so you are not trés originale. So? You will give me satisfaction?"

"Certainly," answered Paul, quivering with rage.

"So! When I demand it — and that will be when you can be spared," he added significantly. "Now you will go to your room and recover from your childish exhibition. This woman will leave the house immediately. She is evidently dangerous to boys."

He turned his back on the maddened Paul, and gave instructions in Arabic to Absalom.

Paul did retire to his room, feeling, immediately the fit of passion had passed, ashamed and very angry with himself. That he, a man who had had his experience, should lose control of himself, as he had never done before, was maddening. He cursed himself, Zolika, the Lady of the Eyes, the scheme, everything and everybody, which resulted in a couple of hours self-abasement before he was restored to a normal frame of mind. Then he suddenly awoke to what he had really done and the significance of the Baron's words. He well knew that the

---

[100] Café chantant or "singing café." A forerunner to the cabaret and music hall, which featured performances of live music.

Baron considered him as everyone else, merely a pawn in the game. The Baron, relying upon the fact that he was an expert duelist himself, would have a good excuse to remove him after he had served his purpose. The Baron's demeanor since the first interview with Abd-el-Kader had changed, and Paul opined that the Baron had either foreseen or read his thoughts, and had determined to get rid of him when opportunity offered. Now Paul, like a fool, had given him the chance. Well, he deserved it, Paul told himself. But yet there was the mortifying reflection that all the trouble had started immediately he had entertained the promptings of his wretched selfish ambitions. Paul could not for very shame offer an apology which he knew the Baron would refuse. He worried himself until he grew peevish, determining to throw the whole thing over.

His reflections were cut short by the timely arrival of Rabbit, who, clad in exceeding fair raiment, sat himself upon a roll of carpet and observed with a judicial air:

"What for you hit Baron?"

Paul glared at him by way of answer.

"You know," Rabbit continued imperturbably, "that Baron not like you. Me tell you long time Baron bad man, what? Baron he like Zolika — you no like Zolika, what? Him awf'ly good girl. You give him me, what?"

"Skut," snapped Paul "Emshi! Get out!"[101]

Rabbit looked at him placidly, puffing at a cigarette.

"You liver dambad, what?" he observed. "I say-ole-chap, you come long me, we go Millah[102] (Jewish quarter). Millah plenty wine, you get drunk, awfly drunk. You orlright tomorrow."

Paul smiled, a thin, peevish smile, which Rabbit responded to by showing a set of yellow, blackened stumps.

---

[101] Emshi (or *imshi*): "go away" / "get out."
[102] Millah: Mellah, the Jewish quarter.

"Me have friens in Millah, come on! Oh, you know every peoples say you Bashador Inglees, what?"

"English Ambassadors? What d'you mean?"

"Mean? Peoples, Sultan he say you Bashador Inglees.[103] Him clever chap," added Rabbit, condescendingly. "Peoples say Sultan Inglees help Moor people, make fight Fransawi."[104]

Paul laughed, interested.

"Some more of his diplomacy," said he.

"'acy? Yes, him clever chap," asserted Rabbit thoughtfully, blowing the cigarette ash into the face of an ormolu clock[105] lying on its back. "Me know Abd-el-Kader long time. Him clever chap!"

"You! Where the devil did you know him?"

"Him? Me know him long time in Marrakech. He young man, jus' or'nary Shareef (saint), sell charcoal. Yes, him clever chap!"

"Of a truth?" queried Paul in Arabic.

"Aye, of a truth, upon the beard of the Prophet," answered Rabat, with dignity.

When Rabat spoke in his native tongue he had the personality of the grave, dignified Moor; as Rabbit, the whole contour of the features changed into the ludicrous character, like nothing on earth – but Rabbit.

"O, my friend," continued Rabat, "mine eyes see that thy heart is grieved, and my heart, too, is sore for thee. Let not this thing grieve thee for, in the heart of Abd-el-Kader, there is great affection for thee, but for the other hath my lord little liking."

Paul brightened.

"How knowest thou?" he demanded eagerly.

---

[103] Cf. British intel memos reproduced in my Afterword below.

[104] Fransawi: a Frenchman, especially a French soldier, official, or trader. Also: any European connected to French influence.

[105] An ormolu clock: a luxurious gilded clock, often of French origin, that became a status symbol. Typically made of gilded bronze, they were usually coated with a gold amalgam. From the French *or moulu*: "ground gold."

"Verily, Omar ben Said spake, saying, thus was the speech of El Hadjib[106] who hath the ear of the Sultan."

Again Paul's ambition flared up, prompting him to action. The fact that he was again contemplating the overthrow of the Baron for self-interested motives was beaten down by the argument that open war had been declared by the Baron, and that therefore any action was justifiable. "Bah!" he thought, and perhaps justly, "almost any man would long ago have not hesitated to discard any scruples and have played for his own hand." Rabat sat quiet, smoking, whilst Paul stared out of the window, thinking. Then, amongst the deeper shadows of the orange trees in the garden grew a pair of eyes, reproachful and passionate. Paul stared for a moment uncertain, and then, realizing this haunting figment of the brain, rose with a violent curse and commenced to pace angrily up and down the room.

Rabat watched him with the placid interest of a scientist observing the gyrations of a new species of beetle. Then his features relaxed and wrinkled into Rabbit, seemingly as if he had decided that Paid needed a check. Said he:

"Well, ole chap, what's matter? You come long Rabbit, get drunk. Me understand plenty peoples want get drunk 'cashun'ly. Me want get drunk — offen: now you want get drunk. Come long!"

Paul stopped in the middle of the room to stare at him. Rabbit dropped his head on one side and leered, presumably intended as encouragement. Paul smiled as if against his will.

"You silly brute," ejaculated he.

"Brute?" repeated Rabbit, not in the least aware of the meaning. "You come get drunk?" — persuasively.

"Yes," announced Paul suddenly. "I will. Not get drunk, but I'll come for a walk."

---

[106] El Hadjib: the ḥājib. A high-ranking court officer or chamberlain who advises the Sultan and manages access to him.

Paul, glad to find something to distract his mind, sallied forth with Rabbit into the streets. Rabbit wanted to turn off to the left on the shortest route to the Millah, but Paul insisted upon another route — just for the walk.

There was little fear that Paul would be recognized as a European. Even his accent would not betray him as other than an Algerian. They made their way on foot, with the peculiar shuffle necessitated by the heelless slipper, down narrow cobbled streets, drawing up against the wall now and again at the cry of Balak![107] Balak! to permit donkeys or mules laden with burdens as big as, and sometimes bigger than, themselves; and anon, for a string of camels with "their silly necks a bobbing like a basket full o' snakes."[108] Then, across a crowded bustling marketplace, elbowed by beggar and prince, past shops, like dark holes in the wall, through a gate and down another lane to the sok of the three gates. Said Paul ingenuously, and for no earthly reason:

"Is this not the place where we tarried to see our lord enter into the city?"

"Truly," answered Rabat, "nigh unto that door yonder."

Which was exactly what Paul seemed to want, for he forthwith developed an extraordinary interest in the precise spot, finding time, however, to glance upon the rooftops where, taking the cooler afternoon air, sauntered the muffled figures of four women. Paul was rewarded, for as he glanced the second time a hooded head was turned and his Lady of the Eyes caressed him with a prolonged look over her haik, whilst he, hypnotized, lost all things in the effort of dumb worship.

---

[107] Balak: "Watch out!" or "Be careful!"

[108] A paraphrase of Kipling's poem, "Oonts," which describes a "commissariat camel," "with 'is silly neck a-bobbin' like a basket full o' snakes." The verse playfully employs Cockney to portray the British military's use of the camel in India. "Oonts" is a phonetic rendering of how the soldiers pronounced the Hindi or Urdu word for "camel."

Then, having deliberately sought and obtained a favor, he cursed the donor and himself and strode away angry at his weakness.

Again changing his mind, he commenced to retrace his steps without explanation to Rabbit, halted, cursed himself afresh, and returned home ignoring Rabbit's whispered entreaties to come and get drunk.

The Baron met him in the gate of the house, and smiled, greeting him as if nothing had happened.

Paul hesitated a moment in doubt, and then with a sudden revulsion of feeling, and wholly unintending to speak, said:

"Ah, Baron, I owe you an apology, I — "

The Baron had raised his eyebrows, appearing not to understand to what he referred, meeting Paul's eye with a frigid stare. Paul hesitated. The Baron bent down to speak to Kismet; then Paul walked on, once more boiling with suppressed rage.

Zolika had left the house and was staying with a family of her tribe in the town. Next morning Paul awoke in a more pacific frame of mind. After a long debate with himself he had come to the conclusion that he was in the wrong; the Baron had brought him into the scheme upon a definite understanding, solely upon his word, and, although he had not actually broken faith, yet he had permitted the temporary success to inflame his private ambition to such an extent that his judgment and actions had been warped. There had been no excuse for the assault upon the other. The Baron, although unnecessarily coarse in his epithets regarding the girl, was from any sane worldly point of view, correct. De Bouche was obviously a man wholly lacking in moral perspective, but that after all was not Paul's concern. He could have adopted quite different methods to protect the girl, and he truly acknowledged — to himself — that that was not the real reason of the blow. So Paul arose in the morning with the firm intention to control his antipathy against the Baron, inflamed by his own jealous ambition, and to continue on with the scheme in the position in which he had accepted service. A disquieting thought was that the Baron obviously did not intend to relinquish the opportunity to remove the instrument when he so pleased; but he might be overestimating his powers; Paul was a fair shot and swordsman too. The irritating part was that Paul could never know when the other would call him out; — a veritable sword of Damocles, of which the Baron was more than probably fully aware.

At mealtimes Paul met the Baron with a smile, adopting the other's attitude of temporary truce. The Baron seemed gratified that the subtleties of the etiquette of a private quarrel should be so understood, and returned the compliment by displaying to the full his powers as a raconteur and brilliant conversationalist. No observer could have possibly surmised that between these two laughing and chatting existed a feud to the death, which at all events one intended should be pursued without scruple — at his own time. Paul, almost unwillingly, found himself falling under the influence of the Baron's personal magnetism once more, and confessed to himself that he was really a charming scoundrel and, moreover, an adversary who understood the art of meeting upon social ground without seeking or displaying any bourgeois traits of character.

Upon the following morning they were summoned to an audience with Abd-el-Kader, who received them very graciously in a private apartment of the Sultan. El Hammo, the Berber chief, was present also, sitting at the Sultan's feet, silent and impassive, with the expression of chronic melancholia characteristic of his sallow Mongolian features.

Sitting cross-legged upon a gilt Louis XVI sofa,[109] Abd-el-Kader talked long and earnestly with the twain, chiefly Paul,

---

[109] Cf. Beadle's essay "A Talk with the New Sultan of Morocco," *Pall Mall Magazine*, October 1908. Beadle relates that when he's received by Moulay Hafid (rendered by Beadle as Sultan Mulai-El-Hafid), Hafid seats himself

who could not refrain from noticing, with an unbidden sense of exaltation, that the remarks were addressed to him. Everything it appeared was going satisfactorily. The Ullema had given their sanction to his nomination as Sultan, so that now Abd-el-Kader was, in the religious eyes of the country, the true and only Prince of the Faithful. He was undisguisedly excited as he related these events. Moreover, several of the surrounding tribes had acknowledged his sovereignty. But the trouble was — his voice trailed into a subdued note — that the army of El Rahman was reported to be leaving for Marrakech, and that consequently the arms and trained men were needed immediately. For the moment the Treasury was comparatively full, due to the contribution by El Hammo of fifty thousand Spanish doubloons, the ancient spoil of some Sallee pirate[110] from a galleon in the golden days of Morocco.

It was agreed that Paul, with a large escort, should ride to overtake the caravan of camels which had already started for the rendezvous on the coast, without delay. Abd-el-Kader was

---

"cross-legged on a gilt Louis XV sofa," while Beadle is positioned in a chair beside the sultan. This is one of several examples of how Beadle imbues the protagonist Paul with character traits and concrete details taken from Beadle's own life. But the military actions of Paul follow the imprint of Beadle's associate Andrew Belton (1882 – 1970), who served as Mulay Hafid's "Kaid" and trained and organized Hafid's forces. Thus, Paul is a "composite" based on these two individuals. (For more on this, see my Afterword.) Historian Douglas Porch notes that, in March 1911, Hafid was "hunched on a gilded reproduction Louis XVI settee" when the French diplomats arrived to pressure him into signing the treaty of protectorate, which would transform Hafid into a "political eunuch." Douglas Porch, *The Conquest of Morocco*, p. 245.

[110] "Sallee pirate": A Barbary corsair, referring to Muslim pirates or privateers who operated from the Barbary Coast of North Africa, especially from the Moroccan port city of Salé. They were active from the sixteenth to eighteenth centuries and were notorious for raiding European ships and Christian coastal settlements. The term *Barbary* derives from the Berbers, the indigenous people of North Africa.

extremely anxious for his present ragtag army to be whipped into shape. At first Paul had intended urging that the Baron should go to the coast whilst he remained to drill the troops, but the Baron, equally alive to the advantage of cultivating the Sultan, had elected to stay, so Paul, having determined to keep his word, raised no objection. The Baron, at all events, was more than capable of instilling the rudiments of military drill and discipline.

Abd-el-Kader had already a number of native and Algerian drill instructors at work upon the men; these Harraba[111] were renegades from the nominal Sultan's army and the French Algerian forces. Paul suggested that Egyptian instructors be imported. Abd-el-Kader eagerly seized at the idea, and requested Paul to write to El Masr — Cairo[112] — for that purpose. Arrangements were completed to the Baron's satisfaction regarding the concessions in exchange for the arms which, if successfully landed, were to count as part payment. As the concessioner was not yet acknowledged Sultan by the Powers, a clause was added in which he agreed to ratify them immediately the Legations recognized him. Almost at the first suggestion of concessions, Abd-el-Kader had referred to an agreement between the Sultan of Morocco and the Powers which forbade any monopoly, but the Baron, with a significant smile, had assured him that he was fully prepared to take the risk of any complications ensuing.

Owing to the Oriental lack of appreciation of time, it was not until the fifth day that Paul found the escort prepared to start.

---

[111] Harraba: tribal leaders, rebels, or bandits, who resisted the central authority (*Makhzen*) and foreign intervention.

[112] "El Masr — Cairo": Moroccan Arabic pronunciation of "Miṣr" (Egypt) as "Masr." Moroccans referred to Cairo as "Masr" because it was the capital of Egypt and, often, the only major Egyptian city they visited, especially on pilgrimage routes.

During that time life flowed evenly at the house of the N'srani Es-Sultan.[113]

Paul had determined that he would banish all thoughts of the Lady of the Eyes from his mind, and had accordingly refrained from passing through the sok of the three gates for four whole days, but upon the fifth and last he relented, telling himself that it did not matter, as he was leaving the city and would probably not see her anyhow. Accordingly, he returned alone from a ride by way of the sok, as the shadows lengthened towards the east. Upon the rooftop a solitary muffled figure met his eye as he rode up the narrow street, which chanced to be deserted. She saw him and, leaning over the parapet, lowered her haik, gazing straight at him. All resolutions deserted him as he mechanically reined in his animal and sat like a figure of stone peering into those eyes as if he would project his very soul. Then, as he gazed, a silvery little voice reached him.

"Tell me, who art thou?"

For a moment he did not reply, whilst his thoughts raced at lightning speed. Did she know that he was a N'srani? What should he say? Then, as in a dream, he heard his own voice saying:

"One who loves thee, O beautiful one. What is thy name that I may sing in my heart?"

"Za-hra!"

The voice pronounced the name like a caress.

"Za-hra!" repeated Paul, devouring her face with his eyes. A flower dropped upon his upturned face, the haik flew up, and with one piercing look, she turned and disappeared.

For a moment Paul sat staring at the empty roof, clutching the flower which he had deftly caught. The sound of hooves disturbed him. He looked down at a fierce hawk-visaged Moor

---

[113] N'srani Es-Sultan: "The Christian Sultan," i.e., the Sultan supported by the European ("Christian") powers.

upon a fiery black stallion. The man scowled fiercely as he passed Paul, and reining in by the door in the wall, hammered upon it.

Paul rode on, looking upon the world through a rosy mist, in which flitted the ghost of dark eyes smiling at him. "Zahra — Zahra!" he repeated to himself.

Rabbit met him at the door, grinning extensively. "Hullo, ole chap," said he, "what?"

"Zahra!" said Paul, smiling dreamily.

"Zahra?" exclaimed Rabbit perplexedly. "No, him name Aisha," he continued, as one suddenly finding light.

"What on earth are you talking about?" inquired Paul, having arrived on earth.

"You come see," said Rabbit, with a mysterious nod. "Him awfly good, whaat?"

He led the way to a vacant room wherein, upon a mat, sat a muffled figure, a pair of bright eyes glancing timidly at Paul over the haik.

"Who the dickens is this?" he inquired in amazement.

"Him Aisha, awfly good," explained Rabbit, adding a sentence in Arabic to the girl, who immediately lowered the veil, disclosing an undeniably pretty face of a girl of about fifteen. "For you!" exclaimed Rabbit proudly.

"For me! What the — " mirabile dictu, Paul swore violently.

"Well, you no like Zolika," protested Rabbit in an injured tone. "Me buy him," indicating the white figure, "in market this morning. Awfly cheap. On'y douro mia khamseen[114] ($150) an' cons'quently — cons'quently — me not know *what* you like!"

"Consequently I'll break your neck — " began Paul angrily.

---

[114] Douro mia khamseen: dūrū miyya khamsin. Although the author translates this as "$150," in marketplace speech it likely signified a payment of about 1 duro (a coin of 5 riyals, or roughly a silver dollar) and 150 copper coins or centimes.

"Me Moor man," said Rabbit sharply. "You no break mineck!"

"I will if you don't take her out of here. Send her back to her owners."

"Owners? Whaat owners?"

"Send her away."

"Me send away! No, no! Me give douro mia khamseen him!"

"Well, take her away — at once."

"Orlright, ole chap, you liver dambad. Aisha, aji!" And, deeply offended, Rabbit stalked away, followed obediently by the young slave.

Next morning, long before daybreak, Paul bade farewell to the Baron, who sat up in bed with Kismet curled on the counterpane, and amicably wished him bon voyage.

CHAPTER IX

Between the Canaries and the Barbary coast a white-painted steam yacht sped through an oily sea, a creamy lip of foam continuously smiling from her graceful knife-edge prow.

Beneath the awning on the poop, where the outer brass works glistened in the sun, sat a group of three in long deck chairs. One of the men placidly slept, an open book upon his white-ducked knees; the other, chewing the stump of a long cheroot, stared at the shimmering horizon; the dark-haired woman indolently read a yellow-backed novel. Stretched out upon a carpet beside the steering gear box slept a dark-visaged Arab clad in his native white robes. Above the soothing seethe of the cloven waters came the pulsing throb of the engines, and the rattle of metal through the fiddley[115] above the stokehole far beneath. A negro cook's mate, leaning over the white rails, spat contemplatively into the sea, and turned lazily to watch a bull-necked fireman, covered in sweat and soot, who had suddenly popped up like a jack-in-a-box. He stood for a moment bathing in the cool air, wiping his face with an oily sweat rag.

"Himmel!" he ejaculated to the negro, "dot vash varm, Zambo, nein?"

"Shuah!" replied the other, exhibiting a specimen set of ivories. "Guess ah've got a bully mouth."

The other swallowed sympathetically and turned to twist a ventilator, which creaked dismally.

The fireman disappeared through the iron fiddley and the negro resumed his meditation.

"Say, Cyrus," said the woman, dropping her book and sitting up. "What's the matter with tiffin?[116] Guess this is hotter'n Noo

---

[115] Fiddley: a vertical space above a vessel's engine room extending into its stack, and usually covered with iron grating for ventilation. (Also applied to the framework around the opening itself.)
[116] Tiffin: a midday meal; a light lunch.

York. I'm done to a turn. What's your idea on the subject, Prince?"

Cyrus returned from the distant horizon, yawned, and contemplated the awning whilst the sleeper, awakening with a start, replied at random:

"Whatefer pleases Madame!"

"Don't believe yew know what I was talking about," said Mrs. Tarkas smiling. "Come. Say, Cy; wake up, dew!"

"What the matter wi' me, anyway? Cyan't ye see I'm awake. Guess yew two more'n lick Rip V. Winkle's stunt holler.[117] Say neow, don't yew get rattled."

He climbed out of his chair reluctantly to disappear into the deckhouse; a bell tingled somewhere below, and he returned to collapse into the chair as if exhausted.

"Say, Cy," remarked Mrs. Tarkas as they sat down to lunch in the saloon, "what time d'yew reckon we're due?"

"Cap'en says 's afternoon sometime. Ought to see land just neow."

"The Captain he does know zis coast, yes?" queried the Don.

"Don't reckon he knows more'n the chart kin tell. Durned few do, I guess. What's the date, anyway?"

"Eighteenth," said his wife.

"U'm. We got bags o' time, then. Any old time fr'm sixteenth to twenty-fifth. No! git me some o' those peaches, steward; too durned hot for flesh."

"Waal!" continued Mrs. Tarkas, "how're we goin' to find that lagoon outfit — the rendezvous place?"

"The Cap'n's got sailin' directions from de Bouche, and old Abdullar here knows the only way in. The only fear is that those

---

[117] "Holler": a reference to Washington Irving's *Rip Van Winkle and the Legend of Sleepy Hollow* (1819).

Frenchies get wind and hev a bunch of cruisers round. 'Cording to international law they kin call our kyards."[118]

"They can't interfere with a yacht," protested Mrs. Tarkas, "and if they dew, guess they'll only find some old cases of canned beef and a piano case or two."

"Sure; but we ain't sittin' on the steps of the Capitol and they kin look inside. No; I guess if we're overhauled we're done, but the old tub's got a slicker pair 'v heels than any durned thing on this coast."

"You mean, Tarkas, dat ve vill run if we zee anythings, eh?" said the Don, with a wily look in his watery eyes.

"You bet!"

"But zey cannot know ze rendezvous, and zen ve can come — return, yes?"

"You bet! But I'm more'n scared o' that Marconi outfit. Wouldn't mind puttin' me shirt on the fact that that feller we passed yesterday ticked out our blessed fam'ly history all up and down the coast. There's always a steam kettle lyin' around Mogador,[119] and altho' that feller didn't make any talkee talkee, he'd got his eyes skinned; 'member ain't any other craft running straight in from mid-Atlantic. Neow, ef it were the old Hassani

---

[118] "They kin call our kyards": phonetic spelling of "They can call our cards," i.e., the demand that a card player must "reveal his hand." Metaphorically, the moment when one must reveal one's true intentions.

[119] Mogador: now known as Essaouira, a city and port on the Atlantic west of Marrakech.

— the Moroccan Navy[120] — guess we'd scrap her with that little bow chaser for'ard, like Spilsbury did with the Tourmaleine."[121]

"And swear we thought she was a pirate," supplemented Mrs. Tarkas, laughing.

"You bet."

"Zen, vat I say vas right, yes?" demanded the Prince excitedly. "I always say: go sout of ze islands and — come up ze coast!"

"Guess you're too cute, Prince," responded Mrs. Tarkas. "Had we cottoned on to your notions we'd ha' run right in the track of steamers on the coast, in Mogador, and over the whole universe.

Say, yew're cute, aren't yew, now? Simply a whole cartful o' bad luck meetin' that feller yesterday — an' what's he doin' there, anyway?"

"Reckon he was lookin' fer fellers o' my kidney," answered Cyrus, depositing a peach stone[122] with care. "Durned lucky that — Say! what the all-fired — ?"

The pulsing throb of the engines had suddenly ceased, the ship gliding on with that eerie sensation and swish-swash of the waters ominously distinct after the familiar throb of the propellers. Tarkas led the hurried rush on deck. A dense white fog enveloped the vessel.

---

[120] The old Hassani — the Moroccan Navy: "Even from the sea, Morocco's quiet decay was apparent. The *Hassani*, flagship of the Sultan's three-boat navy, decorated the entrance to the bay [of Tangier]. But the state of her boilers and the seamanship of her crew seldom permitted a voyage more adventurous than the annual trip to Gibraltar for repainting." Douglas Porch, *The Conquest of Morocco*, p. 8.

[121] "Like Spilsbury did with the Tourmaleine": a reference to British Major A. G. Spilsbury and his 1897 expedition aboard the Tourmaline (misspelled here as "Tourmaleine"). Spilsbury was involved in a quasi-rogue mission to deliver arms to tribal leaders in southern Morocco (outside of the Sultan's control), during a time of European imperial competition. His expedition skirted legality and risked conflict with the other European Powers.

[122] Peach stone: the pit of a peach.

"Say, Cap'en," sang out Tarkas, as he ran up the bridge ladder, "what's all this about, anyway?"

"Nothin' to write home about," answered Captain Elihu Babbs. "Just an or'inary fog raound these waters, so sez the Britisher' Sailin' D'rections. Came up like a blanket from the sou-west. Reckon I saw the land afore this tarnation feller closed in with us."

Mrs. Tarkas and the Prince stood beside them staring into the murky opacity.

"D'you know where we are, anyhow?" queried Tarkas.

The Captain raised his shaggy eyebrows, pulling a goatee beard thoughtfully, as he answered:

"'Cordin' to my reckoning, a bit to the west'ard of the lagoon feller. Kyan't do much in this outfit. Anyway, we'll crawl a bit."

The engine room telegraph tinkled, and the sound of steam snorted up from below as the propellers slowly commenced to revolve. The Captain bellowed some orders, and presently, as the yacht forged slowly ahead, the splash of the lead line[123] and a voice heard droning monotonously: "By th' deep six — an' a half five — by th' mark five — by the deep fower."

"Low lyin' shores heerabouts?" remarked Tarkas. "Yep; reckon won't see land till we're on top of her. Kyan't be far off; we're in four fathom." The engines below snorted and sighed gigantically as if impatient of delay, the leadsman droned monotonously:

"A quarter off fower — and a half three — "

The Captain scanning the water, over the starboard bridge rail, suddenly held up a hand to his chief officer at the telegraph.

"Stop her!"

---

[123] Lead line (or sounding line): a line or wire weighted at one end for sounding. Leadsman: a man who uses a sounding lead to determine depth of water.

"By th' mark three," sang the leadsman.

Again the gliding silence and the caressing swish of waters as the Captain remarked:

"Guess we're right off the mouth of a river; we'll heave to till this yer durned fog lifts some." Over the side the waters had turned to a yellow, murky color full of sediment.

The Prince suggested using the hooter as a signal to their confederates ashore, but as this would talk with equal lucidity to any other vessel in the vicinity, the suggestion was vetoed with usual vigor by Mrs. Tarkas.

All the afternoon they hung about the bridge anxiously listening, and watching for the fog to lift.

Abdullah leisurely made his way to them, and, through the medium of the Prince, made known that they were at the mouth of the Wad Seboo.

The Captain received the information with skepticism, pointing out that as there were two rivers, one some distance each side of their destination, and that as *he* could not be sure which side they were, it was impossible for a durned nigger to know. The afternoon wore slowly away and night fell without signs of the thick mist rising. The Tarkas and the Prince retired to dine, the Captain electing to feed at his post. Hardly had the sweets arrived before the diners heard the clang of the stand-by signal in the engine room. Again a scramble to the deck and the upper bridge where, to their dismay, the rapidly dissolving mists disclosed a line of surf glistening white under the increscent moon, and almost within a cable's length to seaward, the low, gray, vicious-looking shapes of two torpedo craft.

Captain Elihu Babbs swore deep as he wrenched over the telegraph to full speed ahead, but, almost as soon as the propeller commenced to thrash the sea, the churning waters were seen under the sterns of the destroyers, and as they gathered way a puff of white smoke from the bow of one; a pause, and then a report struck the ears, a shot squealed in the air, falling with a splash across the bows of the yacht.

"Hell!" ejaculated Captain Elihu succinctly, as he angrily manipulated the telegraph again. "Heave to! and, by God, we've got to, or they'll sink us."

The war vessels crept slowly up. Tarkas, staring through night glasses at them, ejaculated:

"Euchred, by God!"

For a few moments no one spoke, all intently watching the maneuvers of their prospective captors, who took up a position one on each side of the yacht. From the side of one a small boat full of men put off.

"What d'you reckon they can steam?" inquired Tarkas suddenly.

"Eighteen to twenty knots," responded the Captain.

Tarkas swore. "If we'd only had a start we'd lick the all-fired froggies as easy as we licked Tommy Lipton.[124] Hell!"

"Yep," assented Elihu. "Reckon we kin knock twenty-five outer this old tube, sure."

Meanwhile the rowboat grew closer, the splash of the oars sounding distinct in the silence; a bubbling roar burst from the steam pipe at the top of the funnel.

Tarkas jumped with rage, glancing at the white cloud of steam.

"Gee! full head o' steam goin' to waste! Holy Saints, reckon we ought to make a dash for it! Held up like a bunch of joy riders in Fifth Avenue. Hell!"

Mrs. Tarkas, gazing at the approaching boat through her glasses, suddenly emitted an inarticulate noise.

---

[124] Sir Thomas Lipton (1848 – 1931), a Scotsman of Irish parentage who was the founder of Lipton Tea. He was also a yachtsman who lost five America's Cup races.

"Say, Cap'en," she said, clutching his arm, "how quick kin we waltz round?"

"In two shakes with both screws; but I tell ye we kyan't run, they'd blow us inter the water, sure as I'm Elihu P. Babbs."

"No, no, no! Listen!" and she whispered excitedly in the Captain's ear:

"Gee-hos-o-phat! Bully!"[125] he exclaimed in admiration. "Say, Mr. Tarkas, your wife's cooked 'em sure. Mr. Dermott, see here."

He held a whispered conversation with the chief officer, who ran down the bridge ladder in haste.

"Lower away the starboard gangway there, bo'sen, and throw 'em a line, d'ye hear?"

The Captain left his bridge and whistled down the engine room to the chief engineer, who came flying up the hot iron ladder.

"You've got a full head o' steam, chief?" said the skipper. "Now when I give the signal, I want ye to open her out for every pound she's worth, quicker'n greased lightning and stand by for a hell of a bump."

The chief, a taciturn Scotchman, nodded and disappeared. The Captain returned to the bridge in time to see a gold-braided French officer mount the gangway. Tarkas and the Prince, who had been in close converse with Mrs. Tarkas, advanced to meet him.

"Bon soir, Messieurs!'" exclaimed the Frenchman, saluting. The Prince returned the greeting, and introduced the Tarkas as Mr. and Mrs. Cyrus P. Beethoven, the owners, and then the Captain.

---

[125] Bully: Excellent. Gee-hos-o-phat: Jehosaphat (as in "Great Jehosaphat!" or "Jumpin' Jehosaphat!"). A euphemistic exclamation, derived from the name Jehoshaphat, a biblical king of Judah. Used in old American English as a mild oath or expletive, similar to "Great Scott!" or "By Jove!"

Would M'sieu l'officier be pleased to come to the saloon?

M'sieu l'officier was pleased, and, of course, champagne and biscuits appeared, whilst the Frenchman, with profuse apologies, explained that it was his unpleasant duty to examine the ship's papers.

Captain Elihu complacently produced them. They were drawn up for a yachting cruise between the Port of New York, Canaries and Mediterranean. The Frenchman perused them, smiled, and proceeded to explain that, although he personally deeply regretted, that he was under orders to satisfy himself that there was no contraband goods on board, or arms, he added, with a smile; and that, therefore, would M'sieu l'Americain permit his men to do their duty. Mr. Beethoven, upon receiving the news from the lips of the Prince, waxed indignant as a free-born American subject. A long dialogue ensued between Mr. Cortes, alias the Prince, and the Frenchman, who supped champagne with benign satisfaction. The upshot was that the search must be made, although it wounded the humble instrument to the heart to have to discommode so charming a lady as Madame.

Madame bowed with a sweet smile and retired to her cabin as the officer was politely requested to walk on deck. As he stepped forward Captain Elihu sprang behind, the powerful arm closed round his neck, roughly ramming a serviette into his mouth, and before he quite realized what had happened, the naval officer was lying bound and gagged upon the saloon settee. The electric light was switched off, and he was left to his own wrathful meditations.

In the moonlight on deck four French sailors and their sous-officier, leaning negligently against the taffrail,[126] were suddenly confronted by six rifle muzzles, whilst a mild voice from

---

[126] Taffrail: the upper part of the stern of a wooden ship or a rail around the stern of a ship.

somewhere above bade them in excellent French to put their hands up. For a moment they hesitated, but the ominous click of triggers, and the determined aspect of the rough American sailormen behind the sights, convinced them of the futility of resistance. The one man in the dinghy had been subjected to a similar method of persuasion, and he, with greater excuse, not knowing what had happened to his comrades, surrendered too.

As in all probability the yacht was being closely watched by the war vessels, the Captain and party had remained upon the lower bridge deck. Immediately the prisoners had been secured, the Captain spoke down the speaking tube to the engineer:

"Starboard screw full speed ahead; port screw full astern."

With a seething roar of steam from the cylinders the engines revolved, and the whole yacht, quivering from stem to stern, commenced to turn as on a pivot.

"Now — full ahead," continued Elihu, standing at the tube, watching the bow swing against the stars. "Let her have it and hang on."

Leaping to the upper bridge, he seized upon the steering wheel as the propellers thumped in unison, and the yacht, with incredible swiftness, gathered way. From the torpedo craft shouts floated over the waters. The maneuver had been so sudden and unexpected that their adversaries seemed paralyzed with bewilderment. Their propellers started almost simultaneously to churn the water, but too late to gather sufficient steerage way to avoid the yacht which, in the skilful hands of Elihu, bore down with ever-increasing speed. Two puffs of smoke showed against the gray-black hull, two sharp reports, and two shells tore squealing wide of the yacht's mainmast and funnel.

Mrs. Tarkas hid her face in anticipatory horror of her own idea taking concrete form. Shouts and cries mingled in the air as the sharp steel prow loomed above the low-lying war vessel. The Captain, silent again at the wheel, braced himself against the wheel box as, with a rending crash, the yacht struck the smaller craft nearly amidships, cutting through her eggshell plates like a knife through a length of cheese. Mrs. Tarkas and the Prince, forgetting to hold tight, were flung across the deck. From the upended divisions of the stricken craft men threw themselves overboard amid the babel of escaping steam, shouted commands and gurgle of waters. The white yacht had paused at the crash, seemed to shake herself free as the engines madly thumped, making every bolt and plank quiver, and then continued serenely on her way, gathering speed again amid the ear-splitting explosion of the boilers blowing up astern, on through the wrack and turmoil of waters where once the smart little craft had floated.

The crew of the companion vessel, either stunned by the audacity of the attack, the sudden tragedy, or helpless without their Commander, who lay in the yacht's cabin nearly crazy with anxiety, attempted no reprisals. By the time the yacht had regained her top speed, the group now on her upper bridge could see them busily rescuing those fortunates who had dived overboard in time to avoid the sudden overwhelming cataclysm of the exploding boilers.

"Gee!" remarked Tarkas, sucking in breath. "Won't there be a shine over this! All Yurope'll be shouting like a dog with scalded paws. Guess we'd better get rid of the stuff and take a cruise down Floridah way."

"Oh! Guess I'm real sorry for those poor fellers," said Mrs. Tarkas, with a white face. "Say, but I never thought of what would happen. Oh, my gracious, those awful cries!"

"Say, guess you'd better lie down, Mrs. Tarkas," suggested the Captain. "You're seared some. But don't you worry, we didn't come on this yer outfit fer a picnic."

"That's all right, Sadie, girl," said Cyrus. "You trot right along and lie down. They'd ha' blown us to Hades just as soon, you bet. But say," he added, turning to the Captain, "what're we going ter dew with the officer man? Gee, I'd forgotten him right now."

"Oh!" exclaimed his wife from the top of the ladder. "Can't we land him up there?" She nodded towards the land.

"Guess not," said Cyrus. "These coons would cut his throat durned slick. Waal, let him slide for the present. Good night, old girl! Neow, see here, Cap'n, t'other feller'll be after us quicker'n a monkey after nuts. Say, now, what in hell 're we going ter do?"

"Slip right up to the lagoon and get shot o' this truck right neow, and then lite out fer all we're worth. That feller'll bring half the French navy about our ears afore we kin say George Washington."

"But we're come the wrong way — "

"Yep; I knowed that, don't yew fuss. Get her hull down and slip out to sea and reound back. This feller'll come roaring down here after us in half an hour."

"Are we damaged any?"

"Nope. Bow plates stove in[127] a bit — don't amount to shucks."

For nearly an hour they thumped and quivered down the coast at full speed, and then, sweeping out to sea in a huge circle, they returned to the approximate scene of the sea duel. No sign of the surviving torpedo craft was seen from the lookout in the crosstrees,[128] and acting on the advice of

---

[127] Stove in: past tense of *stave*: to smash a hole in, e.g., to *stove in* the boat. Also: to crush or break inward, e.g., *staved in* several ribs. Cf. the noun form of *stave*: any of the narrow strips of wood or narrow iron plates placed edge to edge to form the sides, covering, or lining of a vessel or structure.

[128] Crosstrees: two horizontal crosspieces of timber or metal that spread the upper shrouds of a ship in order to support the mast. The shrouds are the pairs of ropes leading from a ship's mastheads to give lateral support to the masts.

Abdullah that the river had been the Wad Seboo, they proceeded swiftly up the coast.

The captive officer had been released immediately after the sinking of his colleague's vessel. At first, for the sake of his peace of mind, the Prince had endeavored to persuade him that they had escaped by merely running away, but he had almost reconstructed the scene from the shock and sounds which had reached his ear as he lay bound in the cabin. With a sailor's natural love for his own vessel, he was relieved to hear that she had suffered no harm, and although lamenting the disaster and probable death of his colleagues, he did not conceal his admiration for the reckless daring of the achievement. Accepting his position as the fortune of war, he proved, over a champagne supper, to be a bon camarade. Smiling over his wineglass, which shivered and trembled to the high pressure of the engines, he confessed that he knew the identity of all there from having seen them at Tanga, hence his demand to search the yacht; also that the cruiser which had passed them upon the previous day had Marconied[129] them instructions to keep a sharp lookout.

It was a pure fluke that placed them almost alongside the suspect in the fog.

The supper was interrupted by a sailor arriving with the news that the lookout reported a double light ahead, which the Captain could not determine as yet whether it was the prearranged signal from the rebels ashore or a steamer's masthead lights.

From the upper bridge the lights could be just discerned close in or over, it was impossible to distinguish which, the faint

---

[129] Marconied (early twentieth-century slang): sending a wireless telegraph message using Marconi wireless equipment. Named after Guglielmo Marconi (1874 – 1937), an Italian inventor who pioneered long-distance radio transmission. Cruiser: a warship, typically fast and well-armed, used for patrol, escort, and scouting.

iridescence of the surf line in the silvery half-light of the moon. As, of course, the yacht was not carrying any lights, and all portholes were curtained, she proceeded straight on until, within a quarter of an hour, three lights showed unmistakably over the sheen of the surf. The Baron's sailing instructions stated that "after making landfall from the west, follow the coast northward by night until three lights are seen in shore. When the two *southerly* lights come *in line*, shape a course for the *third*, light and proceed at half speed until the *westernmost* of the two southern lights is full abeam. Then steer for the easternmost light at full speed, straight through the surf, until the westermost of the two southern lights bears *four points* on the *starboard quarter*: proceed dead slow until a hand light is waved ashore. Anchor promptly in three-and-a-half fathoms on sand and shell. A boat will immediately put off[130] to you."

They had all congregated upon the upper bridge to see the yacht make the intricate passage of the reef and bar, the French officer having retired to his cabin after giving his parole not to attempt to escape or even watch through his porthole.

Presently the southern lights swung into line and the Captain took the wheel himself, acting with his Chief Officer up in the crosstrees. The engine-room bell clanged the signal for half speed, and steadily she glided towards the distant line of breakers. The murmurous chant of the surf grew louder.

"Po-rt!" sung the chief from the crow's nest. The steam-steering gear chattered, quickly the mast and bow slewed across the starry heavens, until the Captain, eyes glued to the binnacle,[131] threw over the little brass wheel. As she steamed along almost parallel to the surf the waters eddied and swirled on her port beam indicating the close proximity of a reef.

---

[130] "Put off" = an old nautical expression meaning to "depart from shore" or "set out toward another ship."

[131] Binnacle: the housing for a ship's compass and lamp.

"Hard-a-port!" cried the mate.

Again the fussy rattle of the gear and the flying stars overhead.

"Ste-ady!" and between them and the lights showed the breakers right ahead. Tarkas, at a word from the Captain, signaled three-quarter speed, for they reckoned that the Baron had not calculated upon a speed of twenty-five knots. Rapidly the roar of the surf increased. They could now plainly see the dark of the land beyond. She seemed to be rushing to certain destruction. The steady throb of the engines, the irritable mutter and clank of steering gear, above the increscent roar. Soon they were upon the first gather of the huge rollers, feeling the deck lift beneath their feet. The Captain gave one rapid glance ahead.

"Hell!" he ejaculated.

The next moment she pitched in the thunderous crash of the boiling surf, making them expect a sickening thud upon the bottom; then all in a flash she shot through into placid waters, the sandy shore flying by on each side.

"Ste-ady! Stop h-er!"

The engines were reversed to check the momentum. Presently they found her at rest in a seeming inland lake, the eternal chorus of the sea singing without.

The three signal lights, having served their purpose, winked and went out; several smaller lights bobbed about on the shore like will o' the wisps.

Abdullah, who had been an impassive spectator, now voiced guttural remarks to the Prince who, acting in his apparently only useful capacity of interpreter, translated to the Captain Elihu.

The engines moved reluctantly, as if exhausted with their previous strenuous efforts, the yacht glided slowly until the farther beach gleamed silvery in the moon rays, where hundreds of black objects rushed hither and thither, clustering around a dark blot upon the water's edge.

As the anchor dropped with a rumble and splash, the blot resolved itself into a boat pulling off from the shore. Soon the splash and sparkle of oars, and from a white-draped figure in the stern sheets came Paul's voice:

"Ship ahoy! That you, Tarkas?"

"Hull-o! Yes, that you, Towers?"

The creak and rattle of the gangway tackle, a rope thrown, the excited guttural exclamations of the Arab boatmen; a tall, ghostly figure ran up the accommodation ladder to greet Tarkas and the Prince waiting by the rail.

"Hullo, Tarkas! How d'you Prince? All right, eh? Ah, Mrs. Tarkas, how are you? Scarcely knew me, eh? Well, what's the news? Only got here yesterday. What? Oh, scrap on the road. Oh, nothing; only tribesmen — Beni Hassan."[132]

"Bully! but come right along below," said Tarkas. "Guess we've got to chew the rag some. Eh? Oh! Cap'en Elihu Babbs — Mr. Paul Towers."

"Howdy, Mister Towers? But say, Mister Tarkas, guess it's just on eight bells, and I reckon we've got ter move slick at dawn. Don't cotton to that dandy channel o' yours in th' dark. Moon sets just on eight bells in the morning watch and reckon those Froggie fellers 'll be nosing raound ter-morrow, sure thing."

An animated discussion ensued regarding the most expeditious method of transferring the contraband shipment. Five clumsy barge boats were provided by the shore party and all the yacht's boats were pressed into service. Within half an hour the hatches were open, the steam winches rattled and roared, slinging crate after crate marked canned beef, pickled pork, agricultural implements, into the small craft alongside,

---

[132] "Beni Hassan": an Arab tribal group in Morocco, extending into Western Sahara, Mauritania, etc.

which, with manual aid and the yacht's motor launch, instantly creaked and splashed to the shore.

Meanwhile, leaving the deck in the capable hands of the Captain and his crew, another champagne supper was provided for Paul's benefit at which they exchanged news. Paul, although lamenting the presumable loss of life, expressed great admiration for the exploit, resulting from a woman's wit, of the sinking of the destroyer and fortunate escape. The capture of the yacht and the consequent loss of the arms would have meant a serious waste of money, as well as a heavy blow to the cause of the Rebel Chief they had espoused.

At about three in the morning Tarkas accompanied Paul upon a visit ashore to see that the immediate packing of the caravan had commenced. All the crates had been specially built in the most suitable size for camel transport. Neither party could afford to lose any time.

"Hallo, Mister," said a cheery voice accosting Tarkas as the twain landed upon the beach. "You member me?"

"Who?" queried Tarkas, peering under the hood of the speaker, a Moor.

"Who? Me, intruppter man; you know, ole chap."

"Interrupter man? What in — "

"Interpreter," explained Paul. "It's Rabbit."

"Rabbit?"

"Yes, me Rabbit. Me know you, Tanga, ole chap; awf'ly good Tanga, what? Gotta cig'rette? Ah, Barakolovik!"

"Tanks awfly, straw'n'ry brute!" added Rabbit, gratefully puffing. "These my peoples — they come from Fas — bad peoples Fasi — " He rambled on with his weird notion of entertaining a stranger.

All about was noise and apparent confusion; the shouts, cries and exclamations of the uncouth, ragged soldiers, the excited expostulations of others, the liquid, throaty grumble of camels like a fierce beast growling under water. But as Paul had divided his men into separate companies, each under its own Kaithaha (captain),[133] and each with an appointed task, little time was wasted. Among the sand dunes fringing the lake stood the shadowy forms of a line of camels; each in turn obeyed the voice of the jemmallah,[134] advanced, knelt to receive the load, rose again with their queer jerky motion, to depart and kneel again in line, awaiting the order to start.

The men were all abnormally excited, which for an Arab is a very dreadful state, because they knew the contents of the many bales and packages. Already, in their eyes, the enemy were beaten and themselves triumphant, incidentally covered with much glory in the shape of hard cash, cattle, and many wives.

The moon sank in a glory of silver sea, the hurried work went on in the flickering light of many candle lanterns, the rattle and clash of the winches upon the yacht, working under electric arc lamps, floated across the still lagoon above the harmonious voice of the sea.

"A-urrgh! Kneel, thou son of shame! Skut! Ya Abdul-lah! Ya Oma-r! Rise! E-eeh! Depart, O daughter of no parents! Al-lah! Waali! Waali! Aji! Aji! Balak! Bal-ak! A-mgh! Emshi! Zid! Zid!"[135]

As the first faint flush of dawn appeared in the East, Paul and Tarkas returned to the yacht, relieved to hear that the last of the precious crates were swinging over the bulwarks.

A final magnum of champagne was opened to drink to the success of the cause.

"Vive l'Abd-el-Kader," toasted Paul, looking incongruous in his dignified Moorish robes amid the luxuriously furnished saloon, with a bumper of champagne in his hand.

---

[133] Kaithaha: qāʾid (commander or captain). In Moroccan French / English of that era, *Kaid* or *caïd* was the usual colonial spelling.

[134] Jemmāllah (also spelled "*jammāla*"): camel owners or camel drivers.

[135] Zid: keep going.

"Guess our little show's about over," observed Tarkas, "unless they overhaul outside, which isn't likely if once we get a fair start. Guess I wish I were coming along too. Reckon you'll have some fun before you're through with this. Well, so long, and good luck."

Farewells were hurriedly made, and Paul stepped on board the last loaded barge amid the rattle of the tackle and the chant of the sailors hoisting the yacht's boats to their davits.[136] The lookout in the crosstrees reported a clear horizon; so, with Abdullah as pilot, doomed to return to his beloved country via New York, the screws churned the waters as the yacht circled round the lagoon, to gather top speed for the dash through the surf into the outer channel and on to the open sea, a dull glaucous in the pale dawn, broken by the white freshets of the morning breeze.

As Paul, sitting on top of a Maxim case, watched her, like a great white ghost in the raw light of dawn, glide round and then head at full speed towards the narrow channel, where the surf leapt to caress the placid lagoon waters in clamorous desire, his eye caught a sudden column of smoke against the black of departing night. One or more of the French boats patrolling in search of the culprit who would be just in time to escape the vengeful claws of the insulted tricolor.[137]

Paul could see dim figures clustered on the starboard side of the upper bridge. A rug or wrap waved dark against the paintwork,[138] to which he semaphored[139] with his arms.

The throb of the screws fainted into the paean of the Atlantic rollers as the yacht, flying at full speed, stabbed into a long,

---

[136] Davit: a crane that projects over the side of a ship or a hatchway, used especially for boats, anchors, or cargo.

[137] The tricolor French flag.

[138] Paintwork (chiefly British): paint.

[139] Semaphore: a system of visual signaling by two flags held one in each hand.

curving monster, seemed to pause for a fraction of time, pitch, and then dive forward through the boiling cauldron unscathed. Presently, after she had swerved parallel with the coast, came three loud blasts upon the hooter, another change in her course through the outer channel, the waters eddying and swirling distinctly round the sunken reef, and a succession of long blasts. Paul glanced across towards the stranger, who had apparently already sighted the yacht, for great columns of smoke blackened the horizon.

Paul pointed her out to one of his Kaids. The man laughed, hugely pleased at the prospect of the hated Fransawi being cheated out of their prey.

At about two miles from the shore the yacht, to Paul's astonishment and anxiety, stopped. He sat staring through field glasses as the daylight spread across the arc of the heavens. The approaching vessel could not possibly be more than four or five miles distant. She would be within easy gunshot in a few moments, and if the yacht had broken down it would mean her capture for a certainty. For another five anxious minutes Paul waited and watched, and then, to his relief, the yacht got under way again, disclosing the reason of her delay: a small, dark blob upon the waters represented the captive French sailors, who had been abandoned in open sea for their colleagues to rescue, and incidentally waste valuable time, thus giving the yacht a greater handicap.

Paul explained the maneuver to his Arab companions, and they both laughed consumedly, although the Moor tempered his hilarity by expressing the wish that they had been given the captives when — a significant motion across his throat completed the sentence.

As Paul glanced out to sea again he saw that the small boat had hoisted a sail and was beating out towards the three-funnelled cruiser which now loomed up gray and forbidding, a couple of miles away. As he watched, a tiny puff of white heralded a report, and presently a shell splashed a long way astern of the white yacht, who, by way of answer, gave three sharp defiant blasts.

Paul rose with a laugh and hurried on the final preparations for the march lest the cruiser should proceed to land a party for shore investigation. A long line of camels were silhouetted against the golden glory of sunrise. Paul, mounted again on impatient El Cid, turned for a last look seaward. The yacht, a white dot away down the coast, poured out volumes of black smoke, and opposite the lagoon the huge bulk of the cruiser, stationary, evidently picking up their men. To Paul's surprise, several puffs of cotton wool appeared upon her gray sides in succession, then reports, and shells, screaming away to their south, struck up clouds of sand and dust. The brilliance of the rising sun had evidently blinded their aim, and discretion too. The bombardment of the empty sand dunes continued as Paul, waving a satiric adieu, galloped off into the scrub.

CHAPTER X

Three weeks later Baron de Bouche was seated in the early morning upon an upturned drum in the shade of the wall of the Palace grounds.

In the great open space some four hundred yards long by two hundred yards wide, enclosed by the ancient embattled walls of Mulai Ismael, two thousand men in ragged red tunics and baggy bright blue trousers, and in the dirty gray robes of the tribesmen — the raw, very raw material of the new Imperial Army — sprawled around, resting.

In the vicinity of the Baron a group of gaudily uniformed, heavily-turbaned Kaithahas and Kaids of the military; at a little distance farther along the wall a line of bandsmen in nondescript uniforms, their European instruments at their feet, lounged and squatted, busily engaged in their favorite occupation — dolce far niente.[140] Immediately beyond them rose a concrete platform, a dais upon which stood a vivid green-painted summer house, such as one may see in an English garden. A group of white-robed officials squatted in the cool shade of the southern gateway, all awaiting the arrival of the Sultan, Abd-el-Kader. The slanting rays of the sun still beat with enervating force; flies buzzed irritatingly; the discordant blasts of a ragged soldier boy practicing upon a bugle at the far gate cut the still sultry air; the heat haze shimmered above the olive-clad hills seen above and beyond the walls.

A full beard, clipped and shaven in the Mohammedan style, hid the abnormal length of the Baron's face; only two gimlet eyes and his predatory nose still revealed the personality of the man. As he sat on the upturned drum with the imperturbable patience of the Oriental, a stranger would have had difficulty in distinguishing him from any cruel, hawk-eyed tribesman. The

---

[140] Dolce far niente: "the sweetness of doing nothing."

Baron was rather pleased with himself and with the world at large. Taking into consideration the many risks attached to the venture, all had at present shaped very well. He had succeeded in obtaining all the concessions he desired, which amounted to the practical monopoly of the economical resources of the country, and a messenger had arrived with the news of the successful running of the arms. He smiled to himself as he thought of the international hullabaloo there would be when the time came to disclose the powerful interests which he represented. Already there was trouble in the Diplomatic world; France had accused perfidious Albion of breaking faith in sending a secret agent — Paul — to aid the Pretender, and Germany, laughing up her sleeve, had supported her claim. Of course, Paul had been disowned by the British Foreign Office, which equally of course had been disbelieved, illustrating the maxim that when you wish to be believed, tell a lie, and vice versa.[141]

The Baron attempted to stroke the long yellow moustaches which were not there as he complacently reviewed the situation. The only fly in the ointment was the fact that France, irritated by this unexpected check to the penetration pacifique[142]

---

[141] "Paul had been disowned by the British Foreign Office": Beadle and his colleagues in Morocco were being carefully observed by the British Foreign Office, as evidenced by confidential memos that discuss his presence there. For more on this, see my Afterword below.

[142] "Pénétration pacifique": a French expression that translates to "peaceful penetration," i.e., the use of economic, political, or cultural tools rather than military means to gain influence over another country. The concept of *pénétration pacifique* is often linked to forms of "soft power," such as colonization through economic presence or strategic diplomacy. It usually operates under the more subtle guise of cooperation or development; but the ultimate goal is to increase influence and control. "Lyautey's 'peaceful penetration' followed by indirect-rule theories was indeed a public-relations exercise calculated to mask the brutality of conquest and win over French

might resort to a little quiet filibustering by supplying the much-abused Sultan Abd-el-Rahman with officers, men and guns for his weak-kneed army.

Although this would be strictly against the code inaugurated by France, there would be little difficulty in allowing time-expired soldiers of the Foreign Legion and Algerian regiments to enlist, pro tem,[143] in the service of the nominal Sultan. In such an event the Baron foresaw the result of the internecine struggle between the brothers thrown into considerable doubt.

He looked over at the flower of the army now sprawling its swarthy limbs in the sun, and shrugged his shoulders. It was all a matter of regular pay whether they stayed at all, and although their ranks were well stiffened by trained deserters from Abd-el-Rahman's ill-paid forces, these would desert again with equal promptitude should their pay cease. Money — fluss: it was all a question, as ever, of money, the sinews of war, as aught else.

And upon that the Baron based his greatest chance of success. With the money supplied by his backers he relied upon sapping the strength of any resistance of the enemy, and already the agents of Mulai Abd-el-Kader — or himself — were busy upon the coast, convincing the wavering patriots that the cause of the new Prince of the Faithful was ordained by Allah — and Mammon. The latter invariably won the day — always if in sufficient quantity.

Patriotism! They had no patriotism. Everything a question of profit and loss. The Almighty God Mammon. They did not give their allegiance to any Sultan from any conviction of Divine right, but merely to him whom they calculated, often erroneously, would demand the least of them and subsequently allow them to gain greater wealth. Fanaticism? Yes, because

---

public opinion to the nobility of France's imperial enterprise." See Douglas Porch, "Introduction," *The Conquest of Morocco.*

[143] Pro tem: pro tempore, for the time being.

their religion was one of fire and slaughter, a divine call to kill the infidel and take his goods — if they could. Hence this fiery religious enthusiasm of the ignorant and the placid broad-mindedness of the wise who knew the infidel was far too strong for them. And the Sultan? Power! autocratic power, the greatest intoxicant, save one, inconsistently enough, given to man for his undoing by the Gods. A patriot, risking all for his country's weal?

The Baron smiled, a grim, sardonic smile. Who would not be a patriot for a Sultanate? Absolute power of life and death, the resources of a rich and fertile country under the thumb of the chosen of Fortune! One might persuade himself that only the call of his country's good might claim him. Man is a complex creature, not understanding himself or his motives, deliberately and successfully blinding his own sight to the real motives of his actions. One who gave up life and all things, in obscurity with no possible chance of reward, for the welfare of his country, he was a patriot; some might in religious zeal, but then they hoped for reward in the next world. After all it was only human; egotism is the very essence of human nature, so wherefore could a man be blamed? Many and varied were the forms in which it developed, but in any and every case the same motive was to be found right at the bottom; even if it were only for self-satisfaction, what was that but a form of egotism?

The Baron had seen and studied life too long and deeply to entertain any misconceptions regarding any man or himself. He did not try to persuade himself that any sense of patriotism or sense of his country or his country's weal influenced him the slightest. He wanted Power. The other Great Influence of the Destinies of men had shaken him once — but that was in the distant past. For years he had plotted, schemed and lived for and towards this goal of ambition, and now — ? Well, it seemed near; but — Kismet. The Baron, taught by long experience, seldom permitted himself to anticipate the Future until such had entered the realm of the Present. As for Paul — well, in keeping with the Baron's character and set scheme in life, Paul was merely an instrument, a pawn, inclined to be troublesome and rebellious, therefore to be discarded or destroyed immediately its utility ceased. Paul, Tarkas, Don Carlos, the financiers, Abd-el-Kader, all were pawns in the Baron's game with Fortune. He had been a pawn in other men's games many a time; and he was only endeavoring to profit by the lessons. Among the multitudinous individuals surging about him in the Sea of Life, one only, paradoxically enough, received tender care and solicitude from the Baron with no material hope of reward — Kismet. Yet even this trait was his expression of the inherent demand in every human for a fetish of some sort. The love lavished upon his dog symbolized propitiation of fate — Kismet; the bald conceit amused him and satisfied the shred of superstition.

His reflections were cut short by a discordant crash from the band which, standing in a circle round a white-bearded bandmaster, plunged recklessly into a noisy blare of brass instruments, amongst which, by superhuman intelligence, three or four notes occasionally gave the clue to the air. The whole of the troops scrambled to their feet, the officials by the gate salaaming low, all murmuring "Allah Ibarek F'amur Sidi," as Abd-el-Kader, a tall, dignified figure in white, accompanied by El Hammo and other viziers, walked slowly across to the summer house. The band continued in discordant frenzy long after the Sultan was seated within and had begun to transact business for the day.

The Baron, issuing instructions to the army to resume their evolutions, mounted his horse, and for a couple of hours kept them busy marching and counter marching in open order, galloping about here and there to drive a laggard into line with the flat of his sword, and profuse guttural remarks upon the culprit's ancestry. Away in corners by themselves a squad of swarthy-robed recruits, looking like a boys' school in nightgowns, were initiated into the mysteries of the goose step and rifle drill by native Haraba (drill instructors).[144] The Baron detested the work, preferring the subtleties of diplomacy; but recognizing that such was necessary to the future success, threw himself into it with characteristic energy.

For the most part the men, ill-fed and ill-clothed, took the whole proceeding as a vast joke, condescending, with an amused, tolerant laugh, to attempt to learn the extraordinary methods of the mad infidels. Their attitude was that of a people conforming to the whim of a new Sultan, although they well knew that their immemorial tribal methods of fighting were infinitely superior to this balderdash.

Now and again one, tiring of the monotony of the jest, would calmly stalk away to lie in the sun, when a Kaithahah, or the Baron himself, would wrathfully chase him back. They were a huge family of inconsequent children, these peasant sons of the valley and mountains, neither understanding nor deeply caring, subservient to the will of Allah; ready when a chance to kill or loot appeared as seeming good to them, their thoughts dwelling forever upon their bellies or women. Anon, a dignified merchant shuffled through the open lines of the troops, and producing a little red prayer mat, stopped in the middle, face to the East, to perform his religious calisthenics, oblivious to the scattered battalions thundering round and about him.

Erewhile the Sultan sat within the incongruous summerhouse, holding audiences with Kaids and Sheikhs with one eye upon the troops which meant so much to him. The band blatantly screeched and blared fitfully; two soldier boys trumpeted and

---

[144] "Haraba" possibly a colonial transliteration of *ḥarrāba*, referring to native Moroccan soldiers or instructors, especially those who train others in military drill.

squeaked in the distance as the blazing sun mounted higher, the heat shimmering and the flies exultant.

At length the Baron, hot and dusty, rode away into the shade of the Gate near the dais to cool. The Sultan, ever watchful, saw, and sent a Makhazni[145] to summon him. The Baron strode over, halted upon the steps to salute with his sword, and entering the cool, sat at the Sultan's feet upon a cushion.

"The troops learn well?" queried the Sultan, his eyes shining enthusiastically, after the flowery greetings.

"Truly, Ya Sidi," responded the Baron diplomatically.

"I have good news, praise be to Allah!" continued Abd-el-Kader. "Ben Musa[146] hath arrived, and with him 8,000 valiant men. The Englishman, thy friend, is at Shragna; Marrakech, Azzimoeur, Agadir, Arzila, Al Kazar Kebir,[147] all have acknowledged me. El Mahmud leaves from Marrakech to join me with 10,000 men."

"Mezian bizaff!" assented the Baron.

"But listen! Abd-el-Rahman hath not yet left for Marrakech."

---

[145] Makhazni: Makhzenni. Members or agents of the Makhzen (the central government, royal administration, and security forces). Often elite soldiers, tribal auxiliaries, or government officials loyal to the Sultan / King.

[146] Ben Musa: Ahamed Ben Mussa (aka known as Bā Aḥmad; 1841/42 – 1900): Grand Wazir of Morocco and de facto ruler between 1894 and 1900. Since Ben Mussa died eight years before the battle, Beadle must be appropriating his name as a substitute for some other figure. "The legitimacy of Abd el-Aziz's sultanate had never been universally accepted in Morocco. From the very beginning of his reign, he was not a popular choice to succeed Moulai Hassan, but rather one forced upon Morocco by his father's chamberlain, a cunning black named Ahamed Ben Mussa, and called Ba Ahmed.... Abd el-Aziz, then a boy of only thirteen or fourteen, became the figurehead behind whom Ba Ahmed ruled Morocco. And he ruled it with an iron hand." Douglas Porch, *The Conquest of Morocco*, pp. 56-57.

[147] Shragna: Sraghna. Marrakech: Marrakesh. Azzimoeur: Azemmour. Arzila: Asilah. Al Kazar Kebir: Alcázarquivir (Spanish); or Ksar el-Kebir (Arabic / latinized form most widely used today).

"That is the third time that he hath failed," reminded the Baron.

"The will of Allah!" exultantly. "With thy help and thy English friend, my troops will leave within the month, and, Praise be to Allah! defeat and capture Abd-el-Rahman. But the other, my brother Mohammed, doth worry me. They say he hath drunk with the Fransawi. Moreover, his people gain many partisans in the Shouya. I would that he were here!" his eyes glinted hard.

"Let it be so," said the Baron.

"How?"

"Send thou a trusty servant to negotiate with him to betray thee. The bait will serve to lure him from the town and French protection. Once without — pouf!"

"Good!" assented the other eagerly; "it shall be done. Tell me, how far will the French continue in Shouya? They are now beyond Settat.[148] Is it not against the Act agreed upon by the Christian Powers? Did not the Sultan of Germany promise that my country should be independent? Yet the French continue on and on?"

"Wait!" the Baron gestured with his hands, implying revolution of circumstances. "Ignore the French. We defeat Abd-el-Rahman, the coast towns proclaim thee, then demand recognition as Sultan. The Sultan is the one recognized by the people of Morocco, not any *person*, and demand a new Agreement, which is necessary to make these concessions" — the Baron tapped himself on the chest — "valid. Then — shu-u!" he gestured, smiling. "What I have told thee will happen. I have yesterday from Berlin letters. *They* are pleased."

The Sultan had listened eagerly.

"And the English?"

---

[148] Settat: a city at the northern edge of the Chaouïa.

"They do not want Morocco. They are content with Egypt, and are friends with France."

"Ah! And money?" His eyes shone with avarice.

"Are there not eight hundred thousand dollars Hassani, at Shragna?"

"Truly. But more money is needed to pay my troops."

"There is another eight hundred thousand dollars in gold with the arms," said the Baron, quietly.

"Ah! Good, good! And afterwards? Tell me again?"

"The debts of Abd-el-Rahman to the French shall be paid; then Morocco is free to thee — and my people. Listen, I would speak further."

The Baron paused to glance around. Only El Hammo was present.

"The country of the Wad Sus[149] is rich?"

"Truly."

"They pay tribute to thee?"

"Nay, by Allah, they are a wild and turbulent people. Never since the days of Mulai Ismael have they paid aught. Mulai Hassan,[150] my father,[151] gave presents unto their Shareef to keep the distant border quiet."

"Ma-el-Ainen?"[152]

---

[149] Wad Sus: Oued Souss. A major river in southern Morocco, running through the Souss Valley and flowing westward from the High Atlas Mountains to the Atlantic near Agadir.

[150] Mulai Hassan: probably a reference to Hassan bin Mohammed, aka Hassan I, Sultan of Morocco from 16 September 1873 until his death on 9 June 1894. He was succeeded by his son Moulay Abd al-Aziz bin Hassan, who was later defeated by his brother at the Battle of Marrakesh.

[151] When Abd-el-Kader refers here to Sultan Hassan as his father, this would make him a brother of the warring sultans, the brothers Moulay Aziz and Moulay Hafid. Another possibility is that Abd-el-Kader is here referring to Sultan Hassan as his sovereign "father," not as his biological father.

[152] Ma-el-Ainen: Ma al-'Aynayn (1830/31 – 1910), also spelled Ma El Aïnin). A Saharan religious leader, scholar, and resistance figure of the late

"A-ah! Thou knowest him?"

The Baron ignored the question, staring dreamily out over the hills; the Sultan watched him keenly.

"Once upon a time," commenced the Baron, with the irrelevant air of telling a story, "there lived a great Sultan, who had much wealth and a great army. He conquered many lands, and then, in accordance with the will of Allah, he died. And when his son's son sat under the Imperial canopy,[153] many troubles came to his own land, so that the length of his arm was foreshortened, and certain of his vassal tribes revolted and declared for their own chief."

The Sultan nodded.

"And," recited the Baron, gesticulating; "there came a stranger to him saying: ' I will aid thee to put thy house in order,' upon condition that he should supply the needs of the household. And it was done."

"Eyeh! Eyeh!"

---

nineteenth and early twentieth centuries. As the European colonial powers moved in (notably France and Spain), Ma al-'Aynayn opposed their influence and proclaimed a kind of jihad against what he regarded as the invasion of Muslim lands. He also maintained a complex relationship with the Moroccan central authorities. At times he cooperated (or was supported) by the sultans, because his authority over tribes and his influence could serve their interest in asserting control over distant southern or Saharan frontiers.

[153] The "son" of Ma al-'Aynayn was Ahmed al-Hiba (sometimes referred to as "the Blue Sultan"). After his father's death in 1910, he declared himself Sultan of Morocco in 1912, leading resistance against the French. The "son's son" (that is, Ma al-'Aynayn's grandson) would therefore be Ahmed al-Hiba's son. When the author says he "sat under the Imperial canopy," this likely refers to the symbolic act of claiming the throne or attempting to reign in Morocco. But historical records note it was Ahmed al-Hiba who proclaimed himself Sultan, not his son. So here the Baron is re-imagining the actual genealogy (or making a false prediction), attributing the throne claim to a grandson rather than directly to Ahmed al-Hiba.

"Then the stranger said unto the Sultan: 'See thy garden is tangled and overgrown with weeds. With the servants of thy house, who are now full fed and lusty, will we cultivate the garden that profit may accrue from the produce thereof. This will I do if thou wilt give me the stewardship.' The Sultan said yea, and behold," concluded the Baron, eyeing Abd-el-Kader, "much fruit and goodly vegetable was the product thereof!"

"And," continued the Sultan, smiling quietly, "the garden flourished and seemed good in the nostrils of the kindred of the stranger, that they devoured the garden and drove forth the owner from his house. Inshallah!"

"Nay," retorted the Baron. "The steward waxed strong, and sought to take the garden unto himself."

"But that could never be, for was not the stranger an alien, and how can a man rule an alien face?"

"True," assented the Baron, quickly, "and thus was the Sultan a wise man. Would'st thou have done likewise?"

"Inshallah! Rest thou here," he added abruptly, indicating a cushion at one side and clapping his hands sharply.

"Naam, Ya Sidi![154] Naam, Ya Sidi!" chorused the Makhzenia, flying up the steps and salaaming deeply as their master gave some rapid instructions.

The troops, who had continued their drill, halted and sprawled — they always sprawled — at ease, whilst their officers formed up in an irregular group near the concrete dais. Presently a group emerged from the Gate, in the midst of which walked three men: two white-bearded, venerable old men, the other young and powerful. Opposite the Sultan the escort halted, the three men advancing and performing deep genuflections, their turbaned heads in the dust. At length the Kaid Meshwar, who had resumed attendance, called:

"Sid Mohammed El Fasi!"

---

[154] Naam, Ya Sidi: Nā'am, yā sayyidī. "Yes, sir."

A tall, lanky man, who carried his head on one side and looked like a stork, advanced from the shade of the wall, made his obeisance, and sat himself by the Sultan. A whispered colloquy ensued between the two and El Hammo, El Fasi exhibiting a number of documents. The Sultan handed an envelope to the Baron.

"Read it," said he.

The Baron saw "Dr. Jules Cartier, Casa Blanca," written in sprawling Roman characters.

"El Tabib Jules Cartier, Dar El Baida," he translated, adding "El Fransawi."[155]

As the Sultan nodded, he smiled, just showing the gleam of teeth.

His glance rose to the watching civil guard and on to the three prisoners. His eyes glinted wickedly; he looked full at them and smiled again, as at the same moment his right hand rose quickly and caressed his black beard. On the instant, the waiting group of Makhzenia leapt like wolves upon their victims, tearing off their turbans and robes, so that in a moment their shaven skulls were gleaming in the sun, and nearly bereft of all clothes, they stood calmly awaiting their fate without protest. The Kaid Meshwar whispered instructions to one of the guards, who ran off towards the gate. He had gone for a barber who, upon his arrival, having been fetched from the nearest shop, swiftly shaved all three men of their beards. The two elderly men were now transformed into shriveled monkeys, all suffering the two greatest forms of disgrace — the loss of the beard and bereft of head covering. Still they waited in the sun for they knew not what.

At length a noisy group emerged from the gate, carrying something which steamed. The smell reached the nostrils; it was a cauldron of boiling pitch.

---

[155] "'Doctor Jules Cartier, Casablanca,' he translated, adding, 'the Frenchman.'"

In a few moments the right hand of each prisoner was hacked off at the wrist, the blood from the severed arteries spurting over the executioners, who immediately plunged the stumps into the cauldron, from which arose a suggestive hiss. One of the elder men fainted, but the other two bore their pain with stoical fortitude, not a sound, save a continual hard breathing groan, left their lips. The Sultan watched the proceedings calmly, nodding with grim satisfaction when it was over. The other Moors, callously indifferent, almost bored.

"What have these men done?" inquired the Baron, whose admiration had been won by the demeanor of the victims.

A frown fled across the Sultan's face. El Fasi replied:

"These men are in league with Mulai Mahommed. We have found letters to him in their houses. Mektub. (It is written.) "

The Baron laughed callously.

"Gilbertian!" he muttered in English. "Make the punishment fit the crime!"[156]

He did not make any protest to the Sultan against the fierce cruelty, as many in his place would have done, knowing well that the perspective of an Oriental and a European are so absolutely different that the victims, who had uttered no word of complaint, would have served any man in like manner under the same circumstances; and, moreover, that any such criticism would not be diplomatic, and utterly vain in any case. They were in all probability guilty of treason, and from the Baron's code, should have been shot, or otherwise removed.

Then donkeys were procured, the men tied astride, face to tail, and thus paraded throughout the streets of the City as a warning.

---

[156] A reference to W. S. Gilbert, English dramatist best known for his comic operas with Arthur Sullivan. "Gilbertian" would refer to a world of precise, sometimes exaggerated morality and ironic justice. Born in 1836, Gilbert died on 29 May 1911, just a few months after the publication of *The City of Shadows*.

Immediately after they had disappeared through the gate to perform their pilgrimage of disgrace, Abd-el-Kader, after consultation with the Hadjib — Court Chamberlain — gave audience to one Tahir Ghazi, a tall, gray-bearded, benign old man, who had at one time held the post of Financial Minister to Mulai Abd-el-Rahman, and had, the Baron knew, been a strong pro-French plotter; but the Baron, in accordance with his policy of refraining from interference in the people's business, providing there was nothing to be gained, made no reference to his private knowledge of the man's past career. After paying deep homage, and presenting lengthy and extravagant compliments, begging the acceptance of some costly presents, Tahir Ghazi expressed a desire to place his services at the disposal of the one and only Prince of the Faithful, Mulai Abd-el-Kader, indulging in vitriolic references to all infidels, and the French in particular, strangely in opposition to the views accredited to him.

Abd-el-Kader graciously accepted the material expressions of homage with a calculating eye, welcomed him profusely, literally showering return gifts upon him, and straightway appointed him to a High Court official post. The smiling eye and gentle tone throughout the interview spoke eloquently of high approval and royal liking.

After this .individual had taken his departure, well pleased with the success of his mission, the Baron attempted to make his adieux, but Abd-el-Kader, smiling, mutely gestured him with a slender, taper-fingered hand to remain.

Another stranger, a very wealthy merchant, seeking audience, was summoned, and in due course presented the gifts of homage. Abd-el-Kader frowned disdainfully upon learning the quantity and quality of the presents. The donor, quick to observe the Imperial displeasure, hastened with judicious celerity to add ten thousand douro, which one of his slaves brought at a signal; that wily gentleman had been kept in the background in case he should not be needed. Abd-el-Kader gave a honeyed smile as he nodded in acknowledgment, and whilst the merchant continued to talk, he eyed him keenly. The smile hardened, and the eyes narrowed in warning as the hand again leisurely caressed the beard. Before the startled man realized what had happened, the ever-watching guard of human wolves had exultantly torn his turban and robes from him, and in less than ten seconds he was being haled away to prison, the Sultan confiscating the whole of his fortune and goods.

Afterwards, as the Baron made his adieux, he noticed that Mulai Abd-el-Kader eyed him meaningly; then he realized why he had been detained as a close spectator. It was an object lesson.

CHAPTER XI

The sweetly scent of attar of roses pervaded a room, the floor of which, and the wainscoting to the pillars and walls, were tiled with small glazed blue and white tiles, the particular product of the City of Fez.

Around these whitewashed walls were ranged narrow mattresses covered with gorgeous blue Berber carpets; the glassless windows were barred with scrolled cast-iron, painted a brilliant scarlet; the wooden ceiling beams and the cornices of the pillars, deeply carved and painted in scarlet, blue and yellow ochre, and the cool bluey-white of the whitewashed walls formed a brilliant Oriental setting to a young girl of about fifteen. She reclined upon one of the rich blue rugs, which contrasted with the coppery glory of her hair, around which, loosely tied, was a white gossamer handkerchief splashed with gold. Her large velvety eyes peered lazily at the world, suggesting a sleepy cat. A deep blue, voluminous caftan hid the figure, but the pose of her creamy neck, the swell and fall of hip, and the small delicate pink feet and ankles, beyond which lay a tiny pair of red leather gold-embroidered shoes, gave eloquent suggestion.

Near her, busily employed in blowing a few live embers of charcoal in the small brazier beneath a large silver hot-water urn, sprawled a young half-caste negress slave, in a loose white tunic and baggy trousers. Beyond, lay a silver tray upon which a pear-shaped teapot, small gold-lacquered glasses, a cube of sugar and a bundle of green mint.

Raising herself upon her elbow, her mistress said: "O Raalia, summon Fatma; I would that she tell us more of the story of

Haroun el Raschid[157] from the storyteller of the sok of the cobblers."

Fatma, the abla,[158] by reason of her common caste, was practiced in storytelling from long study of the itinerant professionals in the public marketplace, which amusement was denied to the daughters of the upper classes.

Raalia obediently got up, and ran off, shouting for Fatma. Whilst she was away the young mistress, idly seeking amusement, picked up a silver mirror, and sitting up, viewed her pretty self with some satisfaction.

Holding the glass at arm's length, she made sheep's eyes in the endeavor to get a view of the almost faultless profile. She smiled, showing pearly teeth delightedly, and with the other hand drew her tresses over her shoulder to try that effect; then, with a gurgling laugh, the hair was showered over her face where she let it remain, playing a game of bopeep through the interstices of the strands. Suddenly her mood changed, and twisting over, she swept her hair back, and leaning upon her elbows, propping the mirror against a cushion, contemplated her own reflection for a while with an air of dissatisfied

---

[157] Haroun el Raschid: Harun al-Rashid. The fifth Abbasid caliph, ruling from the late eighth to early ninth century. Rashid reigned from Baghdad and became legendary not only for his political role but also because many of the stories in *The Thousand and One Nights* cast him as a central figure. "On the Bou Djeloud, the open space which separated Fez el Bali from Fez Djedid, circus actors performed and storytellers repeated tales from Arabian Nights or sang ballads of the great feats of the Arabs, which the crowd knew by heart, often joining in the refrain. One raconteur known as Father Driss, an illiterate slipper maker, became so famous that the Sultan Abd el-Aziz wanted to put out his eyes so that he could tell his stories in the royal harem. Fassis amused themselves with evenings spent in conversation, cards or chess, or by taking walks outside the walls often accompanied by a music box or a singing canary in a cage." Douglas Porch, *The Conquest of Morocco*, pp. 48-49.

[158] Abla: a woman of humble background, familiar with storytelling customs, functioning like a domestic entertainer or caretaker within the household.

criticism. She frowned, raised her eyebrows, laughed, coquetted, and then petulantly threw the mirror down, only to pick it up again.

"Ya Aziz (O Beloved),"[159] she exclaimed, as if addressing the mirror, "why dost thou not come? Am I not beautiful? Do I not please thee? Oh, hateful face!" she smacked the mirror, frowning. "It is two months since the light of thy face warmed me! Thou hast returned and yet thou dost not come. Oh!" the mirror flew across the room again as she flung herself among the cushions.

The sound of an excited altercation, the shuffle of slippers, seemed to irritate her. She sat up and clapped her hands. Raalia appeared at the door.

"O Zahra, Fatma, the daughter of a she-ass," commenced the slave, volubly, gesticulating, "hath gone — "

"It is no matter," interrupted her mistress. "I would go to the garden — by the wall. It is warm here. Bring thou the tea."

Raalia clapped her hands three times as Zahra rose languidly and sauntered out to the fountain, where, sitting on the marble edge, she must needs frighten the goldfish with her slim fingers, laughing delightedly to see them dart hither and thither.

Two huge negro eunuchs, answering Raalia's summons, stood awaiting the girl's pleasure.

Ceasing her play for a moment, she pointed with dripping fingers down the garden, the poise of the head and gesture suggesting a charming mixture of haughty imperiousness and childish petulance. The eunuchs, gathering up the tea things, rugs and cushions, bore them after the slim slave girl, whilst Zahra became absorbed in her game anew. With a sudden dart, which sent the water flashing diamonds in the sunlight, she secured the largest of the brilliant-hued fish, and sat watching the frantic struggles of the captive in her little pink hand. Then,

---

[159] Ya ʿAzīz: "Oh dear," or "Oh precious one."

impulsively, she bent her head, pretending to kiss the small, scaly head with lips incarnadine, exclaiming: "Ya llah,[160] would that thou wert my Beloved! Would that I could hold him so. A-ah!" she leaned back gesturing extravagantly, sighed, and dropping the fish back into the fountain, sat pensively gazing down the garden, where amid the scent of orange blossom arose the myriad sounds of insect life of a warm day.

At length, still in pensive mood, she arose, and sauntered down the garden to where Raalia, beside the rugs and cushions in the shade of the wall, energetically worked a small pair of bellows in the brazier.

Lying upon the cushions, Zahra detached one of her huge gold earrings and fell to twisting a garland of wild flowers about the large roughly-cut emerald which adorned the bauble.

When tea was made, the two sat sipping the sweet beverage as the shadows grew longer from the wall.

"O Raalia," said Zahra, plucking the garland of flowers to pieces, and pelting her companion, "tell me once more what news thou hast of him?"

"Truly have I not told thee even a score of times!" protested Raalia, sipping her tea with noisy appreciation. "He hath but been within the City since the hour of noon, and as he rode through the gate his brow was like unto a thundercloud. But Yillah![161] What a man! Tall is he and strong, with a face like unto the sun and eyes as twin stars!"

"And the horse beneath him," chimed in Zahra, with eloquent gestures and shining eyes, "seemed but part of him! O, lucky horse, an[d] that he knew that which bestrode him would he die of delight! Ah! And his voice like unto the soughing of the wind in the trees, gentle and strong! Which hath charmed mine ears

---

[160] Ya llah: "O God" or "My God."
[161] Yillah: yallāh: "Come on!" / "Let's go!" / "Hurry up!" or "OK then" / "Alright," depending on the tone of voice.

but once. Waali![162] Waali! Woe is me! That I die without he look upon me."

Zahra threw herself back on the cushions in extravagant grief, and stretching her arms towards the wall, sighed, bewailing softly: "O Pole, Ya Az-iz (Beloved)!"

"Tell thou me," she demanded, suddenly sitting up, "thinkest thou he hath many wives?"

"How should that be!" responded Raalia. "Is he not an N'srani? And do not they say that it is the custom of the infidel to have but one wife?"

"So sayeth Bu Shaib,"[163] exclaimed Zahra, half suspiciously. "But even if he lieth in his throat yet will I be the favorite wife! A-ah!"

"But how canst thou be?" demanded Raalia. "Is he not an infidel? Thou canst not marry him."

Grief and anger flew across Zahra's pretty features. "I care not! I care not!" she exclaimed, energetically clawing at the cushions. "I will if I die! Yillah! One hour with my beloved and then let me die![164] A-ah, beloved! Come to me! But he will not come! Waali! Waali! He cometh not, and I am desolated. Raalia! Ra-alia! What shall I do? Go, fetch him to me! Tell him I — no, no, o-oh!" With a little scream she buried her head in the cushions, her tawny mane aflame in a stray shaft of sunlight against the blue rug, crying "Waali! Waali! Wa-ali!"

---

[162] Waali: Wā-'alī. A cry of distress or lament, equivalent to "Oh my God!" "Alas!" or "Woe is me!"

[163] Bu Shaib: possibly a reference to the novel *Tafilet* (1895) by Walter Harris, in which the character Bu Shaib is a Moroccan notable. On page 253, Harris introduces him as: "Kaid Ben Bu Shaib, one of the governors of the tribe of Dukála, who owned a great castle not far inland from Mazagan, on the Atlantic coast."

[164] A true testament of her profound love, this highly heretical declaration flies in the face of powerful religious institutions, thus it places Zahra's life in danger. For more on the significance of this courageous act, see my Afterword.

Raalia sat unconcernedly sipping tea, obviously used to these fits of petulant anger and despair. To Zahra, a child of nature, this new trouble that had descended upon her was the most serious affair that had ever troubled her butterfly existence. To the child of a wealthy Mohammedan, the outside world was unknown. The life of the Harem, eating, playing and sleeping, constituted her life. Vague rumors of war and doings of men reached her through the lips of the abla or Raalia, but of men she knew nothing personally. Many seen passing in the street beneath hardly stirred her curiosity. The downfall of Sultans, or the doings of the infidel were heard and interested her in the same way as the secondhand stories of Haroun el Raschid from the lips of Fatma. Education, being a Mohammedan, she had none. The other members of the Harem, the slaves, the guardians, and a white-bearded, haughty old man held in awe, whom she knew to be her father, the gardens, sunlight and flowers, all these were real to her; everything else was vague and half comprehended. She knew no other form of life for a woman; knew no other society; and until lately had scarcely thought of or desired aught else. Sometimes vague longings to know the meaning of things and of life oppressed her. She would, had any opportunity been available, have proved hungry for knowledge and learning.

But all inquiries must of necessity be asked of others as ignorant as herself, and invariably met with the stereotyped answer "Inshallah!"

There came a day when, walking upon the roof to see the Sultan pass, she saw Paul. For no reason that she could fathom, or for that matter, had the slightest inclination to seek, she fell madly in love with him at sight. Then, for a week or more, she had lived in a fever of secret delight. Raalia had been made her confidante, and at her bidding, discovered that he was an N'srani, which, woman-like, had served to quicken her love for him. Flowers were carried in case he might ride by once more.

He did; and she had spoken, bestowing the token upon him without the vaguest conception of any impropriety. She was a purely innocent child of nature, naively free from any taint of false modesty.

Raalia, through the medium of the marketplace, the morning and evening paper of the East, had learned of his arrival that morning, so joy, tempered by impatient disappointment, rioted in the heart of Zahra.

Recovering from her fit of passionate weeping, she sat up with red eye-rims, plaintively disheveled. Raalia, busy making fresh tea, looked up, and noticing her tear-stained cheeks, laughed, at which Zahra, with a little spring, leapt to her feet, and seizing a stick lying handy, belabored her slave over the shoulders, her large eyes flashing in tempestuous anger.

"Thou mule! Thou she-ass!" screamed the mistress between blows. "I will have thee thrashed. "Wilt laugh at Zahra? Thou shalt be killed! Fool! Pig!"

"Waali! Wa-ali! Wa-ali!" moaned the slave, crouching before the blows. "Forgive! ough! I lick thy feet! ough! Mercy! ough!"

Throwing down the stick, Zahra sank back on her cushions, panting with the exertion, her eyes still flashing dangerously.

Raalia, rubbing her injured limbs and muttering to herself, returned to her work at the teapot, as Zahra, her bosom still heaving, fell to playing with her hair, tugging viciously at it. Then, with a revulsion of feeling, she suddenly rolled over laughing heartily, and leaping to her feet, kissed and fondled the docile Raalia with extravagant regard, who showed her gleaming teeth in grinning approval of her mistress's latest change of mood. Zahra, wriggling back on to the cushions, shook her tawny shower of hair from her face, and throwing back her head, sang a few snatches of a plaintive air.

"Raalia!" she stopped to say, "go thou, bring hither my guinbri."

Raalia flew to fetch the two-stringed Moorish guitar, and Zahra, plucking languidly at the strings, commenced to sing, in a low, crooning minor key.

> O, Beloved Moon of my Desire,
> Within me dwelleth eternal Fire
> Of Love consuming, so dire my need
> For one soft, fond look. Ah, thus I plead!
>> Love, could I doubt thee? Nay, but my soul —
>> Faint unto Death — may ne'er reach thy goal.
> O, Twin stars of Love, pity the plight
> Of a lover true in grief bedight.[165]
> So shy my love 'tis mute save in sighs
> Tears of longing bedewing my eyes.
>> Love, could I doubt thee? Nay, but my soul —
>> Faint unto Death — may ne'er reach thy goal.
> O Patience begone! I would implore
> O fairest gazelle, ope[166] wide the door
> That love may enter, where safe installed
> I may thee worship, my soul enthralled.
>> Love, could I doubt thee? Nay, but my soul —
>> Faint unto Death — may ne'er reach thy goal.

Her light silvery voice died away in the hot air. Handing the instrument to Raalia, she bade her sing, which the slave willingly did, for she had been born on the slopes of the Atlas, where among the fierce hill men, she had learned the songs of the Berber poets, wilder and even more barbaric than the Arab music. Cross-legged she sat, plucking the strings in accompaniment to a sad, plaintive air, a note of inquiry and subdued passion ever and again recurring:

---

[165] Bedight (archaic): being dressed or decorated. As a verb form (also archaic): to equip or to array.

[166] Ope (archaic): open.

By what fair shrine did Zahra's parents pray,
That earth and sky grow bright about her way?
My Zahra! Queen of beauty and of grace;
Uncrowned for none save one hath seen her face.
　　All beauty, brothers, is a shrine
　　A gift of Heaven, half Divine.
To match, fair dove, thy dainty, snow-white plumes,
Be straight prepared the Castle's marble rooms;
Wherein I'll pledge thee, Queen of all Delight,
In porcelain goblet, like thyself, all white.
　　The streams in spate, for very joy and pride
　　That Zahra's feet tripped through his crystal tide.

And may the mercy of the Lord belong
To Sidi Hammo, singer of this song.

As the shadows lengthened across the orchard, the two girls sat alternately singing and crooning to each other.

At length, wearying, Zahra signified her pleasure by an imperious wave of the hand, and sinking back upon the cushions, watched a flight of birds.

"Let us go to the rooftop," she said to Raalia. "It is cool, and I would walk."

"Perhaps we may see him walking in his garden," suggested Raalia slyly, for the big rambling grounds adjoined Paul's house, although he knew it not.

Zahra's face lit up with ecstasy, and she laughed, the low, gurgling, caressing laugh of a woman to her lover.

The sound of voices speaking an alien tongue floated over the wall.

"Skut" (be quiet) I whispered Zahra, running barefoot to listen. "'Tis he!"

CHAPTER XII

"AL-LAH — Ak-ba-ah!"

Cynthia's wraith light[167] bathed the white flat rooftops and hills across the valley in mystic glamour, the olive-clad slopes and flower-carpeted Vlei[168] in suggestive shadow and tinted shimmer. A cock crowed afar, the choking lament of an ass, an owl or nightjar; and suddenly silence.

"Al-lah — Ak-ba-a-ah!"

Upon an ethereal rooftop abutting on the crumbling embattled walls, a cigarette glowed, the alien touch in the old-world scene. Paul, up betimes,[169] was listening to the voice of the land, intelligible only to the initiated, to many never, a few seldom.

A stallion neighed shrilly below, a camel gurgled complaint.

"Al-lah — Ak-ba-ah!"

Paul strove to read, interpret that wonderful call; not the mere dictionary meaning, but the inner meaning, which in all probability Muhammad, the deviser, never knew or guessed, let be the humble, ill-equipped mind of the mere Mueddhin, the instrument. There is meaning in all sound, the cry of the seagull, the baying of a dog at the moon. But who reads or seeks to read?

To Paul the cry was eloquent of world forces full strong, the world of joy and sorrow, mixed destiny. He reviewed the past

---

[167] "Cynthia": a poetic reference to the Moon deity. (Cynthia is another name for Artemis, Greek goddess of the Moon.) From the Latin *Cynthia*, derived from *Kynthos* (*Cynthus*): in Greek myth, a mountain on the island of Delos. Hence "Cynthia" is an epithet of goddess Artemis, meaning "of Mount Cynthus" or "born on Mount Cynthus."

[168] Vlei: a South African (Afrikaans / Dutch) word, meaning a shallow, low-lying marshy or grassy depression that sometimes holds water in the rainy season. By extension, in English travel writing it came to mean a flat green valley or lush, damp meadow.

[169] Betimes: early.

rapidly. Every action seemed pregnant with meaning, leading to this — leaning on the parapet of a Moor's house in central Morocco, listening to that call.

"Al-lah — Ak-ba-ah!"

Every incident now seemed as if it had to be, all small bricks building up his life to take the shape and form of himself. Had one brick or incident been otherwise, then, of necessity, the whole structure must have been different, another individuality, therefore not Paul Towers, but — ? It was inconceivable that he could be other than himself; therefore inconceivable that anything should have been other than it had been; therefore — Fate.

From the past to the present, and to the future. What would happen in the future? The throbbing call answered him. "Mektub." It is written. What a comforter! What a solace in an hour of agony or doubt! It is written — already. So will it be: neither more nor less.

Away beyond the hills lay Fez. His journey had been successfully accomplished, and tomorrow he would arrive at Fez to commence a fresh chapter. He pondered upon his attitude towards the Baron. The fires of ambition had not abated in the least, but he had determined to suppress his egoistical promptings and to keep to his word with his accepted Chief. Paul had never ceased to reproach himself for permitting the one slip from his code of honor in even harboring thoughts of infidelity. The temptation was strong; a lesser character would have sought to justify himself upon the ground that the Baron was utterly unscrupulous and only desired to make use of him, and that, therefore, one was at least entitled to fight for one's own interests. The temptation of an Empire, even if nebulous, was not a small one. Ethically it is not a question of the reality of the goal, but the degree of intensity of conviction with which the subject views it. One might murder another for the sake of a gold watch, but if the watch should prove to have existed only in one's own mind, that does not in the least diminish or increase the enormity of the offence.

But, then perhaps, Paul argued, the very weakness to which he had succumbed, although only temporary and abstract, might prove his undoing, for the Baron had undoubtedly read the passing thought and would take the first opportunity, as he had already hinted, to remove him, wholly and naturally oblivious to the fact that the offender had seen the error of his ways and repented. Would the Baron call upon him to give satisfaction for the insult now or when? and if so, was it fated that Paul should be shot as a dog? The thought that he would be simply wiped out of existence in the midst of living ambition irritated him. There was hardly any fear of actual death; Paul had faced the grim angel too often. But the exasperation of such an ignominious end to all his plans and ambition! A little while ago he had protested that life was a burden to him, and death a welcome release; now all had changed, the desire to live had returned threefold, fanned by ambition and — and a wish, which he would not acknowledge, to see a pair of dark eyes once more. Rebellious at the circumstances which had jeopardized his fortune to the Baron, he ended, after analysis, by being wroth with himself for having played his cards so badly in losing momentary control of himself. And although Paul, influenced by the fatalism that throve in the Oriental atmosphere, endeavored to soothe his troubled mind with the panacea of the doctrine of "Mektub," yet he was only humanly inconsistent in endeavoring to avoid the inevitable, or what seemed the inevitable, losing sight of the fact that whatever happened must necessarily have been inevitable from the first.

Throughout the long monotonous journey to the coast and return Paul had devoted considerable time to thoughts of Zahra. He had kept the little flowers in a pocket of his skarrah,[170] although earnestly telling himself that he was quite absurd in so doing and would, after suddenly awaking to the fact that he had plodded along for miles daydreaming of Zahra's dark eyes, angrily extract the offending token, gaze at it speculatively, call himself a fool, and carefully replace it; after which he would force his mind to debate some material problem concerned with the scheme to again awake from a sentimental daydream.

As the dawn broke the clatter of hooves below in the street warned him that it was time to start upon the last stage of the journey and to meet Fate in Fez.

By dint of hard riding, leaving the caravan to arrive in its own time, he entered the Bab-el-Bushat at noon. As he continued straight on he passed a crowd of animals and men, and the clamor arising betokened some unusual excitement. He inquired the reason from one of the native escort.

"Sid Tahir Ghazi[171] lies dead," responded the man after a colloquy with an excited foot soldier.

Paul was told particulars of the previous day's interview, and, knowing the East, inquired:

"Kahawa (coffee)?"[172]

"Eeyeh! Inshallah!"[173]

"Or the Sultan!" added Paul, smiling grimly, at which the man laughed.

---

[170] Skarrah: ṣurra. In Arabic, a pouch, bundle, or small bag. In some North African dialects it can also refer to a pocket-like fold in a garment, where things are kept.

[171] Earlier in the text the narrator describes how Abd-el-Kader "gave audience to one Tahir Ghazi, a tall, gray-bearded, benign old man, who had at one time held the post of Financial Minister to Mulai Abd-el-Rahman, and had, the Baron knew, been a strong pro-French plotter."

[172] Kahawa: Qahwa, or in simplified form, kahwa or kahawa, meaning coffee.

[173] "Yes! God willing!"

Upon his arrival at the house Paul found that the Baron had not returned from the drill, so after a bath and a meal, he awaited him. At the last moment Paul altered his mind and determined to force the hand of Fate by compelling the Baron to agree to a stated policy for the future, or challenge him to the duel and thus settle matters one way or the other. He felt that he could not continue with this sword of Damocles overhanging him — at the Baron's whim.

At length the Baron put in an appearance, bade Paul a placid good morning, and turned his attention to consoling Kismet for his prolonged absence.

For a few moments Paul waited with suppressed irritation for him to cease "fooling with the damned cur." At length the Baron, with easy nonchalance, settled himself on a divan and clapped his hands to summon a servant, remarking:

"El Kader's very anxious for the goods, so I suppose they'll be here today?"

"Yes, this evening," said Paul, ceasing a devil's tattoo[174] on the arm of a chair. "Any news?"

"A little. El Rahman's not left Rabat yet. Mulai Mohammed is getting troublesome. Ben Hama has advanced to Tazza[175] with a reported following of twenty thousand — Ahmed, prepare a bath for me and clean clothes. Go to the Soko and buy me some cigarettes. Remember, fool, Bastos Julienne, not the others. — And — er — ah, yes, the post this morning brings news of trouble at the Legations. I am required — and yourself — to return to Tanga in order to avoid political trouble. Ha ha, they might have saved the postage. M'sieu le Marquis wished to join us here, but I told him to stop where he is — at present. He tells

---

[174] A "devil's tattoo" (chiefly British): nervous or impatient finger tapping, especially the drumming of fingers on a surface while thinking or waiting.
[175] Tazza: Taza. A city in north-central Morocco situated between the Rif Mountains to the north and the Middle Atlas to the south.

me that there's likely to be trouble in the Balkans, which may possibly lead to a European conflagration, and that would be very useful to me — draw attention away from Morocco, so I've instructed him to go over there and use every endeavor to bring the trouble on — and it will keep him quiet. It's worth a million marks or more to us to have a general European War; it would free the air and give us a free hand here. And Kismet has been very ill. I think that the fountain water is impure. I have had it cleaned out. But he's nearly well again now, and I don't think that he'll have a relapse. Well, I think that is about all the news," he concluded, rising.

"Oh, wait a moment," said Paul. "I want to speak about — er — to you a moment."

"So? After tiffin will do."

"No, it *won't* do!" exclaimed Paul irritably. "I want you now for ten minutes."

The Baron raised his eyebrows in protest and reseated himself.

"So?"

Paul stood silent, staring into the courtyard.

"So?"

There was a faint tinge of rising impatience in the Baron's voice.

Paul threw back his hood, tore off the heavy turban, and replaced the tarboosh before he said:

"Well, Baron, I want to come to a definite understanding. The present position is absurd."

"So?"

The Baron gazed interestedly at a fly upon the white wall.

"Well — you won't accept an apology?"

"I am surprised that you ask!"

"Well," exclaimed Paul, wheeling about. "You'll either do that or take your satisfaction now."

"But, my dear Towers," objected the Baron urbanely, "it is for me to choose my satisfaction. I am the insulted one."

"Well, you'll either fight now or not at all."

"But that cannot be possible," protested the Baron, with raised eyebrows. "You are a gentleman, I believe, therefore you must fight if I, the insulted one, demand my satisfaction — it is my right."

"Right, or no right, it's as I say," exclaimed Paul, explosively. "I'm not going to give you my services just as you please and allow you to make use of me."

The Baron laughed softly.

"Now, look here," said Paul with restraint, and walking over to the Baron. "You'll either give me the satisfaction of taking your damned satisfaction now, or I'll heave you into the tank yonder. D'you understand? I will not be made a fool of. Your answer?"

"Don't be absurd, Towers! You're not a coffee-house brawler!"

"Coffee-house brawler or not," roared Paul, passionately. "By Heaven, I'll do as I say if you don't answer. Quick, which is it?"

The Baron lost his equanimity in fear of the athletic, muscular figure threatening above him; acute fear of the possible indignity which many a small man suffers from, and not from any physical cause. To the Baron fear of death was an unknown quantity, as far as such is possible to any human, but fear of ridicule was an all-pervading strong factor. He wished to postpone the duel in accordance with his own plans, but this fear now drove him to acquiesce.

"Very good, Towers. Since you insist upon tasting the waters of Lethe, so be it. Will daybreak, tomorrow suit you? And what weapon do you prefer, revolver or sword?"

"Revolvers."

"Certainly; although the rapier is a much more artistic and well-bred instrument. However, I will bathe now, if that is all you have to say."

"No," answered Paul, "there's no occasion to wait until tomorrow. There's good light now. Let's get it over." He turned away and stood in the doorway, gazing down into the garden.

"Inshallah!" replied the Baron indifferently, picking up Kismet to caress him.

"The garden here will do as well as anywhere," added Paul. "The servants need not know till afterwards. We shall have to dispense with seconds."

"Ja, mein lieber,"[176] said the Baron, addressing Kismet in German. "Thou knowest all things, even the stupidity of a fool is ordained by thee."

"Will you kindly listen to me?" demanded Paul with suppressed rage from over his shoulder.

The Baron laughed softly, caressing the dog.

"Your nerves are very bad, Towers! What do you wish to say?"

"I suggested the garden — " commenced Paul, icily.

"As you will; it is as good as elsewhere."

"And about seconds — "

"Kismet is my second," said the Baron, whimsically.

Paul frowned.

"Are you ready?" asked Paul.

"If you are ready, I am."

"Yes, certainly — after my bath, if you please," returned the Baron, still addressing Kismet. "One should even go to hell clean, eh, mein lieber? Ah, but you have had your bath, have you not?"

Paul stalked away to his room without replying. Sitting down upon a bed, he scribbled letters to solicitors and others in case of

---

176 "Ja, mein lieber": "Yes, my dear" or "Yes, my dear friend."

eventualities. As he sealed the last, the Baron, splashing about in an adjacent room, called:

"Towers? Oh, will you scribble a line about our little difference? I mean to the effect that your death occurred in an *affaire d'honneur*? I do not wish to be charged with your murder when the Legations arrive."

Paul swore under his breath.

"Thank you. I have already attended to that but — merely as a suggestion — will you oblige me in a similar manner?"

"Oh, if you so desire it, I will certainly," answered the Baron, after a series of splashes.

Paul, with knitted brow, paced up and down his room, thinking. The Baron undoubtedly fully intended to shoot to kill. Paul had at first determined that he would fire in the air, half opining that the Baron had only insisted on the duel as a salve to his injured dignity, but now Paul realized that it was a fight to the death in grim earnest. Undoubtedly the Baron was convinced that Paul was a dangerous instrument, and although the time was a little premature, had best be removed. "However," thought Paul, "I am a fair shot, so maybe we shall both be dead in a few hours." The whole thing seemed ridiculous to him. The unnecessary risking of the two lives upon which the scheme depended seemed to him preposterous, but the same idea did not appeal to the Baron, who apparently was confident of the result. To Paul's adversary this was no new experience, and probably his confidence was born of previous successes, but to Paul, although he had faced the long journey many times before, it was never under the deliberate circumstances of a duel. The waiting in cold blood to stand up before another man to be shot at is somewhat disconcerting to the novice.

There was no suggestion of fear, but irritation at the futility of the affair. Then as he paused in his march to stare at the trees in the garden, a pair of deep, dark eyes appeared to his mental vision. He frowned and turned away, suddenly realizing that the thought that he might never see those eyes again hurt.

He searched beneath his robes in the skarrah, and producing the faded flower, contemplated it gloomily. "What an absolute fool I am," he thought. He knew absolutely nothing of the donor beyond her beauty. She might be, and in all probability was, merely the ordinary Arab woman, wholly undeveloped mentally, and incapable of understanding or appreciating anything that appealed to him, and yet — yet the thought of parting was agony. Parting? He had only exchanged a single sentence with her, and yet — he became angry with himself for wondering whether there would be time to ride past her house on the chance of seeing her again, or of postponing the duel until the morrow.

A step on his balcony aroused him. He looked up to find the Baron watching him keenly.

"Are you ready?" asked Paul.

"Certainly. Here are my guns — choose!"

The Baron bowed ceremoniously as he handed Paul an open case of silver-mounted dueling pistols. They walked silently downstairs and out across the long garden. A space at the far end in line with the wall was chosen.

"I exceedingly regret the absence of seconds," said the Baron, precisely, "and also the extreme irregularity of the affair, but you will, I feel sure, act with me in observing the usual etiquette as far as possible. So, with your permission, I will measure the ground."

The Baron proceeded to pace the distance, pausing for a moment to ostentatiously observe his cigarette, held out between two fingers; he smiled grimly in satisfaction. Paul frowned irritably.

"If you are agreeable," remarked the Baron, "I will count three, upon which we wheel and fire?"

"Very good," assented Paul.

They walked to their respective places, the Baron carelessly smoking.

"Oh, do you wish more than one shot, or are we to shoot until one or both of us fall?" inquired Paul.

"Oh, one shot I think will be amply sufficient," answered the Baron, in an insolent tone, over his shoulder.

Paul scowled with annoyance as he drew a tentative bead upon an orange tree. His hand was as steady as a rock.

The sun in the western horizon was well protected by the orchard trees from their eyes. From over the wall Paul heard a woman's light laugh, and thought involuntarily of Zahra. Rabbit's voice, blackguarding a water-carrier, floated across the blossom-laden air.

Paul heard the click of the Baron's revolver hammer as he took his stand facing him. An eerie shiver ran through him.

"Al-lah — Ak-ba-ah!"

The afternoon call to prayer rang out from a neighboring mosque with sinister emphasis.

"Are you ready?" came in even tones from the Baron, standing revolver to earth.

"Al-lah — Ak — — "

"One!"

"-ba-ah!"

"Two!"

"Al-lah — " and a sound of scurrying feet. "Three!"

"-il Al-lah!"

As Paul's arm flew up double reports sounded simultaneously with a vision of a white-robed figure flying between them, and Paul found himself holding the form of Zolika in his arms as the Mueddhin chanted: "El Mahom-ed-rasul — Al-lah!"[177]

---

[177] El Mahom-ed-rasul – Al-lah: Mohammed, the prophet of God.

Paul could not conceive what had happened. For a few moments he was only conscious of the girl lying in his arms, something warm trickling over his wrist, and the high, droning chant of the Mueddhin. He lowered her gently on to the ground, perceiving that she had received the bullet intended for him. He forgot the very existence of the Baron in his anxiety for the wounded girl. She opened her eyes and smiled up at him as he bent over her.

"Thou hast no hurt?" she asked feebly.

"Nay, little one," he answered. "Why hast thou done this thing? and — and how camest thou to be in this house?"

"He — he brought me — hither," she gasped, with white lips.

And as Paul comprehended what her words implied, he heard the Baron's voice calling for Absalom. He glanced in his direction as he rose to run for water for her, and saw him leaning heavily against a tree. His bullet had sped true, then! With rage in his heart, he half prayed that the Baron would die by his hand. Paul seized a jar lying near the fountain, and filling it, ran back to Zolika. She lay still, her white face sideways, eyes glassy — dead. For a moment Paul felt a mad desire to rush at the Baron and hack the life from him.

But he fell on his knees by the dead girl who had given her life for him, and, blinded by tears, kissed her reverently on the forehead. For a while he sat, conscious only of the tragedy of the girl's young life, and dimly hearing the even tones, merciless in their utter indifference, of the cry of relentless fate:

"Al-lah — Ak-ba-ah!"

CHAPTER XIII

Next morning Paul awoke in the small hours and lay listening to the cadences of the Mueddhin in the stilly air. He remembered the dead girl lying silent below, and, although still feeling resentment against the Baron, bitterly blamed himself, arguing that his unreasonable, ill-tempered action in forcing a quarrel upon the Baron, the result of coquetting with selfish ambition, was really responsible. However, there was nothing to be gained for anyone by morbid self-abasement. He determined that in the future he would act strictly to the letter of the course which he would set himself. In his walk during the previous evening he had wished that the Baron's wounds would prove fatal. Such an event would at all events cut the tangled skein. As yet he had not troubled to visit or even inquire after his adversary.

In his heart he wanted the Baron out of the way in order that he might obey the demands of ambition; and at the back of all things, unacknowledged, almost subconscious, was the ardent wish to see and know Zahra. Whenever her image presented itself Paul sternly endeavored to suppress all thought of her, calling himself a fool. Yet he could not persuade himself to throw the flowers away!

As he lay thinking, listening with a curious fascination to the Mueddhin, the chanting cry suggested as ever the voice of Destiny prompting the reflection that everything, the death of Zolika, the quarrel with the Baron, Zahra, all were fated and inevitable, and that as such was the case, the future was equally settled; whatever might happen was already "written." To a tired brain struggling with life problems there was more than comforting solace in the thought. No need to worry! No need to struggle! Mektub, it is written. He thought of Omar Khayyam,[178]

---

[178] Omar Khayyam (1048 – 1131): Persian poet and polymath.

and wondered whether his philosophy had been prompted by the chanting of the Mueddhin:

'Tis all a Checkerboard of Nights and Days
Where Destiny with Men for Pieces plays:
Hither and thither moves, and mates, and slays,
And one by one back in the Closet lays.[179]

Then from without in the near distance came the sound of strife: guttural exclamations, a shot, a scream, a choking sob, silence; and the wailing chant oblivious as Fate itself.

At length came dawn and sunrise. Paul walked round the balcony to the Baron's room, determined to come to some understanding, if he were like to recover, in spite of his recent fatalistic reflections!

In the cool light of his room the Baron lay awake smoking; Kismet, curled as usual upon the counterpane, looked up at the intruder, emitting a shrill snarl.

"Good morning, Towers," said the Baron, pleasantly. "Be quiet, mein lieber," laying a gentle hand upon his dog. "Kismet seems less inclined to smile upon you, Towers, than yesterday, eh?"

He smiled genially, exhaling smoke. Paul, with a faint pang of disappointment, failed to observe any signs of bandages.

"Good morning," he returned, somewhat stiffly. "Er — how are you? I'm sorry I haven't called before, but — but — "

His voice trailed away lamely, at which the Baron raised his eyebrows and smiled cynically.

"So? Sit down! Well, you winged me very nicely. I congratulate you, although Fate was very kind to you — at another's expense!" he added, maliciously.

---

[179] From Edward Fitzgerald's celebrated translation of "The Rubáiyát of Omar Khayyam."

Paul frowned.

"Er — if you're well enough, Baron, I wish to talk this matter out and come to some understanding. We cannot go on like this!"

"So?"

"Yes, so," exclaimed Paul, the extreme cynical placidity of the other irritating him. "Kindly oblige me with your intentions."

"My intentions?" echoed the Baron. "Herr Gott! To lie here until my side is well, thanks to you, dear friend!"

A flush of satisfaction lit up Paul's face, which the Baron observed and acknowledged with a short, dry laugh.

"I'm sorry," commenced Paul.

"Pouf!" exclaimed the Baron lightly, waving the false sentiment aside with brown fingers. "Why lie to me, my friend? The girl saved you and — four inches from my heart! — mein lieber, eh, Kismet?" caressing his dog, which looked up at him affectionately, "saved me! Why apologize? I do not apologize for missing you!"

"That's beside the question," returned Paul, frowning. "What is to happen in the future?"

"So?" said the Baron, with a laugh. "Perhaps Kismet here will tell you; no one else can!"

"Do not fence the question. You very well know what I mean."

"So?"

"What I mean is this. We cannot go on any longer under the same arrangement after what has occurred."

"So? Correct me! I fail to understand. Have you not given your word when joining me in Tanga?"

"Yes, but I do not feel inclined to keep it when I find — after what has occurred."

"A-ah! Why have you not mentioned that little fact before, Herr Towers?"

"Because there was no reason to do so," returned Paul shortly.

"So? But I beg to differ!"

"I don't care a hang about what you beg to do!" exclaimed Paul.

"Well, of course; if you prefer to lose your temper," said the Baron, shrugging his shoulders and lying back upon his pillows.

Paul turned on his heel savagely, conscious that in the matter of self-control the Baron was his master. Rabbit met him at the stairs.

"Mornin', ole chap," he observed cheerily. "Kaithaha come from Sultan, him say want you — Baron and you."

Paul returned to the Baron, repeating the message.

"So?" said the Baron quietly. "Well, you will go, but of course I have been injured in an accident, you understand? It would never do for the only two Europeans in the heart of a Mohammedan country in rebellion to quarrel, would it, Kismet?" he laughed softly, caressing the dog.

Upon arrival at the gates of the Palace, Paul was bidden to wait "a little." Squatted upon a cushion in the shade amongst a crowd of Court officials — two, three, four hours passed. Time is no object to the Oriental mind. In all probability the Sultan, having dispatched the message, promptly forgot all about it in the maze of other affairs.

As the sun commenced to throw oblique shadows, even Paul's laboriously acquired patience gave out, and, hungry and thirsty, he rode back to the house. The evening came on, and when about to retire, another messenger arrived in hot haste.

Paul, led round by devious back ways, was ushered through a small gate to find the tall figure of Mulai Abd-el-Kader pacing leisurely up and down a tiled piazza amid the orange groves. He looked up, nodded to Paul, and with a gesture of the hand, bade him walk beside as the attendants withdrew and the two were left alone. For a while the Sultan walked in silence.

"Tell me, O Englishman," he said at length, halting, "what use hath a man?"

The wholly unexpected dive into the philosophy of life staggered Paul. As he hesitated, the other continued, placing a slim hand on the Englishman's shoulder, looking straight down into his eyes:

"In the days of Suliman[180] all learning was in the East, and in the days of Mohammed the sons of the Faithful taught the world, yet now is the Infidel paramount in knowledge and wisdom. Why?"

"Because," answered Paul emphatically, — without any sense of reasoned thought, rather a flash of intuition — "because the Infidel is weaker in his faith than the followers of Mohammed, and so, depending less upon Allah, have sought and found for themselves many things."

"Thou art a wise man," replied Abd-el-Kader, dropping his hand. "'Tis even as I have thought in my heart and many amongst us. Money is the god of mankind — in his heart. Such thoughts do vaguely disquiet my soul, yet — yet there are better things seemingly."

He paused, resuming the walk.

"And when thoughts disturb my rest, I often rise and soothe my soul with words."

"A favor, Ya Sidi," said Paul, immensely interested; "that I may see thy words?"

"Nay," replied the Sultan smiling, "a true poet doth not show his words to other than his own soul!"

"Yet who was a greater poet than Sid Omar Khayyam?"

---

[180] In the days of Suliman: this likely refers to Suleiman the Magnificent (Sulaymān al-Qānūnī, r. 1520 – 1566), the Ottoman sultan whose reign is remembered for its cultural and scientific advances in the eastern Mediterranean.

"A-ah!" exclaimed the other, his eyes lighting with pleasure. "Thou knowest of him?"

"Truly," replied Paul, and quoted:

> Think, in this batter'd Caravanserai
> Whose Doorways are alternate Night and Day, —

The Sultan stopped him with a gesture, finishing the quotation with a grim smile:

> How Sultan after Sultan with his Pomp
> Abode his Hour or two, and went his way.

"Thy wording is good, but not as Omar hath it,"[181] and good-humoredly he corrected Paul's crude retranslation.

"I have news for thee," he continued, and related details regarding the submission of various tribes, the revolt of others, and the doings of the French in their "penetration pacifique" of Showya. And he concluded: "I have over thirty thousand soldiers without the walls of Fez, with thy arms and guns, and now is the time to move upon El Rahman, who hath left Rabat to advance upon Marrakech. El Hammo hath left for Marrakech; be ready to march with the Legions upon my word.. Tell me from thy knowledge of war, what had we best do? It is now the final test between El Rahman and myself. If he win — which Allah forbid! — then am I lost, but if I win, then every coast town will proclaim in my name."

"Hast thou a map?" inquired Paul, "that I may know the country and where best to give battle?"

The Sultan clapped his hands, whereupon a huge negro slave appeared, and salaaming deep, sped away.

----

[181] Here Beadle makes a witty reference to the fact that, although it's a literary classic, Fitzgerald's "The Rubaiy'yat of Omar Khayyam" is more of a loose, creative reinterpretation rather than a literal translation.

Abd-el-Kader led Paul into a small room adjoining the piazza, where, by the light of electric lamps, the two pored over a French map — ironic omen! — of Morocco till late in the night, Paul questioning, discussing and propounding a plan of campaign.

At length, as the early morning call to prayer sounded, the two moved out into the garden, the Sultan pleased and confident in the prospect of his rival's defeat.

The two, ghostly figures in the brilliant starlight, stood silently staring into the shadows of the gardens, Paul listening to the quavering cry dying in silvery cadence.

"Al-lah — Ak-ba-ah!"

The almost familiar sensation heralding the approach of some act of Fate with that cry crept over him. He glanced round, in half-superstitious fear of the unknown, a rustle of leaves as the cry wailed forth again:

"Al-lah — Ak-ba-ah!"

And from out the dense shadow of the orange grove darted an indistinct figure, the starlight caught and rippled on a naked blade. Paul heard the panting breath as the assassin sprang at the taller figure of the Sultan, who, unconscious of danger, had commenced a sentence addressed to Paul.

With a bound Paul leapt between them, and ducking low to avoid the dagger, hit with his right at the face of the man.

The knife tinkled upon the tiled piazza as the man pitched sideways on to the ground. In an instant Paul followed up his advantage and pinioned the man as the negro slaves came running in response to the summons of the Sultan. They shouted excitedly, bringing others quickly upon the scene, and in a moment the would-be assassin was roughly dragged away, shouting: "Death to the friend of Infidels! Great is the Prophet of the Lord!"

The Sultan had stood apart, calm and collected, and as Paul walked up he smiled, saying, in a deep dignified voice with a suspicion of emotion:

"Barakalofik! Barakalofik!" (I thank thee!)

CHAPTER XIV

The days flew rapidly by. Paul was busily engaged all day in drilling the troops and teaching the half-trained artillerymen the use of the new guns. The Baron, much to his chagrin, was still confined to his bed. The fact of Paul's almost daily attendance with the Sultan evidently disturbed him; and once, in an endeavor to get up, he had broken open his wound, and had perforce to retire again. Although Paul had several times determined to make the Baron agree to some definite arrangement, he scarcely knew what, he had only met with the same satirical fencing as at the first interview after the duel. So he continued with his work as if nothing out of the ordinary had occurred, half believing that the Baron had determined in his own way to wipe out the past, forget his suspicions, and work amicably together. Never by word or look did the Baron betray to him that he had any doubt now of his fidelity to the cause, cleverly suggesting Paul's conclusions in his half-amused, half-satirical refusal to take the subject seriously.

Paul had not forgiven or forgotten the Baron's treachery regarding Zolika, and in his mind it formed the basis upon which he wished to urge a separation of their partnership. Illogical enough, but the subconscious effort to find a tangible excuse for the breaking of his bonds, and so to permit him to work towards his personal ambition. With this idea at the back of his mind, and recognizing the need of future continuity of purpose, Paul steadfastly refused to permit himself to seek Zahra again, although he could not command his thoughts nor his memory.

All day riding in the hot dust with the troop, Paul would return in the evening dog-tired, and then be summoned perhaps to talk to Abd-el-Kader, who began more and more to lean upon the Englishman's opinion. Since the night of the attempted assassination by a man of the mob, one of the workmen in the palace, he had shown more affection and deference to Paul's advice. All this was not without its effect upon Paul, who, fully alive to the fact of the power he was obtaining as the Sultan's favorite, was only human in beginning to slightly lose the right perspective when reflecting that he was, without exaggeration, an active principle in the fate of nations.

He had perforce to definitely postpone the final rupture with the Baron, for so he gradually became convinced that it must end; and in the interim the thirst for power became stronger as the days slipped by and he tasted of the sweets of a position other than that of playing second fiddle to the Baron.

For hours at a time he would pace up and down his room, thinking, planning for the future, taking into consideration the fact that the Baron's supporters would naturally be withdrawn with their representative. In his enthusiasm he was blind to the fact that the Baron would never withdraw, but would instead become an active competitor. The problem of how to nullify the effect of the concessions granted to the German representative and refund or recompense them for the arms supplied, could only be solved by supplying the Sultan with the money to pay exorbitantly for the goods.

The concessions would be an easier problem, as Abd-el-Kader could repudiate them without any political consequences; they were wholly illegal at present, and the concessioner a mere rebel. By aid of London financiers[182] Paul calculated that such

---

[182] Cf. "Morocco's Future," *Sheffield Daily Telegraph* (Sheffield, England), 23 July 1908, p. 8: "Mulai El Hafid offered in return for English (unofficial) assistance to give concessions for the building of railways, mining, the reorganization of the finances, various important political posts, and a partial control at least of the customs. All these things he would grant in return for efficient military assistance from the little English syndicate which Mr. Ashmead-Bartlett promptly formed." (For the complete text, see "Articles About Beadle in Morocco," below.)

could be done. He had now thrown off any pretence of acting otherwise than for himself, drunk with the first sips of power.

Patriotism, he told himself, bade him secure all for the benefit of his country, notwithstanding that his country did not want it; and by a curious process of reason, he still assured himself that the action of the Baron with regard to Zolika was a just casus belli.[183] Had it been possible for Paul to have adjudged his own case from a distance, put in ordinary environment, he would have condemned his own actions without hesitation; but the false perspective engendered by the intoxication of the lust for power threw his mental vision out of focus. Paul, like many before him, saw, not as it was, but as it seemed good to see, as he wanted to see.

Every day added to the strength of the moral drug upon him. Visions of himself receiving the plaudits of the parties for having pulled the Moroccan chestnut out of the fire, the first express running from Tanga to Marrakech, mines making the country peaceful and prosperous, a second Egypt, and Paul Towers — the Cromer of Morocco.

Constant dwellings upon such promptings of ambitious fancy flew to his head like old wine. Given any man with the smallest seed of ambition, and under such a powerful manure it would spring up and flourish like the proverbial mustard seed, choking all moral flowers.

One night at the end of a fortnight, Paul was awakened by a loud hammering at his door, and received an urgent summons to attend upon the Sultan. Hastily mounting a waiting mule, he was soon riding by the flickering candle lantern through the narrow cobbled streets of old Fez. Up under rough leaf-matted sun shelters near lines of small shuttered shops; past open mosque doors with the tinkling splash of the fountain within;

---

[183] Casus belli: an event or action that justifies or allegedly justifies a war or conflict.

through the forbidding darkness of tunnel-like streets, the houses almost meeting overhead, permitting only a narrow strip of starlight overhead; a halt at a ward gate whilst the sleepy guard fumbled with the rusty iron bolts; all amid the murmurous ripple, coming and going like the rustle of leaves, of the hundred and one subterranean channels of the Wad Fas running through the city, and the pungent, spicy, garbagy odor of the Orient, at once repellent and attractive.

As they entered one ward of the city, the sounds of excited voices arose on the still night air, and down the narrow street came a score of white-robed figures carrying lanterns. As Paul drew up against the wall with his people to let the small procession pass, he caught a glimpse in the feeble flickering light of the bare skull of an old graybeard in the center of half-a-dozen hawk-nosed soldiers clutching him by the robes, or striking him wantonly with guns and sticks.

"What meaning hath this thing?" Paul inquired of one of his men.

"When the partridge waxing fat would flee, the hawk swoopeth upon him," answered the man unemotionally.

Paul found the Sultan pacing up and down his favorite garden walk in a state of excitement, two of the Viziers silently squatting in a corner in attendance.

Waving aside the orthodox preliminaries with an imperious gesture, he began immediately:

"A messenger hath but now arrived with the news from one Ali Khabas that El Rahman hath left Rabat these two days with a great host for Marrakech. Tell me, are my troops prepared to leave?"

Paul considered for a moment.

"The soldiers must leave," he answered, "and at once. El Rahman must never cross the Wad Seboo. Summon thy Kiathaha and we leave tomorrow. Is it thy pleasure that I go with them?"

Abd-el-Kader paused for a moment considering; and then turned and expostulated rapidly with his two counselors. The light of the lanterns threw the figures in sharp light and shadow against the blue and white chequered floor, leaving their heads and shoulders and the pillars of the house in mystic gloom.

Paul gathered that the others were objecting to him upon the ground that the presence of an Infidel leading the troops would jeopardize the fidelity of the wild tribesmen, who formed a considerable portion of the whole army. But Abd-el-Kader, obstinate when once having made up his mind, eventually ignored them and commanded that Paul should go. The plan of campaign was discussed anew with the leaders of the Harka — army corps — who had been patiently awaiting their master's pleasure for hours outside the palace gates. Finally Paul departed, upon a new horse and an extremely ornate gold-braided and silver-mounted saddle with which Abd-el-Kader, in an unwonted fit of generosity, had presented him.

However, with the proverbial dilatoriness of the Arab, a thousand and one reasons caused delay; and at the end of the week, despite frantic exertions, and numerous interviews, they were no nearer to the start than before. Fortunately the rival Sultan was not immune from similar weakness, for by every courier arrived news of delay, from desertions and lack of material.

The Baron, upon hearing the news of the intended departure of Paul, smiled amicably and disappointed Paul by exhibiting no sign of regret or satisfaction. The Baron was now convalescent, and Paul, realizing that he would be up and about before the probable return of the army, determined that the definite understanding, as he chose to term it, must be arrived at before he left. He was now in a fever of anxiety to receive the answers to letters which he had written to London. Everything almost depended upon them, for without support in the future he knew that eventually he was bound to lose.

One afternoon he sat in the garden, listening to a young girl's voice singing a plaintive love song about a lover who asked:

> Love, could I doubt thee! Nay, but my soul
> Faint unto death may ne'er reach thy goal.

From thoughts of politics and war, he turned to Zahra. Her memory had not grown dim, merely shelved by force of will and opposing circumstances. And when he took her out of the mental cotton wool the image, he found to his dismay, was as strong as ever.

Recognizing the palpable fact that, do what he would, he could not forget or cease to long for her, he endeavored to compromise by permitting his mind to cherish the vision of those matchless eyes, telling himself that in the struggle for fame, as she was denied to be Cleopatra, then she should be his Egeria.[184] The thought of Cleopatra brought Antony in the thought train, and he laughed scornfully at the idea of a man leaving a kingdom for any woman. Yet — no, no, Antony deserved his fate. A man could not choose two gifts of the gods; he who chose Cleopatra against all Rome was a fool![185]

> Love, could I doubt thee? Nay, but my soul
> Faint unto death may ne'er reach thy goal.

wailed the girlish voice. "Strange!" thought Paul, "even this singing girl might be as Zahra."

---

[184] "She should be his Egeria," i.e., his trusted adviser, confidante, or muse; someone who provides wisdom and guidance rather than romantic passion. Egeria was a nymph who served as the counselor and muse of King Numa Pompilius, the legendary second king of Rome.

[185] Cf. Beadle's treatment of Antony and Cleopatra in his last novel, *Dark Refuge* (1938).

"Hullo, my frien'," broke in Rabbit's voice. "Ruksa come; plenty letter for you."

Paul eagerly took the bundle of letters. The first to open had the Government crest on the flap. An official intimation to the effect that the Legation was neither cognizant of Paul nor could entertain the proposals submitted in his letter, which they had the honor of acknowledging. Paul frowned as he opened the next bearing the London postmark. It was a lengthy epistle intimating that at the present political juncture nothing officially could be done; but that as a general election was imminent and the other side sure to secure power afterwards, the writer bade Paul to continue on the lines suggested with the assurance that before long, and at the critical time, he would be upheld and his claims supported. Another letter from a personal friend of Paul, the senior partner of a firm of influential financiers, assured Paul that if the concessions were obtained as represented and the British Government's support promised, the sum stated would be at his disposal. Paul was elated: that was even more than he had anticipated. Such an assurance from so cautious a political man and the promise of a keen man of business meant practical certainty.

Upon returning to the courtyard he glanced up and beheld the Baron leaning on the balcony rail watching him. Paul instantly regretted that he had allowed any sign of satisfaction to escape him. In all probability the Baron knew from the crests upon his letters who they were from and could with ease solve the reason of Paul's excitement. For a moment he paused to consider what he should do. If the Baron had guessed[,] there was little time to be lost, as in Paul's opinion the issue depended upon who kept the Sultan's confidence. He ordered his horse. On his way down to the stables he had to pass the Baron lounging upon a pile of rugs, playing with Kismet, who looked up and remarked pleasantly:

"Going to overhaul the Imperial Army?"

"Yes," said Paul without looking at him.

"So? We will soon be out to help you. Won't we, Kismet?"

The dog uttered joyful assent and licked his face.

"Will you?" said Paul, in a sepulchral voice, "that's splendid!"

The Baron met his glance with a contemptuous smile, and Paul felt cross with himself and rather mean, if the truth be told.

Upon arrival at the Palace he sent a message to the Sultan, demanding an immediate audience upon important business. A polite answer was returned that an audience would be granted in "a little while." After four hours in which to cool his thoughts, he was led to the top of an old bastion, where sat the Sultan under the shade of an awning.

For a while, in accordance with Eastern etiquette, Paul spoke of the troops, and matters other than the purport of his visit.

At length he remarked, apropos of nothing: "In the days of Mulai Hassan there was friendship between the English and El Mogreb?"[186]

"Truly."

"Wouldst thou that such were today?"

"What news hast thou for me?" inquired Abd-el-Kader, leaning forward.

"Wouldst thou that Germany were the friend of Morocco?"

"Inshallah!"

"And if England were to Morocco as to Egypt?"

"A-ah, good!"

"It shall be so an thou wilt?"

The Sultan nodded.

Then Paul explained the result of his correspondence with London and with the Legation in Tanga. The Sultan smiled upon hearing the contents of the official letter and the private advice. Such diplomacy appealed to the Oriental mind. Without

---

[186] El Mogreb: an older European spelling of al-Maghrib, an Arabic name for Morocco.

hesitation he agreed to repudiate the concessions granted to the Baron, transferring the same to Paul or his nominees with the proviso that no action should be taken until the money was to hand. The Baron would be received as usual, precaution being taken to prevent any suspicion upon his part.

With mutual satisfaction Paul departed to complete the arrangements for leaving with the van of the army on the morrow.

That evening the Baron came in to dine in the mess room for the first time since his injury, and exerted his powers in conversation and manners to their greatest effort, achieving the result of compelling Paul to feel the charm of his attractive personality. Paul at length, not without an effort, retired for the night, uncomfortable under some pricks of conscience. The heat was intense, not a breath of wind stirred, and Paul, unable to sleep, paced the room for a while. A figure moving about upon a distant roof in the brilliant moonlight suggested that he might also enjoy the beauty of the night. As the rooftop is the prerogative of the women under Mohammedan regime, he took the precaution to wind a sheet around him after the feminine manner, and thus attired, climbed through the trapdoor on to the misty whiteness of the flat roof.[187]

Away on all sides a sea of ghostly rooftops, broken and intersected by treetops and the gardens beneath. The narrow high-walled street beneath running between two large gardens, appeared like the bottom of a sewer from the altitude of the roof. After promenading for a while, Paul sat upon the low

---

[187] Speaking of the hazards of living in Fes in the nineteenth and early twentieth centuries, Douglas Porch remarks: "Even the roof terraces were off limits: when Lawrence Harris climbed to his roof to enjoy the splendid views over the city, he was shot at from a neighboring house, a reminder that the terraces were reserved for the women." Douglas Porch, *The Conquest of Morocco*, p. 47.

stone parapet gazing at the moonlit Atlas towering away between the trees. From a low building at the end of a garden on the other side of the street came the rattling throb of drums, and away from the far end of the city a low hum of barbaric music from the palace, where the Imperial household were rejoicing at the marriage of the Sultan to his third wife. Now and again quite close, rattling from a nest of storks in a ruined bastion, the distant barking of a dog, then the murmurous silence under the glamour of the moon.

Paul's thoughts were interrupted by a woman's high ringing laugh quite near and below him. He rose in curiosity and walked round to the far wing of his house in juxtaposition to another large house, the space between cast in dense blue shadow, Paul could not discern anything but the shadowy forms of trees. Another laugh, low pitched and vibrant, guided him to the extreme edge of his roof, from whence he looked down upon a courtyard bathed in the full light of the moon. He uttered an exclamation of astonishment, and kneeling down, leaned forward that he might see the better.

A fountain, in a shower of iridescent diamonds, stood in the center of the brightly tiled courtyard, flanked on two sides by orange trees; and seated on the marble rim, her feet splashing in the water, a young nude girl, ethereal in the soft moonlight. Her glorious mass of hair streamed down her shoulders, clinging in gossamer strands against her gleaming white skin as, with head thrown back showing glint of ivory teeth and whites of eyes in a rippling laugh, she energetically splashed water at another girl lying at length upon the opposite rim retaliating with very shapely arms and anon pushing back her rebellious tresses. Reclining upon the cool tiles at a little distance was a darker-hued girl, propping her head upon her elbows, watching the combat and laughing encouragement. Nearer to the first damsel were candle lanterns, their domes in tricolored glass, the light feeble and yellow in contrast to the moonbeams. The girl, leaping agilely away from the fountain ran round, and before her laughing adversary realized her motive, a deft push rolled her over with a splash into the water amid screams of laughing delight from the culprit and her companion. Rising like a water nymph, all gleaming wet and hair bedraggled, she gave chase, laughing and spluttering, to her nimble assailant, who flew round the silvered water tank like a frightened fawn, emitting shrill little cries of mock fear. Round and round they ran, doubling back, dodging, leaping like deer over their prostrate companion, the patter of feet on the tiles, the panting breath and girlish laughter floated and echoed clear in the still night air, the flying hair and lily-white limbs ethereal in the light of the moon.

At length the pursuer and pursued paused, panting and exhausted. Then out of the shadow of the house a young negress appeared, bearing a brass tray with tea glasses, upon which the combatants, declaring a truce, came and reclined amicably upon the cool tiles, resting their gleaming wet shoulders upon cushions ranged around the lanterns. The other two having joined the circle, the negress prepared tea from a charcoal urn, the live embers glowing red.

The artificial candlelight, in contrast to Diana's beams, materialized the supple rounded limbs and heaving breasts throwing the lithesome curves in harder lines.

The darker-skinned one upon the far side sat up, and in response to an excited duet from the others began to declaim a story, the light flashing upon jeweled ornaments and brown skin as she gesticulated. Peals of laughter from the audience and gleaming teeth of the negress slave busy with the tea testified to her rhetorical prowess. With the filling of the tea glasses her story ended in a paroxysm of laughter. Muttering of desultory remarks, sundry giggles and the noisy sipping of the hot tea, after the Moorish manner, floated up, and with the draining of the first round of tea glasses, the fair supple-limbed girl prepared to add her contribution to the Moorish night's entertainment.

As she moved Paul's heart gave a great leap; he strained over the parapet to see the glint of ruddy bronze hair in the circle of candlelight. The words flowed from her lips, she gesticulated, her head half turned, in profile against the light. Involuntarily Paul craned farther forward whispering "Za-hra!" as his heart gave another great leap like the first explosion of a petrol engine, and raced on, sending the blood pulsing to his temples. With parched mouth and staring eye he peered over the parapet of the roof, feasting his eyes on the unconscious form of the girl as the light gleamed upon the supple figure and firm bosom.

Then suddenly she stopped, as if the thought waves surging in the man's brain made a faint impression, amid a gentle storm of protest, but shaking her head and with a gesture of the hand, she refused, sinking back upon the cushions with petulant, half-despondent suggestion. Another round of tea which Zahra waved aside, and rising, tall and ethereal again in the moonlight, went back to the fountain, mutely suggesting a desire to be alone, and sitting on the edge, fell to gazing into the dim moonlit reflection of her pretty self.

Then, as the group around the lanterns sipping tea chatted in subdued tone responsive to Zahra's mood, came across the warm night the resonant notes:

"Al-lah — Ak-ba-ah!"

CHAPTER XV

Paul lay awake within his tent staring through the V-shaped aperture of the flap door at the faint twinkling stars without. It was a week later, and he, with thirty thousand troops and tribesmen were encamped, waiting to stop the passage of El Rahman and his army across the Wad Seboo upon the other bank of which lay the hosts of El Hammo.

Paul, unable to sleep, was dreamily thinking of that moonlit scene from the rooftop. To his mingled disgust and alarm, it had cost him more than a considerable effort to ride away on the following morning. Paul had not realized the depth of the impression Zahra had made upon him. Absurd, wholly illogical as it all seemed, those eyes had always held a strong attraction to him. Although he had, by the aid of an effort of will and the counter-attraction of ambition, succeeded in making himself immune to any alteration in his affairs, he had had to compromise by endeavoring to place her upon a high pedestal and dub her Egeria. The unexpected ocular renewal of her charms had almost swept away the results of a struggle of weeks. For a moment in the height of the passion that shook him, he had given ear to the strident voice of Nature urging him to claim his mate even if he threw all ambition to the four winds of Heaven.

However, calmer counsels had prevailed, and he had forced himself to ride at daybreak. And now in the wakeful stillness her personality seemed to arise in his memory stronger than ever. There came a moment when, had she been present or it were even possible, that he would then and there have claimed her, even if he had to lay down his life the next moment.

Paul was vaguely frightened by the strength of his passion for Zahra. He had never experienced nor even dreamt of an all-compelling force which can make one individual absolutely necessary to the life of the other. Every nerve and part of his being cried out for Zahra. Yet why? He tried to reason with himself in his saner moments. But only the devouring hunger to clasp her in his arms answered him. Nature does not condescend to answer man's trivial questions. Paul found that the insatiable hunger that filled him became both mental and physical torture. Then, as the spasm died away for a space, his reason ventured to assert itself, bringing as a clean-cut lantern slide the picture suggested by ambition. The future opened before him with all the delights to his self-esteem and vanity, and he cursed, calling every other choice mere madness. Again arose the phantom of Zahra and the call of her glorious eyes, and torn and tortured between the two desires, he sought peace in the futile compromise. She was unattainable to him and must ever be, but in his heart he would erect a shrine to her; all success should be placed at the feet of this abstract divinity, and so for her sweet sake he would be spurred on to greater efforts. This whole idea was unsound and Paul was aware subconsciously that it was so, but he struggled hard to convince himself. It is easy to convince oneself in accordance with one's desires, but so terribly hard at other times to be convinced against them.

Paul striking a match, glanced at his watch. Half past one! Time to arouse the sleeping camp to commence the night march with the object of a surprise attack upon the enemy. He got up, walked to the door, and spoke to the sleeping sentry posted without his tent who, yawning and stretching in protest, stumbled away to awaken the Kaids and Kaithahas.

Paul paused for a moment, looking across the sleeping camp. The lines of tents seemed unreal and filmy in the misty moonlight, the restless champing of picketed horses. A scream of a vicious stallion broke the stillness, a solitary donkey voicing his rasping serenade to the moon, ended in a throttled moan; a cry of a night bird, and then the increasing rustle of the waking host, running from camp to camp, with the rattle of harness, men's low guttural voices, banging of tent poles, and the thousand noises of a great encampment murmuring with awakened life.

The latest deserter from the enemy stated that they were encamped near Sidi Ghalim,[188] some six miles away, where Paul calculated to arrive by dawn. Messengers were dispatched to the Berber Chief El Hammo upon the far riverbank, requesting him — a Nazarene must needs request a Mohammedan — to move his hordes in unison.

Squatting upon his carpet, Paul impatiently and impotently awaited the dilatory methods of striking camp. With all the talking, drilling and badgering, Paul could never succeed in persuading them to adapt their cumbrous equipment to newer methods; they were almost as conservative in their ways as the British War Office. Such had been their way since the days of Khalid, "the Sword of God"; and will continue till they are thrust aside altogether in the race of civilization and the survival of the fittest.

Order and protest as Paul might, and did, the only satisfaction elicited was the universal cry "Inshallah!" (If God wills!); and to Paul's anger and disgust, dawn, gray and glaucous, merged to rosier tints ere the unwieldy masses of troops were upon the road. Sulky, ill-tempered and anxious of the result, Paul rode ahead with the Kaid Bu Hamu, in supreme command, thinking gloomily of the probable result amongst these ragtag and bobtailed troops of a withering artillery fire from the trained Algerian gunners in the army of El Rahman. Paul's position was rather anomalous; nominally in command of the army, he was actually only partially in command of the Moorish Commander,

---

[188] Sidi Ghalim: possibly *Sidi Ghalem*, a small rural locality in the Marrakech – Safi region. It lies in the Haouz plain, southeast of Marrakech, along the road network that connects smaller villages and agricultural lands around the city.

and General Military Adviser;[189] but as the gentleman in question had a well-developed bump of conceit of his own ability coupled with the inherent contempt for the Christian and an irritating belief in the will of Allah, poor Paul's position was hardly a sinecure, except in comparison to his colleagues, inasmuch that if they lost the battle their heads would assume a very precarious position from either side.

The sun had risen some two hours ere, upon breasting a swelling rise, they beheld the red tunics of the regular troops and the white-robed mounted tribesmen, sworn and paid allies of the titular Sultan, spread out across the gentle undulating plains, a sea of yellow barley.

Paul, anxious for a knowledge of the position of the supporting legions of El Hammo, dispatched a messenger to reconnoitre from the opposite riverbank, and endeavored to check the sudden enthusiastic desire of his captains to charge forthwith, helter-skelter, without any formation or plan, upon the enemy. He succeeded in dispatching some excited and confused aides-de-camp with orders to the leaders of the various harkas to deploy to the north. The main body continued to advance straight, with the object of hemming the enemy against the river by a sudden attack of the large force of mounted tribesmen from their circuit round to the north with the simultaneous rear attack of the hosts of El Hammo from the west, after fording the shallow river.

In front of the opposing scattered battalions of men mounted tribesmen began to circle to and fro after the ancient tribal manner; and from the center the artillery opened the ball with a well-placed seven-pounder in the midst of the tattered red-jacketed infantry. Bu Hamu and his staff around Paul began excitedly to protest, call upon Allah and issue contrary

---

[189] After Andrew Belton offered his services to the Pretender Sultan, Moulay Hafid, he was supposedly given the title of "Kaid," or commander.

instructions to each other. Whilst some of the troops halted in dismayed confusion, others advanced at the run, firing off their rifles in the air and into the ground indiscriminately.

Uproar.

Paul sitting disgusted and silent, knowing that orders were useless, noticed, that amid the excitement on the other side, a large body of tribesmen suddenly wheeled out from the ranks of the enemy, galloping madly towards him. Bullets from the enemy and from their own side whistled cheerfully over and about them; some charged aimlessly forward, some bolted, other stood stock still, all shouted and yelled.

Pandemonium.

The artillery succeeded in discharging two seven-pounder shells, which knocked up a cloud of dust at almost one hundred yards ahead of themselves. Upon the other side a similar state of affairs except for the comparatively steady fire from the artillery men. A Maxim detachment near to Paul loudly cried to Allah and everybody, inquiring for ammunition, which had apparently been left behind or in the rear.

Paul had given the whole affair up as lost, when, to his amazement, the contingent of tribesman which he thought were attacking, suddenly wheeled into line with his men, and enthusing them into martial valor, led the whole army in a galloping, straggling, scrambling charge upon their late comrades.

Paul remained upon the rise of ground, watching with mingled feelings the kaleidoscope of color and moving figures of the hosts strewn across the plain. Shots fizzled and popped erratically like so many gigantic squibs, bullets whistled in all directions; shouts, cries, yells, the whole plain a seething mass; men lying down, jumping up, galloping furiously this way and that, some charging, others running away; the whole scene like a vast army of ants suddenly disturbed by an alien body, and scuttling, hurrying, in every direction. It was impossible to discern which was which. Then from the dust appeared a gray cloud of horse, thundering down upon the confused masses. As no messenger or word from El Hammo had returned, Paul could not decide whether these were reinforcements of the enemy or the tribesmen, mounted and foot, of El Hammo; anyhow, it could not matter for his men, and the enemy, for that matter, were all completely out of control. The result could hardly be determined from any view of the proceedings.

The new arrivals, firing from their saddles as they galloped furiously, struck the tremulous main body with the effect of a large river flowing into a wind-whipped lake, concentric ripples and eddies battling against the wavelets, leaping up to fall in an eddying ripple of their own.

Paul sat there surveying the conflict through his field glasses, convinced that his fate lay in the hands of these heaving, swaying hordes of mediaeval tribesmen, fighting, deserting, cursing and praying all at one and the same time. For a moment his heart sickened at the idea that all his plans, and incidentally his wounded self-respect, should be sacrificed at the hands of such a misguided, ill-disciplined soldiery. As his glasses swept the arena of battle, he could discern a continuous stream of flying men radiating from the center in all directions over the country, his own men and the enemy inextricably mixed up. The murmurous roar of excited voices, punctuated with the popping of the squibs— the artillery had long since ceased fire[190] — began to perceptibly diminish, and Paul, wholly unable to determine the state of the conflict, dropped his glasses disgustedly with a monosyllabic "Damn!"

He smiled dully at the incongruity of the sight of a figure near to him engaged with prayer mat, and slippers beyond, face to

---

[190] Squibs: brief, sharp reports of small gunfire or minor explosive discharges; the quick popping sounds of light weapons or powder charges that continue after the main cannon fire has stopped.

the East and back turned in sublime indifference to the tumult, calmly engaged in orthodox worship and genuflections towards Mecca. And then from the villages some three hundred yards away floated the sonorous notes of the call to prayer from the lips of the rural Mueddhin standing at the door of a straw-thatched mosque:

"Al-lah — Ak-ba-ah!"

The placidity of the cry and the obvious note of supreme oblivion to the jarring strife of man suggested the utter futility of worry regarding the result; the philosophy of Mektub — It is written! Paul imbibed calm confidence and raising his glasses anew, took fresh stock of the battlefield. To his joy he discerned a decided set in the tide of fleeing humanity towards the northwest; the scurrying, hurrying masses of his own people had diminished to a mere fraction; within half an hour the enemy were unmistakably in full flight, and in many parts of the field were clusters of joyous victors noisily celebrating the capture of guns and camp paraphernalia of the foe. The chant of the distant Mueddhin seemed to develop a different timbre as Paul realized that, although so utterly unscientific and without the most elementary forms of military tactics, his tattered, half-starved hordes had, owing to fortuitous circumstances and the encouraging desertion of the tribes of El Rahman, really won the day.

"El Rahman," thought Paul as he spurred his horse forward, "has lost the day because, unfortunately for him, his people could run away faster than mine!"

Halfway down towards the river he met the redoubtable Bu Hamu who, now very full of fight, had just emerged from the seclusion of a village corn bin.

Whilst they were talking — Paul could hardly resist laughing in the man's face — parties of deserters from the late opposing army rode or walked up in large detachments, anxious to make their allegiance to Bu Hamu as the representative of Mulai Abd-el Kader. Some excitedly maintained that El Rahman had been captured; others that he had been killed. Paul started off by the riverbank intending to find El Hammo. As he approached a bend in the riverbank, he heard, amid a tumult of shouts and cries, a fusillade of shots. Riding at a gallop, he saw a figure of a European in Moorish military garb standing in the middle of the ford, the water over his jackboots, at bay before a crowd of soldiery upon the bank. His horse had just been shot, and was struggling upon its side in the shallow water.

Without hesitation Paul galloped to his rescue, shouting at the same time to a man amongst the crowd whom he recognized as a Kaid of his own troops, to stop the attack. This man, however, drunk with the triumph of victory, not his own, only yelled encouragement to his fellows to attack the two Infidels. However, the surprise of Paul's unexpected appearance checked the onslaught for a moment, which began again as he reached the man, an unmistakable Englishman, who was quick to accept Paul's assistance, and seizing the proffered stirrup, swung himself up behind. They splashed across to the opposite side amid a shower of bullets flying wide and above them.

Fortunately, the soldiery seemed only possessed of ancient muzzle-loading guns, and so convenient time elapsed ere they could reload. The Kaid, in fact, owned a new Mauser rifle, but had long since succeeded in jamming the bolt.

Once over the rise of ground upon the further side, Paul pulled up to a walk, considering what he could do for the man he had rescued.

"My name's Towers," said he. "Who are you?"

"Sergeant Burnett," replied the other. "I guessed it must be you. Of course we've heard of you," he added with a laugh. "Thanks for pulling me out!"

Paul remembered having heard of him as late of a lancer regiment, lent to the Moorish Army as drill instructor.

"Well, we've licked you, it seems, although no credit to my people. Where's the Sultan? My people say he's killed or captured."

"I don't think! I saw him clearing off at the start, when all my men cleared, leaving me with a Maxim and no ammunition! They are a blooming[191] crowd."

"Yes, I agree with you," said Paul. "The mob who deserted to us did for you from the start."

"Deserted from us!" echoed the other. "Why, we had your people coming in to us for days!"

"That so! Well, so had we!"

"Well, anyway, it was that blooming river attack of yours. I knew that was a European's doing!"

"Well, it wasn't exactly. Where they came from or how I don't know. My plans were absolutely ruined hours before we met you. I intended a night attack."

"Did you! I said they'd try that game if you were with them, but we didn't know for certain whether you were or not."

"What were you doing in the ford?" inquired Paul. "Surely your way lies to the west?"

"Yes, but 'strewth,[192] it got too hot for me with all our own men shooting at me. Lord, you never saw anything like it! Our own men killed more of each other than yours did! Well, I hopped it across here and was trying to get back when that row started. It wasn't my horse; somebody pinched mine, and I collared that one. Lord, they *are* a mob!"

"Well, what do you reckon to do now?"

"Dunno! What do you?"

---

[191] Blooming (chiefly British, informal): used as a generalized intensive, e.g., a *blooming* fool.

[192] The term *'strewth* is a British colloquial exclamation (and mild oath), short for "God's truth," used to express surprise, emphasis, frustration, or disappointment.

"Well, to tell the truth, I'm hanged if I know. I was looking for El Hammo, but I don't see what I'm to do if I find him. Can you get away if we find a horse?"

"Yes, I'll make for Settat as best I can. I'm fed up with this lot."

They had been riding slowly, and at this juncture breasted a slight rise of ground upon the farther side of which lay a small village. Paul pulled up to consider. It was inadvisable to enter the village, as in all probability they would find more trouble awaiting any Infidel.

As they sat together discussing the situation, the clip-clop of an approaching horse sounded. From a track on their right a single horseman rode slowly towards them.

"There is only one thing," said Paul suddenly, "and that is to collar this man's animal. Revolution and loot seems the order of the day, so I'll follow the example of my own troops. Keep still, and I'll cover him as he approaches."

As the man drew nearer the unusual khaki color of Burnett's uniform excited his suspicions, and obviously considering two men beyond his ambition, he sheered off the road. As Paul spurred their animal forward to cut him off he gave rein to his horse, a fine upstanding animal, and galloped away.

Paul pulled up disgustedly.

"I think we had better dissemble if we want to catch our man. If we both lie in the barley, maybe the sight of an unattached horse and saddle may serve as a bait."

They did so, and within half-an-hour another belated warrior appeared on the horizon, leading a spare horse.

When within a couple of hundred yards, he halted, gazing in their direction. The bait was swallowed: two horses were obviously better than one. When he was within fifty yards of the riderless horse, Paul and Burnett simultaneously sprang to their feet, calling upon the Moor to surrender; and as he discovered the shining barrel of a revolver, which any Moor has even more respect for than a rifle because he understands it less, he called upon Allah to witness his dovelike intentions.

With a keen eye for the better animal, Paul bade him mount the led horse, which he did, calling upon the Prophet to save him from thieves and murderers. As soon as he was up, Paul, after commandeering the prisoner's rifle, bade him "Go." The man gazed in blank amazement for a moment, trying to grasp the fact that the Infidels did not want both saddles and horses or his life, which to his mind was inexplicable. With a mournful shake of the head for such stupidity and a pious curse, he turned and galloped off.

"Now we'd best get off, or he'll bring all his mates here," suggested Burnett.

They rode on in the blazing sun down the river.

"Good Lord!" exclaimed Paul, suddenly realizing that he had not breakfasted yet. "I am hungry."

"Me too," assented Burnett. "I ain't had a bite since yesterday morning."

"Not in camp last night?"

"No; every mother's son of 'em cut their own stuff up, and my son of a nigger never turned up at all. But I'll get a damned sight hungrier afore I get anywhere. There's no use you comin' any further, sir. There seems a drift across the spruit[193] here, so I'll say goodbye, and thanks for your help."

"Well, I think you're right, so goodbye, Burnett, and good luck," said Paul, pulling up as they reached the further bank, "Sorry we can't shake, but this brute will savage you."

"Yes, that's the worst o' these here stallions. Shall I say anything about seeing you?"

"Oh, just as you like! — but no, not unless you're actually asked. It may save bad blood between the Europeans. Goodbye."

---

[193] Spruit: a small, often dry, tributary stream in southern Africa.

Paul sat for a moment watching the khaki-clad figure galloping away; then, as the other waved a hand in farewell from the saddle, he wheeled and cantered back up stream.

As Paul neared the battleground, he began to meet parties of horse and foot dotted about the country. Several rode by without recognizing him as an Infidel, shown by the greeting "Salaam alik,"[194] only given to another follower of the Prophet. Another group saluted him as their Harab — drill instructor — and from these men Paul learned the whereabouts of his scattered commandants.

Galloping on, he soon saw upon a distant undulation a large mass of men, their scarlet tunics, blue trousers, and horse trappings brilliant in the fierce rays of the noonday sun.

Here, within a tent, he found El Hammo, grave and taciturn, closeted with the redoubtable Bu Hamu.

As Paul stood waiting for admission, according to etiquette, he noticed that within, behind Bu Hamu, were the muffled figures of four women. The sound of galloping hooves made him turn in time to see the inestimable Rabbit ride furiously up.

"Hullo, ole chap," he shouted cheerily as he scrambled out of the saddle. "You orlright, what? Me look for you everywhere. You see Moor man fight? Plenty strong fight, what?"

Paul smiled.

"Yes, very great fight. Awf'lly good, eh, Rabbit?"

"A-ah!" protested Rabbit, "you laugh! But you wait."

"Wait for what?"

"Yillah! you wait and see what comes out of him! Inshallah!"

"Who are those women — girls there?" inquired Paul, indicating with his eyes.

"Those? A-ah!" drawled Rabbit. "Those new wives Bu Hamu — he take plenty wives in big fight and plenty dollar — awfully good, what?"

---

194 Salaam alik: as-salāmu 'alayk. Peace be with you.

"H'm," said Paul. "He who fights and runs away lives to collar fame and the fair!"

"Him awf'lly clever man," assented Rabbit.

Paul nodded, as he stooped under the tent flap. After the orthodox exchange of flowery compliments, Bu Hamu burst out excitedly:

"Now the Englishman can tell the infidels how we can fight! Yillah, what a fight! They are devoured entirely — Hamdullah![195] — El Rahman is dead and I am triumphant — Praise be to Allah! Yillah, how we fought!"

Paul repressed a smile, thinking of the splendid view obtainable from the village corn bin.

"Hamdullah!" echoed El Hammo gravely.

---

[195] Hamdullah: al-ḥamdu lillāh. "Praise be to God."

CHAPTER XVI

Again at the close of day Paul rode beneath the scarred old walls of Fez the Beautiful. Upon the first time he had ridden in the wake of the Sultan webbed in a romantic mist of ambitious dreams; upon the second time his thoughts were full of Zahra; and now both alternated in his mind, but not with the same flush of enthusiasm.

This time Paul was too coldly sane to imagine himself Hannibal or Napoleon. True he was at the head of a victorious, if not a conquering army, but the knowledge of how the victory had been gained killed the romantic tendency. But in the same ratio as he viewed the immediate past, he saw and contemplated the future with an equally sane perspective. The wild enthusiasm had gone, but in its place was a cool determination weighing the pros and cons with an impartial mind. He saw and knew that the great idea of training the troops and eventually leading them in person to conquer and subject the rebel tribes was utterly impossible with the raw bigoted material with which he had to work. But nevertheless the scheme remained intact, only the method would have to be altered.

And realizing these things, his determination grew harder and more fixed.

Thoughts of Zahra came to him unbidden, and wisely he did not struggle to put her from his mind. He had discovered and acknowledged, no matter how unreasonable and illogical it might be, that he could never forget her — at least not for a long while, and in accordance with the plan formulated as the result of his last mental struggle, he pictured her apart, detached, from an impersonal point of view. Telling himself that her memory was Egeria to him, that never would she, could she, nor would he allow her to step down from her high impersonal pedestal; as a Goddess he could worship her, but he knew and feared that the moment she walked on a common plane, then would he prove but human.

Such had been the tenor of his thoughts away, and now, although the sight of Fez and the close proximity to her excited more vivid imaginations, he still endeavored to keep her upon the pedestal — out of harm's way.

The morning after the defeat of El Rahman's forces, Paul, aware only too painfully that his position was a mere farce, had ridden ahead with Bu Hamu for Fez, leaving the army and all that concerned it to take care of itself.

Soon they rode under the shadow of the Palace wall, where a multitude of Fazi were celebrating the victory after the manner of their kind. Paul, in duty bound, entered with Bu Hamu to await an audience with the Sultan, whilst from without came the murmurous roar of the crowd and the recurrent volleys of the Powder Play.[196]

Abd-el-Kader, Paul learned from the court officials, was immensely excited and pleased at the victory. He had been seated the whole day under an awning up on a bastion overlooking the Wad Fas Valley and commanding a view of the approach of his victorious legions. Also Paul learned that Mulai Mohammed had been captured and brought in chains to Fez, where he had been forthwith cast into prison. Now the Sultan only hungered that he might place the rest of his troublesome fraternity under lock and key.

As Paul sat waiting in the shade of the great gate, his eye wandered near a line of horses picketed along a wall. Upon the saddle of a gray animal, half smothered in the cumbrous Moorish saddle, was a familiar box, like a rabbit hutch, from which peeped the perky ears of Kismet. A short slim figure

---

[196] Powder Play: a traditional Moroccan equestrian performance involving gunpowder, also known as *tbourida* or "fantasia."

came out of the inside of the gate, and a well-known voice greeted him.

"Good morning, Towers!"

"Oh, good morning, Baron."

Paul arose diffidently and held out his hand, which the Baron accepted, smiling genially.

"You see, I am about again — fit for another target, so?"

Paul frowned annoyance, thinking it bad taste to refer to the incident.

"So," continued the Baron, subsiding on his haunches by the wall, "we hear that you had a glorious victory."

He smiled satirically.

"Oh, absolutely disgusting exhibition," said Paul energetically; "but they won — I don't know how myself."

"So?"

"Yes."

They lapsed into silence, Paul frowning at space, wondering what had happened during his absence and determining not to show any anxiety to know.

"There are a lot of letters for you," observed the Baron.

"Oh?"

"If I were you I should go home and have a bath. You won't see Abd-el-Kader for an hour or two yet. He's at the bottom of the gardens with his women — viewing the march past of the conquerors!"

"Well, I will," assented Paul, "although I think he ought to have the decency not to keep me waiting."

"So? You forget, my dear Towers, that you are only an Infidel!"

"Do I? Could anyone forget that — here?" They rode off together, and upon arrival at the house, after shaking hands with all the servants, Paul called for his bath.

The Baron brought him a huge bundle of letters. Paul sensed him watching keenly. He glanced at one or two, and, with an assumption of indifference, pitched them on the floor, and sprawling across his bed, remarked lazily:

"Oh, I'm too tired! I'll have my bath first, they can wait!"

The Baron smiled slightly and sat himself down, proceeding to relate the local news. Paul, with ill-concealed impatience, listened until his bath was announced, which gave him an excuse to escape. Whilst bathing he became suddenly skeptical of the Baron. Could he possibly know? The extraordinary amiability since the duel was in itself suspicious. Was he waiting his chance to strike, or had he already put some plan into execution? Paul felt uncomfortable. His old fear of the man and his ways came over him in a wave. The placid waiting for something, he knew not what, to happen was disturbing — like waiting for someone in the dark to stab or shoot.

He read his letters in peace afterwards, and the excitement caused by the contents of the most important one blotted out his late access of suspicion.

One was from Sir Alfred, the financier, who informed him that he had had a confidential chat with a member of the Foreign Office, and in consequence Paul might draw upon him and enter into contracts on his behalf. Certain agreements were enclosed for his signature. All the old lust for ambition and dreaming of power and success flooded his brain again, and with heightened color, borne of mental excitement which he strove hard to suppress, he went in to dinner with the Baron.

The latter had had some wines and liqueurs sent from Tanga by caravan, and Paul, thoroughly enjoying a moderately decent dinner after his camp fare, found the unaccustomed wine mounting to his head. The Baron seemed more genial and fascinating than ever. Once Paul surprised an impulse to make a clean breast of everything and bring the Baron, in some extraordinary way, to see with his eye. So startled was he at this mad suggestion of a wine-laden brain that the shock almost sobered him. At length he summoned sufficient sanity to retire to bed on a plea of fatigue.

As he lay awake in bed for the few minutes before dropping off to sleep, he felt another pang of fright regarding the Baron and his movements. Paul shuddered at the thought of the terrible faux pas he had nearly made.

From a muddled dream of the Baron, who kept turning into Zahra like a dissolving view, he awoke to find Rabbit with a message bidding him to the Palace. Sleepily cursing any Sultan who summoned people at such an unearthly hour, he splashed and hurriedly dressed in the pale rose-tinted light of sunrise. He found the Baron awaiting him, and together they mounted and set out. Upon their arrival they were led through the great square into the precincts of the private palace, where upon a tessellated piazza they found the Sultan, seated upon a cushion, in the company with El Hammo and a score of favorite Kaids and Sheikhs. At the far end of the piazza, seated upon an empty champagne case, was an extraordinary-looking being, engaged in puffing out his face and wildly rolling his eyes. At the sight of the new arrivals, he ceased for a moment to grimace at them, remarking in a falsetto voice:

"'Tis the Devil, my lord, come to pay homage to mirth!"

A round of delighted laughter from the courtiers and a tolerant smile from the Sultan greeted this sorry quip. Paul and the Baron, obeying a gesture of the Sultan, sat themselves upon cushions, and the entertainment proceeded.

An inflated bladder of a goat, hung round the man's neck, proclaimed his ancient profession.

His hood was thrown back, the better to disclose the facial distortion of features ludicrous in their ugliness. The red Fez cap, stuck jauntily one side of the shaven skull, paled in contrast with the fiery whiskers adorning the sallow, flabby face. The white-lashed, red eyes, the broad, squat nose, and a gash of a mouth, more resembled an animated, anemic potato than anything human.

From the india-rubber lips pursed up on one side came in succession weird sounds imitating the cries of various animals, the hee-haw of a donkey, the liquid grumble of a camel, the neigh of a stallion, crow of roosters and quack of ducks, the while the large hands mimicked the supposed actions of the animal or bird under consideration.

A pause, with inflated cheeks and eyes asquint.

"List to the voice of the Infidel," cried the monstrosity, and forthwith, hammering with clenched fists upon the box, gave a passable imitation of a gramophone suffering from bronchial derangement — probably copied from one of the numerous playthings of the late Sultan.[197]

This contribution was received with great applause. "A song!" cried one.

"Truly, sing, thou fool!" exclaimed another.

"'Tis the voice of the lark!" declared a would-be wit.

"'Tis the voice of a fool singing to fools!" retorted the clown. "But list ye, my lord, a story in verse will I tell." And accompanying himself on the empty box, he chanted:

> Once on a day when Lord Musa rode forth,
> On his white charger in splendor array'd
> With falcon on wrist for the game to be played,
> He bade his courtiers ride far to the North.
>
> And in the train of Lord Musa there rode
> El Karim, the jester, a Zaney renowned
> For white pearls of wit his tongue could redound,

---

[197] One of the numerous playthings of the late Sultan: a reference to the vast sums of money that Aziz squandered on the latest European toys, trinkets, and inventions simply to keep himself entertained. Aziz assumed the sultanship when he was only twelve or thirteen years old.

When El Karim, for reasons, departed the road.

The Sultan, bethinking to enliven the time,
Had the lips of the mule the Zaney bestrode
Sliced off to the teeth — a fantastic mode
Of a practical joke played on a mime!

Laughing full deep they waited the jester,
And shouted in chorus: "Why grins thy beast?"
But El Karim, in horror, cried: "Look in the East,
Robbers of men approach us to pester!"

And then, while the Sultan and Suite stared aghast,
El Karim hacked off the tail of his steed
And quickly untying the bladder and bead,
To the stump of the tail the bladder made fast.

"Look ye, my lords, an answer give I,
A tale-bearer I am, and so is my mule,
And so is a horse as a general rule;
But Lord Musa's is none! Yillah, no lie!

"Even a tale is but breath, that I can swear.
Thus the sorriest mule may laugh full broad
At the sight of thy horse! For true, my Lord,
That a tail never yet was made of thin air!

"And now Lord Musa," he cried in derision,
"A reward is the meed[198] of him who laughs last,
And yillah, 'tis true. As I've won in the past,
Confident now I await thy decision."

After the applause had subsided, the fool, dismissed by a wave of the hand, turned a somersault and went off on all fours,

---

[198] Meed (archaic): an earned reward or wage.

pretending to nibble the grass as he scrambled down the garden out of sight.

The majority of the courtiers, having made their obeisance, departed, and the Sultan, with El Hammo and the Hadjib, beckoned to Paul and the Baron to follow him.

As they entered the Square of the Bab-el-Bushat, the troops were entering from the western gate, amid a brazen pandemonium from both the Imperial brass bands and native reed bands at the head of each tabor[199] (regiment): a blaze of red, blue and yellow uniforms, splashes of green, crimson, yellow and blue banners tempered by the gray white robes of sections of mounted tribesmen against the gray embattled walls; and overhead a gorgeous sky shot with great seas of pale amber, delicate green, vast streaks of russet, blue and fiery-tinted cloud edges of the sunrise.

The Baron and Paul were bidden to wait near the gate whilst the Sultan took up his favorite position in his little green summerhouse. The head of the long column led by Bu Hamu cut off the approach to the Imperial dais.

They stood for nearly an hour watching the march past until the farther gates were closed and the troops massed in a brilliant pageant throughout the large enclosure. The bands, after a wild, discordant finale, stopped; and there was comparative silence save for the murmurous hum of the masses of soldiery and their animals.

A Makhazni beckoned to Paul and led them round towards the Sultan. As Paul approached he suddenly observed a huge pyramid of globular objects which at first sight appeared to be cannon balls, but a few steps and a clearer view disclosed the gruesome fact that they were human heads, hundreds of them, bearded and gory.

---

[199] Tabor: ṭābūr. A military company, troop, or column roughly equivalent to a European battalion or regiment.

Paul felt a hot wave of anger surge through him and he strode forward to the foot of the concrete dais and within a dozen feet of the grim trophies.[200] He marched up the steps and saluted with his sword, which the Sultan acknowledged by an inclination of the head. As he opened his mouth to speak, Abd-el-Kader gestured a negative with his forefinger, saying:

"La, la!" (No, no!)

He motioned to one side, bidding Paul be seated.

Paul frowned angrily as the Baron plucked at his sleeve. The Sultan smiled, and turning to El Hammo, who sat near him, entered into a whispered colloquy. Paul reflected that after all it was none of his business, and if he intended to attempt to reform the East he had better give up all idea of his scheme.

The whole mass of men sat and lolled at ease as if waiting for some event. Presently Paul became aware of a commotion near the opposite wall, and presently, from amid a crowd of white-robed Makhzenia, a rough wooden cross was erected, followed by three more in line against the wall. As soon as they were secured in the ground an order was passed along to the officers, who, leaving their respective tabors, formed in a half circle in

---

[200] "France was happy still to sponsor the new regime and the British who had assisted earned the reward of some prospecting concessions. [Hugh] Pollard asked [Henry Roger] Pocock for a silver Legion [of Frontiersmen] badge to present to the new ruler as an honorary member and thought the new ruler in return might have some useful rewards and jobs for Legion members. Needless to say, the Foreign Office was aghast when they heard of this. Things soon went wrong when Mulay Hafid failed to keep his promise not to exact violent revenge. Belton was disgusted to see public executions, crucifixions and the severing of hands of some of the enemies, being solemnly told that this was their tradition." Roger Pocock, *The Frontiersmen Historian*, "Tasting Adventure and Revolution," 1 June 2016, frontiersmenhistorian.info. For more on the mercenaries and adventurers that composed the Legion of Frontiersmen group (of which Beadle was a founding member), see my Afterword.

front of the dais, saluting their master within, who sat complacently watching proceedings.

Four men of various ages were led from the eastern door and planted in the center of the guard of officers. After bowing low to the ground in homage and submission to their captor, they sat back impassively awaiting their fate, which from their expression they regarded as inevitable.

No unnecessary words passed between the prisoners and their judge, no word of pleading for mercy, no word of regret: either inclination was essentially absent from the characters concerned. The slow keen look from face to face, the grim twitching of the lip comers, and the slim brown hand caressed the full black beard, giving the signal for the wolf pack to spring upon their victims in fiendish, barbaric delight. In a trice the culprits, taken red-handed in arms against the self-appointed Prince of the Faithful, were haled away through the eager, curious throng of soldiery to their doom against the wall.

El Hammo's face the while had retained its resemblance to a yellow Mongolian Sphinx, giving no clue to the thoughts within. Abd-el-Kader, more vivacious, showed a wolfish gleam of teeth between his full lips. The Baron evinced interest, a grim, cynical smile upon his hard-hewn face.

Possibly he was more capable of understanding the motives and emotions of the Eastern Potentate than Paul. Something in one's way to be removed! a warning to the assembled men upon whom one was forced to trust in a limited degree! Ah, yes! Paul's features reflected a combination of anger, pity and the effort of self-control.

Amid much noisy and excited chatter and wild gesticulations the first wretched man, still refusing to show fear or any emotion, was hoisted to his allotted post and spread-eagled thereon upside down, long nails driven in through hands and feet. Within a few minutes the yelping, jeering crowd of Makhzenia had served the other three in like manner. There they hung — lit by the full rays of the morning sun — blood dripping slowly from each limb, their shaven skulls and faces giving the horrid suggestion of crucified apes; their features remained almost impassive, stoical, sweat upon their brows, tears of agony welling from their eyes.

Paul shuddered in sympathy, and glanced at the Baron, who shrugged his shoulders and smiled grimly. Paul felt he could strike him, and knew that other than an Oriental mind was capable of similar cruelty.

Suddenly, with a swirl of sound, one of the bands struck up an erratic version of the Marseillaise, immediately followed by the other, as if jealous, with a different tune. The troops scrambled to their feet and the officers broke and rejoined their tabors. The music ceased as the Sultan emerged from the pavilion, and standing at the edge of the dais, thanked the officers and troops for their valorous service in the cause of the Prophet — with no sense of irony — and blessed the assembly, righthand upraised.

Then as all the bands struck up in clamorous discord, the brilliant-hued pageant commenced to move, marching in columns past their Lord and Emperor, who bestowed a blessing upon each batch of the banners as they paused a moment before him, each and every man bowing low to receive the "baraka."[201]

Paul, sitting behind, saw the tall, upright figure of Abd-el-Kader, the rays of the sun striking from the palace walls, lighting up the silken tassels at the back of the hooded head, in front of which the moving sea of red Fez caps, dotted with white turban denoting officers; a mass of lean, hawk-eyed tribesmen, gray-hooded, riding up, bowing over their tossing horses' heads; and beyond, in splendid isolation by the wall, the four crucified stoics; whilst further still, above the gray walls, the olive-clad hills bathed in glorious sunlight. As he looked he

---

[201] Baraka: a blessing, spiritual grace, or divine favor.

saw gray clouds of horsemen emerge from the blue-black shadows, others still converged from the side hills, all racing in their reckless fashion, like a swarm of white ants, down the hillside towards the city in the plain. Vaguely Paul supposed they were belated tribesmen bound for the general celebrations which were to be held that day.

The head of the long column had disappeared through the Western gate; the figure of the Sultan, a white silhouette against a blue sky, seemed to automatically raise his right hand in blessing, the mumble of words dim amid the musical tornado.

Suddenly a hubbub arose at the far Western gate; a volley of shots, sharp and distinct above the din, and around the inside of the gate the advancing column halted and merged with a seething, struggling mass of men endeavoring to reenter from the outside. For a moment the bands rioted on as the Sultan paused in the act of blessing to watch the distant commotion. The sound of firing increased; and as Paul and the Baron got to their feet, the bands stopped, allowing the cries, shouts and shots of the combatants at the gate to float clear on the hot, still air. The whole mass of men inside the enclosure stood silently watching the fight without realizing what had occurred. A new clamor of strife commenced from the direction of the Bab-el-Bushat as a messenger arrived panting, and throwing himself at the feet of the Sultan, gasped out: "Ya Sidna, El Rogui (the Pretender)[202] is without with a million of men. We are lost! Waali! Woe is me!"

As the news ran like wildfire through the assembled army a storm of excited vociferation arose. The Sultan glanced around

---

[202] A reference to Jilali ibn Idris al-Yusufi al-Zarhuni (c. 1860 – 1909), more commonly known by his nicknames, El Rogui ("the pretender") and Bou Hmara ("the man on a female donkey"). He was eventually captured, tortured, and killed under the orders of Sultan Moulay Hafid.

for a moment with a suspicion of panic in his eyes, but quickly controlling himself, he turned to Paul, asking his advice.

Paul considered for a moment rapidly. The Rogui had either planned an extremely clever coup d'état, or had, by accident, hit upon the very moment when he might bottle up the whole army within four walls.

If the other gate had been successfully stormed and communication cut off with the town, then he scarce knew what could be done. There were only two gates, and any attempt at a sortie from either could easily be stopped by a light gun commanding either.

"Send thy most trusted man to bring news of the Bab-el-Bushat," he advised.

Abd-el-Kader dispatched a man, and together they, the army of thirty thousand, and the crucified prisoners, stood awaiting the news, feeling like mice in a cage with the cat outside.

The sound of desultory firing came from all directions, showing that the rebels were surrounding the town.

The Sultan had resumed his seat, and was conversing with El Hammo, who for the first time showed emotion, anger, when the news came that all the great gates were locked and barred, and the townspeople were attempting to defend the walls.

The Fasi, who little loved a fight, were to be reckoned with when their own houses and dollars were threatened by an invader.

"Will you try to control this crowd whilst I take half into the town?" asked Paul of the Baron.

He nodded, and Paul explained to Abd-el-Kader, who now wore a strained, anxious look, seeming to have aged years in the last ten minutes. He assented, and muttering something to himself, arose and retired through the small private gate to his own quarters.

Paul and the Baron discussed the situation for a moment with El Hammo, what time the army gesticulated and argued with itself. The Baron, collecting some of the excited Kaithahas, proceeded to hoist some of the guns into available bastions whilst Paul, through Bu Hamu, lost much valuable time in herding a few mixed tabors to one side and marching them off into the city, placing as many as possible to guard each gate, from convenient rooftops, with a rifle fire.

Outside, mobs of mounted tribesmen rode round the walls shouting insults and firing at random over the wall. At a little distance away a crowd of excited tribesmen unlimbered a seven-pounder with which they intended to force a breach in the gate. The erratic shooting of the sharpshooters within the walls disturbed them not a little. The roving horsemen, however, began to keep a respectable distance from the walls. The first shot from the seven-pounder flew high over the top of the gate and crashed into a house in the middle of the town. This was quickly replied to by a sweeping fire of a Maxim-Nordenfelt[203] manipulated by the Baron himself with such good effect that they retired hurriedly leaving the gun in the open. The Baron attempted to persuade a party to make a sortie under cover of the gun and capture the enemy's piece, but met with little encouragement.

In the streets of the city confusion reigned. From the interior of the many gardens the howling lament of women rose, whilst in the streets excited men ran hither and thither cursing, praying, boasting. Jews in their somber black garb rent their clothes and bemoaned the prospective loss of their wives and dollars, and above all sang the rippling squib crack of the defenders from the walls.

Meanwhile Paul had reached the lower end of the town in company with Bu Hamu, where he found that a party had rushed one gate and were busily looting a portion of the town.

---

[203] Maxim-Nordenfelt: a type of machine gun or early rapid-fire artillery weapon.

Bu Hamu with much vociferation urged on his unwilling men to rush the narrow streets from whence came shrieks of women, and shouts and cries of men mingling with the guttural triumphant yells of the enemy.

As Paul rode down a narrow dirty street a missile struck him upon the cheek, and a voice shouted: "Kill the dog of an Infidel! This is brought by the Infidel!" and saw a wrath-bound face of a Moor who was in the act of poising another stone. Paul spurred on a little faster, but otherwise ignored the man. It was seldom that he was so insulted, as few recognized him as a European.

Above the pandemonium of shrieks and cries he heard Bu Hamu calling from a side street, and arrived in time to help check an ugly rush of the soldiers in a sudden panic.

Turning down a side street afterwards, thinking that Bu Hamu was right behind him, Paul entered a tunnel-like passage formed by an arch of two houses adjoined. Halfway down, bending over the pommel of the saddle to avoid the roof, he dimly saw some figures rise up alongside him, and felt his feet lifted, throwing him completely out of the saddle. As he fell, his head struck the wall — .

CHAPTER XVII

Black night and loathsome stench: nausea and thirst. Paul feebly raised his head, to heave and sway in flashing darkness and sink back with a groan of agony. For a while he lay still, trying to summon and control his errant faculties and distinguish nightmare from reality.

It was some time before he convinced himself that the darkness and stench were not the figments of a dream. His head throbbed and ached dully. He became slowly conscious of damp, slimy cold damp, of repulsive small creatures crawling over his limbs. His ears registered a medley of sound, a low whining mutter, running beneath a hum of guttural voices pitched low, snarling, and anon the scamper of small feet, squeaks and scuffling. Something hairy and wet ran across his hand, a pair of small bright eyes glinted for a moment in the blackness.

He shuddered as he realized the surroundings and, too shocked to seek the cause for the moment, endeavored to sit up in a spasm of horror. His hand slipped on the inch-deep slime, dropping his body back with a squelch, jerking a stab of pain through his wounded head.

He lay sprawling in an agony of physical and mental torment, telling himself that it was all a dream, that he would wake in a moment to find himself in bed. The awful nightmare sense of the inability to escape the impending horror enveloped him. He tried to scream, with the idea that such would break the spell, but the ecstasy of fright paralyzed his throat; an inarticulate whisper was the result.

Another horror, wet and hairy, brushed his face, and nipped his ear with razor fangs as it vanished in a squelch and a squeak. With a superhuman effort Paul regained control of his muscles and scrambled to a kneeling posture, realizing at the same time that the environment was material, no conjured hell of a dream.

For a while the concentration of his will upon the effort to discover the reason and locality overcame the sense of physical pain. Crouching upright, staring into the murky void, he realized that he had been stripped of clothes, and was incarcerated in a native dungeon. Knowledge gleaned from an outside view and from hearsay sent a wave of panic through him. He knew that Moorish prisons were unspeakably loathsome; underground, dripping, dank, and bedded with the fetid filth of generations of hapless prisoners, innocent, guilty, lepers, victims of indescribable diseases, all herded together, bound together with fetters of steel in a common bond of despair and anguish. Depending for food and water upon the charitable gifts of friends or others, thrown through the iron grating, the wretched prisoner surely died of dread disease if he avoided thirst or starvation. The monotonous hum of voices around was the pleading of those who retained sufficient strength to voice their appeals for sustenance.

Paul, sick with fear and nausea from the humid stench around him, dragged himself painfully towards the voices where he imagined the only ventilation and communication with the outside world would be. Twice his hands came in contact with a corpse of someone who had died in the night. Every day such were dragged away for burial, the only courtesy extended to a prisoner without friends; and few had such, for being cast into prison meant the confiscation of his property, if any, and with no money what man might have friends — in Morocco?

The faintest pale gray glimmer of light, soaking timidly through an iron grating, met Paul's eager eyes as he crawled through the reeking filth. And around this small aperture were crowded a group of men in all stages of strength and weakness, chanting monotonously a pious prayer for alms. Nearest to the window sat a full-bearded man, by right of his superior rude health and strength which a few hours of imprisonment had not as yet undermined. About him others, garbed in filthy rags and prison-soiled fine linen, sulky anger, despair, hunger and disease lurking behind the impassibility of their features.

As Paul crawled near to this motley group, they paused to curse and spit at him. Upon one tattered, vermin-haunted wretch he recognized his tarboosh and rozzah,[204] another wore his silk-embroidered silham over disease-eaten features. No matter how fallen in fortune or wasted by disease, the sorriest wretch had energy left to revile and despoil a hated Infidel consigned to share their dismal fate.

Paul, almost fainting with nausea, shrank down upon the outskirts of the group, suffering the torture of the damned physically and mentally; his limbs and body scalded and stung with the bites of innumerable pests; his beard matted with filth; athirst — he was too ill to feel hunger. In this soul-maddening environment, and the dismaying prospect of a lingering death, Paul had indeed fallen upon an evil day. His thoughts wandered distractedly from the reason of the attack and imprisonment to the result of the assault upon the city and the chances of escape; or how long before oblivion would release him from torture.

From an oblique position to the window a small patch of golden sunlight striking the wall of the street could be seen — an irritating sight. To touch that enchanted spot of sun-kissed wall meant freedom.

No ray of sunlight ever penetrated the noisome den of misery.

Lying prone amid the mire, over which hovered dense clouds of flies in the reek-laden atmosphere, a little sweeter from the street without, Paul gradually lapsed, from sheer weakness, into a comatose condition, to awake hours later with the name of Zahra upon his lips and her image in his mind. All ambitions

---

[204] Rozzah: ruzza. A sash, scarf, or wrap cloth used around the head or waist.

seemed negatived by his sorry plight, and as the sunlight and air appeared never so desirable the sense of his wants and desires were increased. The thought that before long he would be beyond all material things only fanned the desire to live, and magnified the desirability of human things; and to Paul in his agony the greatest of these was Zahra, perhaps because by circumstances and his own choice she had appeared the least attainable. The fire of ambition had been fed, but his love for Zahra had been starved; and now, when every sense was intensified, love was the keener of the twain by reason of its long fast.

The group of motley miserables about him droned their never-ceasing chant with husky voices. A goatskin water bag lay flat and crumpled without the window, its metal-headed neck protruding through the bars, bearing evidence of a gift of sweet water from some charitable Moor in blessed freedom. The clamorous struggle for possession had barely disturbed Paul, who, when he noticed it, became doubly conscious of thirst. His mouth and nose, stung from inhaling the filth-laden air, felt scalding hot and dry, and he noticed vaguely that the sense of smell was deadened. Then he became slowly aware that above the babel and chant of voices came a serene vibrant cry, sinking down through the narrow streets to this dark hell on earth.

"Al-lah — Ak-ba-ah!"

Paul groaned in spirit. The calm tones seemed to set despair within his heart, ever suggesting the relentless march of eternal destiny. That serene call to prayer seemed the sum of man's misery and helplessness ringing throughout all the ages on to the end of time — man's time.

"Al-lah — Ak-ba-ah!"

Paul remembered interpreting it as the voice of destiny pushing him on; now it seemed the same, but relentlessly pushing down — down to oblivion, until he should be oblivious of all things, as the call was oblivious to him, relentless as time itself.

The patch of sunlight had stolen higher up the wall, a natural sundial.

As Paul, pest-ridden, impotently cursed, writhing in torment, and essayed to creep nearer the cleaner air, a noisy storm of invective rose from his fellow prisoners. The hawk-nosed man nearest the window, who had remained in silent contemplation of the sunlit wall of the cul-de-sac, turned his head and regarded Paul closely as he gestured with his left hand in rebuke to the clamorous horde about him. Paul noticed that his other hand was sewn up in leather, indicating another victim of the Sultan's wrath. For a moment Paul wondered whether Abd-el-Kader had been the cause of his own imprisonment, but reason told him that such was against the Sultan's interest, for the death of a European, no matter how, would involve serious trouble with the Legations. No, there was only one man to whom his removal was essential. A particularly venomous fanatic, mumbling curses through a fleshless nose had spat at Paul as if in reply to the hawk-eyed man's rebuke, who, with a guttural oath, leaned forward and struck the disease-eaten bag of bones a crashing blow in the face. Paul, miserable, suffering the agonies of humiliation, thanked his sturdy champion, as he waged a wordy war with the rest of the rabble.

Picking up the neck of the water skin, the man dragged the deflated body through the narrow bars and examined it carefully for water. There was a little still left, the sight of which inflamed Paul's thirst to acute agony; he heard the precious liquid gurgle musically, trying to lick parched lips with a slimy furred tongue.

Suddenly he recognized him — Larbi Gibilo;[205] and then to his astonishment the man handed over the skin, bidding him drink. The first gulp seemed to scorch his mouth and throat; and then, as the pores absorbed the water, he felt new life stir within him. He paused to murmur his thanks, gurgled gratefully, and fell back with a sigh of satisfaction.

But the relief was temporary, for the draught stimulated his flagging senses, causing him to feel the vermin bites and smell the frightful stench ten times more acutely. His benefactor was watching him keenly.

"Tell me, N'srani," said he, "what dost thou here? Has thou not found favor in the sight of the Rogui Abd-el-Kader? Many times have I seen thee with him."

"Yea, but he knoweth not that I am here," responded Paul wearily. "I would that I might send word unto him."

The man laughed softly.

"Thy enemies have full-grown beards! They take good care that thy gaolers are well furnished with dollars. Know ye not who hath cast thee here?"

"No," said Paul, vaguely shrinking from disclosing the perfidy of another European.

"Then, Yillah! know I well!" responded the other.

"What hath happened without?" inquired Paul, turning the subject.

"What meanest thou?"

Paul explained.

"Hamdullah! Praise be to Allah!" exclaimed the other fervently. "May he for whom I have suffered this be successful."

"In what position of the city lie we now?" asked Paul.

---

[205] Earlier in the tale, Larbi Gibilo attacked the Baron in the dancing café; later on, he helps to kidnap Paul.

"By the Bab Djedeed."[206]

From which Paul knew that he must have been carried some distance, arguing that his plight was not due to the men of El Rogui. The Bab Djedeed was on the eastern side of the new town on the plateau near the Sultan's palace.

As they spoke a shadow darkened the window, and the begging chorus rose to a clamorous eager shriek. Paul looked up, and beheld a gray-bearded Moor attended by a black slave bearing a round food basket. The negro lowered the basket at the command of his master, and removing the conical lid, disclosed a steaming mess of stewed meat and couscous. The human animals clamored the louder, struggling in a writhing mass behind the bars of their cage, skinny arms extended, wolfish eyes watering and mouthing lips dribbling saliva. As the dish was placed within reach a dozen hands dived into the mess amid a chorus of "Hamdullahs," yelps and squeaks from those out of reach. In a trice the basket was overturned by too eager hands, and the food scattered outside and inside the bars amongst a heaving, squirming mass of struggling humanity, the weaker trampled and cast aside.

It was an ugly sight. After the fight was over and the combatants, the stronger fed and others tormented by a useless mouthful, lay around panting in the filth, one dying man and one dead were dragged to the side. The donor of this gift of cruelty and kindness, who had stood with the slave watching this bestial struggle for existence with callous interest, walked away amid a chorus of blessings and demands for more.

Larbi, by virtue of his strength and position, had secured the lion's share of the food, and now offered a greasy handful of meat to Paul, who could hardly repress a gesture of disgust as he refused. The ghastly battle between these whole and

---

[206] Bab Djedeed: Bāb el-Jdīd, or "New Gate," which opens northward, toward Old Fes, providing access between the two parts of the city.

loathsomely diseased wretches made him so ill with physical nausea that he could hardly repress another fit of vomiting. He shook his head wearily and shrank away, wishing that he might die to escape the unbearable torment. He felt his whole nervous control deserting him, paroxysms of shuddering attacked him; he jumped violently at any sudden movement or at the touch of a passing rat or human limb. He felt he should presently shriek himself insane.

As he lay quivering in hopeless misery he became conscious of a voice outside speaking. His heart gave a great leap as he imagined this voice to sound like Rabbit's. He hardly dare look up lest he be disappointed.

He summoned courage and turned his head. It was Rabbit.

"Rabbit! Rabbit! O my God, Rabbit!" he cried, in a nervous frenzy of unreasonable fear that Rabbit might vanish.

Rabbit glanced up from his conversation with the hawk-nosed man, looked, started, stared hard.

"Hamdullah!" he exclaimed. "O Pole, I have found thee!"

"Thank Heaven! For God's sake, go to the Sultan immediately — run, run — I shall go mad here. D'you hear? For God's sake be quick, Rabbit, I'm nearly crazy. No! No! No! Don't talk, man. And fetch me some water — and some clothes — and brandy — and run, Rabbit. Oh, do go!" he cried in petulant fury as Rabbit, quick to grasp the situation, paused to gather his instructions. Paul, feeling his heart sink as Rabbit disappeared in the gathering gloom, almost shouted for him to return. However, with an effort he tried to calm himself to await the arrival of freedom.

Although there was now every chance, and hope leaped high in his heart, his misery was intensified by the very approach of freedom, and made almost more unendurable, if that were possible, by the frenzy of impatience that immediately possessed him.

He fell to imagining Rabbit's progress along the streets. Now he should be at the Sok of three gates, now at the Bab-el-Bushat, and now crossing the great enclosure; then he nearly fainted upon realizing that Rabbit might be forced to sit without the gates for hours before he could obtain word or send word to the Sultan, by whose orders only any effective rescue might be accomplished. And, with another spasm of horror, he remembered that he did not know what had happened since the surprise attack upon the town. That must be yesterday, or was it to day?

He tried to comfort himself with the reflection that Rabbit would have stopped to tell him had anything serious happened.

Quickly complete darkness settled down; the monotonous chorus died down to an occasional whimper, and steady, gurgling, coughing, breathing; squeaks of the hosts of rats running riot in the dark, fighting, scuttling, already commencing their ghastly work upon the dead; the horrid rending of flesh and snapping of jaws, shrieks of horror from live victims. Paul sat erect, hitting wildly at the ghastly forms flung out of the darkness, straining his ears to catch the sound of approaching footsteps, his eyes for a glimmer of a lantern. He felt that his reason would give way before morning. Every minute seemed an eternity.

A score of times he almost persuaded himself that Rabbit had been murdered en route, that the Sultan had been killed or captured; any wild suggestion that would prevent help ever coming was entertained for a distracted moment, to be cast aside for another.

Amidst the darkling horror a silhouetted figure of a devotee rose and fell against the lesser blackness of the window, bowing and kneeling in the slimy filth in prayer, apparently oblivious of the ghastly sounds around him.

The night wore on to the accompaniment of groans, muttered prayers, and half-stifled shrieks of pain, sickening squelch of limbs in the slime, shrill squeaks, snapping of sharp teeth, and much scuttling of the rodent carnival; a dreadful dirge of human misery unspeakable. One crazed wretch flung himself madly against the bars, shrieking inarticulate oaths and prayers, to fall in a crumpled heap, exhausted, too feeble to protect himself.

Paul passed from frenzy into semidelirium merging into a comatose condition from sheer exhaustion, only to be spurred into frantic energy by the warning nip of a rat.

Periods of strained gazing in search of a glimmer of an approaching lantern which never came, mechanically keeping his arms beating the air; anon despair and consequent indifference to his fate except that it might come quickly. Several wet hairy forms, a glint of evil eyes, fetid breath, a bite on ear or limb stinging him to a frantic fight against those vermin assailants of the night.

Then again from out in the silent streets floated the calm serene notes:

"Al-lah — Ak-ba-ah!"

Paul heard and cursed in his abject misery, shuddering at the reminder of remorseless destiny. Four hours to dawn. Would he keep his reason, would help ever come? Too feeble to be violent, he whimpered in impotent misery.

Suddenly, as the cry seemed to fade and swell to his half-delirious senses, a flash of a lantern caught his eye from the black depths of the dungeon. He turned with a half-articulate scream. The light grew. A pale yellow flare lit up the sky-blue pantaloons of a soldier swinging a candle lantern, picking his way, barefoot, between the huddled, whimpering wretches, over the half-eaten corpses, bloody and ghastly in the filth, a score of black forms scuttling in retreat.

Paul tried to scramble to his feet, slipped feebly and fell prone at the feet of the man, who lowered the lantern to examine the filthy, naked object.

"Ashkoon?" he queried.

Paul, with an effort, raised himself on an elbow, staring wildly at his interlocutor.

"Ana N'srani,"[207] he gasped, and fainted.

---

[207] Ana N'srani: ʾanā n-ṣrānī, "I am a Christian."

CHAPTER XVIII

Paul, recovering from his fainting fit, was vaguely aware that he was being borne rapidly along the narrow streets, inhaling vigor with the fresh, clean morning air. A troubled dream of a hot bath diluted with strong disinfectant, brandy and beef tea, and his wounds being skillfully dressed by the Baron, strangely solicitous; then he had fallen into a sound sleep.

It is only by privation and suffering that one can truly appreciate peace and plenty; and Paul found that in proportion to the indescribable agony of mind and body endured during that one night the appreciation of freedom and sunlight had never been so keen; never a sheeted bed such a thing of delight, the air never so sweet and the sun so cheerful. Fortunately the human memory cannot wholly reproduce the pain of the past. To Paul, as he lay awake in bed and looked out into the sunlit yard, the previous night seemed but a realistic nightmare.

He lay quiet for a while, thinking over the situation, trying to determine what attitude he would adopt towards the Baron. There was no proof whatever against him. No official would have cast Paul into prison unless bribed by someone; fanaticism or robbery might account for the assault, but in such circumstances he would have been killed outright or left unconscious in the street. But an interview with the governor of the prison, aided by silver dollars, would perhaps solve the riddle; meanwhile he must treat the Baron as Caesar's wife. It was unlikely that Rabbit could throw any light upon the subject; the Baron would be far too clever for mistakes of that sort.

A footstep sounded on the tiled balcony. The Baron appeared, with Kismet in his arms.

"Ah, Towers! awake? So! feel better?"

"Yes, thanks," said Paul, striving to drown a note of irony. "Gad! I'm hungry! How's Kismet? — You haven't treated me well of late, old man," he added, caressing the dog, which the Baron had deposited on the bed.

"The ways of Kismet are past understanding," observed the Baron smiling. "Sometimes he frowns upon you, and then, ach! he smiles when you least expect it! Kismet was in a bad temper this morning. I gave him two pills, eh, mein lieber? I wonder what Kismet has in store!"

"Well, I hope — breakfast — or is it dinner? But tell me what has happened, Baron?"

"Oh, pah!" replied the Baron, shrugging his shoulders as he lit a cigarette. "These people are but playful children. They like not the artillery. They are gone to the hills again. We made a sortie — mon dieu, what canailles! They fled faster than they came. The gates are well decorated, assure you. M'sieu le Sultan is pleased. And you? How did you fare? I thought you were killed in the streets."

Paul met the Baron's eye, with a quiet smile, and felt as a duelist en carte. He related briefly what had happened.

"So?" commented the Baron, playing with Kismet. "It is strange! Perhaps with the aid of the Sultan the governor can be made to speak. I will mention it to him."

"Thanks!" said Paul drily.

"So," continued the other unheeding, "if you feel well enough to get up we will have dinner." They dined in the starlit courtyard, a fairy dinner of dainty dishes, luscious fruits and nectar of the gods — or so it seemed to Paul. He was still rather weak, and derived more pleasure from toying with the food than eating it. The Baron, as usual of late, waxed entertainingly reminiscent.

Paul, pleading fatigue, retired early, leaving the Baron to smoke innumerable cigarettes and contemplate the stars in company with Kismet, installed upon his own chair.

Rabbit appeared at Paul's summons.

"Tell me all you know," demanded Paul.

Rabbit shook his head, gesturing towards a glowing cigarette in the courtyard beneath.

"Well, what do you know?"

"Know? Me tell you long time — " commenced Rabbit.

"Never mind what you told me!"

"Me come home," he related resignedly. "You not here. Nobody see you. Bu Hamu say you go — sssf! — me go look. No see you. Look — look everywhere. Me hear people talk in Sok Nsrani in prison. Me look, find you, go Sultan, now you here. Hamdullah! That all. But Rabbit know — ssh!" breaking into Arabic. "This man hath the heart of a snake; unless a man kill the snake the snake kill him. Inshallah!"

"Well, what shall I do?" queried Paul.

"Do? Me tell you!"

"No, no, I can't do that, Rabbit."

"Orlright ole chap: You see what will come out of him!"

With a despondent shake of his ugly face Rabbit departed.

For a while Paul lay awake, trying to determine what he should do. He could have no shadow of doubt that the Baron meant to remove him; it was so easy in the Orient! He would not entertain Rabbit's hint, but sought a means of rendering the Baron impotent physically and politically.

Next morning Paul sought and obtained an interview with the Sultan. He particularly desired, for obvious reasons, to see him alone, but notwithstanding all his maneuvers to attain that object, the Baron refused to be outwitted.

To his surprise he learned that the wretched Kaid of the prison had met a rapid death for direct disobedience of the Sultan's explicit commands; months ago he had issued a threat to the effect that any assailant of a Christian would be torn to pieces; he had relentlessly kept his word. An expression of satisfaction flitted across the Baron's face upon hearing the news. Dead men tell no tales.

Paul, remembering with gratitude the hawk-eyed Berber Larbi Gibilo, pleaded for his release, which the Sultan granted, dispatching one of the civil guard on the spot.

The Rogui, disappointed at the failure of his raid and perhaps a little demoralized at the unexpected strength of the artillery, had fled back to Tazza, leaving many of his followers to decorate the gates of Fez with their heads. This news had had the good effect of encouraging several recalcitrant tribes to send their deputies to make their submission to, and their recognition of the new Prince of the Faithful, in the shape of money and presents. Upon the morrow the celebrations of the Feast of the Ram were to be held, after which for three days the Sultan would appear in the Bab-el-Bushat to receive the homage of the tribes.

For the next week Paul lived in a state of indecision. Now he determined to tax the Baron with treachery, only to realize the absurdity of the charge. One night he awoke almost in a sweat of terror, half imagining that the Baron or some hired assassin was about to attack him in the dark. By day, he took the precaution to guard against street attacks by never riding alone. He found himself suspicious of food, watching to see the Baron eat of a dish or drink before he dared partake himself. The position grew intolerable. It was like living with a viper in one's shirt, never knowing when it would strike. Yet what could he do? He thought of removing to another house, but on second thoughts there was no feasible excuse; and moreover, would offer an easier opportunity than ever.

Several times his thoughts wandered to Zahra, ever with longing, but not in the same key in which she had appeared to him during that night when despair and misery gripped his heart. A man ever turns to a woman in times of the blackest agony only to wonder vaguely upon recovery of a normal state of affairs. So it was with Paul. Now with his feet set again more or less firmly on the track he turned with more energy than ever to struggle towards his goal of ambition. He could not yet keep his thoughts from her, it is true, but by dint of constantly reiterating the statement that she was unattainable, in fact, was rather a mental personification of Egeria, he had almost succeeded in auto-hypnotizing himself into that belief. His strength, he knew, lay in keeping away from sight or sound of her, and although, inconsistently enough, he found himself riding past her house and once, intent upon viewing the glorious night from his own rooftop, had cast a wistful eye across the adjacent gardens, the Fates seemed to accord with his reason and adverse to the dictates of his heart.

A more charming and courteous companion than the Baron during these days would have been hard to find, the world over. All reticence and distrust seemed foreign to his nature, and Paul, angry with his own foolishness and against his sane reason, began to reproach himself for having committed a serious injustice to the Baron in doubting him. He recalled all the various incidents, real and deduced, against the man only to surprise a sneaking affection and an insane desire to confide in him.

At the end of the week a special courier arrived from Tanga with news of the Proclamation in favor of Abd-el-Kader in all the coast towns save Dar-el-Baidas.[208] The news quickly spread, and another three days of festivities commenced.

During the whole of this period both Paul and the Baron were necessarily idle, the Sultan attending to no business save that of Oriental pomp and ceremony. In the late afternoon he would ride out upon his white charger and lead a select party of his favorite officials in the Powder Play outside the walls of the city amidst a vast concourse of townspeople and tribesmen, gorgeous in color and sound. Every day large batches of tribesmen, on their wild-maned stallions and afoot, arrived to

---

[208] Dar-el-Baidas: al-Dār al-Bayḍā’ or Casablanca.

do homage to Abd-el-Kader, now, ipso facto, Sultan in the eyes of Morocco; only the official sanction of the European Powers and the arrival of their respective diplomatic missions remained to qualify his claim to the Sultanate.

Paul was aware that the crucial moment was at hand when the whole of his schemes depended upon the Sultan keeping to his word in granting to him the concessions immediately after the official recognition by the Doyen of Legations at Tanga, which would compel the Baron to withdraw defeated; unless Germany were to support his claim, which would assuredly lead to international complications. France would strongly object to either concession party as against her interests and contrary to the International Moroccan Agreement, but if England stood firm there was little chance of war. France would never join hands with Germany, and the latter was not ready for war with Great Britain. There would be strained relations, much newspaper excitement, and in the end Germany would climb down and add one more item to the account against England.

As the days flew on Paul's fear of another attack began to diminish. He grew to think that the Baron would not make another attempt upon his life, but rather would depend upon a diplomatic battle for the Sultan's favor.

One night he was awakened from sleep by Rabbit shaking his shoulder.

"Well, what is it?"

"Ssh! Baron he go now to Sultan. He not want you know."

Paul sat up in bed.

"The Sultan sent for him?"

"No; he go see Sultan."

Paul began to dress hurriedly.

"What do you think he has gone for?"

"What man can see in the heart of another?"

"Truly. But what thinkest thou?"

Rabbit grimaced.

"We shall see what will come out of him!" he replied, and went off to see to the horse.

Paul, knowing that Absalom — the whole household were divided into opposition camps — was spying upon him, made no effort to conceal his movements, riding boldly away with Rabbit carrying the lantern. Since the episode of the gaol he had made it a practice to carry a loaded Webley,[209] handy.

Upon arriving at the Palace gates, he awoke the sleeping guard, and after a lengthy argument and much baksheesh, persuaded him to go in search of the Hadjib — Court Chamberlain — whom Paul had bought with a heavy bribe. However, whilst waiting for the return of the messenger, Paul sadly reflected that the gentleman in question, fanatically anti-European unless soothed with more silver, was in all probability profiting from the Baron's pocket with cheerful impartiality.

The time passed slowly as Paul crouched in the shadow of the gate whilst the disturbed guard resumed their slumber, one man storing up dreams of Paradise from the slender stem of a kif pipe.

Rabbit crouched silent beside the lantern throwing a yellow glare upon the iron knob-encrusted gate, odd points of light from rusty bayonets. From near at hand floated the seething bubble of subterranean waters, an occasional neigh, or a donkey's choking sob distant, pathetic under the starry heavens.

At length shuffling footsteps, a knock upon the door, exchange of words between the newcomer and a kif-dazed

---

[209] Webley: a type of revolver widely used by the British military in the late nineteenth and early twentieth centuries.

guard. It was the messenger with the information that the Hadjib had long since retired to his house in the city. Paul, on principle, classed this as a terminological inexactitude of a common order; and so, bidding Rabbit disgorge more dollars from the heavy bag brought for this express purpose, he dispatched the man with a promise of a further present to the wily Hadjib, who, after another long wait, appeared, turban awry, scratching his shaven poll. Squatting down upon the cushion, which an attendant carried, with the air of one settling down for an all-night sitting, he gave the interminable greetings in a soft, sleepy voice. At length Paul was enabled to state his object.

"La, la!" exclaimed the other, waving a negative finger but without conviction.

Paul explained that he must see the Sultan immediately. No good, the Sultan was in his harem. "It was worth much money to him," Paul added. The other mumbled that he would lose his head if he accepted a present.

"A fat mule shall be lost at thy door," suggested Paul.

"A large mule?" dreamily contemplating his bare toes.

"A large, strong mule!"

"If Allah wills!"

He nodded, and rising, shuffled off through the gate, a tall white ghost in the flickering light of the lantern.

An hour passed away slowly, and Paul, huddled against the wall, dozed fitfully. The flash of a light in his eyes awoke him. He glanced sleepily up at the figure, the head in deep shadow, and started violently as a familiar voice said placidly:

"Good morning, Towers!"

"De Bouche!" exclaimed Paul.

"So. You take the air early this morning?"

"Er — yes," said Paul, rather at a loss how to meet the situation.

"You are returning with me?"

"No," returned Paul. He could not see the Baron's face, but he felt the familiar, contemptuous smile.

"So?"

"Yes — so!"

"Aji — come!" interpolated the voice of the Hadjib, with that faint, but ever-present note of a contemptuous courtesy used by an Arab addressing an Infidel.

Paul frowned irritably as he arose.

"I may as well tell you, Towers," the Baron was saying, in an openly hostile level tone, "that you are a trifle too late."

"What do you mean?"

Rabbit, holding the lantern high, let the light fall on the two men facing each other.

There was no humor in the Baron's face; the eyes were hard, the mouth snarled slightly. He laughed sardonically.

"Merely this: that your plot to overreach me has failed. The official recognition arrived from Tanga this night, and I hold the concessions — valid, my good Paul — in my pocket."

Paul felt the blood desert his face. The Hadjib, whom he had bribed heavily to get the news first, had played him false.

"You will quite understand that there is nothing to be gained by approaching the Sultan. You will quite comprehend that in future I cannot trust you, nicht wahr?"[210] — Paul winced — "but if you return with me, there is no reason why you cannot still be of service to me. I mean that you are harmless, you understand?"

"You played me false before ever I — " began Paul hotly.

"Qui s'excuse s'accuse!" retorted the Baron. "Verbum sapienti![211] Come, Towers!"

---

[210] Nicht wahr: Isn't that so?

[211] Qui s'excuse s'accuse: He who excuses himself accuses himself. Verbum sapienti: A word to the wise [is sufficient].

"I'll see you damned!" exclaimed Paul angrily.

"Don't be melodramatic, Towers," returned the Baron, his voice suddenly softening to an ingratiating purr. "I don't blame you, you know that! It was merely a fair fight for the prize — which I have won. I should have done the same in your place; you're not the fool I thought you in Tanga, that's all."

"Come! Aji!" from the Hadjib, who had stood watching the faces of the Europeans.

"Good night," said Paul, shortly, turning on his heel to follow the Hadjib.

The Baron shrugged his shoulders and smiled, his face falling into shadow as Rabbit turned to follow Paul.

"Eile mit Weile,"[212] returned the Baron ironically as the great door slammed.

Paul despondently cursed the treachery of the white-robed figure of the Hadjib in front of him.

"Him liar!" announced Rabbit succinctly.

"Eh? Who? What do you mean?"

"Him liar," repeated Rabbit emphatically.

Paul had forgotten for the moment that Rabbit understood some English.

"What — you mean the letter from Tanga?"

"What letter?"

Paul explained.

"Yes: him come tonight."

"Then why the devil didn't you tell me?" demanded Paul explosively.

"You get plenty recited."

"Recited?"

"Yes — br-r-r!" Rabbit pantomimed lucidly.

---

[212] Eile mit Weile: "More haste, less speed" (i.e., take time to do things properly even when you are in a hurry).

"Why the dickens don't you do as you're told!" exclaimed Paul angrily.

"No," said Rabbit obstinately. "Me know. We shall see what will come out of him."

They arrived at a smaller gate at the end of the long courtyard, where they were bidden to wait. Presently the Hadjib returned and bade Paul enter, leading him through the gardens. As they approached a single-storied building Paul could see the tall figure of the Sultan pacing slowly up and down in the starlight.

When the Hadjib had retired at the Sultan's bidding Paul hastened to offer his congratulations upon the recognition of the Powers.

Abd-el-Kader's eyes gleamed whimsically.

"Inshallah!" said he nodding.

"Hath the master of the little dog sought speech with thee?" inquired Paul at length.

"Even so!"

"He sayeth that thou hast given him that which was promised me?"

"A man may be a liar, yet wot not of the lie!"

"But he sayeth that he carried away the words of the affair?" persisted Paul, feeling his heart leap with relief.

"Seek ye! Are my scribes to write within the hour?"

Such an agreement could not be prepared within five minutes!

"Are ye of the same mind when last we spoke upon the matter?" inquired Paul.

"Even so! The French have written word that they would send Haraba for my army, govern my treasury; that you should leave my service; that your Government know ye not; that France is my friend, and that El Bashador Fransawi hath left Sidi Absalom for Malai Idrees — Inshallah! What news hast thou?"

Paul translated portions of letters in code which caused Abd-el-Kader considerable satisfaction.

"For long have the dogs quarreled over the bone," said he; "and now shall the strongest defend the bone against the multitude. It is good."

"And the papers?"

"S'bah Inshallah![213] (tomorrow — if God wills!)"

"Who knows what the morrow may bring forth?"

"It is as Allah wills. Bring then the documents, and I will affix the seal. But the money — what of the money?"

"Have no fear. The document which, as thou hast read, is conditional upon the debts of thy brother being paid to the French, thus freeing thee from their hands."

Abd-el-Kader watched him keenly.

"Good! But of the Germans — they would help me, too."

"Have they helped thee now?"

"Nay, but they would!"

"S'bah Inshallah!" retorted Paul, ironically. The Sultan laughed.

"When will the Bashadaw Englees tell to the world of his friendship?"

"When they receive the signed concessions."

"A-ah! The soldiery clamor for money, but the chest is empty!"

"The papers signed, and in ten days the soldiers will be paid."

"Good! Bring them today."

"Barakalofik!" said Paul, smiling.

When Paul in high spirits mounted his horse he exchanged El Cid for Pegasus, soaring high, unmindful of the fate of Bellerophon[214]. In the midst of his thoughts, as his body was

---

[213] S'bah Inshallah: ṣ-ṣbāḥ in shā' Allāh. Tomorrow morning, God willing.

[214] El Cid: the famous Spanish hero Rodrigo Díaz de Vivar (c. 1043 – 1099), known as El Cid ("the Lord," from the Arabic, al-Sayyid), who symbolizes chivalry and earthly martial glory. Bellerophon: in Greek myth, the mortal who tamed Pegasus and rode him to Olympus. Like Icarus, due to his hubristic attempt to enter the realm of the gods Bellerophon is thrown off

borne by El Cid pacing in the wake of Rabbit, a pair of reproachful eyes seemed to stare at him out of the darkness, and he felt a sudden pang of regret, although Zahra's memory no longer held him in thrall. Just that passing regret for something that could never be; that was all. Higher still rode his bewinged thought to the realm of Moroccan Empire-builders, not now a wild dream but fait accompli; or so he almost considered it.

The clip-clop of El Cid's hooves upon the cobblestones seemed music to his ear The lantern swinging in Rabbit's hand threw the sharp-cocked ears and rippling black mane in sharp relief. Over the brooding silence of the night a familiar sound:

"Al-lah — Ak-ba-ah!"

Always that cry embodying the very soul of Morocco, of the ancient Mohammedan East. That sense of inevitable destiny, of romantic beauty to the sight yet sordid ugliness to the nose; beautiful fancies and ugly facts; through all running a current of brooding mystery and unthought-of crime. Behind each wall and barred door no man knew what ghastly acts. The words of Poe recurred to Paul as he rode listening to the resonant notes:

> And much of Madness and more of Sin
> And Horror the Soul of the Plot.

A side thought suggested the likeness between the Baron and the country; in both the force of attraction and repulsion.

The thought of destiny, the negation of free will, implying that not to him the power but to Fate. He was but the puppet. The thought damped his ardor, wounding his vanity.

---

and falls back to earth. Hence he represents an incautious leap from mundane heroism to lofty, immodest ambitions. In similar fashion, Paul abandons a grounded, heroic ideal (El Cid) for one fueled by inflated, unrealistic goals (Pegasus), ignoring the cautionary tale of Bellerophon who is punished for overreaching.

"Al-lah — Ak-ba-ah!"

A fit of depression fell upon him like a cloak.

They turned the corner into another lane, crossing over a small bridge upon which the horses' hooves rang loud, the rushing of the waters a musical accompaniment to the plaintive cadence of the call to prayer.

As El Cid reached terra firma again he suddenly reared at a spurt of flame in the darkness followed by a report and a scream of pain from Rabbit, who dropped the lantern. Paul, startled by the sudden plunge of the horse, was almost unseated, and before he could control the frightened brute, encumbered by the voluminous robes, a second shot rang out. El Cid collapsed, hurling Paul to the ground; before he could regain his feet a cloak enveloped his head, hands seized him, and he was half lifted, half thrown over the parapet, striking the turbulent waters with a splash.

CHAPTER XIX

Zahra awoke from her midday siesta in a very bad temper. Sitting up upon the cushions, she brushed back her disheveled Titian hair with an impatient slender hand, and sat for a while frowning through the barred window at the deep-blue sky, her two tiny bare feet below the green silk trousers, pink and white against the dark-blue Berber carpet.

It is very annoying to want something one cannot have; and exasperating when that something is desired more than anything ever before. The Englishman had been back in Fez for weeks, Zahra knew, and not once had she seen him; although she told herself he was an Infidel, cursed and reviled him, and had beaten Fatma as his deputy, yet she could not forget him, and knew she wanted him more than anything else on earth. In her sheltered life she had had most things which had happened to take her fancy — a limited selection, it is true — and so this affair was au grand serieux. A child of nature, she had neither been taught nor sought to disguise or deny her emotions. Her simple mind always went straight to the point: she hated, liked, feared with transparent simplicity, knowing no subtleties.

Paul had come into her life with a suddenness and force dwarfing all childish delights, awaking the woman in her, filling her with a riotous joy of life, to love and be loved. Religion and consequent fanaticism was almost a negative quantity. Women are taught little theology, and if it were otherwise, love, the soul of a woman, would well have swept religious scruples aside, as it has done aforetime with women of the Eastern world.

She did not question the reason of her love for Paul or the consequences. She loved: that was enough. The world was small. She lived, ate, slept, played; there was the sunlight and storm, the garden and a phantasmagoria of men and things passing and repassing in the world without.

A mild curiosity of the author of the light and heat and of the world without had needs be satisfied with a garbled version of Mohammedan teachings from the lips of Fatma or her abla. Above the seven heavens, below the seven hells; and the whole supported by a blue cow with spotted horns standing on a fish, was Fatma's curious belief, founded upon a slightly inaccurate account, as regards the color scheme, culled from the Koran. Also with commendable ingenuity and knowledge of bovine weaknesses the Deity had provided small flies to sting the cow in order to prevent her falling asleep and dropping the whole fifteen-story tenement, with God in the attic and the Devil in the basement. But when Zahra had expressed great concern to know what the poor fish rested upon[,] Fatma's store of knowledge, and Mohammedan lore, be it said, ran dry; she found refuge in the safe and universal Arabic phrase for the unanswerable: "Only Allah knows!"

Zahra was suffering from boredom. All her old toys palled: she wanted the new toy.

Zahra sat up and clapped her hands to summon Fatma, who upon arrival was bidden relate for the twentieth time the latest bulletin gleaned from the marketplace. The account of Paul's wrongful imprisonment was stale news. The body of the narrative was concerned with detailed description of his looks, his horse; in which Fatma proved an enthusiastic reporter. A volley of questions regarding the ways of Infidels and their womenkind followed, to which Fatma, drawing upon a fertile imagination, sketched a truly amazing account of the manners and customs of the English.

All Englishmen lived on ships; England was a rock in the middle of the ocean, to which they moored their ships; Englishmen only had one wife at a time, but each one was killed after the birth of the first child, or murdered if there were none, so altogether the men had many wives; the Germans were another tribe who lived on another rock.

"Are the ships of the Infidels big?" inquired Zahra meditatively.

"A-ah!" exclaimed Fatma, gesturing, "very ve-ry big! Abdullah Bu Shaib, the baker, hath two sons who went upon one of the ships of the English. They lost each other and wandered for seven seasons (years) before they fell upon each other's neck again."

"Eh! Eh!" murmured Zahra in admiration. "And the waters, what are the waters like?"

"A-ah!" said Fatma, who had never seen the sea, "they are full of djinns who cause it to go — " she seesawed realistically.

"Ugh!" ejaculated Zahra, wrinkling her pretty nose. "But the Infidels have much wealth?"

"All Englishmen have more dollars than we can count in a lifetime!" stated Fatma.

"And I shall have many jewels," exclaimed Zahra, betraying the trend of her thoughts.

"Who can refuse anything to a gazelle with a face like the moon?"[215]

"Sing to me," demanded Zahra, lolling back upon the cushions.

But the sound of shuffling steps arrested the song. A muffled figure of a woman appeared at the door, and discarding the slippers on the threshold, murmured as she unveiled, disclosing a yellow wrinkled face. Squatting down before Zahra, she made obeisance and mumbled salutations, to which Zahra replied, petulant at the interruption.

After a lengthy preamble of desultory conversation the Abla approached the subject of her visit, Fatma meanwhile busy preparing sweet tea brought by a black eunuch.

---

[215] [Author's note in original text:] This conversation is taken, almost verbatim, from the lips of a Moorish woman in Fes.

"O Zahra," said the old woman, "Mulai Abdullah thy father — may Allah be good to him — hath weighty news for thee."

"May Allah be good to him!" murmured Zahra, parrotwise.

"Sidna es-Sultan[216] hath commanded that the daughter of Abdullah be given him in marriage as his fourth wife."

"E-eh!" ejaculated Zahra, opening wide her eyes in startled surprise, whilst Fatma dropped her bellows in amazement.

"It is much honor — it is written," mumbled the old woman.

Such a union was naturally the summit of ambition to any Arab maiden; and for a moment a vista of Oriental splendor, as the wife of the Potentate, dazzled Zahra's little heart. But almost before she had realized the meaning she thought of Paul, and, loyal in her love, she hesitated but a moment before the superlative attraction of the marriage arranged for her. As her mind grasped the fact that from her point of view Paul was lost to her, the tears welled in her great round eyes, and hiding her tawny head in the cushions, she sobbed, crying: "Waali! Waali!"

As an Arab girl she had no choice in the matter; such do not even see their husbands until after the ceremony.

The Abla, surprised beyond all measure — she had expected an outburst of delirious joy — gasped like a fish on dry land, speechless with astonishment.

Fatma, in the light of her knowledge, sat motionless among the tea paraphernalia, watching.

"O-oh!" protested the Abla. "Hath not our Lord Mohammed been good to thee? Art thou not favored of Allah! He is in stature nigh five cubits, a beard like unto the Prophet, eyes like twin stars, and teeth of snow! Yillah, he is a man! What wouldst thou? Come, let us prepare for thy lord, the Sultan. Much feasting and rejoicing will there be for Zahra, the moon face, peerless among women!"

---

[216] Sidna es-Sultan: Sīdnā as-Sulṭān. "Our Lord the Sultan."

"Waali! Waali!" moaned Zahra disconsolately. "What aileth the girl?" exclaimed the Abla, turning to Fatma.

"Nay, by Allah, I know not! Have I the knowledge and wisdom of Allah who knoweth all things?"

"Hast thou a lover?" demanded the old woman of Zahra in sudden suspicion. "For yillah, an thou hast the house of thy father is shamed before all people."

"Nay," denied Zahra vehemently, sitting up, her velvet cheeks bedewed with crystal drops. "Nay, thou liest! I am weeping with the great joy of the honor to come to me!" and indeed, she smiled like the sun through a rainstorm.

The Abla eyed her suspiciously.

"Tell me, O Abla Azizah, what time is it written that our lord would summon me? My heart grows pale at the thought of time!"

"Ah, Azizah, the sound of preparation is now within the harem of the Prince of the Faithful. Praise be to Allah! Ere the moon hath yet grown again will Sidna summon thee. He is ever impatient for thy charms!"

Zahra sighed, struggling to subdue another outburst of grief, her thoughts racing to seek some plan of escape.

"My heart is full with gratitude to Allah," she murmured mechanically. "Would that my lord be pleased with his servant. Hamdullah! Praise be to Allah!"

And during the next half-hour, whilst the twain sipped tea, Zahra fought valiantly to appear pleased at the prospect of her Imperial union, which had been arranged for political reasons: to secure the powerful family of the Shareef of Wazzan[217] to the cause of Abd-el-Kader. Since his arrival in Fez he had married three other wives for the same purpose, dispersing his former wives to the outer realm of the harem by the simple procedure

---

217 As noted earlier, the Sharif of Ouazzane (Wazzen) was Sīdī al-Ḥājj ʿAbd al-Salām (aka Sidi Mohammed, 1835 – 1891).

appointed by the Koran: the formula "I divorce thee" repeated three times in the presence of witnesses. Zahra was chosen to form the complement of the four official wives sanctioned by Mohammed to every true believer.

Zahra, *mirabile dictu*, succeeded in wholly removing any suspicion of an unorthodox liaison from the mind of the old woman, although the little features worked painfully at times. The Abla, a most important person in Mohammedan households, accredited with almost supernatural powers, at length departed satisfied with her mission; and Zahra, loosing the flood of pent-up anger and grief, sobbed unrestrainedly.

As the shadow of night fell she, red-eyed with weeping in the seclusion of her own apartment, suffered herself to be laved by the sympathetic Fatma. As she sat on her cushions, dry-eyed and miserable, Fatma crouched behind her[,] combing the long tawny tresses, discussing over and over again the dreadful fate which had befallen her mistress.

Fatma, although equally conscious of the honor and magnificence attached to the latest addition, and therefore favorite, pro tem, of the harem, quite understood Zahra's attitude: truth to say, she was as much in love with Paul herself, and hoped and argued that if her mistress succeeded in capturing Paul she, too, would be always near him; although neither could have suggested how this object was to be effected; both, earnestly desiring, vaguely imagined some wonderful genii to pop up from nowhere, upset the universe, if need be, and make them live happy ever after, in the manner of the Arabian Nights; and without effort a parallel case may often be found among enlightened Western maids.

Several times Zahra, in the middle of this half-tearful dialogue, collapsed weeping in the arms of her faithful little slave, who, out of sheer sympathy, sobbed in unison.

"O-oh!" gasped Zahra. "If Allah would but send my love to me! Oh that I might die in his arms! Oh!" pushing Fatma from her, starting up with glistening eyes, "look! look! See what height he has! What a beard! What eyes like flashing stars! See how his horse leaps under him! Yillah, what a man! See, he looks at me, and I swoon! A-eh! Waali — Waali!" And throwing herself violently on the mattress, she writhed in an ecstasy of grief and longing.

During the evening Zahra alternately sulked peevishly, and gave rein to passionate outbursts of temper, a child of nature, untaught to hide emotions except when cunning or fear bade her. The evening meal she rejected, and spent with grief and temper, crawled early to bed, to sob, tearless, to sleep.

She awoke with the first call of the Mueddhin filling the silent chamber, and restless, still miserable, she arose, gently shot back the bolts of the gilded prison door, and stepped out into the courtyard, an ethereal figure in the light of the gorgeous stars overhead. Fatma, asleep upon a mat in the corner of the verandah like some faithful terrier, stirred sleepily at the patter of Zahra's slippers.

Flitting past the fountain down the orchard, she sped to her favorite spot beneath the wall which separated her from Paul, there to weave with the fairy wand of imagination pleasant fancies of him.

Her hot flushed face, scorched with sleep-falling tears, cried out for cooling water, suggested by the laughing gurgle of the adjacent stream.

Rising, she made her way to the brink, pausing a moment to listen at the sound of two distant shots breaking the tenor of the Mueddhin's chant from the mosque nearby. The crack of firearms by night was nothing unusual, and stooping, she commenced to bathe her face.

Suddenly as she bent over her dark shadow in the flowing stream a great black object, like some large fish, was vomited out of the adjacent tunnel, and seemed to rush at her. She started back with an inarticulate cry of fear. The object, caught on the turn of the bank, swung round and over, exhibiting the dim whites of eyes. In a flash she saw that it was a man, and involuntarily stooping, clutched at the floating robes.

Something prompted her to look closely at the face, awash; with a gurgling cry of excitement and pleasure, she recognized Paul. The fear of something unknown fled, to be replaced by a cold clutching at her heart that he was dead. With frantic hands she dragged him on the bank, and catching his head within her arms, fell to madly kissing his face, as if determined to kiss him back to life, the while murmuring "Great is Allah! Allah hath given him to me! Praise be to Allah!"

Paul, all unconscious of these gifts, lay inert. Of a sudden realizing that her caresses met with no response, no sign of life, she placed him on the sward and stood up, glancing wildly about her, trembling with fright, impotent. Fatma would know! Loath to leave him, she cried once for the slave, but fearing to rouse the others, she summoned courage, and flew up the orchard barefoot, regardless of the loss of her tiny slippers.

But Fatma knew no more what to do than her mistress; together they sat on each side of him, whispering prayers and objurgations to the night wind among the trees, whilst overhead floated the imperturbable cry of destiny.

As Zahra fell again to kissing the pallid face, whilst the little slave surreptitiously kissed a hand, the eyelids flickered and Paul moved, immediately welcomed by a rapturous outburst of pious phrases from the two maids. For a moment or two he lay staring up at the stars, and then, with an effort, turned his head, wincing with pain. Had he been a Mohammedan quite possibly he might have imagined himself in Paradise in the hands of ministering houris. As it was he vaguely imagined himself to be dreaming until a second twinge of pain brought reality. A confused memory of the struggling horse, the plunge into water from which he arose to bump his head against the arch of the water tunnel, a mad struggle in pitch darkness clawing at slimy bricks, sucked under again by the rapid current, sensation of drowning, and with a crash against some hard object, he had lapsed into insensibility, to awake with the stars blinking at him and two dim figures bending over him.

Vaguely the voice of one calling upon him, interlarded with references to Mohammedan saints, seemed familiar to his dazed senses.

"Ya Mulai Idrees! he lives! Zahra, Allah hath sent him to thee — Barakolofik! Barakolofik!" another voice was saying.

Zahra? Zahra? Who was — A-ah! in a flash his memory returned. But how came Zahra here? Where was he?

"Zahra?" he whispered.

"Eyeh! It is I! Thou art not dead, O Pole?" He lay passive, looking up at her.

"Nay, I am not dead, little one, but where am I?" he whispered at length.

"Thou art in the garden of Mulai Abdullah, my father, O Pole. Allah hath sent thee in answer to my prayer."

"But how came I hither?"

"The waters vomited thee forth — it is a miracle! Praise be to Allah!"

He essayed to sit up, groaning in the attempt.

"Ah!" he exclaimed, resting on his elbow as he drank greedily of her eyes, dim and beseeching in the starlit shadow, whilst the stream rippled in ghostly laughter, and the cry of the Mueddhin wandered amid the gentle whisper of the trees.

For an eternity it seemed to little Fatma, the twain sat in motionless ecstasy, unconscious of any presence save their own.

"Za-hra!" he whispered caressingly.

"Az-iz (Beloved)!" she murmured.

Paul dropped his eyes, gazed at the stream which suggested material things bringing in its train the consciousness of pain.

"Ah, I understand now," he exclaimed in English. "Heavens! what a lucky escape! — Ashkoon hiya?"[218] he inquired, staring at Fatma.

"It is Fatma, slave of the pearl amongst women, Zahra the Moon face!" exclaimed the ebony maid, salaaming low in Oriental extravagance.

"O Pole!" whispered Zahra plaintively. Zahra resented any interest save her own.

But the nervous force of love, slackening for a moment, allowed physical pain to supervene. Paul sank back, faint and dizzy, moving Zahra to a fresh outburst of solicitous sympathy. A European maid would doubtless have been concerned at this stage with her lover's damp clothes, but Zahra was too far up in the clouds of romantic bliss to be aware of such mundane affairs; so it was left to Paul to suggest a change of abode other than the cool bank of the stream, where Zahra, in her newfound happiness, was content to stay forever apparently, gazing in ecstasy, while Fatma, in the background, sat upon her haunches, similarly occupied.

"Zahra," said Paul quietly, his head upon the rack, "I would that thou help me! Tell me where I may seek a way to my house?"

"La, la, la!" exclaimed she, suddenly alarmed at the thought of losing her lover so abjectly in her hands. "No, no, no!"

"But I will see thee again, Azizah!" returned Paul, smiling, half divining her thought.

"No, no! Thou canst not leave now, for the gates are locked, and it is death for thee to be seen leaving here."

"Nay," objected Paul, "hath not Allah brought me here? Also, they dare not hurt me openly, for fear of the wrath of the Sultan."

---

[218] Ashkoon hiya: 'ashkūn hīya. Who is she?

"No, no!" protested Zahra, in a sudden frenzy of fear as she thought of the consequences to a European found in the harem of the Sultan's betrothed. "No, *no*! Who hath eyes to see through stone walls?"

"What then must I do?" queried Paul. "The dawn will soon be here."

"O Fatma, O Fatma!" cried Zahra distraught, beating her breast in agitation. "What may we do with him? Speak! Where may we hide him?"

"Listen!" said Fatma, who, less excited, thought more quickly. "At the end of the garden is an old mosque. There will he be safe. We will bring him food and drink."

"O wise Fatma! I will give thee my new earrings!" exclaimed Zahra delightedly. "Come thou, O Pole! Come!" and forgetful of his infirmities, she leapt to her feet and sped excitedly away.

Paul, dragging himself together, tried to rise unaided. Fatma flew to help him. Zahra, pausing to see if he was following, saw and flew back, jealous and angry with herself.

Paul, assisted by the two girls, staggered through the orchard, faint with nausea caused by the pints of water swallowed involuntarily and the throbbing of his wounded skull. In the small mosque, an equivalent to a private chapel in Europe, he fell asleep, damp and exhausted, upon a heap of cushions brought by Fatma, whilst the two girls kept watch until dawn.

Fortunately there was little risk of Paul's discovery, as nobody lived in the house except womenfolk and slaves, who were not expected or accustomed to require a house of prayer. During the morning Paul, left to himself, reviewed the events of the preceding night. To his vague annoyance the enthusiasm for the success of the scheme seemed to have evaporated. He thought over the situation with detached placidity, much as if they were another's affairs. He told himself that he ought to return immediately and secure the contracts from the Sultan, that he was malingering, and yet he lay passive, content, making no endeavor, growing ever more impatient at the absence of Zahra. His wounded head was still a little painful, but certainly insufficient to warrant inert apathy. It was not his fault, he plaintively argued; he had tried to keep Zahra out of his thoughts, had succeeded until Fate had actually flung him, an unwilling victim, right at her feet. It was cool and sunny in the garden; pleasant to sprawl, gazing into those limpid, childish eyes of this Moorish Dryad, to watch the lithesome curves of her fine figure suggested through the silken Zouave dress[219] and the tawny masses of hair burst into flame under chance rays of sunlight percolating through the branches.

A delicious thrill enthralled him at the chance contact of her hand. Longing to clasp her in his arms and kiss that perfect mouth, yet content was he to mutely worship with his eyes, and she with her eyes answered him. It was only when alone that any thought of affairs touched him.

Towards the close of day Paul and Zahra sat together in the cool of the mosque, double sacrilege of an Infidel and a woman on holy ground! Outside among the trees the gnats whirred in the shimmering heat, the refraction of the whitewashed wall glimmering through the trees as the distant stream gurgled sleepily. Zahra's slim figure reclined upon red cushions, ever watching Paul with eyes of devotion as he, clad in clean white robes purloined by Fatma from some unknown wardrobe, told her how Fate had hurled him to her through the medium of midnight assailants.

And as they talked of these things with their lips, their eyes spoke an eloquent language of no nationality, common to all the world.

---

[219] Zouaves: light-infantry regiments in the French Army, originally recruited from North African Berbers, especially in Algeria. A "Zouave dress" refers to a style of women's garment inspired by the uniforms of the French colonial Zouave soldiers of the nineteenth century.

"And so," concluded Paul, "I awoke in Paradise."

Zahra smiled, showing pearly teeth.

"And who is he that seeketh thy life?"

"What is a man's life to seekers of money?" he replied evasively. "It was written." They remained silent awhile, feasting.

"Thou art beautiful, little one," whispered Paul.

"My heart rejoiceth that I please my lord," she replied softly, flushing with pleasure.

Again silence held them, till Paul, suddenly conscious that all will-power was fading within him, shook himself as one struggling to be free from a spell.

"O Zahra," he commenced. "Listen. I must leave thee. I have work to do which must be done. I — "

"O Pole," she whispered, interrupting. "I love thee! Thou canst not go!"

"Nay, I must. I will return."

He half rose, as if to go on the instant. She sat back, looking at him. He paused, averting his eyes, and said as if it hurt him:

"Let me go, O Zahra! I will climb by yonder wall to my house, and I will — by Allah! — I will come back to thee."

The harder tone of his voice and the determined look in his eyes frightened her. She suddenly bent forward, clasping his face between her hands, at which he quivered, and forcing him to look at her, murmured: "O Pole!" a message insistent in her eyes.

He sighed heavily; as their faces grew closer the murmurous silence was broken:

"Al-lah — Ak-ba-ah!" and as the cry died in quivering cadence, their lips met — for the first time.

He released her and sank back. She laughed, a low, gurgling laugh of supreme happiness and triumph.

"Thou wilt not leave me?" she murmured, her lips hovering about his.

"Nay," he whispered, "thou knowest!" and again their lips met.

And indeed Paul, as he lay with his head upon her lap, was in that condition in which neither the whole world, the heavens above nor the waters beneath are aught in comparison to one woman's love.

A delirious joy rioted through him. What were Sultans and empires compared to this one fragile girl? Who could give him that sense of perfect peace and content save her? Away with the strife of the world, the life struggle for empty honors and selfish power. Here was power — of a woman's love; and over him, crushing him in delicious happy defeat. He did not want to move lest the magic spell be broken; to lie and bask in her presence was heaven. He felt he could not bear her to leave him for ten minutes else he would starve for her love.

And for an hour or more they chatted, intermittently, as lovers will, upon those themes so dear to them, so ludicrous to a cynical, unbelieving world.

"Hast thou seen Sidna es-Sultan?" queried Zahra, *apropos des bottes*,[220] her thoughts reverting to her late future; for in blind faith of her lover she considered that he would subvert all decrees of conventional destiny in some miraculous manner.

"Yea, many times."

"What looks hath he?" curiously.

Paul described him enthusiastically.

"E-eh!" commented Zahra, in a noncommittal manner.

"What thinkest thou?" asked Paul, as Zahra sat watching him wistfully.

---

[220] "Apropos des bottes": literally, "concerning the boots." A humorous way of introducing a change of subject, in the sense of "speaking of something completely different" (something as random as boots), thus signaling a topic shift.

"When Allah shall decree that we shall go upon the sea —
thou and I — "

"Upon the sea?" echoed Paul startled.

In Empire scheming he had, necessarily, planned in the
future, and in his endeavor to strangle the fact of his love for
Zahra, he had scarcely permitted contemplation of a future;
even after her conquest of him he had been so lost in the
delirium of her presence that no thought had been given to the
morrow.

"When thou and I are beyond — together," she answered
dreamily.

Paul, busy digesting the new suggestion, did not reply. He
had surrendered to her without fully realizing the
consequences. The death of ambition, of the scheme he knew
and to his own amazement, accepted content. But the
immediate future? They could not stay here indefinitely, nor
even in Fez, for the father of the girl would never consent to her
marriage with an Infidel.

She was a mere child, incredibly ignorant of everything from
a European standpoint. For a moment he hesitated, fearing to
ruin his own and her life. And again, could he be happy with
her?

He glanced at her, and she, seeming to divine his thoughts,
leaned forward and kissed him on the mouth. The clinging
warm lips drove the blood madly through his veins, banishing
all doubts and fears. Yes, he would have her for always, if it cost
him ten kingdoms! As he held her in his arms, gently,
reverently kissing her smooth forehead, some imaginary
likeness in the form of her eyebrows suggested Irene Trevelyan.

He leaned back to look at Zahra afresh and smiled. Physically
there was no comparison between the exotic flower-like beauty
of the child face and the cold, unsympathetic Northern features:
the English girl brought up in worldly knowledge and worship

of place and the Moorish maid, blissfully ignorant, trusting wholly in his love, an unspoiled child of nature.

And here a paradox: the child love wielding supreme power over him in whose hands she placed unreservedly her life to mold and keep.

The thought attracted him; he saw a vista of years in which she, taught under his tuition, should develop and enjoy her right as a seeing, understanding woman and wife, freed of Mohammedan bondage. No preconceived ideas to jar against his world experience; a virgin mind to which he would unroll the scroll of the world, a kaleidoscope of wonders, all under his guidance, to him would she owe everything! It was a fascinating idea and enthralled him. The months of scheming, risks and pains were consigned to oblivion. He had lived but for this moment and the future with her; summoning a new Pegasus, Zahra pillioned[221] beside him, he flew up to a new realm of fancy, guided by a soft-winged Aphrodite.

---

[221] Pillioned (chiefly British): on or as if on a pillion (a light saddle for women consisting chiefly of a cushion).

CHAPTER XX

A whisper from Fatma summoned Zahra away to the evening meal, absence from which would excite dangerous chatter among her women slaves; and Paul, lying in the gloom by the mosque, slowly awoke from his dream of love. The presence of Zahra seemed to stifle reason, so he told himself; the magic of her lips had hypnotized him, and as he gazed out at the gathering darkness, the bonds seemed broken, and with almost a shock he realized what he had decided to lose for her sake. Was it worth it? A fit of depression seized him, the finger of Ambition seemed beckoning to him. No, no! He must have been mad to have thought of it. No good could possibly come of such a rash union. They were as far apart as the Poles. In a month he would tire of her — and she of him. All Eastern women were fickle; they could not well be otherwise as children of nature.

Then a new point of view presented itself. Ought he not to have thrashed all this out before? Well, he had, with much satisfaction to himself; but Fate, that fickle jade,[222] had played him a scurvy trick! Hurled him right into the arms of the enemy, a most seductive enemy. Of course he ought to have retained his cast-iron reserve, but — her eyes — her lips! The very suggestion recalled the subtle thrills!

Scrambling to his feet as if affrighted at the possibility of her return ere he could summon courage to escape, he walked towards the door, and then paused as if loath to leave his prison. He conjured up her dismay and grief upon her return to find him flown, and bitterly he blamed himself for not having had the strength to save her fruitless pain.

He turned and looked back into the room. Poor little Zahra! How beautiful she was! He could see her, in imagination, sitting there, looking up at him with a world of devotion in those

---

[222] Jade: used here in the sense of a disreputable woman or flirtatious girl.

wonderful eyes. Love for her welled up in his heart. He took another step forward; then a flash of cruel memory showed him the past. He had had no doubt of Irene all through those weary months and years of captivity, and — well, all women were the same. True, he had not worshipped her so madly as he did Zahra, but in the first love there had been a stratum of cold sanity percurrent, while in this case, he admitted to himself with a dry laugh, there seemed little but midsummer madness. Belike[223] love is synonymous with insanity! O fortunate mortal who never recovers!

What should he do? Torn between the two desires, he swung first one way and then the other, until at last, in sheer terror and delighted anticipation lest Zahra might return, when he knew he would have no will at all, he turned and fled out into the violet-black shadows of the orchard. Stumbling over shrubs and stones, he groped his way back to the bank of the stream, pursued by a phantom Zahra bedewed with reproachful tears. He paused to consider where he should attempt the escape, but finding that his thoughts flew back to Zahra, he stumbled blindly forward lest he give way at the eleventh horn. Following along the bank, he came to the wall under which the stream gurgled into forbidding blackness. Stooping low in an unreasoning attempt to fathom the length of the tunnel, he saw to his surprise the twinkle of the stars at the other end. He stood up, casting a wistful look over his shoulder, hesitated, and then, hounded by the fear of love, plunged into the stream.

In a moment he found himself scrambling up the bank upon the other side. Something dark and furry rushed out of the darkness with a familiar shrill bark, which turned into a whimper of recognition. It was Kismet. Paul picked up the little dog, who whined disconsolately. Thinking that the Baron must be away, possibly endeavoring to mend his fortunes now that

---

[223] Belike (archaic): most likely; probably.

his competitor was bound for Acheron,[224] Paul made his way down the garden towards the house. A light glimmered yellow from the windows of the servants' room on the ground floor, from which floated the tinkle of someone playing the guinbri.

Advancing, Paul opened the tall, heavy doors and looked within. A candle, stuck in a bottle, feebly lit the hooded figure of Absalom lolling in the corner, the instrumentalist, who ceased abruptly. A smothered scream of fright drew Paul's attention past a group of other Moors to a shadowy figure lying upon a mattress wrapped in a djellaba, peering at him with startled eyes from under the hood.

"Ashkoon?" it gasped.

Paul recognized the voice.

"Don't you know me, Rabbit?" he asked in astonishment.

"Hamdullah!" ejaculated Rabbit. "Thou art alive!"

"Hamdullah!" echoed Absalom from the other end of the room, testifying to Paul's popularity by such exhibition of emotion.

"Yes, of course I'm alive," answered Paul, walking across to him, Kismet still in his arms. He had forgotten for the moment the tragic circumstances in which he had parted from the other.

"Heavens!" he exclaimed as memory returned, "where's El Cid?"

"El Cid? El Cid dead!" answered Rabbit in a normal voice, sinking back. "Where you go? How you not dead?"

"Poor brute!" said Paul; "and you, Rabbit — weren't you injured?"

"'Jured?"

"Yes, shot."

"Shot? Him ibn Iblees shot me here" — he pointed to the region of his right side.

"Poor old Rabbit! And then?"

---

[224] Acheron: a river in Hades.

"Then?"

"Yes, what did the man do?"

"Throw you in water — you not know? — and run away. 'Nother chap he come bym-by[225] and con-s'quently — cons'quently — "

"You're here, eh?"

"Yes, me here, ole chap. Where you go?"

"Oh, I came up — on the other side — all right — only a bang on the head."

"Awfly good, ole chap! Den where you go?"

"Where's the Baron?" inquired Paul, ignoring the question.

"Baron? He dead, too."

"What!" exclaimed Paul, startled.

"What!" mimicked Rabbit solemnly. "Baron he dead — Praise be to Allah!"

"How?"

"How? dunno, ole chap," answered Rabbit cheerfully.

"Absalom," said Paul, turning round. "Where is the master-of-the-little-dog?"

"Nay, I know not, O Pole."

"What the devil's the matter with you all?" exclaimed Paul angrily, looking round at the others. "Speak, Absalom! A man cannot disappear as a dog!"

"No?" interrupted Rabbit, grinning. "You disappear orlright — two times!"

And Paul was compelled to admit the truth of that statement.

"Be quiet. You, Absalom, speak!"

"Yillah, we know not," answered Absalom. "Today at the hour of ten in the morning, he rode forth. We have not seen him since. Neither is he at the Palace. He was seen by the soldiers

---

[225] He come bym-by: phonetic rendering of "he came by and by" (i.e., he came later).

who sit at the gate of El Bushat. We know no more —
Minshallah!"

"Why did you say he was dead?" demanded Paul of Rabbit.

"What the heart desireth the tongue would speak," answered
Rabbit oracularly, and with solemn dignity he turned away.

Paul frowned in perplexity.

"What thinkest thou hath happened?" he enquired of
Absalom.

"Minshallah! (It is as Allah wills!)" replied Absalom, picking
up the discarded guinbri.

"Rabbit, confound you!" cried Paul, irritated, "d'you hear?
Tell me what you think. You must think something?"

"Minshallah!" echoed a muffled voice, and after a pause: "we
shall see what will come out of him! — Goo' night, ole chap."

Paul tossed sleepless all night. The thought of Zahra, grief
stricken, haunted him, interrupting speculations upon the
position of affairs now that the Baron had apparently been
removed. Of course he might return at any moment. It was only
Rabbit's surmise that he was dead. Rabbit, Paul thought, knew
or guessed more than he would say. Paul tried to feel really
grieved at the thought of de Bouche's death, but in fact he felt
callously pleased. He was confident that only the mysterious
ways of Providence had saved him from a like end at the
Baron's hands or instigation. The news, in fact, gave a fillip to
the scheme. Now there would be small likelihood of any
international complications. All evidence, practically, for and
against the German party disappeared with the Baron. All Paul
had to do was to secure the signed concessions, and the rest lay
with the British Government, whose promise of support rested
in his dispatch case. Yet Zahra? He felt a wave of longing surge
afresh within him. He turned over, face to the wall, as if
banishing her memory. Racked between the two greatest forces
which move humanity, Ambition and Love, he tossed till the

summons to prayer vibrated in the still night air, heralding the coming dawn.

Late in the morning Paul awoke, harassed and tired with the mental struggle. For the present Ambition held the lead again.

His first inquiry was for news of the missing Baron, solely lamented by the disconsolate Kismet. The Baron had not returned; neither was there news of him. Rabbit, with determined cheerfulness, insisted that he was dead.

Haunted by the feeling of invisible hands trying to hold him back, Paul made his way, with the papers in his pocket, to the Palace, to which, after an unusually short wait of an hour, he was admitted. He found El Hammo, who had just returned from Marakesh where he had been acting as Viceroy, in audience with the Sultan, together with a stranger, magnificently robed, wearing a gilt embroidered turban, indicating a native of Algiers. This man Paul guessed to be Drees Ali[226] the dragoman-envoy of the French Legation, and accordingly determined to avoid any reference to the concessions in his presence. To Paul's surprise and annoyance Abd-el-Kader, who beamed upon the French agent with genial affability, went straight to the point as soon as etiquette permitted.33

"And the papers concerning the affair which thou wouldst have?" he asked, in a cold, contemptuous voice.

Paul felt the agent's eyes watching him keenly.

"It is of no matter — " he commenced nervously.

"La, la! no, no," the Sultan interrupted angrily. "Hast thou them with thee — as I commanded?"

Paul flushed with annoyance and silently withdrew them from his pocket, wondering what course the Sultan was about

---

[226] Drees Ali: an English phonetic rendering of a person named Idrīs 'Alī, whom the author portrays as an interpreter or go-between (dragoman) from the French legation.

to take. He had imagined that Abd-el-Kader had wished to ignore or pretend indifference in the company of the French representative. To his horror, the Sultan, with a glance at the agent, unrolled the manuscript, and with a quick twist of his wrist, tore it in half. The Frenchman smiled triumphantly; the Sultan looked calmly at Paul, who bit his lip in the endeavor to suppress his anger and annoyance. El Hammo, as usual, wore the expressionless mask of a Burmese idol. The papers rustled to the floor, and for a while no word was spoken, all eyes watching Paul in his almost futile effort to appear unconcerned. He saw himself made a fool of before this sneering agent by the man whom he had suffered much to help, who had sworn and professed such enmity to the French. His friends would laugh, too, to see a newcomer snatch the reward of months of toil, hardship and risk from beneath his nose. How they would laugh at Tanga at this man who was going to build empires, alter destinies of nations! And harder still was it to sit there and appear indifferent. He felt that he could give the world to be able to thrash the two sneering Moors. How they would laugh at the infidel! He felt he dare not trust himself to speak. There the three sat, El Hammo the only merciful one in his impassivity, smiling at the baiting of the Christian!

With an effort he rose, bowed ceremoniously, and backing out of the little house, stalked down the steps and away to the gate, impotent fury and chagrin surging within him. And as he mounted his horse, angrily refusing the customary tip to the attendants, there rang out, clear and resonant, the call of the Mueddhin:

"Al-lah — Ak-ba-ah!"

There seemed a mocking note mingling with the ever-present suggestion of implacable destiny. The very Fates were laughing at this presumptuous puppet! He drove his horse recklessly along the narrow crowded streets towards the city gate, raising an angry chorus of curses in his wake. Once out in the open plain, he gave his restive horse his head, and out of sheer mad impotence, drove his spurs home savagely.

The shadows had crept far across the plain as the sun sank below the western hills when Paul turned his reeking besweated steed towards Fez. Riding at a saner gait along the silver stream of the Wad Fas, where the tortoises flopped in amphibious play and the wild duck sailed upstream, he, in a saner mood, endeavored to readjust the perspective. Of course Zahra had immediately occupied his thoughts, and although the longing for her was intensified by the collapse of the house of ambition, he felt that he would be a sorry lover who returned to his mistress when all other charms had vanished. Yet, argued another view, such a course would be the better as apart from his own feelings, it would give her happiness. He had already forgotten the arguments anent the fickleness of Moorish women and the general incompatibility of their personalities: views are so often the child of inclination by selfish ambition. A reaction after the ebullition of violent anger set in; he felt morbid, pessimistic. What was the use of anything? He had failed miserably and ignominiously. And Zahra? No, he could not bring himself to think of returning to her. He would never forgive himself if he did so; and moreover, it would mean many complicated responsibilities. He dare not undertake anything again. He would return to the coast and bury himself in the Far East somewhere, away from the scene of his ignoble and eternal disgrace.

It was dark as he rode up to the nearest town gate to find it closed. All are shut at sundown save the main gate of El Bushat. He hammered irritably on the door for admittance. No answer; although he could hear the noise of soldiery within. With angry humiliation he rode away, thinking that they knowing him to be an infidel, contemptuously refused to stir; always sensitive, though this undercurrent of Mohammedan contempt for the Christian he morbidly exaggerated.

Half-an-hour later he rode under the big main gate, and passed through the jostling mob of the outer market. Under the next inner gate he caught sight of a familiar face in the glare of a candle lantern. It was Larbi Gibilo. Paul pulled up beside the man, a sudden thought suggesting that he might know something about the mystery of the Baron's disappearance.

"Salkhair, ya Larbi!"

The man peered up, asking "Ashkoon?"

"El Pole."

"Salkhair!" exclaimed the other, extending his left hand in greeting.

Paul bent over the saddle to watch the man's face.

"What hast thou done with the-master-of-the-little-dog?"

Larbi hesitated a moment and then laughed.

"Allah knoweth!"

"Thou knowest also!"

"Inshallah!" smiling broadly.

"Hath Abdullah come into his own?"

The other nodded, still smiling.

"How?"

A significant sweep of the fingers across the throat answered him.

Towards midnight Paul, still suffering from insomnia, miserable, and unable to make up his mind to leave Fez without seeing Zahra once more, wandered upon the roof under the brilliant heavens.

A gentle wind whispered lightly among the treetops; a dog yelped dismally afar, and from the quarters below came the twanging of Absalom's guinbri. Paul ceased his peripatetic promenade and rested himself upon the low parapet overlooking Zahra's garden. His thoughts wandered back over all the occasions upon which he had seen her.

The nocturnal idyll fantasized in his mind. How superbly beautiful and graceful was she! A Moorish Cleopatra! And apropos a thought suggestive of himself as Antony! But alas! he had no kingdom now to throw away for sweet woman's sake. Was Antony's choice wiser than his choosing? Well, what did it matter? Fate had already settled that for him. How cruel were the caprices of Fate! Why had he not been left alone to seek oblivion and obscurity in his own way? Why drag him into this maelstrom only to be buffeted cruelly between ambition and love and in the end to fling his choice in his teeth with contumely?

What was Zahra doing? Sleeping, or awake, thinking, grieving for him? Should he go to her? He had through his cursed weakness and indecision caused her pain before. No! he should crawl away somewhere where he could neither make a fool of himself nor hurt innocent people.

The sound of voices arose from the street, and he idly noticed the pale yellow glare of a lantern in the blue darkness, flitting along like a huge will-o'-the-wisp. Will-o'-the-wisp, yes! He had been fluttering like a foolish moth between two distant lights, and the chosen one had proved but a will-o'-the-wisp.

The light below became stationary, the hum of voices in excited argument rose. What were those belated men intent upon? More madness and sin tainted with horror! He looked up and across the filmy white roofs and minarets, ghostly, tall, losing themselves amid the whispering trees, violet black against the crystal-studded blue of the night sky, the east growing faint and paler in homage to fair Cynthia's dawn.

An impatient hammering upon a door reverberated. The chant and accompaniment of Absalom's voice floated up serenely from below. The knocking recommenced with greater vigor. A voice shouted "Absalom!"

Paul realized that the summons was at his own door. What could they want? His entrée to the palace was a thing of the past. Absalom's voice continued singing, weird in the peculiar minor key what time the pounding of the door increased.[227] At length the tall doors of the room opened, someone came out and went to the street door. Commotion, expostulations, and the man returned and mounted leisurely to the balcony. Paul heard him knocking at his door, and wondering, went down.

The Hadjib sent word that the Sultan commanded Paul's presence immediately. What could it mean?

The light of hope shot up in Paul's heart. He was ready, and proceeded to the door to await his horse. A thought struck him. He had a duplicate of the concession papers, why not take them? He did — in case!

After several halts at the closed gates of each ward they emerged outside the city walls. Paul recognized where he was being led. Along the open plain in the shadow of the palace garden walls to the end; round over a cobblestone bridge spanning the Wad Fas before it enters the town to be split up into a thousand subterranean channels; and down the eastern wall as far as the disused tramway, running beside an aqueduct, to the summer palace two miles away; here, at a small gate, they entered.

In a brilliant flood of electric light within a plain, whitewashed room, Abd-el-Kader was seated upon a low divan, a mass of papers and heaps of coins beside him. Nearby sat the Hadjib in attendance.

The Sultan acknowledged Paul's reserved greeting with an amused smile. After the Hadjib had been dismissed, he said quietly:

"Truly, by Allah, thou art an Englishman!"

Paul looked bewildered, at which Abd-el-Kader laughed.

"Didst not know that it is good to fool the dog of a Frenchman?"

---

[227] In this sentence the word "what" is an archaic or literary adverb meaning "while" or "at the same time that."

"Ah!" exclaimed Paul eagerly.

"Hast thou the papers?"

Paul produced them quietly, with an assumed air of astuteness.

The Sultan nodded as he took them.

"Yillah! Thou art not so foolish! The Frenchman hath a cheap victory!"

"But why shouldst thou so dissemble?" inquired Paul.

"Yillah! Thy government hath not yet befriended me. Should I offend the lion before I know the gun is loaded? He is well pleased, and will make a report to his people so that they will not press me."

He commenced to read the Arabic version of the proposed articles of the concession, pausing now and again to discuss afresh and question various clauses, and upon finishing, bade Paul translate the English portion, shrewdly comparing it with the version in his hand.

"Good," said he upon completion. "It is as we have agreed."

He called aloud for the Hadjib, bidding him produce the seal.

After all the formalities were over and the concession with the Imperial Seal affixed to the head in Paul's pocket, the Sultan dismissed the Hadjib and invited Paul to walk with him in the garden.

The crescent moon, now well above the horizon, lit up the garden in ghostly radiance as the two, white clad, walked and talked.

"Tell me, O Nazarene," the Sultan had said, "what think thy people of me and my people?"

"Few understand," answered Paul veraciously. "The majority know little of thee and thy country, The taste of the days of Mulai Ismael remains still upon their tongue, and to them it is a far-distant country where all is darkness."

"Darkness? Where then is light? Is not life but as a garden of shadows: so fair to look upon in moonlit glamour, yet lurking within denser shapes of horrors grim, felt, not seen. That is my life and my country. Is it not the same with thine, or do ye scorn us as we do ye because we are the chosen of Allah?"

A note of irony crept in the Sultan's voice.

Paul smiled covertly.

"Aye, that is so. A man ever hath hate in his heart for those that believe not as he believes. Yet our life is lived in a fiercer light, perhaps for the better — Allah alone knows."

"True," returned Abd-el-Kader. "And yet in the days of El Mahmud were the infidels in the darkness and Islam the seat of the learning of the world, and before him, in the days of Sidna Ali and El Khalid, the Sword of God! — Yillah, what a man! — we drove all before us and ruled the world. Yet are we fallen on harder times, alas! Wherefore is it?"

"History telleth us ever the same story. When a man waxeth great and fat, he becomes gross and given to indulgence and pleasure; the enemy, hard with fasting and strife, riseth against the great man, who, as a mighty tree overburdened with branches, falleth to the ground. So has it been with ye and with the empires of the Infidels aforetime!"

"A-ah! Sidi Assmai hath so prophesied:

> Lest eyes do turn in cold despair,
> Remember! Once we too were hound
> And chased far the trembling hare:
> Much credit to us then redound,
> Our super-prowess heed!
> But see, if ye would further seek:
> The eagle hovers still above
> The soft-eyed yet arrogant dove.
> An eagle! But with palsied beak
> From glutton-bellied feed!

They are true words — yet would I be the champion of my faith to rise again," he added, after a pause. "But — Mektub!"

"Inshallah!" from Paul quietly.

For a moment or two the Sultan was lost in thought.

"Thou with all thy race, look with arrogance and contempt upon the Mohammedan world?" he observed, a note of resentment in his voice.

"Some, yes: but who looketh with more contempt upon the Infidel than the True Believer?"

"The people, yes; for so it is written" (in the Koran) "but those amongst the learned know full well, though they will never acknowledge, that the power of the Infidel is supreme — now."

"It is ever the same," replied Paul. "The masses are ever blind in thought and deed, Infidel or Mohammedan."

The Sultan nodded.

"Aye, they are but children. But what think thy wise men?"

"Who knows?" answered Paul.

"Aye," said Abd-el-Kader smiling. "A wise man revealeth not his heart! And thou?"

"Am I not a wise man?" queried Paul smiling.

The Sultan laughed in response.

"El Bashador Fransawi is at Shragna. What wilt thou say, for they will surely question thee?"

"By what right?" inquired Paul. "I am not compelled to answer to them. And thou?"

Abd-el-Kader smiled craftily.

"Is the Frenchman my father? As Allah wills!"

"And the Rogui — what of him?"

"Bu Hamu hath sent word that the son of Iblees hath lost the confidence of the Kabyles; they return to their homes and to me, to swear allegiance. The days of El Rogui are numbered."

"Is his price high?"

"Allah knows; but they have the greed of El Rumi (Romans); however Bu Hamu hath sent three hundred trophies of his victories."

Paul smiled at the remembrance of the valiant Bu Hamu.

"I would speak with thee concerning that custom," said he.

"Of what custom speak ye?"

"Of the cutting off heads and hands, and the crucifixion of prisoners. Such doth thee much harm in the eyes of the nations of Europe; of England in particular. Thy enemies use it against thee. The French cry out that — "

"Enough!" interrupted the Sultan angrily. "Why should I conform to the womanish practices of the Infidels? Hath England helped me that I should strip my beard in the eyes of my people for her sake?"

He continued to pace up and down, more perturbed and angry than Paul had ever seen him.

"Ye speak with the words of a fool! What think ye they would do to me an they could? What saith the Prophet? 'Pursue them with fire and sword the unbelievers and they that ill treat ye until not one is left in the land.' Am I to be disgraced before all men and branded a coward, afraid to punish mine enemies in the sight of all men, a warning and a threat to those who scoff at the word of the Prince of the Faithful? What am I? A poltroon? a coward? Am I to take the men whom the Prophet hath delivered into my hands, feed, clothe, and keep them, that in due course they may go forth, well and strong, to raise their hand and voice against me, crying: 'See Abd-el-Kader, the fool, who is weak and would conciliate his enemies, in the words of a woman or a slave?' Have not the nations agreed to respect the independence of Morocco? Where are the words of the Sultan of Germany at Tanga, to protect the integrity and independence of Morocco? Yet would ye have them dictate my own affairs! If in my wrath I wound thee or thy fellow Infidel — 'tis well. I will pay as my father before — since Islam hath sickened. There were other days when ye paid tribute to the Faithful of Mahommed! Yillah! would that I had the hosts of Khalid, the Sword of God! But in the time of the father of Mulai Hassan came your infidel envoys upon their bended knee to the footstool of the King of Fez, pleading that the slaves of Nazarenes, who built yonder wall," — he pointed an imperious hand — "should be released for their weight in gold. Think ye that we can forget the Alhambra or the mighty Empire of Istamboul?"

In silence Paul had watched this ebullition of haughty rage, the Sultan's eyes flashing angrily.

"And now" — the angry voice dropped to a soft resigned whisper — "what Allah willeth!"

A pause ensued, during which a cricket shrilled its contempt for the affairs of men and nations; the increscent moon sailed swiftly through a ruck of wind-whipped clouds; a peal of woman's laughter echoed afar, the gurgling whisper of running water from out the violet-black shadows of the vast gardens.

"I am not a child," resumed the Sultan's voice, in a calm tone. "I know those things, but think ye 'tis easier to bear, knowing?"

"Nay," answered Paul. "I know too. I did but speak for thy policy's good."

"Aye, that is so. But see ye not that mine enemies would account such leniency mere weakness — fear?"

"Yea, I know that too, for have I not lived amongst the tribes, as I have told, and eaten of the fruit of experience? But is it not wise to weigh native expediency with foreign diplomacy?"

"Thine are true words. I will think on it."

As Paul rode home with the first call to prayer ringing above him, ever mindful of capricious Fate, his brain bade him be joyful, for the thing which he desired was certain of accomplishment; but yet he could not, for a gentle hand tugged persistently at his heartstrings.

Zahra! her eyes haunted him as of yore. He felt in the hour of his triumph as if he had done a mean action, something to be ashamed of. Yet what man, worldly man, would not have applauded his decision? yea, and even scoffed at the pain it had cost him.

As he rode through the narrow streets, the sounds of a melee, the glimmer of lanterns, came from a side street.

Another victim being hailed away to a living death, his goods confiscated to the rapacity of the god in the car. For what? Merely perhaps a difference of opinion, or inability to pay some extortionate sum demanded of him. Would the country ever be anything but a den of barbarians, even with progress and a modicum of civilization? Could the leopard change his spots? Paul in a moment of pessimism (or sanity?) doubted it. The people, by means of a really efficient army and police, might be kept in to a nearer semblance of sane law and order; but the rulers? From the Sultan to the meanest water carrier, all were utterly corrupt. Yet, thought Paul, short of a complete revolution in the environment they could never be ruled otherwise; at least, not for a generation or two. The law of "might is right" had been born and bred in them for centuries, and however much any individual might cry out against the iron hand of the Sultan, each and every man did the same when opportunity permitted. The preceding Sultan had been a weak man, who listened to the advice of rapacious European advisers, filling their pockets at the expense of the country, and treating the people with a gentle, civilized, hand, with the consequence that he depleted the treasury and turned his people against him; they forgot to fear him, knowing that he was weak, a ruler afraid!

And yet the poetry emanating from the people and the country! Light, color and sunshine never seen in a Northern clime. The filthiest beggar "a joy and delight forever"[228] in the eyes of an artist. The glamour of the East, with its baffling odors, wondrous unconscious artistry — and that all-pervading horror and mystery. The very houses with their windowless exteriors and forbidding metal-bound doors seemed pregnant with numberless ghastly secrets of vice and crime.

Ragged clouds were massing near the distant virgin peaks of the Atlas, through which struggled the soaring moon in fitful gleams, heralding the commencement of the rainy season.

As Paul dismounted the man hammered on the door, picturesque and mediaeval in the lantern's yellow glare. The knocking reverberated through the silent house. A scream rang out in the night air, breaking in upon the chant:

"Allah il allah ilia la il alla-ah!"

Paul started. Silence till the Mueddhin intoned again the callous cry. Zahra? No; in the wrong direction, but — she might be dead by now. Anything was possible in this city of dreadful horror! He felt himself go icy cold at the idea. Kismet's shrill bark sounded within, followed by Absalom's low voice muffled through the heavy iron-studded door. Kismet! Allah akbah!

But the puppet of Fate! He frowned at the suggestion of relentless Destiny pervading the whole atmosphere. Bah! enough of moralising in the moonlight, the glamour of night was affecting his nerves. Tomorrow, glorious tomorrow, with the goal of ambition golden-hued in the rising sun!

---

[228] A paraphrase of "A thing of beauty is a joy for ever," from Keats' poem "Endymion."

CHAPTER XXI

A certain fox once coveted some grapes — an old story. His disparaging remarks were human, but one might wonder whether, had the fox tasted of those grapes, would they have been as sweet as he anticipated? Hardly — at least, if human nature be consistent at all. Paul awoke, to his surprise, to find the first few grapes of success singularly dry and flavorless. He had long contemplated this moment, when the first vital rung of the ladder had been won. The joy of success seemed turned to ashes. He felt as if he had bought this empty triumph with the happiness of another, of an innocent Zahra's. He had struggled hard to suppress those insistent tuggings at his heartstrings, but they would not be denied. And now it seemed that whatever happened, whatever further honors awaited him, even as the Cromer of Morocco, that a bitter flavor of regret would ever tinge the sparkling draught of worldly success. A mental picture sprang unbidden: of himself in years to come, an honored power in the land, driven from the scene of his triumph by haunting big eyes and childish face in a tawny halo of hair. Himself the British Resident, wearing full orders bestowed for services to the country, presiding at the ceremony of the first railway train to enter Fez, sad-eyed, and loathing himself and everybody else for the fantasy of that girlish face. Many a man is ever haunted by the face of her whom they have sacrificed for the bauble of Fame! She might marry! The thought stung him like a whiplash. And be happy? He knew too well that the fate of a Moorish wife — to any woman, even one with an animal temperament — could be naught but a living hell.

He tried to put an end to his tormenting thoughts by the stern resolution that no matter what it cost him now he had passed the Rubicon at his own choice.

As he sat sunning himself upon the balcony after a late breakfast, and while the last firm resolution lingered in his mind, came the soft twanging of a guinbri across the orange-scented gardens, accompanying a girl's voice:

Love, could I doubt thee? Nay, but my soul
Faint unto death may ne'er reach thy goal.

The familiar minor plaint seared him like a hot brand. The aura of the Lady of the Eyes seemed to envelop him, stifling all sordid ambition, and fanning the slumbering embers of love to flaming fire. He almost writhed in torture exquisite[,] summoning all his strength to resist, conscious that all his being bade him yield, yet feeling a savage delight in denying himself. The song ceased in a choking sob halfway through a verse, whereat Paul, to relieve his feelings, ejaculated "Damn!" and incontinently fled below, calling for his horse.

As he reached the bottom step, in a frenzy of haste to flee from the plaintive voice, a thunderous hammering came upon the outer door, and amid a babel of guttural sounds, a hoarse voice rang out, erratic but triumphant:

It orlrig — hic — right in shumma time — hic — luf — hic — ly!

and the door, opened suddenly by Absalom, disclosed the estimable Rabbit, rampant, in the arms of four black-garbed Jews. For a moment his rolling eyes stopped, and he ceased from struggling as he gazed stupidly at Paul.

"Hurra — y!" he roared, wildly waving one free arm, as the Jews bore him bodily inside.

"It orlright — hic — " he began again.

"Be quiet, thou son of a pig," exclaimed Paul sharply, as Rabbit developed a paroxysm of rage, struggling frantically with his bearers. He became passive at the sound of Paul's voice, and leered at him stupidly.

"Hullo, ole — hic — chap," he mumbled. "Awfly good — ge' drunk. Why — hic — you no ge' drunk — hic — whaat?"

Paul, instructing the men to carry the reprobate to his room, mounted his horse and rode off.

Rabbit, lying upon his bed in the servants' quarters, became maudlin confidential to Absalom, who, grinning hugely, listened to this wayward son of the Prophet.

"Yillah," spoke Rabbit, "who can understand the heart of an Infidel? — hic — Many years have I dwelt — hic — in Tanga and many Infidels — hic — have I seen. Is it not — hic — the will of all to drink — hic — of the grape until Allah smiteth them — hic — with the road upon which they walk? — hic — Yet my friend hath ever been wont to walk upright — hic — strange — very strange. Yow!" he shouted hoarsely, clinging to the side of the bed. "Iblees gallops beneath my bed — a-ah!"

"O Absalom," he continued after the devil had consented to stand still, "I have a great love for El Pole, yet — hic — will he not drink of the grape with me. Waali! Waali! — And again, thinking to find favor — hic — in his sight, did I buy a maiden like unto the moon for him — hic — yet did he scourge me with whips — hic — driving her forth whence she came — hic — ." He shook his head slowly and despondently. "Yet all other Infidels — hic — would have showered much gold upon me — a — hic — ah! strange are thy ways, O Pole — hic."

Rabbit cautiously clambered to a sitting posture, looking mournfully at Absalom.

"Thou son of a fool!" he suddenly shouted. "Thou pig of a Mohammedan! — hic — Truly am I a N'srani. It is good to be a Christian," he adjured Absalom, lapsing into a quiet tone. "Ah! mezian bizaff![229] — hic — Truly a N'srani doeth what seemeth good to him — hic — in particular of the grape. All — all except El Pole. Why doth not El Pole wallow in the grape — hic?" he

---

[229] Mezian bizaff: Mzyān bzāf. Very good.

demanded querulously, and then, lapsing into English, "My fren' Jack — y'know Jack — hic — Lefften't Ro'ley? he get drunk — hic — offen. Very drunk — offen. Awf'ly good — Awf'ly — hic — ge' drunk. Me ge' drunk offen — awfly offen, ole — hic — chap, conshewuently — "

He collapsed on the bed, and clutched it wildly, staring horror-struck at the ceiling. "Oh yow — yow!" he bawled, pouring out a string of English oaths, until exhausted he fell asleep.

In vino veritas.[230]

Meanwhile Paul rode on immersed in thought of the probable immediate results of his schemes, punctuated by thoughts of Zahra. As he returned from a long ride amongst the olive-clad hills to the plain without the town, his eye was arrested by the unusual sight of a figure in European garb, an alien spot in the Eastern scena, crying aloud in a sharp contrast. The man rode at the head of a small mule caravan, plodding in the shade of the old walls towards the Bab-el-Bushat.

As Paul galloped on he took stock of the stranger, noting the leggings, Norfolk jacket, a suggestive bulge in one pocket, and felt hat that immediately classed him as a correspondent; a closer view confirmed the diagnosis in the person of an old friend. He experienced a sense of mild curiosity at the familiar yet strange garb of civilization which he had not seen for so many months.

The stream of Moors passing and repassing afoot and mounted regarded the daring Infidel with mixed expressions. He glanced up as Paul thundered alongside, but no light of recognition stirred behind the calm gray eyes.

Paul rode silent at a walk alongside him, amused that this man whom he had known for years, a fellow clubman,[231] should fail to penetrate through the oriental mask.

---

[230] In vino veritas: In wine there is truth.

Alan Netherby stared quietly at him as if faintly annoyed by the close scrutiny, until Paul suddenly laughed.

The look of mild amazement at this incongruous hilarity faded to delighted surprise as Paul said quietly:

"Come and have a cocktail, Bunny?"

"Well, I'm damned!" exclaimed Netherby, reining in. "Towers!"

"Yes, me all right," responded Paul, shaking hands. "Gad! but I'm glad to see a Christian!"

"Are you? You don't look one yourself. Gad, what a splendid makeup!"

"Makeup be hanged, I'm perfectly natural. But how come you to be here?"

"Oh, for the 'Courier' as usual. Just got back from the Balkans — oh, what a giddy time! tell you later — and the old man sent me off here at three hours' notice. Found the French Mission ahead of me, so came along on my own, but skirted their camp last night. Two other parties of Europeans behind, too. German crowd and a Spanish doctor along with the Britishers. Now come the ruck,[232] you see."

"Yes," said Paul smiling. "Fez will be too common soon with all you tourists arriving!"

Netherby laughed.

"Gad, man! but you have set 'em talkin'. Oh, Ho! what a lot of ink spilt over you! Old man's great on you. Got to make a special feature of you. Gad, you're a daisy. Radicals say you

---

[231] The character Alan Netherby is based on Beadle's friend and fellow Frontiersman Alan Ostler, a correspondent for the *Daily Express* who was in Fes during this period. Ostler filed reports about the situation in Morocco, particularly after the Battle of Marrakech, and conducted the first published interview with the new sultan on 24 September 1908: "Mulai Hafid's Policy: Message to Europe from the Moorish Sultan." For more on Ostler, see my Afterword.

[232] Ruck: the usual run of persons or things.

ought to be caught and hung; Tories say you ought to be given a peerage."

"Why, what d'you know anyway?" inquired Paul, with a conscious thrill of pleasure.

"Know? Why, you've been the salvation of the hour in the dead season. Boomed you all over London, and someone's been talkin' — inspired information. You're top-hole, sonny. France started shrieking blue murder, Kaiser thundered threats and — climbed down as usual. It's all been settled quietly as a matter of fact; and you and Abd-el-Kader are the heroes of the hour. Come along, I'm dying for a drink. Can you put me up?"

"Yes, of course. M'm — er — yes."

Netherby, understanding, rode along in silence, giving Paul time to digest the latest news.

CHAPTER XXII

That evening Paul and Netherby sat long over cigarettes and coffee in the courtyard. Paul, shut away from the world, had not realized the fame he had attained as the man who by his daring had pulled the Moroccan chestnut out of the fire and had nearly embroiled Europe in a general conflagration. Although not prone to vulgar flattery, yet he had not been human had the news not acted as oil to the fires of ambition. For a while at least the promptings of his heart were stilled, the haunting ghost of Zahra laid.

Netherby, tired with the day's hot ride, retired early to bed, leaving Paul to ride Pegasus as high as he listed. A little after midnight the moon arose, and Paul, too excited to think of sleep, arose to go upon the rooftop. As he strode across the courtyard, a dark, furry shadow trotted after him. He lifted Kismet up in his arms.

"Well, little man, how is it?" said he, as the little dog licked his face. "Kismet, old man, you have to smile upon me at last. Thy ways are varied but sure. Come, little one, tell me that all is settled — for the best."

A short, sharp bark answered him. In his arms Paul carried him to the rooftop, a fitting companion in his hour of triumph.

From what Netherby had told him, he gathered more than sufficient to corroborate the views he had formed, which again were far more than he had dared to hope. The initial struggle was over, and barring physical accidents, his success was more than assured. No dream now; one of those wildcat schemes, such as Clive and others dreamed of, fait accompli.

He suddenly thought of Irene Trevelyan. She would have heard of him. How she would wish that she had waited and how envious she would be of his brilliant future! He felt doubly thankful now that all had happened as it had, and caressed Kismet anew with tender gratitude.

Zahra! Ah! he had banished her name and image from his thoughts, and although he resolutely remained at the far end of the roof, he was conscious of a force impelling him to have just one glimpse.

As a sort of charm against the influence he repeated to himself a list of honors awaiting him.

As he sat upon the low parapet, the distant sound of Moorish music floated over to him. It was from the direction of the palace, and he vaguely wondered for what occasion the rejoicings might be. Another marriage festival for Abd-el-Kader, thought he, with a smile. Then his ears, more keenly attuned, caught a faint sobbing from out the violet darkness of the gardens. Zahra? He had started nervously; and, angry with himself, returned below, plunged in torment afresh at the bare suggestion of a plea from Zahra.

Then again, as he worked round to his golden future, successfully consigning Zahra to oblivion, and in the midst of pride of accomplishment, came the cry of the Mueddhin, to remind him to whom the credit.

"Al-lah — Ak-ba-ah!"

All the vanity died within him at the first tremulous notes. Of what use was fame, place and honor? Only in vain imagination, illusion. Puppets of Fate! He tossed Kismet off the bed irritably.

"Oh, go to the devil!" he exclaimed petulantly and as if addressing an unseen person. "Oh, let me alone! Why can't you let me alone. And you, Kismet, you beast! I'm not happy now I have got it! What is the matter with me?"

A murmur of voices arose in the courtyard beneath, the slip-slop of native shoes up the stairs and along the terrace, and the figure of Rabbit loomed in the doorway.

"Ya Pole," he whispered excitedly.

Paul lay still, feigning sleep.

"I say, ole chap!"

Kismet barked shrilly as Rabbit advanced into the room.

"Well?" said Paul, sitting up.

"I say, ole chap," began Rabbit, by the bedside. "Him come see you."

He paused to chuckle wheezily.

"Him? Who?" queried Paul angrily.

"He! he! he! You no like girls, eh?" returned Rabbit in the darkness. "He! He! Awf'ly good! Awf'ly good!"

"What the devil are you talking about, you infernal fool? You're drunk again. Go to bed!"

"Bed? Me no drunk — not now. Me very bad head — me walk in garden — me meet him. Yillah! awf'ly good girl! — awfly — "

"Confound you," exclaimed Paul irritably, sitting up. "What d'you mean?"

"Mean? Him awf'ly — he, he!"

"Oh, damn you! Don't giggle like an hysterical girl!"

"Girl? Yes, him girl want see you. Awf'ly —"

"Girl wants see me? Me?"

"You wait — me bring — he-he!"

Rabbit shuffled out of the room, whilst Paul, still uncomprehending, sat on the bed, perplexed, half imagining it to be some new vagary of Rabbit's.

"Come thou!" he heard Rabbit's voice whisper outside. Then the shuffle of small feet, and the muffled figure of a woman stood in the doorway, water dripping from her soaked draperies.

"Ashkoon?" inquired Paul nervously, his heart giving a great leap as he caught the glimmer of the big eyes peering over the haik, and heard the half-controlled sobbing breath.

Kismet ran towards her, sniffing an investigation, and whimpered in approbation.

"O Pole!" whispered the gentle voice of Zahra.

"My God! Zahra," he exclaimed, and leaping off the bed, rushed to her, enfolding the dripping figure in his arms.

"What doth thou here, little one?" he inquired tenderly.

In answer she buried her head against his shoulder, sobbing unrestrainedly, whilst Paul held her trembling form the closer and Kismet wagged his absurd tail delightedly, peering up at the twain. Paul, glancing across the moonlit gardens, beheld Rabbit leaning against the rail, grinning extensively.

"Go away! Go to the devil!" whispered Paul, in sudden anger. "Go away! Emshi!"

"Me?" queried Rabbit placidly.

"Oh, damn you, will you go away! You fool!"

"Fool? Oh, you — you liver dambad, ole chap. Goo' night!" said Rabbit, gathering his robes together. "And you no like girl, eh?" he muttered as he walked away. "Oh! no like girl! Oh! Goo' night!"

Sitting on the threshold, Paul held the quivering girl in silence until the paroxysm of weeping had given place to a clinging calm.

"Tell me, O little one," he said again, "what hath happened?"

"O, my Beloved, canst ask why the flower would ope its petals to the kisses of the sun? O Pole, I love thee! Life is no life to me without thee. Can a flower grow if the sun be hidden? And moreover I have much to tell thee — much that thou couldst not know, O Pole. Hearest thou the sound of the cymbal and the guinbri in the gardens of the Prince of the Faithful? They are for me! Oh, waali! waali! Woe is me!"

"For thee?" exclaimed Paul, unconsciously clasping her the closer.

"Yes, for me, woe is me. Yet will I never be his bride. By Allah I swear it. Never! If thou wilt not take me, then is my life sped,[233] for without thee there is no life."

---

[233] Sped (archaic usage): the past tense and past participle of the verb speed, meaning "to bring to a conclusion, to dispatch, to kill" (Middle English / early Modern English). Hence, "my life is sped" = "my life is over."

"What meanest thou, little one? They would betroth thee — to whom?"

"Listen!" With an impetuous gesture she loosed herself from his clasp, and with a quick movement cast aside the haik and outer cloak, standing, a tragic figure, on the threshold of his room, the moon rays bathing the glories of her face and figure in glamorous beauty. "Listen! But two moons ago I, Zahra, played in the gardens of my father with my women and my slaves, and all the world was beautiful. No sorrows had I, no sadness dimmed my eyes. Till upon a day I walked upon the rooftop and ye came! And ye burnt the heart of me, but never sang the birds so beautifully, never shone the sun so bright as when ye looked upon me. Thy madness and passion entered in and rioted in the heart of Zahra, so that I too was made mad, mad with happiness, mad with love for thee. And mad am I now, and rejoice in my madness. Then, when ye came no more, was the sun darkened, and the birds sang no more, all the world mourned in the heart of Zahra for that which she had not. A-ah! Wa-ali — wa-ali!

"Then on a day came Fatma with great news for me, news which would have made glad the heart of any maiden not drunk with the love of thee. News that he, the Prince of the Faithful, desired my charms. Great honor and jewels awaited me. Such that no maiden had e'er yet refused; yet born out of my love for thee came the strength to resist. Nay, why should I lie? I could not hesitate. Thy presence claimed me, and I knew not how to kill the love which burnt within me. Then came a day when — Praise be to Allah — he cast thee at my feet, and I attained Paradise within thy arms! A-ah! And again was the sun extinguished when in the hour of my joy that thou didst flee from me! Ah! waali, waali! What could I do? What could I say? They came and bathed me and prepared me for — him. But I could not — Nay, thy arms called to me, and I would fain have died.

"But Raalia in her love for me showed me a way where I might put thee to the last test, for never will I lie in any other man's arms save thine. See, thou Infidel! I, Zahra, daughter of the Shareef, Ben Fileli,[234] descendant of our Lord Mohammed, plead with thee!" Her bosom heaving, great tears welling afresh, she cast herself at Paul's feet.

"Choose! Thou shaft take me to thy arms, or then shall I be the willing bride of — Choose!"

A short curved dagger rippled light in the moon rays, as she poured her very soul through her eyes, the disengaged hand clutching at Paul's sleeve.

With lightning rapidity the whole of the accomplished past and the alluring, ambitious future flew before Paul's mental vision, and on the instant he sacrificed, and joyfully, with full consciousness, the whole of his past and future for this one frail alien girl; he swept her passionately into his arms, sealing his compact with the gods in one long clinging kiss.

Before he had always hesitated upon any decisive action, seeing both sides of the question, yet now no suspicion of hesitating crossed his mind. Almost for the first time in his life, and that at the most critical moment, he acted with conscious precision.

In a flash, more of intuition than reasoned thought,[235] his mind mapped out the course, and he obeyed. All his plans, the schemes, everything could go its own course; only one thing mattered: to save the girl before it was too late. Picking her up in his arms, he placed her on the bed, bidding her wait, and walking downstairs, quietly awoke Rabbit. He walked and

---

[234] Fileli / Filali: a well-known nisba (family or geographic name) meaning from Tafilalt, the Saharan oasis region in southeastern Morocco that produced the ʿAlawī dynasty.

[235] Note how Paul's rigid mindset and all-or-nothing perspective is suddenly vanquished. The eruption of the feeling function, coupled with intuition, usurps the cold, "logical" trap of "black or white" thinking.

acted as if in a dream, or hypnotized. Rabbit, half awake, at length appeared.

"Saddle El Cid Joos and Hassani," Paul commanded the startled Rabbit. "Put on both saddlebags. Do this quickly and quietly. Tell no one. Go!"

There was something new in Paul's voice which made Rabbit, for the first time, go and do as he was bid without question.

Returning to the room, he heard a voice singing softly:

My soul sings for joy! Hath not my heart
Told me we've met, love? never to part!

And on the bed sat Zahra, a misty halo of hair about her face, her eyes aglow, ethereal in the soft moon rays from the open window.

Paul, in silence more eloquent than speech, knelt and kissed her fingertips in ecstasy. As he rose to open his dispatch ox, his lips were tight and drawn as one battling with emotion. Small bags of gold were thrust in his skarrah and two revolvers strapped underneath his robes, whilst Zahra's large eyes followed every movement with devotion.

Lighting a candle, careful to avoid meeting her eyes, Paul scribbled a short note to Netherby:

"DEAR OLD BOY, — Do not ask questions nor even wonder. There are actions in a man's life which only he and the woman concerned can understand. Do all you can to help me by hindering pursuit if you can. To those who have helped me say what you like. I care not. I think you will understand. Goodbye and good luck."

Snuffing the candle, he stood in the doorway listening for a moment to the sounds of horses' hooves moving in the stable beneath.

A dolorous whine attracted his attention. He picked up the little lop-eared dog.

"So this is your decision, Kismet, is it? And, by Heaven, you're right. It is the best thing, only — only your method of teaching is devilish painful. Goodbye, little dog. God, what a fool I've been! Blind! Blind! — Is that you, Rabbit? Are they ready?"

"Yes, sir!"

Putting down the dog, Paul turned towards Zahra.

"Come, little one!"

"O Pole," said Rabbit's voice behind. "Take thou this djellaba that the guards may not know she be a woman."

Paul thanked him gravely, and taking the proffered garment, enveloped the girl in it, the hood well over her face.

"Why tremblest thou, little one?"

"Nay, it is but for the great joy within me, O my lord!" said she, kissing his hand.

The gleam of the discarded dagger on the carpet caught Rabbit's eye. He picked it up without question, and led the way to the stables. As the two crossed the courtyard Kismet suddenly barked shrilly and rushed into the shadows of the trees. The water dripping from his robes, a tall figure stalked out into the open. The moon rays revealed a heavy black beard and hawk nose which Paul recognized. Zahra gasped affrighted, and shrank behind Paul as the man spoke.

"Thou pig of a Nazarene, what dost thou with the daughter of a true believer? Thy and her life shall pay forfeit."

A scimitar twinkled in the moonlight and the hawk eyes gleamed viciously.

At the same time Rabbit thrust the dagger into Paul's hand, exclaiming:

"Quick! Pistol make plenty noise!"

Paul had loosened a revolver, but recognized the value of Rabbit's advice. With a deft motion he cast off his heavy cloth silham, and quickly rolling it around his left forearm, bade Rabbit care for Zahra.

Paul knew that to escape he must kill this man without rousing the house; the duel must be silent and swift. The man, who had paused for a moment, now advanced cautiously. Paul edged round into the open courtyard to give more room for play and kicked off his slippers.

And there in the moon-swathed courtyard, soft with the perfume of orchards, began a duel appropriate to the mediaeval environment.

Rabbit crouched against the wall, beside Zahra, her large excited eyes anxiously following her lover, straining her breath at every thrust or leap.

Paul's opponent seemed to catch the spirit, and, one arm holding up his skirtlike robes, the other clutching the murderous weapon, advanced and retired, feinting for an opening. Paul, equally cautious, determined not to strike until his opponent gave an opening for a fatal thrust. Once, as they circled round each other on stealthy feet, the Arab feinted in one direction to leap aside and delivered a downstroke; but Paul, ever alert, countered it upon his cloaked arm. Again the Arab tried a crosscut, which Paul skillfully parried, leaping out to stab beneath the raised arm. The attempt failed, the Arab agilely doubling to avoid the blow.

The Arab muttered wrathfully in his beard, and fought the more cautiously.

Round and round they circled, ever intent upon the other's eyes, Paul resisting the temptation to attack with an effort.

If only he would lose his temper! thought Paul, and on the instant a ruse came to him.

"Thou filthy bearded pig!" he exclaimed.

The ruse answered. Sentiment overcame reason.

With a call upon his Prophet to avenge such insult, the man rushed blindly in, striking furiously downwards. Paul, ready, caught the descending blade upon the cloak, at the same time springing in and thrusting home under the armpit. The man dropped on his knees, and lay prone.

For a moment Paul stood over him. The man moved feebly, looking up at him with unconquerable hate, and attempting to speak, collapsed, the blood dyeing his beard.

Paul turned away, discarded the slashed cloak, and picking up Zahra in his arms, walked to the door. As they were about to mount, Paul, who had not spoken since the fight, said to Rabbit:

"Go thou, fetch me one of the caps of Omar the Makhazni. Quick!"

Rabbit soon returned, and Paul, discarding his turban, put on the small cap.

In a moment the two were mounted.

"Now listen," said Paul to Rabbit from the saddle. "Get that man away — the river hath many mouths. Speak not one word concerning me. Ye know not, if any ask ye. Feed and care well for Kismet, you understand? Bring all my goods to Tanga. I will write there and send money. If ye would follow me, ye shall — afterwards. If we never arrive at the coast, hand my goods to the Consul at Tanga. And — mark well — care for Kismet. And now," he added in English, shaking hands, "Goodbye, Rabbit!"

"Goo'-bye, ole chap," answered Rabbit, his vast mouth working between a grin and a howl. "Goo'-bye! an' — an' — may Allah bless thee and watch over thee!" he finished in Arabic, with the dignity consonant with his native heart. Bending low, he kissed the hem of Paul's cloak, and turning, disappeared into the black of the horseshoe arch. "Come, little one," said Paul to the muffled figure beside him. "And who was he?"

"Hadj el Roos," replied Zahra, "one who would have taken me in marriage. My father would have none of him, but well would he ever watch over me."

They rode in silence, save for the jangling of harness, the sharp clop-clop of the horses' hooves and the knocking clatter of disturbed storks, until the first ward gate was reached.

A gruff salutation to the sleeping sentry, and the sight of the little cap of the civil guard which Paul wore, and with a rusty jangle of bolts, they were passed without question.

A few more dark lanes and passages, redolent with the odor of garbage and spices, and they were past the last and outer gate in safety.

As they climbed the hill towards the olive gardens, no word was spoken; each conscious that the other was content. Paul, in truth, was lost in wonderment at this strange, calm peace that had fallen upon him. No wrangling strife, only the bliss of perfect happiness in her presence. He sought no reason, having learned, at last, the fallacy of questioning the decrees of nature.

As they reached the cactus-girt road, alive with the shadows born of the moon, he turned in his saddle to take a last view of the ethereal beauty of Fez the Beautiful, wrapt in that mystic, brooding silence. And as he looked soft clouds crossed the face of the moon, and great shadows like hovering birds of ill-omen fled across the city.

The brooding silence seemed as ever pregnant with meaning of unspeakable horrors and vice indescribable; the calm, placid beauty of a pool of water showing but the shadowy ripples of the loathsome denizens in the depths.

That brooding sense seemed abnormal, full of hypnotic suggestions of evil, as if in reality djinns hovered about ever ready to drag a soul into filth and crime. Paul shook himself, as if endeavoring to throw off a spell, and turned to Zahra. Her large eyes peered from under the hood upon him, a world of love outpouring.

"Look, little one," said he, pointing to the filmy road lost in the darkness of the olive-clad hills. "There lies our road. Together we go because — because — "

"Mektub!" whispered Zahra. And as she spoke the brooding stillness of the city was broken by the voice of Destiny.

"Al-lah — Ak-ba-ah!"

For a moment they listened, her hand within his hand safe clasped.

"Come!" cried Paul, kissing her fingertips.

Together they wheeled their horses, and fled into the violet shadows of the night, their hoofbeats beating the rhythm of the sonorous call.

"Al-lah — Ak-ba-ah!"

FINIS

Romance in Morocco:
An Afterword by Rob Couteau

Although Charles Beadle played a brief role in the chess game enacted between the colonial European Powers, a complete chronicle of his gambit remains enshrouded in a tessellation of shadow – just like the history of Morocco itself.

A case in point concerns the Battle of Marrakech: a pivotal event that occurred on 19 August 1908 and that forms the narrative nucleus of *The City of Shadows*. It resulted in the defeat of Sultan Aziz, who was deposed by the forces of his brother, the Pretender Sultan, Moulay Hafid. While Aziz personally took part in the battle and was lucky to escape with his life, Hafid remained in Fez while his soldiers routed his brother on the battlefield. Although Hafid's men emerged victorious, the details of what actually occurred during the skirmish remain murky. According to contemporary historian Roger Pocock:

> Events were as complicated as could be expected, but at a totally confused pitched decisive battle it became evident that Mulay Hafid's army had won. It was suggested that was because Abd El Aziz's army was able to run away faster than Mulay Hafid's.

Roger adds that, "strangely," Beadle's novel offers the "best account" of the event; and that the hero was partially modeled upon Beadle's associate, Andrew Belton (who is also referred to in various accounts as "Sergeant" or "Captain" Belton).[236]

---

[236] Roger Pocock, "Tasting Adventure and Revolution," Frontiersmen-Historian.info, 1 June 2016. This site was created by Roger's father, historian Geoffrey Pocock, author of *One Hundred Years of the Legion of Frontiersmen* (Chichester, UK: Phillimore, 2004). They are unrelated to the legionnaire author (Henry) Roger Pocock.

Additional information is included in the memoir of (Henry) Roger Pocock (1865–1941), who in 1905 founded the Legion of Frontiersmen: a volunteer paramilitary group largely composed of filibusters, adventurers, and former military men, several of whom were in Morocco during the conflict. Beadle and Belton were both founding members of the Legion. In his *Chorus to Adventurers* (1931), Henry reports that Belton was also known as "Kaid Belton, Commander-in-Chief to Prince Muley Hafid." Accompanying him "at Fez were other Legionaries: Hugh Pollard as Minister of the Interior, Alan Ostler the War Correspondent,[237] Arkell Hardwick, and hovering on the coast was Charlie Beadle … and three other gentlemen I did not know" (i.e., three participants who were not Legion members). "Assisted by our adventurers, Muley Hafid overthrew the Emperor Abdul Aziz, succeeded him as Sultan, and presently opened Morocco to European trade. I was sick with envy of our adventurers, and disgusted with the French for chasing them out of Morocco." Then he refers to Beadle's novel, wryly observing:

> The author splits poor Belton into two rival Generals who, at the close of a perfect day, find themselves in command of the wrong armies. Last time I met Major Belton and we had a tea

---

[237] As noted earlier, Alan Ostler makes a brief appearance near the end of *The City of Shadows* as "Alan Netherby": a correspondent for a British paper and a "fellow clubman" (i.e., a fellow legionnaire) whom Paul "had known for years." In fact Ostler was covering events in Morocco as a correspondent for the *Daily Express*, particularly during the fall of 1908, and he published the first interview with Sultan Hafid after the Battle of Marrakech. Like many other Frontiersmen, he lost his life while serving in the Great War, as a lieutenant with the Royal Air Force. Severely wounded, he died on 16 September 1918 and is buried in Sains-les-Marquion, France. While Ostler was missing in action, a fellow journalist wrote of him: "He has a greed for adventure" – an epitaph that might be applied, for better or worse, to many Frontiersmen. See *Daily Express*, 23 September 1918, p. 2.

together, he told me that he did not altogether approve of Beadle. He [Belton] had all good gifts except a sense of humor.[238]

Although Beadle remained near the coast,[239] he later incorporated Belton's account into *The City of Shadows*.[240]

When I contacted historian Geoffrey Pocock, founder of the Frontiersmen Historian website, he further clarified Beadle's role and elaborated upon the nature of the Legion. "An accurate version of the life and adventures" of the Legion's men is "difficult to find," he said, adding:

We usually describe them as men who got together round a fire winter evenings smoking their pipes and telling "camp-fire yarns" of their adventures, which they often embellished. Their fiction books can be useful because they often based them on their own escapades and were able to put words into the mouths of fictional characters, which they could not use in their factual accounts for fear of the laws of libel, etc.

It was only Belton who was enlisted in Moulay Hafid's army. The others stayed back. With such events in such countries it is impossible to say what is 100% truth. Beadle's book is important, as he was in Morocco at the time and spoke to all the Englishmen. But obviously, he had to vary his tale from the truth in order not to cause legal complaints. I have

---

[238] (Henry) Roger Ashwell Pocock, *Chorus to Adventurers* (London: John Lane, The Bodley Head Ltd., 1931), pp. 60-61. The forces of the opposing Sultan, Abd al-Aziz, were commanded by Sir Harry Maclean (1848 – 1920), aka "Kaid" Maclean: another soldier of fortune, from Scotland.

[239] A British paper reports that Redman and Beadle "were the only two Europeans in Fez during the 1908 revolution, and were present at the arrival of Muley Hafid." See "Swindon Doctor in Fez," *Swindon Advertiser and North Wilts Chronicle*, 5 May 1911, p. 10. (Reproduced in full, below.)

[240] Beadle also published a short story, "A Pinch of Fever," in the June 1915 issue of *The Badminton Magazine* that features a character named Sergeant BOLTON, who was probably based on Belton.

always said that with many historical events we will never know the exact truth.[241]

But the bane of the historian may serve as a blessing for the novelist, who examines the scattered facts and replants them as seeds, hoping they may sprout into a creative reimagining. In Beadle's case, however, his novels are so deeply grounded in autobiography that it's no surprise that much of *The City of Shadows* is rooted to actual experience. Although it's a highly imaginative novel, Beadle later complained: "[It] isn't a book; it's drivel – or journalism, which is prostitution."[242]

It isn't clear why he was so acutely critical of such a fine effort twenty years after its publication. One possibility is that he's using the term *journalism* metonymically: as a pejorative stand-in for a "prosaic tale" as opposed to a more innovative, inventive one. Perhaps, by tethering the narrative to a historical scaffold of real life, Beadle felt that his creativity was unduly hemmed in. (It was also challenged by the staid, uninspired demands of commercial publishers in Great Britain.) He would finally cast all creative caution to the wind when he unleashed his daemon with the publication of *Dark Refuge*, in 1938: another autobiographical novel, but one that contains an explosion of surreal imagery, set largely in Paris between 1915 and 1920. But his first attempts to compose fiction occurred during his sojourn through a war-torn Morocco.

When we examine Beadle's literary biography at the turn of the century, two keynotes emerge. One is that his African travels would inspire some of his best writing in the decades ahead. But how did he end up there? In a personal account

---

[241] Email from Geoffrey Pocock, 1 July 2022.

[242] See Beadle's letter to his niece Isabel, composed circa 1930. For a transcript his letters, see Charles Beadle, *A Passionate Pilgrimage. Edited with an Introduction and Afterword by Rob Couteau* (New York: Dominantstar, 2024), pp. 462-463.

published in *Adventure* magazine's "Camp-Fire" column on 3 July 1918, he says:

My infancy was spent around Siam and the farther East: early memories, fireflies, mosquitoes, and ayahs. ["Ayah": a nurse or maid native to India.] Educated at boarding schools in England; hence no home life and consequent atrophy of the sentimentalities. Parental Government required me to become a consulting marine engineer; but a congenital dislike of work and a gaudy poster persuaded me to learn poker, to starve in Cape Town where I held down a waiter's job for four hours and to join the British South African Police.

Too late for big rebellion but kindly chief got up a small one to console me; saw Boer War in B. S. A. P. [British South African Police], Morley's Scouts (unpaid Looting Corps) (if any of the Scouts should read this should be glad to hear from them) and Stock Recovery Dept. After Peace held various jobs from three days to a week – in a news office, a bar, hawker, insurance agent – and peddled cheap jewelry for three months (and made money!); served in Transvaal Customs and became Asst. Compound Manager to the Witwatersrand Native Labor Association.

Then I raised a syndicate to support me for an exploring-trip on the headwaters of the Zambezi. Returned to London to promote a company; failed – of course. A head on a coin sent me to British East Africa and Uganda; native trading, running transport from Victoria Nyanza to the Kilo Mines, Congo; shooting and various ventures. England again, company promoting; and failed again.

Went to Dutch Borneo, rubber planting. Afterward returned to go to Morocco; penetrated into interior in disguise during rebellion; met Pretender Sultan, Mulai Hafid; instead of cutting my throat or crucifying me as predicted he gave me a palace and an escort and treated me as an ambassador; eventually I failed and Hafid lost his throne. We both had a royal time, anyway.

More specifically, in November 1898, a month after his eighteenth birthday, Beadle enlisted in the British South African Police, Matabeleland Division, and was stationed in southwestern Zimbabwe. Between 1899 and 1901, during the Second Boer War, he was in Transvaal (now the South African Republic), serving with Morley's Scouts. So it's possible he met some of the other legionnaires there, either during or after their military service. Legion founder Henry Pocock fought in the First Boer War, which lasted from December 1880 until March 1881. Geoffrey Pocock, who published a biography of Henry Roger Pocock (*Outrider of Empire*), says that Henry served as a corporal in a Scout unit. And he confirms that "A very high percentage of early Frontiersmen were ex-Boer War – often, like [Henry] Roger Pocock, serving with irregular troops."[243]

Participating in the Second Boer War (October 1899 – May 1902) were Beadle's friend Ellis Ashmead-Bartlett[244] and the Frontiersmen Andrew Belton and Alfred Arkell Hardwick, the latter who also served in the British South African Police (BSAP).[245] As we shall see, along with Beadle, these last three

---

[243] Email from Geoffrey, 28 October 2025.

[244] Author of contemporary history books such as *Some of My Experiences in the Great War* and *The Uncensored Dardanelles*, Ellis Ashmead-Bartlett (1881 – 1931) was a lieutenant in the Second Boer War and a correspondent during WWI. He was the eldest son of Conservative Party MP Sir Ellis Ashmead-Bartlett, the civil Lord of the Admiralty between 1885 and 1892.

[245] Alfred Hardwick (1878 – 1912) served as a trooper in the BSAP in Rhodesia in 1896 and in Mashonaland in 1897. In the fall of 1900, Beadle was in Mashonaland as the guest of an Englishman named Mason. (See his "My Narrow Escape From a Lioness," *The Brooklyn Daily Eagle*, 7 August 1910.) Hardwick also published a memoir, *An Ivory Trader in North Kenia* (London: Longmans, Green, and Co., 1903). He was killed in an airplane crash in north London on 15 December 1912.

Besides archiving Hardwick's service record, both the Casus-Belli and Anglo Boer War websites contain data on several of the other Frontiersmen. But often just a first initial is included from the forename, making positive

would later work for a London-based syndicate that attempted to gain Moroccan concession rights from Moulay Hafid. Beadle's other travels through Africa included expeditions into Zimbabwe, Zambia, Uganda, the Congo, and Mozambique. Such locations would later serve as settings for his short stories and novels.

The second keynote that resonates in Beadle's biography is the versatility of his writing, which spans diverse forms: travelogues, interviews, essays, literary novels; and then, later on, more commercial forms of adventure fiction and romance. Twenty-six of his short stories appeared in *Adventure* between 1918 and 1925.[246] The fact that he could so easily alternate

---

identification difficult. A record for an "H" Pocock says that he served as an "agent" with the Field Intelligence Department and in an "unknown" capacity with the Oudtshoorn District Mounted Troops. (But Geoffrey Pocock advised me that "H Pocock may or may not be Roger. He tended to slip through the mesh until he joined the National Scouts.... Pocock is quite a common name in the west of England, from Berkshire, through Wiltshire to Bristol.") An "A" Ostler was a bugler in the 2nd Battalion, Duke of Cornwall's Light Infantry. Private "C" Beadle served with the Kimberly Town Guard and as a trooper with the Nesbitt's Horse unit. (Charles Beadle's service in the latter group has been positively confirmed elsewhere.) An "E Bartlett Ashmead" (and with such a unique name, it must certainly have been Ellis Ashmead-Bartlett) was with the 2nd Battalion, Bedfordshire Regiment. Andrew Belton is recorded as a private in the Westmoreland and Cumberland Company, 8th Battalion, Imperial Yeomanry; and as a corporal with the Midland Mounted Rifles unit.

Notorious for self-promoting exaggerations and fanciful prevarications, Belton often went by the title, *Captain*. In his "Tasting Adventure" article, Roger Pocock says that, in 1906, Belton "was the officer in command of the Capetown Command of the Legion of Frontiersmen." In his "An Oddity: 'The Imperial Legion' and the Kaid," Roger adds: "The very reliable pioneer Frontiersman Robert A. Smith in a letter described Belton as 'a human kaleidoscope' and 'not invariably accurate in his facts.'" Posted on the Frontiersmen Historian website on 1 October 2021.

[246] In 1927 *Adventure* published a serialized novella, "A New Found World," by Henry Roger Pocock, under his usual byline, "Roger Pocock."

between these various forms of fiction and nonfiction may explain why his novels so seamlessly intertwine reality with a fabric of fantasy and imagination.

Beadle first began to publish nonfiction at the age of twenty-five, when his travel essay, "Our Trip Down the Zambezi," appeared in the May 1907 issue of *Wide World Magazine.* The subtitle of the periodical illustrates what a perfect fit it was: *An Illustrated Monthly of True Narrative, Adventure, Travel, Customs and Sport.* The piece chronicles his August 1904 expedition to Zambia, when he was only twenty-two years old (and which occurred three years before the publication date). It features a riveting account of a rambunctious hippo that rises out of the river's depths, overturning fragile canoes and killing as many travelers as possible – a fate that Beadle himself narrowly avoids one morning, while dozing in his craft:

> A huge, speckled black mass – a monster hippo – seemed to be rising underneath the boat; all the paddlers had jumped and were swimming for dear life…. I leant forward to pick up my gun, and at the same instant the hippo raised the bow of the boat out of the water, throwing me backward…. Presently the brute rose again about ten feet away and came at me open-mouthed. Firing point-blank into his gaping jaws, I leaped for the bank, now only a few feet away, hearing a crash and a snort as I scrambled through the reeds and up the bank.

Other highlights include a meeting with a stocky, 250-pound African queen who, until recently, had the right to strangle her husband if she decided she was growing bored. The domineering diva also developed a reputation for being a "bloodthirsty young woman." A few years earlier, she had demanded the execution of one of her councilors; but when the executioner balked, she picked up an ax and completed the task by herself.

A year after this publication Beadle headed for Fes, hoping to arrange an interview with the Pretender Sultan, Moulay Hafid. (Two months later, Hafid would be recognized as Morocco's official sultan). His subsequent photo-essay, "A Talk with the New Sultan of Morocco," was featured in the October 1908 *Pall Mall*: another widely circulating magazine. The article was so well received that excerpts were reproduced in many other mainstream papers both in England and abroad. Rather heady stuff for a fledgling author who would turn twenty-seven that same month! And thanks to his essay, we can construct a more detailed chronology of his Moroccan adventure.

On 23 April 1908, embarking from the Port of London aboard the SS *Agadir*, Beadle headed south for El Jadida (then known as Mazagan), about ninety-nine km (or sixty-two miles) southwest of Casablanca, off the Atlantic coast. His name is the first to appear on the ship's manifest, traveling "First Class." This sort of luxury was atypical for the author, who often led a penurious life; but he was probably feeling flush after having received a substantial inheritance from his father, in 1906.

Arriving in El Jadida on 4 May, Beadle secures the services of William Redman, a British merchant born in El Jadida who was the son of Alfred Redman, Vice-Consul at Mazagan from 1873 to 1896. (The Redman clan formed a virtual dynasty that served as Vice-Consuls and Consuls at Mazagan from 1837 to 1896.) William is well-versed in the local customs and is fluent in Arabic and Shilha, a Berber language spoken primarily in southwestern Morocco.[247] (He would later become Sultan

---

[247] Speaking "both Arabic and Shilha like a native," by 1910 Redman would be working as a noncommissioned officer for the French military mission, performing exemplary work in training the native cavalry. (See Douglas Porch, *The Conquest of Morocco*, p. 217.) On 1 June 1912, during a battle near the crest of Jbel Zalagh (the largest mountain overlooking Fes), he was fatally wounded. The French generals Brulard and Lyautey both spoke of Redman's courage during his funeral service, held on 2 June at the French

Hafid's official interpreter.) Together they travel to the nearby town of Azemmour, about seventeen kilometers (or ten miles) back up north, along the coast.

There they are received by the governor, who provides Beadle "with a letter of introduction to his brother, the Grand Vizier to Mulai-El-Hafid." After a fortnight in the Mazagan region, on 19 May they embark on the *Gibel Kebir*, a steamer headed further north, back to Tangier (429 kilometers, or 267 miles, up the coast). We may assume that Beadle made this enormous U-turn because he needed to secure that precious letter.

"On arrival at Tangier," he continues, "I found Captain Belton impatiently awaiting the start; but, to our great disappointment, we were held up for many weary days." Due to the "present state of anarchy and civil war" they are prevented from traveling from Tangier to Fes and are warned that their trip can only lead to "capture or massacre at least."

---

military hospital at Fes. A Newcastle newspaper from 4 June reports: "Sergeant-Instructor Redman was originally a member of the disbanded British mission in Morocco. He, however, remained behind, and, being regarded as an excellent soldier, was gladly accepted by the French mission, and promoted to a privileged position. There remains at the military mission another English non-commissioned officer, who is serving on the same conditions as Redman." (This is probably a reference to Thomas Bolding, formerly a sergeant with the Thirteenth Hussars, who, along with Redman, had trained the Moroccan cavalry under the French military command.) See "An Anglo-French Soldier" and "Improved Situation in Morocco," *North Mail Newcastle Daily Chronicle*, 4 June 1912, pp. 6 and 12. An article published that same day in the *Daily Telegraph* ("Englishman's Fate," p. 9) reports: "The whole of the French colony and the representatives of the different Powers were also present," including the British Consul Macleod. And the French Minister of War, Alexandre Millerand, telegraphed Lord Haldane, the British Secretary of State for War, "expressing his condolences at the death of the English instructor Mr. Redman, who was killed at the head of his men in the fighting near Fez." For information on the Redman consular "dynasty" in Mazagan, see the online Historical Text Archive.

Undeterred, Beadle follows the advice of a local and decides to proceed to Fes from a different direction. At midday on 8 June, he boards a steamer, the *Quetzil*, and arrives at 6 a.m. at the coastal city of Larache, about eighty-nine km south of Tangier. Redman and Belton are awaiting him there, having arrived earlier on the *Gibel Dersa*.

The men wend their way through a swarming mob near the Custom House ("I had but my camera and revolver"); dine at the Hotel Lucas "with the other European visitors"; and secure accommodations in a local Jewish household (as the hotel is fully booked). The following morning, under a "fierce" sun, they prepare for the next leg of their trip: to Alcázar el-Kebir, now known as Ksar el-Kébir. (A traveler moving from Larache toward Fes would naturally pass through Ksar el-Kebir along one of the main overland routes.) This stage of the journey will take them further inland, about 30 km southeast of Larache. But for this arduous and dangerous trek they're provided only with "some sorry looking pack animals" that are "peeping from under their cumbrous straw pack saddles."

Beadle says that it proves to be a "wretched journey" in "intolerable heat," but the worst part is the "thousand unprincipled ways in which every attendant imposes on the credulity or good nature of the traveler." And so, as a necessary precaution, he's "disguised in the native garb." He catalogs some of the pitfalls that would otherwise await them minus such a disguise: "In the disturbed state of the country, with one sultan superseding another, and the army in a state of utter division, we should have stood a chance of decorating the country roadside with a heap of our devoted bodies." This fanciful turn of phrase, infinitely preferable to "we might have been killed," highlights the young author's nascent literary bent.

The various dangers facing Europeans traveling to Fes are such that his team is "required to procure the necessary escort from the British vice consul." Even so, after some troublesome interactions along the way, he remarks:

> I might have had reason to view some of these encounters with even more miscellaneous feelings, had I known that my guide accounted for my complete disguise by confiding to our assistants that I was a dancing girl bound for the household of a distinguished native official. At other times I was, it seemed, a holy man, a *shereef*.[248]

Beadle as a shrouded dancing girl is also captured in one of the photos included in the essay. The enveloping veils were a godsend, given the author's pale British skin and slate-blue eyes, which could have easily given him away. He concludes: "There is plenty of humor, and lying, in Morocco."

Thus camouflaged, he's transported through the suburban olive groves, arriving at Fes on 14 June. Following "many days' rest considerately appointed for us after our journey" and a series of meetings with high-level intermediaries (including the grand vizier and the minister of foreign affairs), they're finally granted an audience with the Pretender Sultan, Moulay Hafid.

After embarking on a mule-back ride to the Government House, they're formally introduced to the sultan, who remains seated "cross-legged on a gilt Louis XV sofa." Beadle portrays him as a refined, intelligent man, even making note of "his really beautiful hands and feet, tapering fingers, and filbert nails." The discussion is wide-ranging but focused on Morocco's relationship with the European Powers. At the conclusion of their two-hour tête-à-tête, Hafid honors the twenty-six-year-old with a grand gesture:

> He thanked us for having been the first Europeans to visit him in Fez as Sultan, as also the first to enter since all Europeans

---

[248] Shereef: another variant spelling of *sharif*.

left at the outbreak of revolution in August of 1907. We were to go anywhere we liked, to see the sights of Fez; his Ministers had orders to see that we were provided with an escort and anything else we might require, and he bade us make our stay as long as possible. After present topics had been exhausted in an interview lasting about two hours, we arose and, shaking hands with His Shereefian Majesty, departed.

Beadle was lucky to have met Hafid while the latter was in such a good mood. The following summer, shortly after he defeated El Rogui's rebel forces, the sultan's reputation for spectacular forms of torture became even more legendary. By mid-August 1909, sacks stuffed with salted human heads soon festooned the gates at Fes. "One group of sixty prisoners was made to parade through the streets each carrying the head of a fallen comrade. For the next three days, the 320 prisoners were publicly tortured in the *mechouar* or at the Bab Mahrouq under the placid gaze of Moulai Hafid."[249]

Beadle's biography is replete with examples of traveling in close proximity to such grave danger, including stampeding elephants and leaping lions; the outbreak of decimating plague; ritual cannibalism; and bloody tribal warfare. Not to mention an avaricious French landlord who absconded with his most treasured possessions – Beadle's typewriter and diary – then ejected him onto the street, once he could no longer pay the bill.

* * *

Following this promising nonfiction debut, Beadle began to compose fiction while he was hunkered down in Morocco. In an essay published in a forum titled "Contemporary Writers and Their Work," he describes his first attempt to construct a novel:

---

[249] Douglas Porch, *The Conquest of Morocco*, p. 211.

I began when I was 28 or 29. I was stuck in the center of Morocco, isolated, and finding a library abandoned by – well, no names, no pack drill! – I read to pass the time, novels, and became so bored with them that I swore that if I could not write a better yarn than those in particular I would eat my hat and other clothes! […] I began a novel there and finished it in London when I returned – broke; and being broke took it into my head that I would be a writer or bust! Every publisher in London turned it down; Public won't stand for it, etc. A friendly critic said to me, "Stick your tongue in your cheek, old man, and write something to please 'em!" I did. First publisher to whom it was offered gave special terms. My hoary aunt, I actually made money! Not much, but real money! That book is selling in cheap edition.[250]

Since *The City of Shadows* portrays a heroic English protagonist (Paul) whose life is threatened by an evil German "Baron," it's not surprising that it found favor with the British reading public. (A reviewer for the *Globe* even chortles: "The hero is an Englishman, and the villain a German Baron – which, to begin with, offers the fairest promise!") And if Paul and his London-based financiers are successful, England will beat the other European investors to the punch, gaining valuable access to Moroccan resources. He continues:

I sat down again to write "something that would please 'em!" Then occurred the process to which I have already referred. My "creations" would not obey their god (how very human). They would insist upon making a tragedy of it. After the fourteenth publisher I took to sending it round in couples. Two publishers, young, made an offer simultaneously. I accepted the better offer. My publisher on the day of publication eloped to Morocco with his typist and incidentally

---

[250] See *The Editor: The Journal of Information for Literary Workers*, 25 February 1920, pp. 156-157.

the firm's funds – and a few months afterwards the other fellow was in gaol for embezzlement. Fate "got me going and coming," as they say!

The second book referred to here, whose characters "would insist upon making a tragedy of it," might be *A Whiteman's Burden* (1912), which is set in the Congo, Zambia, and Uganda during the African sleeping sickness epidemic, which killed hundreds of thousands throughout the continent. And yes, Beadle was right there, at the peak of the devastation, in all the most dangerous places. Another somewhat tragic candidate would be Beadle's third novel, *A Passionate Pilgrimage* (1915). A provocative coming-of-age confession set largely in South Africa, it depicts amorous encounters between unmarried partners as well as a "mixed-race" romance – the latter considered to be an utterly taboo subject. But the novel that he began in Morocco and finished in London was most certainly *The City of Shadows*, which foreshadows such literary improprieties by climaxing with a radiant, romantic bonding between an Englishman and a native Arab teenager. And like the interracial pairings in his other novels, such a romance would never have been sanctioned by either of their societies.

Beadle said that he began to write fiction when he was twenty-seven or twenty-eight years old, but a clue to more accurately dating this debut is found in an essay, "What Has Happened to Muley Hafid," featured in the July 1909 issue of *The Sphere* (London). A byline states: "By Charles Beadle, who has just returned from Morocco." Since he repatriated before the publication date in July, he would have been twenty-seven while working on *The City of Shadows* during the first half of 1909. (He turned twenty-eight later that year, in October.) He must have finished it no later than 1910, since notices about the forthcoming novel appear in February 1911, with reviews cropping up by early March. His name is also registered in the

April 1911 English census, listed as "author" and residing at 69 Antrim Mansions, Hampstead, London.

So we can conclude that Beadle was writing fiction by his twenty-seventh year at the latest. Judging from the vivid imagery contained in *The City of Shadows* and in dozens of other stories that he'd publish in the years ahead, Morocco played a crucial role in feeding his prodigious, fruitful imagination.

*   *   *

Several newspaper reports published before and after the Battle of Marrakech go into elaborate detail about the efforts of Beadle and his fellow Frontiersmen to secure concession rights in Morocco for a British syndicate. One in-depth account is featured on page one of the 23 July 1908 *Daily Express*: "King-Makers at Fez," excerpts of which are cited in many other papers. From this we learn that Beadle and his crew represent an investment syndicate based in London, which is hoping to gain lucrative concession rights from the Pretender Sultan, Moulay Hafid. They are referred to as "the six English kingmakers"; and the "audacity and enterprise of this little band of Englishmen" is duly lauded. The article describes how the group's leader, Ellis Ashmead-Bartlett, "was convinced that much benefit would result from the success of Mulai el Hafid and determined that, with the aid of certain friends, he would furnish that aid, on various conditions":

> After sundry negotiations it was made clear that Mulai el Hafid was prepared to grant sundry concessions, which, given a settled state of the country, would be exceedingly valuable. He offered, in return for English (unofficial) assistance, to give concessions for the building of railways, mining, the reorganization of the finances of the country, various important political posts, and a partial control, at least, of the

Customs. All these things he would grant in return for efficient military assistance from the little English syndicate which Mr. Ashmead-Bartlett promptly formed.

These were prizes worth working for. It is undeniable that there is considerable mineral wealth in the country, and also railway concessions, if granted by one whose authority was genuine, might very well prove to be a source of considerable profit. Indeed, so widely recognized are these facts that the English company were by no means without competitors.

It is asserted that on one occasion the Standard Oil Company of America offered no less than £200,000 cash down for the right to build a railway in a rich mineral district, the conditions being that they should have mining rights for thirty miles on either side of the line, the property to revert at the end of eighty years to the Moorish Government.

There were also German and Portuguese competitors in the field. One German company claimed that they had sufficient money, put up by Berlin financiers backed by the German Government, to reclothe and arm Mulai el Hafid's entire force. The main point about these gentlemen, however, appears to be that they could not leave Tangier and come to close quarters with Mulai el Hafid in order to negotiate.

With the English party, however, it was different. As soon as their scheme had got well under way, Charles Beadle, one of the party, went out to Morocco to join the agent already there. This latter – Redman by name – had been in the country for a considerable period prior to the inception of the scheme, and from the first was in touch with the chief advisers of Mulai el Hafid.

Mr. Beadle joined him in March, the expenses having been raised by Mr. Ashmead-Bartlett, who had lost no time in entering into an agreement with a firm of London financiers. By this agreement it was arranged that any profits should be divided in equal parts by the syndicate and the other parties to the agreement.

The first emissary of the syndicate had no sooner landed in Tangier than he came into contact with the German party to whom we have already referred. A second man, Belton, was promptly sent out to reinforce him; and the three members of the English party—Beadle, Belton, and Redman—were tentatively approached by the German party, but did not disclose their own plans. Instead, they made every effort to get into personal communication with Mulai el Hafid himself. In this they appear to have received valuable assistance from El Glawi, brother of the Vizier and Mulai's right-hand man. Mulai el Hafid was at this time in Mequinez, and was hourly gaining adherents from all parts of the country.

It was now imperative that the syndicate should strain every nerve if they did not wish success to slip through their fingers. Accordingly, Mr. Ashmead-Bartlett sailed for Morocco, leaving affairs in the hands of a thoroughly capable member of the party, Mr. Hardwick, with whom he regularly corresponded, and to whom he proposed to send word when the time should be ripe for the rest of the party to follow him. On arriving at Tangier he found that his three friends, unable to wait for him, had started up country. He therefore decided on the very risky plan of making his way direct to Fez, where the Moorish Pretender had by this time taken up his quarters. Luckily for him, his plucky attempt succeeded. Disguised as a native of the country, he reached the Moorish capital, recruiting on the way two more Englishmen from a town near the coast.

Before long there were thus six Englishmen in Fez, and they were quickly successful in gaining the approbation and attention of Mulai el Hafid.

The whole story is one of enthralling interest, and when the time comes for it to be told in full, it will add another page to the vast record of daring private enterprise by Englishmen. With this, however, we are not so much concerned as with the probable results of the action of the party concerned. As a matter of fact, it almost seems as though they may afford the solution of more than one difficult problem. Where national interference in Moroccan affairs was impossible, this private and unofficial intervention may have the result of laying the foundations of a strong, self-governing Morocco.

France, it is fairly safe to say, will welcome an easy way out of what is daily becoming a more difficult situation. The less trouble Morocco gives her, the better will her people be pleased. Then again, there is the question of the opening up of the country—undoubtedly a rich one if properly developed—to European trade.

But the actual result was quite the opposite: France turned Morocco into a subservient "Protectorate," bleeding her through military and economic means. And Beadle and his friends were forced out (although Redman stayed behind, serving as a noncommissioned officer at the invitation of the French). And while the Protectorate officially ended in 1956, to this day France continues to exercise enormous control over Morocco.

Oddly enough, the reference to "six" Englishmen is cited again and again in various periodicals, but the reports name only five participants. A likely candidate for number six might be fellow Frontiersman Hugh B. C. Pollard[251] (1888 – 1966). In August 1908 Pollard traveled to Fez with Frontiersman Alan Ostler, the *Daily Express* journalist who published the first interview with Hafid after the Battle of Marrakech. "Pollard

---

[251] Known for his pro-Nazi and Fascist sympathies, Pollard was one of the more unsavory of the Frontiersmen crew. A key player in an MI6-engineered coup that brought Spanish dictator Francisco Franco to power, in July 1936 Major Pollard helped to fly Franco from the Canary Islands to Morocco. Once there, Franco assumed command of Spain's Army of Africa and participated in the military uprising that would trigger the Spanish Civil War, lead to the overthrow of the democratically elected Republican government, and result in decades of horrific dictatorship. Pollard considered himself to be on the "extreme right," and he later published a letter in the *Times* in which he stated that the bombing of Guernica was "perfectly legitimate." See Graham D. Macklin, "Major Hugh Pollard, MI6, and the Spanish Civil War," www.cambridge.org, 24 February 2006.

reported to [Henry] Pocock on 28 August: 'Ostler and I have been in Fez for a fortnight, and have had a very good time. I have interviewed the Sultan twice, and been to tea etc. with all his ministers.'"[252]

Pollard is also the main subject of Roger Pocock's "Tasting Adventure" article. Roger reports that, in 1908, the twenty-year old Pollard joined the "Redmond-Hardwick exploration syndicate on an allegedly prospecting venture in Morocco" but that "prospecting was only part of the adventure. A photograph exists of a William Redman serving as a Lieutenant under Belton, so, knowing how commonly surnames were misspelt especially in newspapers and magazines, there has to be the likelihood that this ["Redmond"] was the same man and prospecting was only part of the adventure." (A reproduction of the photo is included below.) This possibility is reinforced in Fred Boalt's "A Twentieth Century Kingmaker," an article about Belton published in Michigan's *Yale Expositor* on 16 September 1910:

> Belton was in South Africa in 1908. He came to London on six months' leave. Two weeks of London fogs and drizzle and the prospect of a half year of inactivity filled him with disgust. Then a friend wrote him that he had been commissioned by a syndicate to secure a mining concession in Morocco from a pretender to the throne named Mulai Hafid. Would Belton like to go along?

Note the aforementioned "mining" concession.

---

[252] Peter Day, *Franco's Friends: How British Intelligence Helped Bring Franco to Power in Spain* (Hull, UK: Biteback Publishing, 2011), e-book edition, pp. 17-18.

He met the friend in Tangier, and the two were joined by a third Englishman, Redmond, who had been brought up in Morocco, knew the natives and spoke Arabic fluently.

Other details in the report lead us to conclude that the "third Englishman" is Charles Beadle. Many of the same highlights from Beadle's essay about meeting Sultan Hafid are repeated in Boalt's piece, including the fact that they're disguised and "dressed as Moorish women." Boalt also adds a fresh ingredient: "The sultan had issued an edict forbidding natives to assist Europeans. Their muleteer refused to go further than Alcazar, as the tribes were carrying on the jehad (holy war) against the Christians. So they employed a notorious brigand and horse thief, one Abselem, to take them through to Fez." One wonders if Abselem forms the basis of the character "Absalom": a quick-witted native guide who makes his first appearance in chapter three of *The City of Shadows*. A guide with a similar name also appears throughout Lawrence Harris' *With Mulai Hafid at Fez*: an "Absolem" who accompanies Harris and Frontiersman Alfred Hardwick to Fes.

But how does the syndicate saga relate to our novel? Quite directly, as it turns out; for the reader may recall a passage in which Paul, inflated by the success of his recent maneuvers, reflects:

Taking into consideration the many risks attached to the venture, all had at present shaped very well. He had succeeded in obtaining all the concessions he desired, which amounted to the practical monopoly of the economical resources of the country, and a messenger had arrived with the news of the successful running of the arms. He smiled to himself as he thought of the international hullabaloo there would be when the time came to disclose the powerful interests which he represented. Already there was trouble in the Diplomatic world; France had accused perfidious Albion of breaking faith in sending a secret agent – Paul – to aid the Pretender, and Germany, laughing up her sleeve, had supported her claim. Of course, Paul had been disowned by the British Foreign Office, which equally of course had been disbelieved, illustrating the maxim that when you wish to be believed, tell a lie, and vice versa.

In fact, both the British Foreign Office and the British War Office were growing increasingly vexed by the unauthorized adventurism of Beadle and the other Legion members. An index of confidential reports from the Foreign Office summarizes a 21 June 1908 memo as follows: "Englishmen at Fez. Refers to [memo] No. 105. Informs of their names. They are being treated as if on mission from His Majesty's Government. Steps taken to counteract this impression. Encloses copy of letter from Lord Mountmorres relative to Mr. Beadle, one of the Englishmen in question." (The "steps taken" may have involved the planting of clarifying information in the press.) A memo from Mr. Herbert White, the Chargé d'affaires at Tangier, reads in full:

> *Mr. White to Sir Edward Grey. – (Received June 29th.)*
> (No. 118.) *Tangier, June 21, 1908.*

Sir,

I HAVE the honor to transmit herewith translation of a letter received by Mr. Consul Macleod from his Arabic Interpreter reporting the arrival of two Englishmen, alleged to the Emissaries from His Majesty's Government.

On the 11th instant [11 June] the Consular Agent at Alcazar wrote to inform me that two Englishmen, accompanied by Mr. Redman, a British merchant at Mazagan, had arrived from Gibraltar via Larache and were proceeding to Fez. Mr. Carleton did not mention their names, nor the object of their intended visit to Fez. Upon receipt of Mr. Carleton's letter, I at once instructed him to call the special attention of these gentlemen to the warning issued in April last, but I have heard nothing further from Mr. Carleton on the subject.

It is difficult to say whether these travelers have alleged that they are Emissaries of His Majesty's Government to give themselves importance and ensure a good reception, or whether the report originated with Mulai Hafid and his officials, and is intended to lead the people to believe that His Majesty's Government have recognized him, or at any rate are in negotiation with him.

I have, &c.
(Signed)

HERBERT E. WHITE.

Enclosure in No. 106.

Lord Mountmorres to Mr. White.

5, Central *Chambers, South Castle Street, Liverpool,*
June 4th, 1908.

Sir,

I HAVE the honor to enclose herewith a letter address to Mr. Charles Beadle, who has been staying in Tangier. He is leaving today, and is likely to be absent from Tangier for about a fortnight. On his return, about the 17th of this month, his address will be Hotel Cavilla, Tangier.

As I have reason to fear that if the letter lies there it may be tampered with by persons into whose hands I am particularly anxious it should not fall, I should esteem it a very great favor if your Excellency would see that this letter safely reaches Mr. Beadle.

Your Excellency will probably have received from the Foreign Office, prior to the receipt of this letter, information which will indicate to you my reason for being anxious as to the safety of the accompanying letter.

I have, &c.

(Signed)

MOUNTMORRES.[253]

This provides us with another example of how the novel's chief protagonist, Paul, is imbued with details taken directly from Beadle's own life. And note the threatening German contingent described above, which Beadle may have condensed into a single figure: the vile German "Baron." Paul's mercenary role, however, is more closely aligned with "Kaid" Belton, who trained and organized Hafid's forces.

*   *   *

Beadle's traveling companion William Redman and the Frontiersmen Belton and Hardwick are also sketched in Lawrence Harris' memoir, *With Mulai Hafid at Fez*, which chronicles Harris' September 1908 trip to meet Hafid. When he arrives at the palace to interview the newly victorious sultan,

> two officials from the palace, garbed in a curious-looking uniform, paid me a visit. They were Mr. Belton, the new drill instructor, and his Khalifa, Mr. Redman. As a very great compliment to me, they were sent by the Sultan to act as my escort to the palace, and to be present at the interview.

The presence of Belton and Redman at the sultan's court is confirmed in an article published in the 29 August 1908 issue of *The Graphic*. A photo titled "Three Englishmen at the Court of Mulai Hafid" is captioned: "On the left is Mr. William Redman,

---

[253] "Foreign Office: Confidential, Part 37, Further Correspondence Respecting the Affairs of Morocco." April to June 1908, pp. ix, 75-76, National Archives (Kew, UK), accessed at archive.org. Thanks to my colleague Christopher Sawyer-Lauçanno for unearthing this memo on 20 July 2022.

son of a former British Vice-Consul at Mazagan, who is a lieutenant under Kaid Belton. In the centre is Kaid Belton, described elsewhere. On the right is 'Bibi' Carleton, British Vice-Consul at Alcazar, who wields more power throughout Morocco than any other European."[254] A side-bar photo, titled "Mulai Hafid's Right-hand Man," displays a portrait of Belton with the caption: "Kaid Belton has served Mulai Hafid in the same capacity as Kaid Maclean served Abdul Aziz. Our photograph, taken recently at Fez, shows Captain Belton in Moorish costume." Lawrence goes a step further and describes the Redman / Belton getups as "something like a clown's dress." And Ellis Ashmead-Bartlett seems to be taking a direct dig at the duo when he writes in his memoir:

The Moorish army is drilled under extreme difficulty, and its efficiency has not been added to by Hafid's unfortunate choice of instructors. One of these gentlemen is an ex-non-commissioned officer of some colonial corps; and the other, who acts as his interpreter, comes from Masagan. He knows naught of military matters, but wears a uniform and carries a sword and struts up and down exceedingly pleased with himself, endeavoring to make his companions word of command understood by the troops, who gaze in open-mouthed astonishment at the hoarse cries of "Right turn," "Halt," "Stand at ease," "Present arms." Both these gentlemen came up to Fez early and impressed the Sultan with a sense of their military efficiency, and as there was no one there to gainsay them, they were appointed by Hafid, who imagined that by doing so he was pleasing the British Government and sowing the seeds of discord amongst the nations. He now greatly regrets his precipitate action. As the instructors do not understand Arabic and the troops do not understand English, it is impossible for them to drill, and the morning's work consists in marching this disorganized rabble round and

---

[254] See Lucien Wolf, "The F. O. Bag," *The Graphic*, 29 August 1908, p. 252.

round the square to the opening bars of "The British Grenadiers," "The Cock o' the North," and "The Marseillaise." Nevertheless, what the Moorish Army lacks in efficiency it certainly gains in picturesqueness.[255]

Returning to Lawrence's chronicle, the passage quoted above marks the only appearance of Redman and Belton in Lawrence's memoir, but Hardwick appears throughout Lawrence's text, and his talents are engagingly described. After Lawrence departs from London with orders from his newspaper editor to interview Hafid, he encounters a "quiet, mild-looking, blue-eyed Englishman," seated at a dining room table at his hotel in Tangier. Upon making "direct inquiries in the right quarter," Lawrence discovers that, "for all his lamblike appearance," Alfred Arkell Hardwick

> was just such a man as I should wish to accompany me. An ex-member of the South African Police, he had seen service in the native wars in Rhodesia. As a big game hunter and trader in ivory he had written a successful book on sport and travel in East Africa. He was, in fact, a wanderer of many years experience in most of the wilder parts of Africa…. His knowledge of transport and camp equipment was invaluable. A good rider and an excellent shot, he proved throughout the expedition an ideal traveling companion.

It's also thanks to Hardwick that, once again, we encounter the irresistible guide Rabat (Lawrence renders his name as "Rabet"), who plays such an important role in *The City of Shadows*. Hardwick brings Rabat into the picture when he attempts to hire him for their expedition to Fes. But note

---

[255] Ellis Ashmead-Bartlett, *The Passing of the Shereefian Empire* (Edinburgh and London: William Blackwood and Sons, 1910), pp. 351-352.

Lawrence's patronizing, colonialist tone when he describes their meeting:

Hardwick brought to my room at the hotel a truculent-looking rogue named Mohammed Rabet. He had been to Fez and produced the usual sheaf of testimonials from former alleged satisfied patrons. His English as well as his manners led me to believe that his former tourist patrons had treated him with greater freedom than is politic with men of his breed. "Hallo! old cock," he observed, in a matter-of-fact tone, as he entered the room and appropriated the only other chair. His air of pained surprise when ordered to stand up and exhibit more restraint both in speech and manner in my presence was almost ludicrous.

Questioned as to the possibility of leaving Tangier for Fez in forty-eight hours, he gave me to understand that he approved of me, he approved of the expedition, and if I would leave the whole matter in his hands he would 'see me through, in less than no time.' As a preliminary, would I disperse a small advance on account of his salary? Also a little on account of the expenses he would be compelled to incur while slaving in my service. The next morning he brought me his friend, Muhammad Moktar, the muleteer. After much swearing by A'llah, he agreed to a price for the animals, but I must give a substantial deposit. Hardwick had secured tents and camp equipment, and everything was ready for our departure on the following morning. Late the same afternoon the ubiquitous Rabet appeared and declared that we should all be murdered if we did not take a soldier. He would not venture without one. On a promise of more money, he agreed to risk it, if we would consent to go disguised as Moors. While we went to buy the necessary dresses, Hardwick and I visited the nearest barber's and had our heads shaved and beards trimmed in Moorish fashion. We looked hideous, and slunk back to the hotel and took refuge in my bedroom. Later, Rabet brought the clothes, which we donned. We were to start at three in the morning to escape prying eyes. But the next day neither Rabet nor Moktar appeared. The sun rose, and it was impossible to think of starting even if they did arrive, for we should be observed. I learned afterwards that official pressure had been applied to intimidate Rabet, and he had run away.[256]

The story of "official pressure" is quite possible, since by that time the new sultan had issued an edict forbidding native Moroccans from helping Europeans. But it's also tempting to imagine that Rabat vanished because he was fed up with the demeaning treatment meted out by the pretentious, supercilious Harris. This profoundly nettled, class-obsessed gentleman is quick to take umbrage at Rabat's playful imitation of British aristocrats – drawling with their stodgy, hidebound Victorian idioms in the proper King's English – especially when Rabat twists, tangles, and scrambles it up so unwittingly, resulting in the greatest mockery of all.

We should note that even the British book reviewers were critical of Harris' acidic tone and the extreme, broad-stroke negativity that he displays toward Moroccans:

Mr. Harris is one of the few Europeans who have visited Fez, and his book is a description of a journey that he took as correspondent of the "Graphic" at the end of 1908 from Tangier. It says he remained for some considerable time, and had audiences with Mulai Hafid, who treated him well and wanted him to edit a paper at Fez. He seems, besides, to have met most people who were worth meeting in Fez – he dined once with Raisuli at the house of the Foreign Minister. His journeys, moreover, were full of interesting incident, and all together he had abundant opportunities of understanding

---

[256] Lawrence Harris, *With Mulai Hafid at Fez: Behind the Scenes in Morocco* (London: Smith, Elder, and Co., 1909), pp. 10-13, 83. Excerpts from Harris' account appear in the 20 November 1909 issue of *The Graphic*, the paper that commissioned him to conduct the interview.

Morocco. Unfortunately, Mr. Harris was not able to make the best use of them. A vein of familiar humor mars his narrative, and with Mulai Hafid he seems to have felt like a Yankee at the Court of King Arthur. He disliked Mulai Hafid, though for what reasons is not very apparent, and, indeed, has a hearty contempt for nearly everything and everybody in the country. Enough has happened since to show that his opinion of Mulai Hafid is prejudiced, and the future of the country not so hopeless as he affects to think. Mr. Harris went to the country in the wrong spirit, and the result is that his book is lacking in serious interest.[257]

A far more sympathetic portrait is found in Ellis Ashmead-Bartlett's *The Passing of the Shereefian Empire*. The first part of chapter XV is subtitled "Rabbit," and it goes into vivid detail about this unpredictable guide who often seemed to annoy as much as he seemed to charm.

Ashmead departs from London in June 1908 with the intention of meeting Moulay Hafid in Fes. Despite the dangers involved, and the rumors that Hafid "hated the sight of foreigners," Ashmead concludes: "from my private advices, I had reason to believe that the presence of Europeans would be far from unwelcome to Hafid, and I decided to slip quietly up country unobserved." But at first, he faces the same obstacles that Beadle did earlier that May:

I speedily realized that it would be impossible to start from Tangier, as Moorish authorities had strict orders to allow no European to pass the town gates. I was advised to go to the little port of Larache, forty-eight miles down the coast. My first step was to find someone to go with me who could speak the language…. In the end I was obliged to accept the services of a guide called the "Rabbit," on account of the peculiar shape of his ears and nose, which gave him a very general

---

[257] *The Guardian* (London), 23 December 1909, p. 5.

resemblance to that harmless animal. Rabbit is the most famous guide in Tangier. His character is peculiar, and his society is much sought after by tourists and diplomats. His knowledge of the English language is confined to those words which public decency prohibits from appearing in the dictionary. But it is surprising how perfectly a man can make his meaning clear and comprehensible by merely using the unorthodox expletives of a language. Every master under whom he serves adds a few expressive phrases to his rapidly swelling vocabulary. They cannot help doing so, however modest their demeanor and gentle their upbringing, for Rabbit in his off-moments would try the patience of a Job. On landing at Tangier he greets you with insolent familiarity. A raucous voice shouts out from the crowd on the quay, "How are you, old pal?" or, "How are you, old fellow?" or, "What have you come here for?" "Want a guide? Colonel Pleydell and the American Minister are my friends." He then proceeds to rattle off the names of his distinguished acquaintances in Tangier and Gibraltar, telling you the peculiarities of their habits and lives, and dividing them into two classes, those whom he calls "Good man" and those whom he calls "No good man." He will also tell you that he has many friends amongst the officers in garrison at Gibraltar, and that in a day or two he is off to stay with them at their barracks. Rabbit, in spite of his faults, has a good heart, and when sober is most obliging, if not very hardworking, but the curse of his life is his delight in going on the spree. During these lighter moments he gets hopelessly drunk, has a fight, and usually wakes up on the following morning in the noisome atmosphere of the local Moorish jail. Now you may stay in a Moroccan jail indefinitely until you can pay a sum to the keeper to release you. But Rabbit is never lacking in friends. He is so intimately acquainted with the private lives of the leaders of society in Tangier, and he has so many difficult and delicate missions thrust on him (for he is absolutely reliable), that he is always in a position to call upon some client to pay up the necessary, and to release him from durance vile. Thus he has become part and parcel of the life of

Tangier, and he is the most familiar figure on board the boats which ply between that town and Gibraltar; and in the little *soko*, where he may be found any afternoon sipping his coffee or drinking the vilest whiskey neat – for he despises mixing it with water, declaring, like the Scotsman, that it ruins two good things. Rabbit was pleased at the prospect of going to Fez, prophesying that Moulai el Hafid would be delighted to see him, and assuring me that, under his auspices, I would be certain of a good reception.

On June 30th, at 11 p.m., Rabbit and myself slipped out of Tangier and boarded the little steamer, *Gibel Musa*, without telling anyone of our intentions or of our eventual destination.[258]

The vessel appears to be the same "red-and-black funnelled *Gibel Musa* in which Paul Towers had traveled from Gibraltar," as the narrator of *The City of Shadows* informs us when describing the ship idling in the harbor, moments before Paul encounters Rabat.

It's also of interest to compare Lawrence's "Rabet" to Beadle's portrait of the initially annoying but ultimately lovable guide. Beadle as the intrepid traveler would have appreciated this irreverent, transgressive escort who deftly transcends class boundaries through the force of his personality and wit. Not to mention the inestimable value he possesses as a guide in the wilderness, where the British caste system no longer serves any useful function. Beadle as narrator clearly enjoys a laugh at the expense of Beadle the squirming protagonist, "Paul." But even Paul gradually comes to cherish Rabat, especially once he realizes that Rabat has been attempting to guide not only Paul's body but also his heart and soul. In so many ways, Paul has severed himself from the vitalizing stream of life. Almost

---

258 Ellis Ashmead-Bartlett, *The Passing of the Shereefian Empire*, pp. 204-207.

immediately, Rabat senses that it's his job to reconnect this overly ambitious Westerner to the things that truly matter: wine, women, and song. (The later invocation of the Rubaiyat of Omar Khayyam is far from incidental.) When Rabat encounters Paul suffering in a gloomy mood and Paul tries to shake him off by handing Rabat a cigar, we witness a sudden shift in their interpersonal dynamic. Rabat says

> "Tanks," accepting proffered cigar with alacrity. "Awfly good o' you, ole chap!"
>
> Paul completely failed to repress a broad smile.
>
> "Where on earth did you get that expression?"
>
> "Me learn Englees in school."
>
> "You didn't learn that in school?"
>
> "Wha-at? Awfly good o' you, ole chap? My frien' Jack — Lefften'nt Ro'ley, y'know — he always say that. Now, you come along me, ole chap."
>
> "You're an extraordinary brute" observed Paul again, and then relapsed into gloom as if suddenly remembering that laughter was a crime. As a matter of fact, Rabbit seemed designed by a kindly Fate to give Paul the only tonic he really needed, laughter and forgetfulness.

All of which leads to a pivotal scene in the story, when Rabat invites Paul to witness the sultry undulations of Zolika, a local dancing girl who falls so passionately in love with Paul that she would gladly sacrifice her life for him. Which is precisely what happens later on, when she takes a bullet fired from the Baron's gun so that the object of her unrequited love will not perish. But until then, despite her continual attempts to ignite Paul's ardor – not to mention her successful efforts to save his life more than once – Paul keeps Zolika at arm's length, ignoring Rabat's playful attempts at matchmaking.

One senses that what also separates them (from Paul's point of view) is the gulf between their vastly different cultures and intellectual perspectives, not to mention their class differences. Yet none of that matters to Zolika, who lives purely through her heart. Due to an earlier infatuation with one Irene Trevelyan, Paul's heart is broken and has yet to heal – especially after "the joy of life and success turned to bitter ashes." Instead, we're left with his obsessive focus upon materialistic ambition as a means of forgetting his loss. But when Zolika dies in his arms, Paul's heart is suddenly reawakened.

Her supreme self-sacrifice ultimately serves as a stepping stone to Paul's engagement with Zahra. For his empathy has been triggered, his heart opened, his spirit ripened and made ready for life's core dynamo – the vivifying presence of love.[259]

We shouldn't forget, however, that it's Rabat's love and respect for Paul that delivers him to this essential path, aided by "Mektub" – the fate that has already been written.

*　*　*

Although Paul (or as Zahra calls him, "Pole") is a composite figure molded upon Beadle and Belton, his general life philosophy and tendency to alternate between an adoration of the eternal feminine (especially when it's personified by a "goddess" figure) and a rejection of said goddess to instead pursue worldly ambition is pure Beadle. This represents a central theme in nearly all Beadle's confessional novels, especially when the hero takes flight after being spurned by an overidealized woman. To allay their grief, Beadle's alter-ego protagonists embark on a quest, expatriate to foreign lands, and yearn to accomplish something of value – despite being

---

[259] Beadle explores a similar dynamic in *A Passionate Pilgrimage* when Jim, a stiff British protagonist, is chided by his Irish counterpart, Biddy, to loosen up and engage in life. It also features a tragically devoted native girl, Haiwani, whose self-sacrificing acts trigger Jim's otherwise entombed sentiments.

continually confronted by life's apparent meaninglessness and tragicomic absurdity. And quite often, after detaching themselves from the allure of the feminine, they suddenly become enraptured by it once again. Or, as in the more pessimistic *Dark Refuge* and *A Whiteman's Burden,* they grow jaded and embittered by the loss of meaningful relationships – resulting in the soul's eclipse by cynicism and despair, once the goddess has flown the coop. But in *The City of Shadows* we encounter a more optimistic pattern: a seeker whose journey culminates in a profound romantic bonding.

The unfolding of weighty historical events; the stalwart endeavors of brave men and their trials of courage; the unspeakable horror of bloody war ... all this pales in significance when Zahra assumes her proper role, appearing and reappearing like a persistent, arduous genie:

Waali! Waali! Woe is me! That I die without he look upon me."

Zahra threw herself back on the cushions in extravagant grief, and stretching her arms towards the wall, sighed, bewailing softly: "O Pole, Ya Az-iz (Beloved)!"

"Tell thou me," she demanded, suddenly sitting up, "thinkest thou he hath many wives?"

"How should that be!" responded Raalia. "Is he not an N'srani? And do not they say that it is the custom of the infidel to have but one wife?"

"So sayeth Bu Shaib," exclaimed Zahra, half suspiciously. "But even if he lieth in his throat yet will I be the favorite wife! A-ah!"

"But how canst thou be?" demanded Raalia. "Is he not an infidel? Thou canst not marry him."

Grief and anger flew across Zahra's pretty features. "I care not! I care not," she exclaimed, energetically clawing at the cushions. "I will if I die! Yillah! One hour with my beloved and then let me die! A-ah, beloved! Come to me!

This heretical action flies directly in the face of two all-powerful institutions, the State and the Church – or, in this case, the Mosque – by proclaiming the divine value of personal love even when threatened by punishment, banishment, or death.

Viewed from a contemporary perspective, it remains difficult for us to gauge the significance of Zahra's courageous declaration. As with the legends of the troubadours, through the vehicle of unsanctioned but authentic love, rigid traditions and constricting religious conventions are transcended, to be replaced by actions that support our precious individuality and unique destiny – hence, posing the greatest threat to the established collective order. The divine is no longer made accessible only through the intercessor of religious institutions: divinity is immediate, palpable, and made personal through the wonder of the essential human organ, the heart.

Zahra's proclamation is also reminiscent of the romance of Tristan and Isolde, whose love violates fundamental social hierarchies and religious traditions. And like Tristan and Isolde, even if the temporal duration of personal love remains brief because it may be punished by death, Zahra concludes that this is a small price to pay for incarnating such eternal values.

Commenting on the mythic dimension of Tristan and Isolde, the scholar Joseph Campbell remarks:

> The usual marriage in traditional cultures was arranged for by the families. It wasn't a person-to-person decision at all. In India to this day, you have columns in the newspapers of advertisements for wives that are put in by marriage brokers....
>
> In the Middle Ages, that was the kind of marriage that was sanctified by the Church. And so the troubadour idea of real person-to-person Amor was very dangerous....

Not only [was it] heresy; it was adultery, what might be called spiritual adultery. Since the marriages were all arranged by society, the love that came from the meeting of the eyes was of a higher spiritual value....

The true marriage is the marriage that springs from the recognition of identity in the other, and the physical union is simply the sacrament in which that is confirmed.... It starts from the spiritual impact of love – Amor....

And every marriage was such a [spiritual] violation when it was arranged by the society and not by the heart. That's the sense of courtly love in the Middle Ages. It is in direct contradiction to the way of the Church. The word AMOR spelt backwards is ROMA, the Roman Catholic Church, which was justifying marriages that were simply political and social in their character. And so came this movement validating individual choice, what I call following your bliss.

But there's danger, too, of course. In the Tristan romance, when the young couple has drunk their love potion and Isolde's nurse realizes what has happened, she goes to Tristan and says, "You have drunk your death." And Tristan says, "By my death, do you mean this pain of love?" – because that was one of the main points, that one should feel the sickness of love. There's no possible fulfillment in this world of that identity one is experiencing. Tristan says, "If by my death, you mean this agony of love, that is my life. If by my death, you mean the punishment that we are to suffer if discovered, I accept that. And if by my death, you mean eternal punishment in the fires of hell, I accept that, too."... What he was saying is that his love is bigger even than death and pain, than anything. This is the affirmation of the pain of life in a big way.[260]

---

[260] Joseph Campbell, Bill Moyers, *The Power of Myth* (New York: Penguin Random House, 1991), e-book edition. Transcribed from Campbell's televised interviews with Bill Moyers, recorded between 1985 and 1986. For their complete discussion, see *The Power of Myth with Joseph Campbell*, Episode V, "*Love and the Goddess.*"

In a similar fashion, when Zahra announces to her hand-maiden Raalia that she intends to be Paul's favorite wife, Raalia demands: "But how canst thou be? Is he not an infidel? Thou canst not marry him." Nearly overcome by anger and grief, Zahra exclaims: "I care not! I will if I die! Yillah! One hour with my beloved and then let me die! A-ah, beloved! Come to me!"

The spirit of adventure urges us to venture forth – to engage in the trials of the mundane world and to conquer. But the soul yearns for a holy grail of heartfelt human connection: "One hour with my beloved and then let me die!" Paul's heroism lies in the fact that he rejects mere worldly ambition to instead quench his heart's true desire. And this, more than anything, is the keynote of *The City of Shadows*.

Sultan Abd al-Aziz with his bicycle.

Sultan Aziz, who often appeared to be uncomfortable in his role as leader of Morocco.

Left:"MOROCCO'S DEPOSED SULTAN. The cause of Abdul Aziz received its death-blow at Marrakesh. Abdul is now a refugee with the French."

Right: "MR. ELLIS ASHMEAD-BARTLETT, who made his way to Fez in native costume and interviewed Mulai Hafid on behalf of the 'Morning Post.'"
Source: *The Graphic*, 29 August 1908.

"THREE ENGLISHMEN AT THE COURT OF MULAI HAFID. On the left is Mr. William Redman, son of a former British Vice-Consul at Mazagan, who is a lieutenant under Kaid Belton. In the center is Kaid Belton, described elsewhere. On the right is 'Bibi' Carleton, British Vice-Consul at Alcazar, who wields more power throughout Morocco than any other European." Source: *The Graphic*, 29 August 1908.

Kaid Belton. Lawrence Harris describes the "curious looking uniform" of Redman and Belton in his memoir: "Their uniforms were certainly most gorgeous, and I was given to understand that they were designed by the Sultan himself, in order to impress the natives. His Majesty's artistic conceptions were evidently most bizarre. The style was a mixture of Moorish, Turkish, and Albanian brigands' costumes; unfortunately, the native tailors are very primitive in their methods of 'cutting out' and 'fitting,' and the result of the Sultan's ideas, together with their workmanship, was something like a clown's dress with a short Zouave jacket, all of it being elaborately trimmed with a profusion of bright yellow and gold braid, twisting and turning about in grotesque patterns among the tortuous folds of the heavy material, which tormented the royally appareled but uncomfortable wearers."

Portrait of Moulay Hafid taken by J. Giry and gifted to Ridder van Rappard, special envoy of the Netherlands, on 13 February 1913. In later years Hafid would remark to the writer Walter Harris: "Is not the wisdom of God manifest? Has He not given intelligence even to a dog? A little less, it is true, than to the elephant. But a little more than He bestowed upon the French administration."

Hugh Pollard, a Frontiersman who participated in the 1908 revolution in Morocco and who later worked as a right-wing British intelligence officer during WWII. Pollard asked Henry Pocock to present Sultan Hafid with a silver badge and to make him an honorary member of the Legion.

Alfred Arkell Hardwick, circa 1903. From the frontispiece to his memoir, *An Ivory Trader in North Kenia*.

Ellis Ashmead-Bartlett as a junior officer in the Bedfordshire Regiment, circa 1900.

"Alan Netherby," a journalist who appears near the end of *The City of Shadows*, is based on the Frontiersman Alan Ostler, who was a correspondent for the *Daily Express* and filed reports about Morocco, particularly after the Battle of Marrakech. While Ostler was missing in action during WWI, a fellow journalist wrote of him: "He has a greed for adventure."

Henry Roger Ashwell Pocock, who founded the Legion of Frontiersmen in 1905. Photo courtesy Archives Canada.

Beadle's Essays About Sultan Moulay Hafid

"A Talk with the New Sultan of Morocco," *Pall Mall Magazine* **(London), October 1908, pp. 473-479.**

A Talk with the New Sultan of Morocco.

An Englishman entertained at the Court of Mulai-El-Hafid.

The new ruler's prospects and relations with the powers, with some remarks from the sultan on his high opinion of the English, and his arrangements with regard to his deposed predecessor.

By Charles Beadle, F.R.G.S.

ILLUSTRATED WITH THE AUTHOR'S PHOTOGRAPHS.

ARRIVING at Mazagan[261] on May 4, I was fortunate in securing the services of Mr. W. Redman, a European resident, speaking Arabic fluently, and well conversant with the customs of the country. At his suggestion we paid – in Moorish garb – a visit to the neighboring town of Azzimour, at this period in the hands of Mulai-el-Hafid, the rival Sultan. We were received most hospitably, and entertained by the Governor, Sid Hassi ben Mansar Glawi, who obligingly provided us with a letter of introduction to his brother, Grand Vizier to Mulai-el-Hafid.

A fortnight was spent in Mazagan and vicinity, and we left on the 19th by the steamer *Gibel Kebir* for Tangier. Owing to the lack of accommodation, I found on investigation that a blanket on deck, amongst a motley crowd of Jews and Moors, was preferable to the comforts of a small cockroach-infested cabin.

---

[261] Mazagan: El Jadida.

The whole population were soon in the throes of *mal de mer*,[262] and this added a certain piquant charm to the summer voyage.

On arrival at Tangier, I found Captain Belton impatiently awaiting the start; but, to our great disgust, we were held up for many weary days. Everybody was cheerfully insistent that our proposed trip was impossible, and that, if attempted during the present state of anarchy and civil war, it would lead to disaster – capture or massacre at least. After several futile attempts we abandoned the effort from Tangier, and, thanks to the suggestion of a native scribe, decided to try from Larache.

Captain Belton and Mr. Redman, having preceded me by the *Gibel Dersa*, I left Tangier at noon on June 8 on the steamer *Quetzil*. She was really little better than a launch, dependent on fine weather for her trips round the coast. I happened to be the only Britisher on board, and, having omitted to bring provisions, fared but ill in consequence. I managed, however, in execrable French, combined with signs, to persuade the Spanish steward to provide me with a sumptuous lunch of dry bread and oranges. At length, towards 6 a.m., we sighted Larache, and navigating the narrow channel of the bar,[263] came to an anchor in the river opposite the town.

My two companions were already awaiting me, and together we made, or fought, our way through the mob, past the Custom House – I had but my camera and revolver – and up through dark and evil-smelling streets. Stumbling over garbage and loose stones we at length reached our lodging in a Jewish house; the hotel (!) being full, my friend had engaged this room as the best accommodation available. Entering the low archway – flush with the street wall – a hand pump faced you; we went through another arch or doorway into the family living room, otherwise courtyard. Around the square were the bedrooms

---

[262] *Mal de mer*: sea sickness.
[263] Bar: a sandbar or sandbank that lies across the river's entrance.

through another arch or doorway into the family living room, otherwise courtyard. Around the square were the bedrooms, ours being that lately occupied by mine host; about twenty feet long by six feet wide, furnished with two absurdly cumbrous beds with huge cloth canopies, and a collection of weird and wonderful crockery-ware and clocks decorating the walls. I immediately availed myself of soap and water, the performance of my toilet being watched by an admiring and amiable group of daughters squatting in the courtyard.

Then to dinner at the Hotel Lucas. After having exchanged stares with the other European visitors, and fed – we certainly did not dine – we returned to our rabbit hutch to compose ourselves, with the kind permission of certain small tenants, for the night.

At sunrise the next morning we arose – still scratching – and proceeded to prepare for the first stage of the journey to Alkazar. Our talib (scribe) had reported the previous day that animals and saddles were ready; but now he arrived with his usual self-satisfied air, and gravely informed us that it was utterly impossible – I discovered weeks later that "impossible" meant a little trouble in obtaining his desired article or action – to hire a single animal. It proved waste of breath to remind him of his statements on the previous evening; he calmly ignored the point, simply irritatingly reiterating, as usual, half a dozen irrelevant excuses. However, he was at length dispatched with strict orders to procure animals, or expect instant destruction.

We sallied forth in search of breakfast to the hotel, only to find it still closed up and in the hands of the sweepers. The proprietor was awakened from his beauty sleep, and after the usual display of explanatory palms, a window was opened, a table cleared, and an awful concoction entitled cafe au lait, with two "election" eggs[264] apiece, came to light. After this sumptuous repast we paid a visit to the British Vice-Consul, and were most hospitably received. Breakfast was insisted on; of course we most politely protested that we had already broken our fast, but reluctantly contrived to devour all food within sight. Our future plans were discussed; but we were compelled to perjure our immortal souls by disclaiming or rather carefully avoiding any mention of a trip to Fez. Our paternal Government takes good care of its children; and, having visions of heavy ransoms paid to wicked brigand persons, insists that its subjects shall be good, and kindly refrain from placing their dear little necks in jeopardy. The country between Larache and Alkazar not being within the prohibited area, we therefore only desired to view the same, as any guileless Cook's tourist[265] might.

On our return we beheld some sorry-looking crocks peeping from under their cumbrous straw pack-saddles, which the scribe informed us were secured as far as Alkazar. Moorish saddles were not obtainable, and European saddles, kindly lent by the Vice-Consul, had to be returned because our muleteer objected to all the inventions of the infidel, and gave us to understand that it was only by a great favor – and hard cash – that he agreed to transport our unworthy selves. The animals having been loaded with our blankets and traps, we followed on foot through the town to the outer sok (market). Here packs were adjusted afresh, and, with assistance, we were at length perched on our respective animals (one cannot possibly secure any sort of grip, and feels for some time extremely uncomfortable and ridiculous. One consolation – my particular

---

[264] In travel writing from this period, calling something "election" implies that it's exceptional or remarkable, e.g., "the eggs were unusually big – fit for an election!"

[265] Cook's: Thomas Cook & Son, a British travel company that pioneered organized tourism in the nineteenth and early twentieth centuries.

animal would certainly fall down if he attempted anything more ambitious than a gentle jog. A trot would have meant certain disaster). After several false starts and noisy arguments, we finally got under way at 11:30 a.m. The sun was fierce, and the road was sandy and dry. As we plodded steadily along, following the ridge above the river, a beautiful view was obtained of the whole valley and the open sea beyond, with Larache, white and cool, nestling on the southern lip.

Presently several unkempt specimens of humanity came running towards us, shouting and waving their arms. We halted, whilst Redman, the scribe, and these gentry engaged in a lively bout of voices and explanatory palms. On inquiring, I learned that they demanded money. "What on earth for?" I asked. "Oh, they are soldiers (of Abdul Aziz) – outposts, you know – and say that you must give them a present before they allow us to pass." "What a brilliant idea," I remarked; "tell 'em I won't, and see what happens." More talkee, talkee, and waving palms; then finally the amateur banditti retired towards their tents on a neighboring rise. "Is this the usual custom?" "Yes," I am told, "they always seize any opportunity that offers. They seldom get any pay, so try to make it up in other ways." What a charming and interesting country! The army whiles away the dreary hours by playing at Robin Hood.

I will spare my readers any details of the wretched journey stage by stage to Fez – the fearful discomfort of a Moorish saddle, the intolerable heat, and the thousand unprincipled ways in which every attendant imposes on the credulity or good nature of the traveller, even though (as we had to be later) he is effectually disguised in the native garb. Otherwise, in the disturbed state of the country, with one Sultan superseding another, and the army in a state of utter division, we should have stood a chance of decorating the country roadside with a heap of our devoted bodies. At Alkazar we found a native dignitary – an Abdul Azizite – who had sworn unutterable penalties to any Moor hiring animals or helping any European on the road to Fez or Mequinèz;[266] and it was only through the courtesy and help of Mr. Bibi Carleton, the British Vice-Consul, that we procured the necessary escort – an absolute necessity, as I found more than once when we had to face the gentry of a Moorish country highway. I might have had reason to view some of these encounters with even more miscellaneous feelings, had I known that my guide accounted for my complete disguise by confiding to our assailants that I was a dancing girl bound for the household of a distinguished native official. At other times I was, it seemed, a holy man, a *shereef*; and so on. There is plenty of humor, and lying, in Morocco. But let us come to our destination, with its suburbs of olive gardens, and the Mehalla, or army corps, encamped along the valley stretching away in a southwesterly direction towards Mequinèz, at which I arrived[267] on June 14.

After much waiting and reconnoitering and negotiation on the part of scribes, we gained a hearing with the Grand Vizier, to whom I carried letters, and he informed his master, the Sultan, who appointed us a handsome house in a good quarter with a guard of soldiers to do us honor.

After visits from the British Agent, a Moorish merchant, and exchange of visits with the Grand Vizier and other important people, and many days' rest considerately appointed for us after our journey, we waited on the Minister for Foreign Affairs; and it was during our second visit to this great functionary that we had the honor of being received by the Sultan, Mulai-el-Hafid, himself.

---

[266] Mequinéz: Meknes.

[267] The sentence structure is a bit confusing here. Beadle means that he arrived at Fes ("our destination"), not Meknes (which stretches back west, from the direction that they came).

It was about three in the afternoon when we received this second summons from the Foreign Minister, Sid Eisha ben Omar. After shaking hands he suddenly apologized, and at a short distance produced his praying mat, and forthwith, facing Mecca, commenced his devotions. This naturally, to our European ideas, seemed rather embarrassing; but it is the custom to pray thus, no matter where the true believer may be. They are, I believe, supposed to pray about a dozen times in the twenty-four hours; needless to say, few indeed do this, some not at all. As far as I can gather, it is all more or less hypocrisy – as usual, the greater the scoundrel, the more parade he makes of his devotions. A Moor once told me that, no matter what crimes a man commits, as long as he prays regularly and gives charity, in short, attends to all the ceremonies of the religion, he is sure of going to heaven – in the form of seventy thousand *houris*! Mark the conception of perfect bliss! The faithful son of Mahomet carries always a circle of beads, which he fingers as he mutters the prescribed prayers, usually contenting himself with reiterating "Allah!" one bead; "Allah il Allah!" another bead; "Allah il Allah!" still yet another, on through the cycle of the rosary. This becomes purely mechanical, for while the pious man is talking business, he is trying to get the better of you. I often noticed the Foreign Minister thus fingering his beads and praying whilst discussing State business.

Arising, he returned and opened the conversation. Tea followed, then a huge basin of roast beef and wheat bread, which, after we had washed in orthodox style, we tore and ate with our fingers. Presently bidding us follow, he proceeded to the entrance and mounted his mule. We followed suit; but I had not the faintest idea where we were going, nor could Redman enlighten me. Belton on starting was slightly ahead of me, and he, unused to the Moorish saddle, turned to speak, resting his weight on the off stirrup. Slowly the cumbrous saddle turned turtle – they ride with the girths loose – and the rider, with amazement written on his face, disappeared. A rush was made by the numerous Court attendants to his assistance. I had to bite my lip in a frantic endeavor to keep from railing with laughter – the whole incident was inexpressibly funny – for it would not be politic to be so undignified. However, at length we found ourselves entering the Government house which is devoted to official business, and apart from the Sultan's private quarters and harem. Whilst waiting in a small antechamber I observed three Ministers gravely squatting on the pavement in the courtyard, holding perhaps a Cabinet Council. The courtyard in question was large and cobble paved, flanked by a high embattled wall on one side, and blank walls of the Palace on the other, the orthodox pond and fountain in the centre. Around the gates lounged the soldiers of the guard, only distinguishable from others by their high fez caps without turbans. Most of these have been trained by Kaid Maclean or others in former times.

At length we received the summons to the audience. Mounting a narrow flight of steps, after passing through an inner courtyard, we, leaving our slippers at the top, entered a long narrow tiled room, with high windows on the left overlooking the Wad Fas Valley. At the far end of the room seated cross-legged on a gilt Louis XV sofa was the Sultan, Mulai-el-Hafid. Advancing barefoot to within a few feet I, as before instructed, saluted military fashion, and sat on his left in a chair provided. On his right sat the Foreign Minister, and the Grand Vizier Hadj Marani el Glawi.[268] An individual whom I had not observed until then preceded us with a long staff, bowing and scraping right and left; he, it seemed, was the

---

[268] Marani el Glawi: Madani El Mezouari El Glaoui (1860 – 1918). Moulay Hafid appointed him to the post of Minister of War and married his daughter, Lalla Rabia. In May 1908, Si El Madani was promoted to the post of Grand Vizier.

Master of Ceremonies. In appearance the Sultan was undoubtedly a handsome man, with large black humorous eyes alight with vivacity, a black well-groomed beard, and olive skin, high forehead and rather prominent cheekbones – the lower part of his face, if anything, was the weaker. Particularly I noticed his really beautiful hands and feet, tapering fingers, and filbert nails. He was of medium height, slim, and well formed. He immediately took stock of us, and smiled as if pleased, whispering something to his Grand Vizier, which I heard later was to the effect that he liked these Englishmen.

In conversation he proved to have a very broad mind, and showed a keen insight into foreign politics. Speaking of the present situation he expressed his intention of acknowledging the debts contracted by his half-brother Abdul Aziz up to the time when he (Mulai-el-Hafid) was proclaimed Sultan, at which time he had notified the Foreign legations that he would not hold himself responsible for further liabilities incurred by Abdul Aziz. He intended to endeavor, when acknowledged Sultan by the Powers, to have the Conference of Algeciras amended, and to ask them to adjudicate between him and France regarding the war indemnity. On the subject of the war in Shaoaya[269] he protested that he had used every means in his power to stop further bloodshed, that his intentions were strictly pacific towards them, fully realizing that he and his country could obtain a more satisfactory result by peaceful methods. The French were undoubtedly helping Abdul Aziz both by arms and the Press, which he considered was a distinct breach of neutrality; his quarrel was with his brother Abdul Aziz, on behalf of his people, and not with the French. If Abdul Aziz had ruled wisely, and kept the hearts of the people, no

---

[269] Shaoaya: Chaouïa. In his fight against his brother Aziz (the reigning Sultan), Hafid was supported by various tribal leaders and factions, including those from the Chaouïa region.

such incident as the Casa Blanca disaster could have occurred.[270] Of the present state of anarchy in the country he was fully aware, and was daily dispatching his governors to their various districts to restore order; for the tribesmen were like children, who, when the ruling hand was withdrawn, immediately commenced to quarrel among themselves. If the protection of French guns was withdrawn from the ports they would immediately proclaim him Sultan.

This, I may interrupt to say, is perfectly true, as witness the Mazagan incident. The French, on the very day the Moors had decided to proclaim Mulai Hafid there, landed guns and men, and took the adjacent town of Azzimour, on pretence of assisting the police!

Then, in the same frank and reasonable tone, Mulai went on: His desire and ability was to rule his people peaceably for the country's welfare, and to open the country, as soon as affairs were settled and outlying tribes brought to order, to European enterprise and civilization, and prove to the Powers that not only were Europeans and European interests safe in Morocco, but that she was fit to continue as an independent State. The English had always been the friends of Morocco since the days of Mulai Idrees. Why was it that France was allowed to carry such a high hand in Moroccan affairs? The Algeciras Conference was not with the people of Morocco, but with Abdul Aziz. Mulai asked me many questions regarding the occupation of Egypt, and of the French operations in Algeria. At some of the answers to his naive questions he laughed heartily. He particularly requested us to don European clothing; but to this we were unable to accede, having not a stitch with us. We explained that, having to come disguised as Moors and travel

---

[270] From 5 August to 7 August 1907, French warships bombarded the city of Casablanca resulting in widespread destruction and the death of 1,500 to 7,000 civilians.

fast, we had only brought such gear as was absolutely necessary. He thanked us for having been the first Europeans to visit him in Fez as Sultan, as also the first to enter since all Europeans left at the outbreak of revolution in August of 1907. We were to go anywhere we liked, to see the sights of Fez; his Ministers had orders to see that we were provided with an escort and anything else we might require, and he bade us make our stay as long as possible. After present topics had been exhausted in an interview lasting about two hours, we arose and, shaking hands with His Shereefian Majesty, departed.

"WHAT HAS HAPPENED TO MULEY HAFID:
The Story of the Inevitable Counter-stroke.
By Charles Beadle, who had just returned from Morocco." *The Sphere* **(London), 3 July, 1909, p. 14.**

[Photo caption:] Muley Hafid. The new Sultan of Morocco on his white charger. The former Sultan, who loved bicycles and gramophones, is living quietly with some of his wives in a villa at Tangier.

Commenting upon the latest news regarding the defeat of the troops of Muley Hafid it has been remarked that as the weakness of the ex-Sultan, Abdul Aziz, proved his downfall so the strength and independent character of Muley Hafid may cost him his kingdom.

Personally the present Sultan is a man of fine physique, high-spirited, with a quick and subtle intellect. But no matter how clever the ruler it is extremely difficult to steer the Moroccan political barque between the Scylla of Europe and the Charybdis of his own people.[271]

Towards the Powers he has throughout the negotiations held a firm and decided hand, realizing fully, whatever his private and religious inclination might dictate, that the time has arrived when his country must bid farewell to medieval methods and make a step to modern civilization, and equally well that Morocco owes its past immunity to international jealousy. The knowledge of the latter point has been the motive strength and support in his somewhat high-handed manner of late. When the writer had the honor of the first interview accorded to a European in his role of Sultan, Muley Hafid laid particular stress upon that point and made no effort to conceal the fact

---

[271] Scylla and Charybdis: in Greek mythology, two sea monsters located on either side of a narrow strait. A sailor attempting to avoid one monster risked being destroyed by the other. Thus, a choice between two equally hazardous alternatives.

that his future policy would be to play off one Power against the other. His weak point was, and is, principally lack of money and consequent inability to purchase the support of his pseudo adherents. The ethics of patriotism are absolutely incomprehensible to the egotistical Moorish mind. Of this national trait the Sultan is fully aware, and consequently conducts all business personally no matter how trivial, unlike his predecessor, who left all the affairs of state to his various ministers.

His Shereefian Majesty has expressed the desire to meet the demands of the Powers strictly according to the terms of the Algeciras conference, which, by the way, is a contradictory act providing for the development of Morocco in one clause and annulling any effect in the next. The aim and object of the conference, as it states, is the integrity of Morocco as a sovereign state. This point the Sultan quoted to the French representative when demanding the evacuation of Shauia province, which argument is at least logical and in strict accord with clauses of the said act referring to military occupation of the country.

The strained relationship between the Sultan and the Spanish mission rested mainly on the complications ensuing from the occupation by the Roghi of the Rif country and some concessions and other rights sold to Spanish interests. As Sultan he claimed that Buhamara[272] had sold property which did not belong to him, hence his refusal to acknowledge any rights granted by an outlaw. He was supported in this action by the rivalry of the respective Powers, who, although nominally at a

---

[272] As mentioned in an earlier note, a reference to Jilali ibn Idris al-Yusufi al-Zarhuni (c. 1860 – 1909), more commonly known by his nicknames: El Rogui ("the pretender") and Bou Hmara ("the man on a female donkey"). El Rogui was captured by Hafid's forces about a month after Beadle's article appeared in print. Under Hafid's orders, he was horribly tortured and then killed on 12 September 1909. Rif: a mountainous region in northern Morocco, along the Mediterranean coast.

perfect understanding, wear a different complexion in the political intrigues at Fez.

On the other hand, the people in the immediate vicinity of the Sultan openly declared their dissatisfaction with his autocratic and from a European point of view – cruel actions. Muley Hafid is attempting to adopt the methods of his father, Muley Hassan, who was the only Sultan of recent times who understood his people and succeeded in ruling Morocco in anything approaching peace and prosperity.

But times and circumstances have changed. The Berber tribes, mostly mountaineers, have refused to acknowledge this Sultan as they are on principle, like the proverbial Irishman, "agin" every government. Disorder and chaos mean to them freedom from irksome taxes and liberty to pillage and loot, so dear to their souls. The people in the bulk care little who may be Sultan, their preference being for he who squeezes them least; or it is, rather a local matter, for the governor who squeezes least.

Regarding the recent defeat of the Sultan's troops it is by no means abnormal. The material from which they are recruited can only cause surprise if they should by accident defeat the hardy Berber tribes, who have probably from monetary consideration elected to temporarily support the Roghi instead of carrying on their favorite amusement – intertribal raids varied by an occasional smack at the reigning Sultan. This is quite the normal state of affairs as sanctified by custom since the beginning of Islam. The Sultan Muley Hassan used to collect taxes successfully by perambulating the country with a large force and sitting down quietly to persuade each individual tribe to render unto Caesar and then passing on to the next in rotation. Until the present Sultan can afford to keep a large paid army for this purpose similar disasters will be the order of the day.

Another factor in the problem before the Sultan is the control of the fanatical classes. The religious bodies are against all progress and civilization irrespective of reason or circumstances. In the early days of the Sultan's struggle for the throne he recruited the majority of his followers from the fanatical masses, promising them as a party cry that he, when Sultan, would endeavor to free Morocco from all Christian or infidel interference, intending, as he has frankly admitted, that having gained their support he would then act for the best as his superior wisdom dictated. Hence the natural consequence that his friendly attitude towards the Christian Powers has been misconstrued by these adherents, who now accuse him of breach of faith and perfidy.

The Moroccan problem can only be settled satisfactorily from any impartial point of view by either the Sultan being assisted financially to support a large and well-equipped army and adopting the methods of his father, Muley Hassan, as he wishes to do, or that France or some other Power deputed insist upon policing and garrisoning the interior.

Illustrations

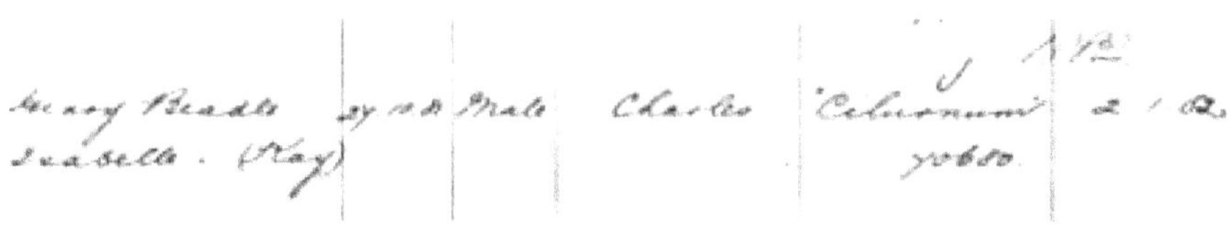

12 July 1873: Marriage of Henry Beadle and Isabella Kay at St. John's, Hackney, London. Both Henry and Isabella's father, Peter Kay, were master mariners. Henry's father, William, is listed as a "gentleman."

27 October 1881: Record of Beadle's birth aboard the SS *Cilurnum*, from "UK Registers of Births, Marriages and Deaths at Sea, 1844-1890." Other documents, such as his draft registration card, indicate he was born the day before, on 26 October 1881.

(Above:) The brothers Henry, Charles, and William Beadle. (Below:) Various portraits of Beadle from a family album. Courtesy of Beadle's great-niece Patricia and her daughter Liz.

Circa fall 1900 or 1901: Beadle in Mashonaland, South Africa. Courtesy archive of Patricia and Liz.

During this period Beadle received various decorations and service awards. The "Roll of individuals entitled to the South Africa Medal and Clasps, April 1901" includes trooper Charles "Marmaduke" Beadle, who served in the National (Waldon's) Scouts and Orange River Colony Volunteers, Nesbitt´s Horse, Regiment Number 1014. Beadle may have fictionalized his middle name in order to enlist a second time.

Rickshaw driver, Durban, South Africa. Photo courtesy *Six Thousand Miles Of Sunshine Travel Over The South African Railways*, p. 68.

Undated photo of Henry Beadle (1844 – 1906), father of Charles. Courtesy of Patricia and Liz.

Another photo of Henry Beadle, courtesy of Patricia and Liz.

Photo of Charles Beadle featured in *The Wide World Magazine*, May 1907.

Passenger list of the SS *Agadir*, 23 April 1908, with Beadle on his way to Morocco, where he would interview Sultan Mulai-El-Hafid.

Beadle disguised as a dancing girl or, alternately, a holy man, during his June 1908 expedition to Fez, published in the photo essay "A Talk with the New Sultan of Morocco," *The Pall Mall Magazine*, October 1908.

"Your [affectionate] nephew Charlie." Courtesy of Patricia and Liz. "I might have had reason to view some of these encounters with even more miscellaneous feelings, had I known that my guide accounted for my complete disguise by confiding to our assistants that I was a dancing girl bound for the household of a distinguished native official. At other times I was, it seemed, a holy man." ("A Talk with the New Sultan of Morocco.")

Hotel Cavilla, Grand Square, Tangier, circa 1910. According to a secret memo generated at the British Foreign Office, after an absence of a fortnight Beadle was expected to return to Tangier on 17 June 1908 and to reside at the Hotel Cavilla.

(Sideways view:) Rare dust jacket of Beadle's first novel, *The City of Shadows: A Romance of Morocco*, published in the spring of 1911.

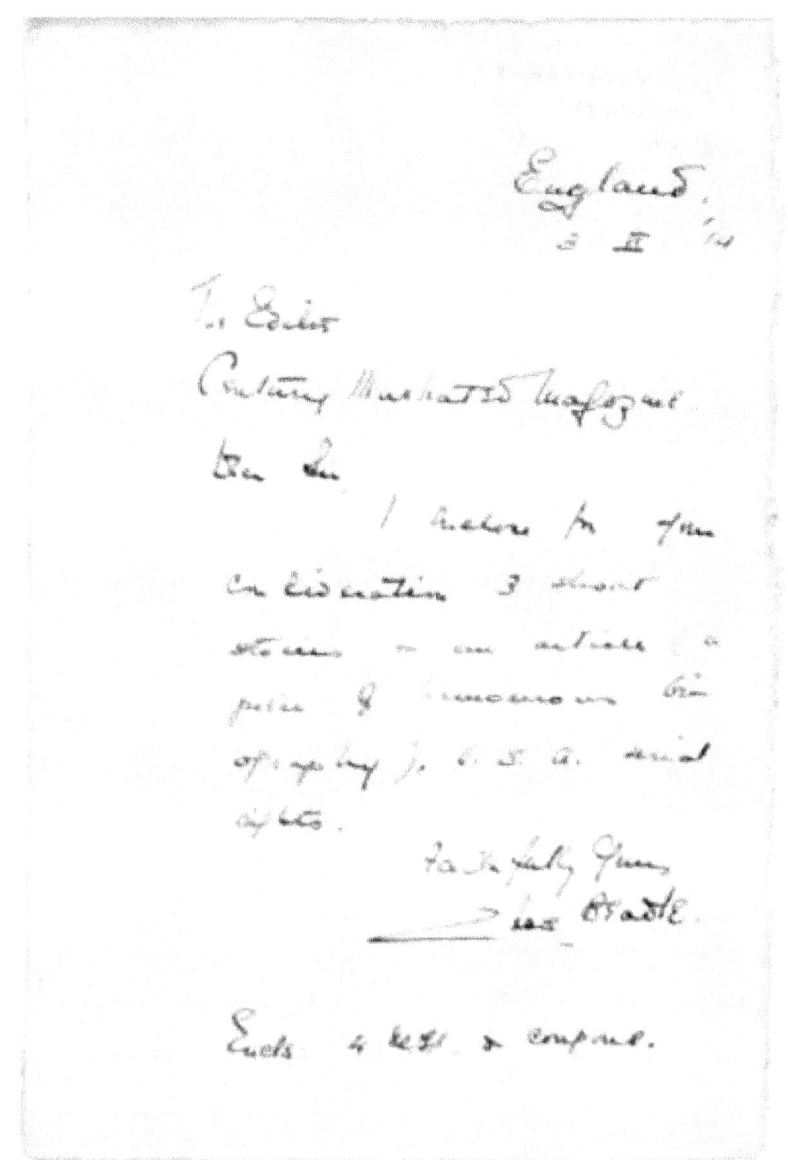

3 June 1914: A letter to the editor of *Century Illustrated*: "England. / 3 VI 1914 / The Editor / Century Magazine / Dear Sir, I enclose for your consideration 3 short stories & an article (a piece of humorous biography) for USA serial rights. Faithfully Yours Charles Beadle Encl. 4 Ms. & coupons." A watermark on top reads: "Creek Cottage, Bosham, Sussex." Courtesy of New York Public Library, Century Company records, Series I.

A PASSIONATE PILGRIMAGE

By CHARLES BEADLE

September 1915: Publication of *A Passionate Pilgrimage*. Hardcover edition, embossed with an image of Beadle's handwriting in red ink.

Copy of Sylvia Hornsby's death certificate, retrieved by Céline Cardon on 30 June 2022. The French vital statistics bureau had misspelled her surname (it appears in their index as "Homsby"), making its retrieval a particularly tricky task. From this document we learn that Sylvia died at the Hotel Beau Rivage (now known as the Hotel Majestic). This was during a period in which the villas and hotels of Cannes were used as hospitals, especially for the soldiers of WWI. So she essentially died "in hospital" on 13 September 1915.

Early twentieth-century train compartment, South African railway: the setting of Jim's first steamy encounter with Joan in *A Passionate Pilgrimage*. Photo courtesy C. Carlyle-Gall, ed., *Six Thousand Miles Of Sunshine Travel Over The South African Railways* (Johannesburg: South African Railways & Harbours, 1937), p. 13.

REGISTRATION CARD

SERIAL NUMBER 4661 ORDER NUMBER 1337

Charles Beadle

PERMANENT HOME ADDRESS: King George Hotel Mason St. San Francisco Cal
Will be 119 Central Av. Sausalito Cal

Age in Years 36 Date of Birth Oct 26 1881

RACE
White ✓ Negro Oriental Indian Citizen Noncitizen

U. S. CITIZEN ALIEN
Native Born Naturalized Citizen by Father's Naturalization Before Registrant's Majority Declarant Non-declarant ✓

If not a citizen of the U. S., of what nation are you a citizen or subject? England

PRESENT OCCUPATION EMPLOYER'S NAME
Novelist

PLACE OF EMPLOYMENT OR BUSINESS:

NEAREST RELATIVE Miss Jane Beadle
Address 22 Gordon Road Boscombe England

I AFFIRM THAT I HAVE VERIFIED ABOVE ANSWERS AND THAT THEY ARE TRUE
Charles Beadle

P. M. G. O.
Form No. 1 (Red).

ORIGINAL

REGISTRAR'S REPORT 4-1-24. C

DESCRIPTION OF REGISTRANT

HEIGHT			BUILD			COLOR OF EYES	COLOR OF HAIR
Tall	Medium	Short	Slender	Medium	Stout		
21	22 ✓	23	24 ✓	25	26	27 Blue	28 Grey

29 Has person lost arm, leg, hand, eye, or is he obviously physically disqualified? (Specify.)

12 September 1918: A month short of his thirty-eighth birthday, Beadle registers for the military draft in San Francisco, just before relocating to Sausalito. Under the heading "Description of Registrant" it notes that he's of medium height, with a slender build, blue eyes, and gray hair. His occupation is "Novelist." Under "nearest relative" he lists his daughter (then living in Boscombe, Bournemouth, England).

Circa 1915: A Modigliani portrait of Charles Beadle, titled *Le Pèlerin* ("The Pilgrim"), pencil on paper, 42.5 x 24.5 cm., featured in a Sotheby's catalog for Sale 6019, held in New York on 17 May 1990. The estimated value was set at $40,000 – $50,000.

The catalog caption quotes a passage from *Artist Quarter* in which the narrator says that Modi represented him with "the head of a hunting dog protruding between my thighs." The catalog adds: "There are three similar drawings of young pilgrims in private collections, but none include the dog…. [Modigliani biographer Pierre Sichel] "ascribes much of the [*Artist Quarter*] biography … to Charles Beadle … He attributes the anecdote concerning *Le Pèlerin* to Beadle rather than Douglas."

The anecdote in *Artist Quarter* includes Beadle's statement that the drawing was stolen: "Some years after Modi's death the drawing was on show at Zborowski's gallery – just before the latter's death – and was stolen." (*Artist Quarter*, page 227.) Léopold Zborowski died in Paris on 24 March 1932. Therefore, the portrait was still in circulation in 1930, the year that *Expatriates at Large* was released.

Sotheby's dates it from 1916 to 1917, but by November 1916 Beadle was in New York. A more likely time frame is 1914 to 1916, when Beadle's friend and neighbor Beatrice Hastings was involved with Modigliani. (Note how the date corresponds to the 1915 publication of *A Passionate Pilgrimage*.) Regarding the related "Pilgrim" drawings mentioned above, the Sotheby's catalog cites the authoritative J. Lanthemann, *Modigliani, Catalogue Raisonné*, Barcelona, 1970, pp. 345-346, illustration nos. 774, 778, 779. One of these drawings, titled *Le jeune Pèlerin* ("The Young Pilgrim"), was sold at a Christie's auction on 18 June 2007 for $55,636.20. On page 209 of Beadle's novel *The Esquimau of Montparnasse* (1928), the Esquimau protagonist remarks: "I'm merely a pilgrim, I seek and never find."

Collectors are searching all over the world for pictures by Modigliani, the artist who died in obscurity, who has now become a sensation in the world of art. A new Modigliani has just come to light, a portrait of the novelist, Charles Beadle (above), whose new book, "Expatriates at Large," is soon to be published by Macaulay.

From the *Omaha World-Herald*, 23 February 1930, p. 57. On 9 November 2024, John Locke discovered a fifth Modigliani "Pilgrim," and one that includes a hunting dog. Note Modigliani's signature at the top left and the words "Le Pèlerin" at bottom left. If this was the portrait that was stolen and never recovered, its disappearance could explain why it doesn't appear in any catalogs and has, until now, been lost to history. As noted above, Lanthemann's *Catalogue Raisonné* includes three other "Pilgrim" portraits "but none include the dog." The newspaper caption unequivocally identifies it as Modigliani's "portrait of the artist Charles Beadle," which we know was still in circulation in 1930, when *Expatriates at Large* was first published. So, it appears that Modigliani made at least *two* portraits of Beadle as the "Pilgrim."

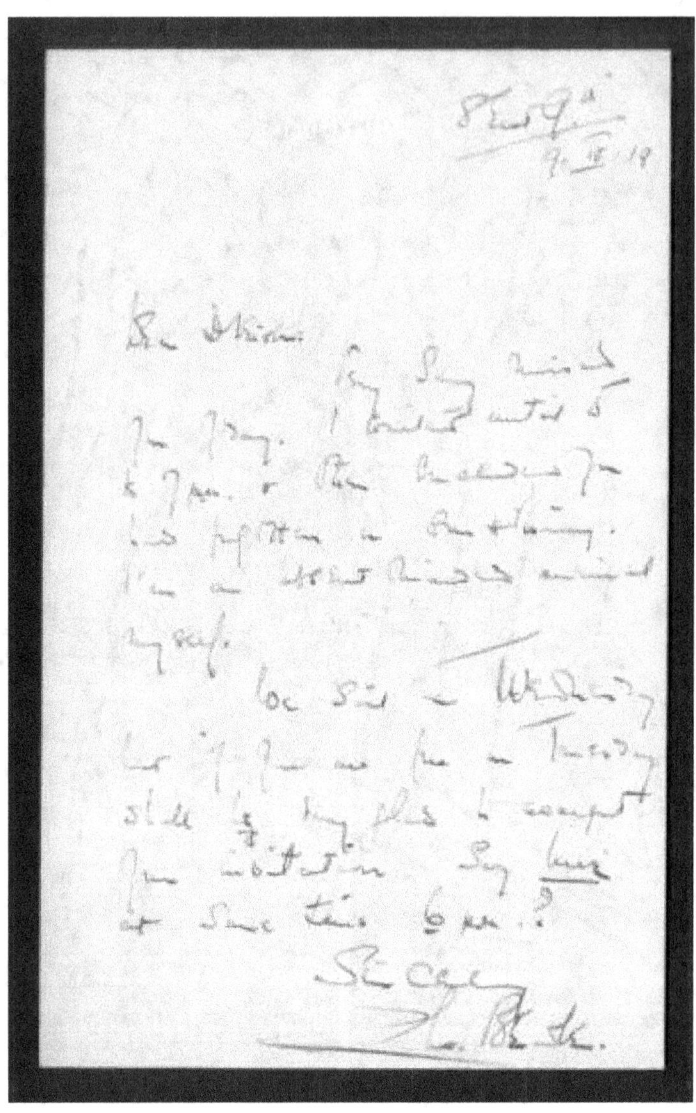

19 October 1919: Letter to author Theodore Dreiser: "8 East 9th / 19.10.19 / Dear Dreiser: Very sorry missed you y'day. I waited until 5 to 7 p.m. and then concluded you had forgotten or something. I'm an absent minded animal myself. We said on Wednesday but if you are free on Tuesday shall be very glad to accept your invitation. Say here at same time 6 p.m.? Sincerely Chas. Beadle." Beadle's flat was located between University Place and Broadway, three blocks north of Washington Square Park. Dreiser lived at 165 West 10th, a half mile west of Beadle. (Courtesy of the University of Pennsylvania, Kislak Center for Special Collections.)

Autographed copy of *Witch-Doctors*, inscribed "To Frank Harris from Charles Beadle." (Obtained in February 2025.) After Harris self-published his banned multivolume memoir (*My Life and Loves*; 1922 – 1927) it was republished by Jack Kahane's Obelisk Press in 1931: the same publisher who later issued Beadle's *Dark Refuge* (1938). Following the outbreak of WWI, both Harris and Beadle expatriated to New York. Harris became editor of the American edition of *Pearson's*, while Beadle published his stories in *Adventure* and occasionally served in an editorial role. They also traveled to London, Paris, and the South of France at roughly the same time and moved in many of the same circles. Harris settled in Nice in 1922, the same year that *Witch-Doctors* and *My Life and Loves* were published; and he died there in 1931, while Beadle was also residing in the Côte d'Azur. It's possible that Harris introduced Beadle to Kahane or suggested that he approach the innovative publisher with his *Dark Refuge* manuscript. *My Life and Loves* was banned in the United States until 1963, when it was republished by Grove Press.

An artistically enhanced photo of Beadle from the 6 April 1930 edition of the *Buffalo Times*, featured in their "Important Books of the Week in Review" column. Reviewer Kate Burr writes: "'Expatriates at Large' is a novel of genuine power. But the power is impaired by a splurge at brilliancy. Too often the cynicism is forced. The dialogue oscillates too sharply between wit and vapidity. Why ignore the intervening gamut?" Thanks to John Locke for uncovering this rare image.

On 18 May 1930 the *Sioux City Journal* published a copy of the same publicity photo but without any enhancement. Writing about *Expatriates at Large*, reviewer Vera Edwards opens her piece ("Paris Quartier Latin Sans Romantic Gloss") with the sentence: "A portrait of Charles Beadle has just come to light, by Modigliani, the artist who died practically unknown and has now become a sensation in the world of art."

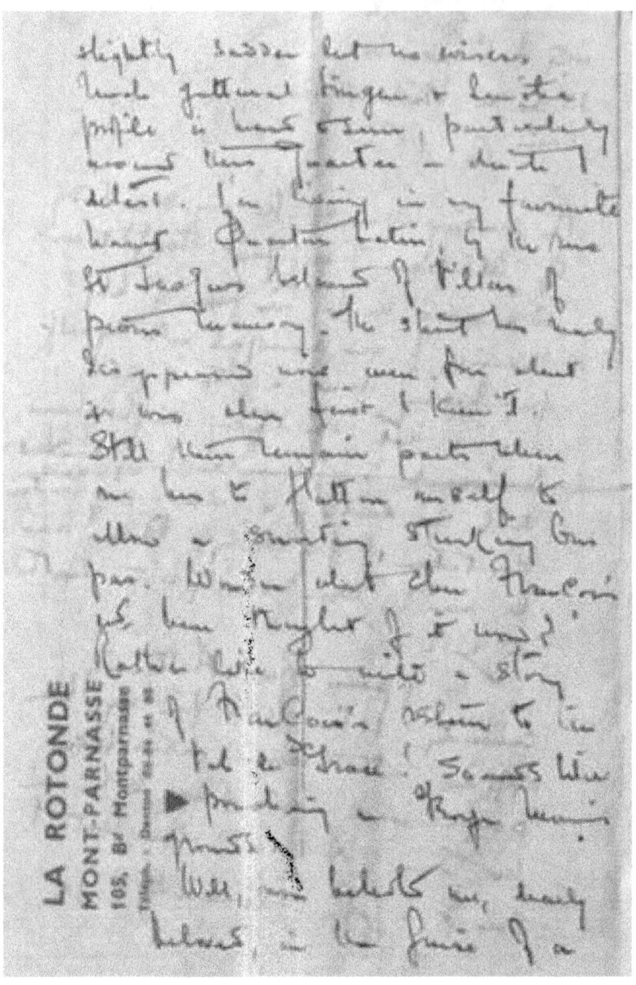

Circa spring 1933: Second page of a letter composed by Beadle and sent to his niece Isabel, with the return address of "Hôtel des Capucines, 13, rue des Feuillantines, Paris." The letter is written on stationery from the Café de la Rotonde, which was located just a few blocks from the Hôtel des Capucines. Courtesy of Patricia and Liz.

Passport-sized snapshot of Isabel Hettie Beadle (1904 – 1999), daughter of Charles' older brother William. If Isabel is thirty years old here, the photo would date from 1934, when she was corresponding with her uncle. Charles severed contact with the rest of his family, but he conducted a lengthy correspondence with his niece, writing from various locations in France. Courtesy of Patricia and Liz.

7 August 1946: Birth of Elizabeth Owen Bely, daughter of Jane Beadle and Igor Bely, at 9 Saxonbury Road (about four miles east of Jane's residence at 14 Dean Park Road, Bournemouth, England). Igor is identified as a "Chemical engineer of 29, rue Assalit, Nice, France."

Elizabeth Bely died at the age of sixteen on 23 August 1962 at her home at 99, Avenue Cyrille Besset, Nice. Her death certificate identifies her as the daughter of Igor Bely, "translator," and his wife Jane Beadle, "interpreter." Jane's address is listed as 20, rue Parmentier, Nice.

ACTE DE DECES
COPIE INTEGRALE

N° 005012 / 2002 Jane BEADLE

Le vingt six novembre deux mil deux à une heure treize minutes, est******
décédée avenue des Roses "Rimiez", Jane BEADLE, née à Saint-Tropez (Var)
le 8 juillet 1915, en retraite, domiciliée à Nice (Alpes-Maritimes) 8,**
avenue Georges Clémenceau, fille de Charles BEADLE, et de Sylvia Grace**
Ellen HOMSBY, décédés ; veuve de Igor BELY.************************
Dressé le 28 novembre 2002 à 9 heures 28 minutes sur la déclaration de**
COPPOLANI Tony, 39 ans, Chef de Bureau à Nice (06), 3 rue Alexandre******
Mari, qui, lecture faite et invité à lire l'acte, a signé avec Nous,****
Andrée GUILLAUMIN, fonctionnaire de la Mairie de Nice, Officier de******
l'Etat Civil par délégation du Maire.***************************

Nice,
le 7 juin 2022,
Pour copie conforme,
L'Officier de l'Etat Civil délégué,

Aurélie FAREY

Jane Beadle's death record, retrieved by Céline Cardon on 13 June 2022.
(The surname of Jane's mother is misspelled, and it appears as "Homsby"
instead of Hornsby.) Jane lived at 8, Avenue George Clémenceau, but at
the time of her death on 26 November 2002 she was at the Avenue des
Roses, in the Rimiez quarter of Nice. This quarter also hosts the Hôpital
Les Sources, a geriatric institution. The record also includes the name of
Jane's husband, Igor Bely (1916 – 1978).

EB 83322

Beadle
Charles

Le *sept* [...] mil neuf cent cinquante-sept, [...] heures [...] est décédé [...] avenue de la voie Romaine, Charles *Beadle* domicilié [...] 4 avenue Victoria, né à *Londres (Angleterre)* le vingt-six octobre mil huit cent quatre-vingt-un [...] sans profession, fils de *Henri Beadle* et de *Isabelle Kay* époux décédé [...] veuf de Sylvia *Honsby*.

Dressé le *trente et un [...]* mil neuf cent cinquante-sept, [...] heures, sur la déclaration de *[...]* qui, lecture faite [...] a signé avec Nous [...]

Paulin GASTAUD
Officier Légion d'Honneur, Médaille Militaire
Adjoint au Maire de Nice, Officier de l'État Civil par délégation.

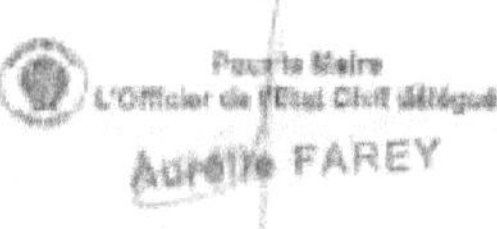

CERTIFIÉ
Conforme à l'acte original

Nice le 1 4 MAI 2025

Pour le Maire
L'Officier de l'État Civil délégué

Aurélie FAREY

Thanks to her dogged determination while navigating labyrinthian French bureaucracy, my research assistant Céline Cardon finally unearthed the elusive death certificate of Charles Beadle. Though it doesn't reveal where he's buried, it says that he lived at 4, avenue Victoria, in Nice; and that he died on 27 January 1957, at 20, avenue de la voie Romaine, Nice. It also includes the names of his parents and of his wife Sylvia. The Pasteur Hospital is located at 2, avenue de la voie Romaine; so perhaps #20 was part of the Hôpital Pasteur Urgences complex. The cert states: "Born London 26 October 1886. Without profession. Son of Henri Beadle and Isabel Kay. Only spouse deceased, widower of Sylvia Honsby." (Note the misspelling of *Hornsby*.)

Timeline

2 January 1844. Birth of Charles' father, Henry Beadle, in Barking, Essex, England.

23 May 1849. Birth of Charles' mother, Isabella Kay, in Liverpool.

12 July 1873. Marriage of Henry Beadle to Isabella Kay at St. John's, the parish church in West Hackney, London. According to the marriage certificate, Henry Beadle and Isabella's father, Peter Kay, were both master mariners. Henry's father, William, was a "gentleman." The newlyweds live on Dunlace Road.

12 July 1876. Birth of poet Max Jacob in Quimper, France. Max will later play a major role in Beadle's novel, *Dark Refuge* (1938), portrayed as the character "Isidore 'Izzy' Ginsberg."

27 January 1879. Birth of Beatrice Hastings (née Emily Haigh) in Hackney. Hastings was romantically involved with Amedeo Modigliani while she was Beadle's neighbor in Montmartre and is portrayed in both Beadle's fiction and nonfiction. She also produced the first English translations of Max Jacob's poetry.

25 October 1881. Birth of Pablo Picasso in Malaga, Spain. Born just days apart, Beadle and Picasso will move in similar circles in both Montmartre and Montparnasse.

26 or 27 October 1881. Birth of Charles Beadle at sea, aboard a Merchant Marine vessel, the SS *Cilurnum*, to Isabella and Henry, the ship's captain. Charles is the youngest of four children. (Henry junior, born in 1874, is the oldest, followed by William, and then Catherine, who died after less than nine months.) The family resides in West Hackney, where Charles is raised.

[Age 2] 2 July 1884. Death of mother from "consumption" (i.e., tuberculosis) at sea, while aboard the SS *Cilurnum*.

[Age 2] 12 July 1884. Birth of Modigliani in Livorno, Italy. In *Dark Refuge*, Modi is portrayed as "Ceccilini" (or "Cecci"), and his biography forms a major part of Beadle's *Artist Quarter* (1941). Modigliani composed a pencil sketch of Beadle circa 1915, a reproduction of which was recently rediscovered by John Locke and included in our new edition of *A Passionate Pilgrimage* (Dominantstar, 2025).

[Age 3] 22 October 1885. Sixteen months after the death of Beadle's mother on the SS *Cilurnum*, the ship is destroyed by fire. A court rules "the explosion and the subsequent loss of the said ship was due to the fire generated by spontaneous combustion in the coal which she had on board, and that the master, officers, and crew used all proper measures ... to save the vessel." Source: Merchant Shipping Acts, 1854 to 1876.

[Age 9] 5 April 1891. English census records that the Beadle family is still residing at 80 Benthal Road, West Hackney.

[Age 9] July 1890. Death of maternal grandmother Catherine Owens, who raised Charles while his father was at sea. Perhaps as a tribute of his enduring affection for her, he will later give his daughter, Jane, the middle name of "Owen." (And Jane will give her daughter, Elizabeth, the same middle name.) On 8 March 2009, Beadle's great-niece Patricia wrote to biographer Neil Pearson and said that Charles "had an odd upbringing." When I spoke with Patricia on 6 October 2022 and asked what she meant by this, she said Beadle's father Henry and his second wife, Sarah Killick, "were frequently away at sea on long voyages, so we think the children were cared for by Henry's sister Sarah Beadle, and by Catherine Owens, Charles' grandmother, who lived with them. Catherine was wealthy and blind."

[Age 17] 6 November 1898. Enlists in the British South African Police (BSAP) as Charles "Marmaduke" Beadle, Regimental No. 1019, Matabeleland Division. (Stationed in southwestern Zimbabwe.) According to Beadle's great-niece Patricia, "Charles and his brother joined the South African Police to fight in the Boer War. London was rife with recruiting posters back then. Henry later went missing. He was possibly killed in the war, although there's no military record of his death. I also heard that Henry may have died in a bicycle accident." Source: Conversation with Beadle's great-niece Patricia on 6 October 2022.

[Age 18-21] Abt. 1899 – 1901. Transvaal, South Africa. Serves in the Second Boer War (BSAP), in Morley's Scouts, Stock and Recovery Department. (Source: autobiographical sketch in "The Camp-Fire" column, *Adventure* magazine, 3 July 1918.) During this period Beadle receives various service awards.

[Age 18] September 1900. At age sixteen, Modigliani contracts pleurisy, which develops into tuberculosis.

[Age 18] Fall 1900. Mashonaland, South Africa. Guest of an Englishman named Mason, who owns a large farm. Beadle is nearly killed by a lioness during a hunt organized there on his behalf. (Source: "My Narrow Escape From a Lioness." *The Brooklyn Daily Eagle*, 7 August 1910.) Historian Geoffrey Pocock informed me that "the only Mason who is listed as a Founder-member of the Legion of Frontiersmen in London is Charles "Chinese" Mason, whom Beadle would have known and have met at early meetings." Source: email from Geoffrey, 18 August 2022.

[Age 19] 18 July 1901. Discharged from British South African Police.

[Age 21] Abt. 1902. Transvaal, South Africa. Employed by Transvaal Customs as Assistant Compound Manager, Witwatersrand Native Labor Association. Source: *Adventure*, 3 July 1918.

[Age 22] August 1904. Travels along the Zambezi River, Chikoti, Zambia. The expedition is chronicled in Beadle's essay, "Our Trip Down the Zambezi," published in the *Wide World Magazine* in 1907.

[Age 23] 1905. Henry Roger Pocock forms the Legion of Frontiersmen; Beadle is a founding member.

[Age 23] December 1905. Government House, Fort Portal, Uganda. "Engaged in recruiting and registering fresh porters" for an expedition into the Congo. (Fort Portal: aka Kabarole, formerly of the Toro Kingdom.) Source: Beadle's essay "Two Close Calls" in *The Captain: A Magazine for Boys and "old Boys,"* June 1910.

[Age 23] 5 January 1906. Beadle's expedition embarks from Fort Portal and enters the Congo, where he's attacked by a buffalo and almost killed by stampeding elephants.

[Age 24] Abt. January 1906. Modigliani expatriates from Italy to Paris.

[Age 24] 19 March 1906. Death of father in Buenos Aires. Charles receives a substantial inheritance, including assets that would normally have gone to his brother Henry, who disappeared in South Africa. This allows Charles to finance future expeditions. Source: conversation with Patricia, 6 November 2022.

[Age 24] Abt. 1906. London. Elected as a Fellow of the Royal Geographical Society (FRGS).

[Age 25] January 1907. Residing at 98 Cazenove Road, Stoke Newington, near the street where he grew up. Source: Masonic registry, listed below.

[Age 25] 11 January 1907. London. Initiated into the Masonic Commemoration Lodge No. 2663. Source: United Grand Lodge of England Freemason Membership Registers, 1751-1921; Folio Number 153.

[Age 25] February 1907. Northumberland Avenue, London. Elected to the Royal Colonial Institute. Source: *Journal of the Royal Colonial Institute*, February 1907, p. 138.

[Age 25] May 1907. Publishes photo-essay, "Our Trip Down the Zambezi," in *The Wide World Magazine*. One photo portrays Beadle with his back to the camera, sporting a pith helmet.

[Age 26] June – July 1907. Picasso paints *Les Demoiselles d'Avignon*. Modigliani visits his studio and sees the painting. In the first volume of *A Life of Picasso* (1991), John Richardson calls it a work that "established a new pictorial syntax" and "the first unequivocally twentieth-century masterpiece, a principal detonator of the modern movement, the cornerstone of twentieth-century art."

[Age 26] September 1907. Resigns from the Masonic Commemoration Lodge.

[Age 26] Abt. February 1908. Travels to Borneo. (Source: diary of Roger Pocock, housed at the Bruce Peel Collection, University of Alberta.) In his autobiographical "Camp-Fire" sketch from 3 July 1918, Beadle notes: "Went to Dutch Borneo, rubber planting. Afterward returned to go to Morocco."

[Age 26] 23 April 1908. Embarks from the Port of London aboard the SS *Agadir*, heading for Morocco.

[Age 26] 4 May 1908. Arrives in El Jadida (originally known as Mazagan), a port city on the Atlantic coast. There he secures the services of William Redman, a British merchant and mercenary versed in the local language and customs. Together they travel seventeen km (about ten miles) north along the coast, to the nearby town of Azemmour.

[Age 26] 19 May 1908. Beadle and Redman embark on a steamer, the *Gibel Kebir*, heading further north to Tangier, where they will join Andrew Belton.

[Age 26] June 1908. A confidential memo penned at the British Foreign Office notes that, after departing from Tangier for a fortnight, Beadle will return around 17 June, to reside at the Hotel Cavilla. Source: letter from Lord Mountmorres to Hubert White, Chargé d'Affaires, Tangier, archived at the British Foreign Office. (Appended to 21 June 1908 memo, as noted in Timeline below.)

[Age 26] 8 June 1908. Prevented from traveling from Tangier to Fes due to civil war. Beadle then boards the *Quetzil*, a steamer headed south, to the coastal city of Larache.

[Age 26] 9 June 1908. Arrives in Larache, where he's joined by Redman and Bolton, who had arrived earlier on another vessel.

[Age 26] 10 June 1908. Redman, Bolton, and Beadle travel inland to Ksar el-Kebir, about thirty km southeast of Larache.

[Age 26] 14 June 1908. After a "wretched journey" during which Beadle is disguised as a dancing girl, the expedition arrives in Fes. Source: Beadle's interview with Moulay Hafid, published in *Pall Mall Magazine*.

[Age 26] 21 June 1908. Following Beadle's successful interview with the Pretender Sultan, Hafid, a memo from the British Foreign Office expresses concern that Beadle, Redman, and a third man (presumably Andrew Belton) "are being treated as if on [a] mission from His Majesty's Government. Steps taken to counteract this impression." The memo adds that Beadle and Redman "arrived from Gibraltar via Larache."

[Age 26] 19 August 1908. According to a contemporaneous newspaper report, Beadle and Redman remain in Fes during the

Battle of Marrakech: a decisive encounter between opposing sultans that results in the forces of Moulay Hafid defeating the army of Sultan Aziz. (Source: "Swindon Doctor in Fez," *Swindon Advertiser and North Wilts Chronicle*, 5 May 1911.) Beadle later portrays this conflict in his novel, *The City of Shadows*.

[Age 26] Early October 1908. Publishes photo-essay, "A Talk with the New Sultan of Morocco," in *Pall Mall Magazine*. It includes a picture of Beadle in disguise, his face obscured by veils.

[Age 27] 17 November 1908. Camping in South Africa with fellow members of the Legion of Frontiersmen. Source: Roger Pocock's diary, which notes: "Beadle to camp."

[Age 27] January 1909. Socialite Natalie Barney moves from Neuilly to 20, rue Jacob, Paris, where she hosts a famous salon for the next sixty years. Beadle uses her as the model for his character, "Theodosia" (a wealthy sybarite, poetess, and self-identified "androgyne") in the novel *Dark Refuge*.

[Age 27] Circa early 1909 – June 1909. Morocco. Begins to write fiction. Source: Beadle's contribution to the forum "Contemporary Writers and Their Work," published in *The Editor*, 25 February 1920.

[Age 27] Circa May – June 1909. Repatriates to London from Morocco. Source: "What Has Happened to Muley Hafid," *The Sphere*, 3 July 1909.

[Age 28] 9 December 1909. Henry Roger Pocock's diary notes that Beadle was one of several friends who "visited Pocock the day after an operation on his foot," but their whereabouts are not recorded.

[Age 29] October 1910. The first issue of *Adventure* (dated November 1910) appears on newsstands. Beadle will become one of its major contributors.

[Age 29] abt. February 1911. Publication of *The City of Shadows: A Romance of Morocco* (London: Everett and Co.). According to historian Geoffrey Pocock, Beadle's novel offers the "best account" of the Battle of Marrakech. Source: private communication with Pocock, 12 September 2022.

[Age 29] 2 April 1911. Resides at 69 Antrim Mansions, Hampstead, London. Source: 1911 English census, which identifies Beadle as "author."

[Age 29] July 1911. Café La Rotonde opens at 105, Boulevard Montparnasse. (Source: Luc Bihl-Willette, *Des tavernes aux bistrots: Une histoire des cafés*, Paris: L'Age d'Homme, 1997, p. 174.) The Rotonde is prominently featured in Beadle's novels, *The Esquimau of Montparnasse* and *Dark Refuge*.

[Age 30] 23 September 1912. Picasso leaves Montmartre to rent a flat in Montparnasse, at 242, Boulevard Raspail. His studio is a ten-minute walk from La Rotonde, which he patronizes along with Modigliani, Max Jacob, André Salmon, and many other artists and writers, including Beadle.

[Age 31] October 1912. Publication of Beadle's second novel, *A Whiteman's Burden* (London: Stephen Swift and Co.).

[Age 32] 1914. London. Elected as Fellow of the Royal Geographical Society.

[Age 32] 14 March 1914. British Consulate General, Paris. Marries Sylvia Hornsby (1891 – 1915), daughter of Edmund Hornsby (1861 – 1908) and Teresa Ashwell (1866 – 1940). The couple resides at 4, rue de la Grande Chaumière, a few doors away from the famous Académie de la Grande Chaumière (located at 14, rue de la Grande Chaumière), where Modigliani, Gauguin, and many other artists drew from the model. Source: certified copy of marriage certificate, in possession of Beadle's great-niece Patricia, who recalls having a Picasso print in the house, "for which Sylvia probably modeled."

[Age 32] 3 June 1914. Posts a letter from Sussex to New York's *Century Illustrated* magazine, submitting "3 short stories & an article (a piece of humorous biography)." A watermark at the top-right corner of the stationery reads: "Creek Cottage, Bosham, Sussex." Source: New York Public Library, Century Company records, Series I.

[Age 32] 28 July 1914. Austria-Hungary declares war on Serbia.

[Age 32] 1 August 1914. Germany declares war on Russia. The French General Staff issues the Order for Mobilization.

[Age 32] August 3, 1914. Germany declares war on France. The following day, Britain declares war on Germany.

[Age 33] c. 1915. Modigliani creates a pencil drawing of Beadle, composed in Beadle's flat at Place du Tertre. Titled *The Pilgrim*, the portrait is described in detail in Beadle's Modigliani biography, *Artist Quarter*. (See Illustrations, above.)

[Age 33] January 1915. The hallucinatory drink absinthe is banned in France by presidential decree.

[Age 33] 8 Jul 1915. Birth of daughter, Jane Owen Beadle (1915 – 2002), in Saint-Tropez.

[Age 33] 20 August 1915. Letter from former U.S. President Theodore Roosevelt to Charles Beadle, addressed to Beadle's residence at Villa Robinson in St. Tropez, thanking him for sending his book (probably the forthcoming *A Passionate Pilgrimage*).

[Age 33] September 1915. Publication of Beadle's third novel, *A Passionate Pilgrimage* (London: Heath, Cranton, and Ouseley), while Beadle resides at Villa Robinson, St. Tropez. Source: Last Will and Testament of Sylvia Beadle.

[Age 33] 13 September 1915. Death of Sylvia Beadle, in Cannes. According to her death certificate, she died at the Hotel Beau Rivage (now known as the Hotel Majestic) during a period in which the villas and hotels of Cannes were requisitioned as hospitals, especially for the soldiers of WWI.

[Age 34] 13 November 1915. D. H. Lawrence's novel, *The Rainbow*, is banned in Britain. Censors burn over 1,000 copies.

[Age 35] 30 October 1916. Embarks from Cadiz, Spain aboard the SS *Montserrat*, heading to New York. On the ship's manifest Beadle lists Beatrice Hastings as his "closest friend living in country of departure," noting her address at 13, rue Norvins, Paris (Montmartre). His contact information in Manhattan is Paul Tausig, 104 East 14th Street. An ad for the company Paul Tausig & Son appears in the 28 July 1910 issue of New York's *The Call* newspaper, advertising "Steamship tickets to all parts of the world. Railroad tickets to all parts of the United States and Canada. Money orders and drafts sent to all parts of the world. Foreign money bought and sold. Located in the German Savings Bank Building." The manifest indicates that it's Beadle's first trip to America.

[Age 35] 14 November 1916. Arrives in New York City.

[Age 36] March 1918. Outbreak of the Great Influenza Pandemic, with the first documented case occurring in Kansas. By the end of the pandemic in 1920 about 500 million will be infected worldwide, resulting in fifty million to one-hundred million deaths, with 675,000 fatalities occurring in the United States.

[Age 36] 3 April 1918; 3 May 1918. *Adventure* lists Beadle as a travel expert in its "Ask *Adventure*" column. ("A Free Question and Answer Service Bureau on Information on Outdoor Life and

Activities Everywhere and Upon the Various Commodities Required Therein." His area of expertise is Africa: "Transvaal, N. W. and Southern Rhodesia, British East Africa, Uganda and the Upper Congo ... Covering geography, hunting, equipment, trading, climate, mining, transport, customs, living conditions, witchcraft, opportunities for adventure and sport." Beadle's contact info is still c/o Paul Tausig & Son. This is the first of many mail-drop locations that the peripatetic author will provide to *Adventure*: a useful resource for tracking his whereabouts.

[Age 36] 18 May 1918. Publishes "The Christman," the first of twenty-six stories that Beadle will publish in *Adventure*. His contact info is still c/o Paul Tausig & Son.

[Age 36] August 1918. Residing in, or traveling through, Grand Isle, Jefferson, Louisiana. (Source: announcement in *Adventure*, 18 August 1918.) Around this same time Beadle may have visited nearby Mexico.

[Age 36] 12 September 1918. A draft registration card in San Francisco notes that Beadle was living at the King George Hotel on 334 Mason Street, and that he would soon be moving to 119 Central Avenue, in nearby Sausalito. Under "Description of Registrant" it says that he's of medium height with a slender build, blue eyes, and gray hair. His occupation is "Novelist."

[Age 36] 3 October 1918. Contact info in *Adventure* is still Authors' League of America, New York. (Repeated in issues 3 January – 3 February 1919.)

[Age 37] 11 November 1918. Armistice. End of World War I.

[Age 37] 23 April 1919. Departs from New York aboard the SS *Rotterdam*, traveling second class, headed for Paris. His address is registered as 7, Place de Tertre, Paris. Source: Rotterdam, Netherlands, Passenger Lists of the Holland-America Line, 1900-1969.

[Age 37] Late April or early May 1919. Arrives in Paris and resides at the Grand Hotel. Source: Rotterdam, Netherlands, Passenger Lists, etc.

[Age 37] 15 March 1919. *Adventure* publishes the first installment of Beadle's *Witch-Doctors* (a four-part serial appearing between March 15 and May 1, 1919). Published in book form in 1922 by Jonathan Cape (UK) and Houghton Mifflin (U.S.).

[Age 37] 3 April – 3 May 1919. Contact info in *Adventure* is still Authors' League of America, New York.

[Age 37] 18 August – 18 September 1919. Contact info in *Adventure* changes to 7, Place de Tertre, Paris. Repeated in the 3 December 1919 and 3 March 1920 issues.

[Age 37] 19 October 1919. Corresponds with novelist Theodore Dreiser while residing at 8 East 9th Street in Manhattan. Source: University of Pennsylvania, Kislak Center for Special Collections, Rare Books and Manuscripts.

[Age 38] 8 January 1920. Spotted in Paris by occultist Aleister Crowley: "I ran around Paris, and walked into Lapérouse for lunch to find Beadle and Willy!" (The latter was the Pulitzer Prize-winning journalist Walter Duranty.) Source: Aleister Crowley, *The Magical Record of the Beast 666. The Diaries of Aleister Crowley, 1914 – 1920* (London: Duckworth, 1972), p. 90.

[Age 38] 17 January 1920. Volstead Act goes into effect in the United States, prohibiting manufacture and sale of alcohol. Prohibition Era continues until 1933.

[Age 38] 18 January 1920. *Adventure*'s "Camp-Fire" column publishes a letter from Beadle postmarked from Paris.

[Age 38] 24 January 1920. Death of Modigliani.

[Age 38] 25 January 1920. Death of Modigliani's companion, Jeanne Hébuterne, by suicide.

[Age 38] 3 August 1920. Residing in Westminster. Source: announcement in *Adventure*, August 3, 1920: "Care Society of Authors and Composers, Central Buildings, Tothill St., Westminster, London." This same info is repeated in the 18 October 1920 and 16 March 1921 issues.

[Age 38] 3 October 1920. The "Camp-Fire" column publishes a letter from Beadle, postmarked from Paris.

[Age 39] 6 October 1920. Hôpital Cochin, Paris. Death of Modigliani's lover, Simone Thiroux, from tuberculosis.

[Age 39] 18 January 1921. *Adventure*'s "Camp-Fire" column publishes a letter from Beadle, postmarked from Paris.

[Age 39] 21 February 1921. After *The Little Review* publishes excerpts from James Joyce's *Ulysses* in its 1920 issue, the magazine is successfully prosecuted for obscenity, effectively banning *Ulysses* from publication in the U.S.

[Age 39] 3 May 1921. "Camp-Fire" column publishes a letter from Beadle, postmarked from Paris.

[Age 39] 1921. Max Jacob is portrayed by Picasso as a monk in his two large paintings of the *Three Musicians*.

[Age 40] 2 Feb 1922. Sylvia Beach publishes Joyce's *Ulysses* in Paris.

[Age 40] June 1922. After serialization in *Adventure* in 1919, *Witch-Doctors* is issued as a book by Jonathan Cape in London and by Houghton Mifflin in Boston.

[Age 40] 20 June 1922. Beadle's contact information in *Adventure* is now "Île de Lerne," a small island off the northwest coast of France, in the Gulf of Morbihan.

[Age 41] 1923. The Dingo Bar opens at 10, rue Delambre in Montparnasse: the site where Hemingway will meet Fitzgerald, two years later. One of the only all-night pubs in Paris, it will eventually become one of Beadle's favorites. Frequented by artists and writers during the 1920s and Thirties, the clientele includes Pablo Picasso, Aleister Crowley, Nancy Cunard, and Isadora Duncan, who lived in a flat across the street.

[Age 45] April 1927. Publication of Beadle's fifth novel, *The Blue Rib: A Romance of the Riviera* (London: Philip Allan and Co.).

[Age 45] August 1927. Residing in the vicinity of Nice. Source: Beadle's letter to his niece Isabel.

[Age 46] July 1928. An unexpurgated edition of D. H. Lawrence's *Lady Chatterley's Lover* is privately published in Florence. The novel is subsequently declared "obscene" and banned in Britain until 2 November 1960; and in the States until 21 July 1959.

[Age 47] Fall 1928. Publication of Beadle's sixth novel, *The Esquimau of Montparnasse* (London: John Hamilton). A quasi-autobiographical satire about Parisian expatriates, it includes characters based on Modigliani, Beatrice Hastings, Simone Thiroux, and Beadle (as the "Esquimau").

[Age 48] 29 October 1929. A stock market crash ushers in the Great Depression.

[Age 48] February or March 1930. *The Esquimau of Montparnasse* is republished as *Expatriates at Large* (New York: Macauley).

[Age 48] 18 May 1930. The *Sioux City Journal* features a fuzzy image of Beadle, standing in profile, which accompanies a review of *The*

Esquimau of Montparnasse, "Paris Quartier Latin Sans Romantic Gloss."

[Age 49] Circa 1930. Teaching English as a second language at the International School, located at 1, Avenue St-Hilaire, Grasse, Côte d'Azur, France. Source: letter to Isabel.

[Age 49] 19 February 1931. Residing in the vicinity of Nice. Source: letter to Isabel.

[Age 50] Circa October 1931. Visits Paris but doesn't return again until circa May 1933. Source: letter to Isabel, circa spring 1933.

[Age 50] 1 January 1932. Breaks his ankle. After recovering, works as "a cabin boy on a yacht." Source: letter to Isabel, circa spring 1933.

[Age 51] Circa May 1933. Returns to Paris after an absence of "about 18 months." Source: letter to Isabel, circa spring 1933.

[Age 51] May 1933. Paris. The Palais-Royal Press publishes Beadle's seventh novel, *The White Gambit*.

[Age 52] 5 December 1933. End of Prohibition in America.

[Age 52] May 1934. The Dingo's charismatic barman, James "Jimmie" Charters, publishes *This Must Be the Place; Memoirs of Montparnasse*, edited by Morrill Cody, with an Introduction by Ernest Hemingway. Beadle is included in a list of notable patrons mentioned at the back of the book; his favorite drink is said to be a glass of white wine.

[Age 52] 1 September 1934. Jack Kahane's Obelisk Press publishes Henry Miller's novel, *Tropic of Cancer*, which is banned in the U.S. until 1964.

[Age 53] October 1934. Beadle writes a letter to Isabel addressed from the Promenade des Anglais, Nice, which includes the remark:

"The few friends I have are as broke almost as I am. Others don't know me ..."

[Age 56] June 1938. Jack Kahane publishes Beadle's eighth and final novel, *Dark Refuge*. It features thinly disguised portraits of Modigliani, the art dealer Léopold Zborowski, Max Jacob, Beatrice Hastings, and others from the Parisian demimonde.

[Age 57] 6 June 1939. Beadle visits Aleister Crowley at Crowley's home in Chiswick, England: the first of five dinner engagements there, lasting through 23 October (see below).

[Age 57] 1 September 1939. Germany invades Poland.

[Age 57] 2 September 1939. Publisher Jack Kahane dies from heart failure, possibly induced by a suicidal consumption of alcohol.

[Age 57] 3 September 1939. Two days after Germany invades Poland, both France and England declare war on Germany.

[Age 57] 29 September 1939. Beadle is residing at 331 Homewood Road, St. Albans, Hertfordshire. Source: 1939 England and Wales Register. The National Archives; Kew, London; 1939 Register; Reference: RG 101/16681.

[Age 57] 23 October 1939. Chiswick, England. After Beadle's fifth dinner engagement chez Crowley, the occultist notes in his dairy: "Here to pick my brains regarding Montparno" (Montparnasse). Beadle is gathering material for his only nonfiction book, later published as *Artist Quarter*.

[Age 58] 14 June 1940. German troops enter Paris and march on the Champs-Élysées as Nazi tanks rumble around the Arc de Triomphe.

[Age 58] 20 June 1940. Death of Beadle's mother-in-law, Teresa Ashwell, at La Maison Jaune, Chemin de St. Claude, Antibes. She leaves behind an estate worth £113, 17s, 1d. Source: England and Wales, National Probate Calendar (Index of Wills and Administrations), 1858-1995.

[Age 59] June 1941. Faber and Faber publishes *Artist Quarter: Reminiscences of Montmartre and Montparnasse in the First Two Decades of the Twentieth Century*. Coauthored by Charles Beadle and Douglas Goldring under the portmanteau pseudonym "Charles Douglas," the chronicle will eventually be recognized as a seminal work on the life of Modigliani.

[Age 62] October 30 or 31, 1943. Convinced that she's suffering from a terminal illness, Beatrice Hastings commits suicide in Worthing, Sussex. Shortly afterward, Beadle and Goldring receive a manuscript from her estate: a surrealist novella titled "Minnie Pinnikin," written by Hastings in French, which dramatizes her relationship with Modigliani. According to Modigliani scholar Kenneth Wayne, the curator of the Museum of Modern Art, William Lieberman, was preparing for a 1951 exhibit of Modigliani's work "when he was put into contact with Goldring and Charles Beadle by the art historian Douglas Cooper," and "through them he obtained a copy of Minnie Pinnikin." Source: Kenneth Wayne, *Modigliani and the Artists of Montparnasse*, New York: Harry S. Abrams, 2002, p. 205; and private communication with Wayne.

[Age 62] 24 February 1944. The Gestapo arrest Max Jacob in France.

[Age 62] 5 March 1944. Two days before being shipped to Auschwitz, Jacob dies at the Drancy internment camp.

[Age 63] 2 September 1945. End of World War II.

[Age 64] 7 August 1946. Birth of Beadle's granddaughter, Elizabeth Owen Bely, daughter of Jane Owen Beadle and Igor Bely, in Bournemouth, England.

[Age 65] 10 June 1947. *Short Stories* magazine publishes "Nameless Spy," Beadle's last known original publication.

[Age 70] February 1952. *Short Stories* republishes Beadle's "The Idol," a tale that first appeared in their 10 October 1933 issue.

[Age 75] 27 January 1957. Beadle's death certificate states that he passed away at 20, avenue de la voie Romaine, Nice (which was probably part of the Hôpital Pasteur Urgences complex). It also notes that he was residing at 4, avenue Victoria, Nice. Neither the cause of death nor his burial place are mentioned. The date and location of Beadle's death remained a mystery until 14 May 2025, when Céline Cardon located his death certificate in France. A reproduction of the document appeared for the first time in our newly revised edition of *A Whiteman's Burden*, in August 2025.

Articles About Beadle in Morocco

"King-Makers at Fez." *Daily Express* **(London, England), 23 July 1908, p. 1.**

KING-MAKERS AT FEZ.

———

DARING ADVENTURE OF SIX YOUNG ENGLISHMEN.

———

TO RULE MOROCCO.

———

BACKED BY A BRITISH SYNDICATE.

There are at least six English king-makers at present in Fez, or—if it be true that the popular favorite for the Moorish throne is now on the march—in the immediate entourage of Mulai el Hafid.

What they are doing, and how they come to be in the heart of Morocco at a time when resentment against European influence is the direct cause of the present upheaval, is a story which could only come from the land of perpetual adventure and romance.

Six enterprising young Englishmen are doing their utmost to establish Mulai el Hafid firmly on the throne of Morocco, in the belief that if they succeed the country will be opened up to foreign enterprise, internal troubles will cease, and Morocco will no longer be a constant menace to the peace of Europe. On the other hand, the restoration of the deposed Abdul Aziz will restore the affairs of the country to the deplorable state in which they have continued for so many years.

The audacity and enterprise of this little band of Englishmen is really astonishing. At a time when the whole country is in a turmoil for the very reason that the Moors resented the influence of foreigners with Abdul Aziz, these six venturesome men have actually penetrated to the very heart of the country, and have even succeeded in attaching themselves to the immediate entourage of Mulai el Hafid.

VOICE IN COUNCIL.

How far that chief's remarkable progress is due to the presence of his English advisers we have yet to learn. Their very presence in Fez at present, however, shows that their influence with the man whom the majority of the Moorish people are anxious to have as ruler over them does not count for nothing.

In the middle of last summer, when the internal troubles in Morocco were at their height, it became evident to Mr. Ellis Ashmead-Bartlett, son of the late Sir Ellis Ashmead-Bartlett, M.P., who had just returned from a visit to the country, that no settled state of affairs was likely to be brought about without intervention of some kind. Neither Abdul Aziz nor Mulai el Hafid was likely to gain the mastery, for the simple reason that neither was able to maintain any efficient fighting force in the field.

If, however, either of the rival claimants to the throne were furnished with effective foreign assistance, the scales would be turned in his favor. Now, officially, no Power could intervene in the matter, which was purely a private one so far as Morocco was concerned. France, it must be borne in mind, sent her troops and warships to the country for the protection of French interests and of Europeans threatened with danger, but not to meddle with the internal politics of Morocco. Any support which France has given to Abdul Aziz appears to have been strictly limited to moral support.

CONCESSIONS OFFERED.

Nevertheless, Mr. Ashmead-Bartlett was convinced that much benefit would result from the success of Mulai el Hafid and determined that, with the aid of certain friends, he would furnish that aid, on various conditions. After sundry negotiations it was made clear that Mulai el Hafid was prepared to grant sundry concessions, which, given a settled state of the country, would be exceedingly valuable. He offered, in return for English (unofficial) assistance, to give concessions for the building of railways, mining, the reorganization of the finances of the country, various important political posts, and a partial control, at least, of the Customs. All these things he would grant in return for efficient military assistance from the little English syndicate which Mr. Ashmead-Bartlett promptly formed.

These were prizes worth working for. It is undeniable that there is considerable mineral wealth in the country, and also railway concessions, if granted by one whose authority was genuine, might very well prove to be a source of considerable profit. Indeed, so widely recognized are these facts that the English company were by no means without competitors.

EAGER RIVALS.

It is asserted that on one occasion the Standard Oil Company of America offered no less than £200,000 cash down for the right to build a railway in a rich mineral district, the conditions being that they should have mining rights for thirty miles on either side of the line, the property to revert at the end of eighty years to the Moorish Government.

There were also German and Portuguese competitors in the field. One German company claimed that they had sufficient money, put up by Berlin financiers backed by the German

Government, to reclothe and arm Mulai el Hafid's entire force. The main point about these gentlemen, however, appears to be that they could not leave Tangier and come to close quarters with Mulai el Hafid in order to negotiate.

With the English party, however, it was different. As soon as their scheme had got well under way, Charles Beadle, one of the party, went out to Morocco to join the agent already there. This latter—Redman by name—had been in the country for a considerable period prior to the inception of the scheme, and from the first was in touch with the chief advisers of Mulai el Hafid.

Mr. Beadle joined him in March, the expenses having been raised by Mr. Ashmead-Bartlett, who had lost no time in entering into an agreement with a firm of London financiers. By this agreement it was arranged that any profits should be divided in equal parts by the syndicate and the other parties to the agreement.

The first emissary of the syndicate had no sooner landed in Tangier than he came into contact with the German party to whom we have already referred. A second man, Belton, was promptly sent out to reinforce him; and the three members of the English party—Beadle, Belton, and Redman—were tentatively approached by the German party, but did not disclose their own plans. Instead, they made every effort to get into personal communication with Mulai el Hafid himself. In this they appear to have received valuable assistance from El Glawi, brother of the Vizier and Mulai's right-hand man. Mulai el Hafid was at this time in Mequinez, and was hourly gaining adherents from all parts of the country.

It was now imperative that the syndicate should strain every nerve if they did not wish success to slip through their fingers. Accordingly, Mr. Ashmead-Bartlett sailed for Morocco, leaving affairs in the hands of a thoroughly capable member of the party, Mr. Hardwick, with whom he regularly corresponded, and to whom he proposed to send word when the time should be ripe for the rest of the party to follow him. On arriving at Tangier he found that his three friends, unable to wait for him, had started up country. He therefore decided on the very risky plan of making his way direct to Fez, where the Moorish Pretender had by this time taken up his quarters. Luckily for him, his plucky attempt succeeded. Disguised as a native of the country, he reached the Moorish capital, recruiting on the way two more Englishmen from a town near the coast.

TRIUMPH OF DARING.

Before long there were thus six Englishmen in Fez, and they were quickly successful in gaining the approbation and attention of Mulai el Hafid.

The whole story is one of enthralling interest, and when the time comes for it to be told in full, it will add another page to the vast record of daring private enterprise by Englishmen. With this, however, we are not so much concerned as with the probable results of the action of the party concerned. As a matter of fact, it almost seems as though they may afford the solution of more than one difficult problem. Where national interference in Moroccan affairs was impossible, this private and unofficial intervention may have the result of laying the foundations of a strong, self-governing Morocco.

France, it is fairly safe to say, will welcome an easy way out of what is daily becoming a more difficult situation. The less trouble Morocco gives her, the better will her people be pleased. Then again, there is the question of the opening up of the country—undoubtedly a rich one if properly developed—to European trade.

POLITICAL ISSUES.

Great Britain has always, in times of comparative peace, done a larger trade than any other country with Morocco; and, given fair opportunities, that trade might prove to be capable of wonderful expansion. Mulai el Hafid has given out that he is willing, if recognized as Sultan by the Powers, to safeguard the interests of foreigners trading in his country, and to afford them such facilities as lie in his power. He has also this recommendation, that he is a strong man, capable of keeping his unruly subjects more or less in order. They would never have been at rest under the discredited Abdul Aziz. Under Mulai el Hafid they will probably at least remain quiescent for some years.

Altogether, his establishment on the throne of Morocco seems likely to be the best thing that could happen not only for Morocco, but for Europe in general, and for England, it may be, in particular. The adventures of the handful of Englishmen now in Fez, and of those of their party who will subsequently join them, will, at all events, be worth watching. It is not an uncommon sight to see Englishmen making or marring a kingdom, but the spectacle loses none of its interest on that account.

"English Kingmakers." *London Evening Standard*, **23 July 1908.**

ENGLISH KINGMAKERS.

PLAN TO PLACE MULAI HAFID ON THE THRONE.

The story of a daring and ambitious adventure by six young Englishmen is told in this morning's issue of the "Daily Express." There are, it is said, "six English kingmakers in Fez at present, or—if it be true that the popular favorite for the Moorish throne is now on the march—in the immediate entourage of Mulai Hafid." Their object is to establish Mulai Hafid firmly on the throne of Morocco, and they believe that by this stroke of statecraft the country will be restored to peace, and will be thrown open unreservedly to foreign enterprise.

Mr. Ellis Ashmead-Bartlett, who had visited the country last summer, was convinced that much benefit would result from the success of Mulai Hafid, and he resolved that, with the aid of friends, he would supply assistance. Mulai Hafid was prepared to grant certain concessions for railways and mines and part control of the Customs in return for unofficial assistance from England. As soon as the project was well thought out, Charles Beadle, one of the party, went to Morocco to join an agent, Redman, who had been in the country for some time. This was in March, and the expenses were raised by Mr. Ashmead-Bartlett, through a London firm of financiers. A second man, Belton, then set out, and finally Mr. Ashmead-Bartlett himself set sail, leaving control of affairs in England to Mr. Hardwick. Other members of the party are yet to join their comrades in Morocco.

"Morocco's Future." *Sheffield Daily Telegraph* **(Sheffield, England), 23 July 1908, p. 8.**

MOROCCO'S FUTURE.

———

Remarkable Scheme

———

DARING ENGLISHMEN.

Six enterprising young Englishmen are doing their utmost to establish Mulai El Hafid firmly on the throne of Morocco, says the "Daily Express." Last summer, when the internal troubles in Morocco were at their height, it became evident to Mr. Ellis Ashmead-Bartlett, son of the late Sir Ellis Ashmead-Bartlett, M.P., who had just returned from a visit to the country, that no settled state of affairs was likely to be brought about without intervention of some kind. Neither Abdul Aziz nor Mulai El Hafid was likely to gain the mastery, for the simple reason that neither was able to maintain any efficient fighting force in the field.

Mulai El Hafid offered in return for English (unofficial) assistance to give concessions for the building of railways, mining, the reorganization of the finances, various important political posts, and a partial control at least of the customs. All these things he would grant in return for efficient military assistance from the little English syndicate which Mr. Ashmead-Bartlett promptly formed.

Various foreign competitors, including Americans, Germans, and Portuguese, were in the field, but they were at the disadvantage of being unable to leave Tangier. This was not the case with the Englishmen. One, named Redman, was already in touch with Mulai El Hafid, and he was joined by Mr. Charles

Beadle. Then a Mr. Belton joined the little party, and efforts were made to get into personal communication with the Pretender.

Next Mr. Ashmead-Bartlett sailed for Morocco, leaving affairs in England in the hands Mr. Hardwick. He decided on the very risky plan of making his way direct to Fez, where the Moorish Pretender had by this time taken up his quarters. Luckily for him his plucky attempt succeeded. Disguised as a native he reached the Moorish capital, recruiting on the way two more Englishmen. Before long there were thus six Englishmen in Fez, and they were quickly successful in gaining the approbation and attention of Mulai El Hafid.

The whole story is one of enthralling interest, and when the time comes for it to be told in full it will add another page to the vast record of daring private enterprise by Englishmen.

Where national interference in Moroccan affairs was impossible, this private and unofficial intervention may have the result of laying the foundations of a strong self-governing Morocco. Mulai's establishment on the throne of Morocco seems likely to be the best thing that could happen not only for Morocco, but for Europe in general, and for England, it may be, in particular.

The adventure of the handful of Englishmen now in Fez, and of those of their party will subsequently join them, will, at all events, be worth watching. It is not an uncommon sight see Englishmen making or reviving a kingdom, but the spectacle loses some of its interest on that account.

"King Makers at Fez." *Staffordshire Sentinel* **(England), 23 July 1908, p. 4.**

KING MAKERS AT FEZ.

———

Daring Adventure of Six Young Englishmen.

The "Daily Express" publishes an article today in the course of which it is stated that there are at least six English king-makers at present in Fez, or—if it be true that the popular favorite for the Moorish throne is now on the march—in the immediate entourage of Mulai el Hafid.

What they are doing, and how they come to be in the heart of Morocco at a time when resentment against European influence is the direct cause of the present upheaval, is a story which could only come from the land of perpetual adventure and romance.

The Englishmen are doing their utmost to establish Mulai el Hafid firmly on the throne of Morocco, in the belief that if they succeed the country will be opened up to foreign enterprise, internal troubles will cease, and Morocco will no longer be a constant menace to the peace of Europe. On the other hand, the restoration of the deposed Abdul Aziz will restore the affairs of the country to the deplorable state in which they have continued for so many years.

The article indicates that the young men are backed by a British syndicate, and it goes on to say:—The whole story is one of enthralling interest, and when the time comes for it to be told in full, it will add another page to the vast record of daring private enterprise by Englishmen. With this, however, we are not so much concerned as with the probable results of the action of the party concerned. As a matter of fact, it almost seems as though they may afford the solution of more than one difficult problem. Where national interference in Moroccan affairs was impossible, this private and unofficial intervention may have the result of laying the foundations of a strong, self-governing Morocco.

"Under Which Sultan?" *Dundee Evening Telegraph* **(Dundee, Scotland), 25 August 1908, p.3.**

UNDER WHICH SULTAN?

———

POWERS AND POSITION IN MOROCCO.

———

The Pretender's Claim.

Confirmation of the defeat of Abdul Aziz, Sultan of Morocco, and of the proclamation of his brother, Mulai Hafid, as Sultan, has been received the Foreign Office in a dispatch from Mr. White,[273] Charge d'Affaires, Tangier.

By the terms of the Algeciras Convention[274] the signatory Powers are pledged not to intervene in internal affairs of Morocco. The choice of an Emperor is reserved for the people, and the Powers have no intention of forcing on the Moors either Abdul Aziz or his brother, the Pretender. If the Sultan has still

---

[273] This may be the same Herbert E. White whose letter of 21 June 1908 is quoted in a secret Foreign Office memo, in which White expresses concern about Beadle's presence in Morocco, stating: "It is difficult to say whether these travelers have alleged that they are Emissaries of His Majesty's Government to give themselves importance and ensure a good reception, or whether the report originated with Mulai Hafid and his officials, and is intended to lead the people to believe that His Majesty's Government have recognized him, or at any rate are in negotiation with him." After receiving this information, a memo from the Foreign Office concludes: "They are being treated as if on mission from His Majesty's Government. Steps taken to counteract this impression." And Beadle is identified as "One of the Englishmen in question." (For more on this, see my Afterword.)

[274] As noted earlier, an agreement reached in 1906 that attempted to resolve the First Moroccan Crisis between France and Germany, which opened Morocco to international trade.

the strength and the will to recover his heritage no obstacle will be put in his path.

On the other hand, if is found that the proclamation of Mulai holds good and is accepted by the country without further opposition, the Powers may be invited to recognize his claims. For the present, however, the signatories see no reason for intervention. The initiative must come from France, which is the country chiefly concerned. Spain also must be consulted, not merely because of her territorial interests in Morocco, but because the great majority of the European residents are of Spanish origin and nationality.

France and Great Britain will abandon Abdul Aziz only as a last resource, for they acknowledge in him a ruler well affected to reform. Germany, on the contrary, though it has withheld any sign of official support, is prepared to acknowledge the accession of Mulai Hafid as un fait accompli.

THE MEN BEHIND HAFID.

How much of Mulai Hafid's success is due the six enterprising young Englishmen who arrived Fez in the middle of last month has yet to come out.

The story of how these English Sultan-makers arrived in Fez is a most interesting one.

The principal of the contingent is Mr. Ellis Ashmead-Bartlett, who was convinced that much benefit would result from the success of Mulai Hafid, and determined that, with the aid of certain friends, he would furnish that aid on various conditions.

Hafid offered in return for English (unofficial) assistance to give concessions for the building of railways, mining, the reorganization of the finances of the country, various important political posts, and a partial control at least of the Customs.

Three Englishmen named Charles Beadle, Redman, and Belton left for Fez, and their reports made it imperative that Mr.

Ashmead-Bartlett himself should sail for Morocco, leaving affairs in England in the hands of Mr. Arkell Hardwick.

On arriving at Tangier he found that his three friends, unable to wait for him, had started up country.

He therefore decided on the very risky plan of making his way direct to Fez, where the Moorish Pretender had by this time taken up his headquarters.

Luckily for him, his plucky attempt succeeded. Disguised as a native of the country, he reached the Moorish capital, recruiting on the way two more Englishmen from a town near the coast.

On 30th July Mr. Arkell Hardwick left London for Tangier, and the last that was heard of him was that he was on his way to Fez across the desert.

"Old Order Changed," "The New Sultan," and "Daring Adventure of Young Englishmen," *The Observer* (Adelaide, Australia), 29 August 1908, p. 45.

Old Order Changed.
Sultan of Morocco Defeated.
Fled from country.
Mulai Hafid Proclaimed.

London, August 24. The fighting between Abd-el-Aziz, who has been Sultan of Morocco since June 7, 1894, and Mulai Hafid, his brother and Viceroy of Southern Morocco, for the possession of the throne, has ended in the complete defeat of Abd-el-Aziz and his flight from the country. Last year the then pretender was proclaimed Sultan at Marakesh, the southern capital, and after varying fortunes he entered Fez, the Holy City, where he was received by the populace and acclaimed as the rightful ruler. His brother in the meantime had withdrawn to Rabat, on the sea coast west of Fez, to await developments in his favor. Here he was disappointed, for indications all pointed to the loss of his prestige, and on July 12 he started with the Maghzen for Marakesh to reconquer the districts which had declared for his brother. Later advices stated that the circumstance that he contented himself with such a short day's march on the first day as about 10 miles that separated Rabat from Tmara, a kasbah on the coast where he was reported to have spent the night, was not regarded as evidence of much energy. On two previous occasions his mehallas started with a great flourish of trumpets for the conquest of the interior, only to "march back again" shortly afterwards with their task undone. Afterwards his prospects seemed brighter. The principal notables of Saleh and Rabat saluted their ruler, and expressed their devotion to him, while a certain number of them accompanied him on his march to Marakesh. The Shawia and other tribes sent him mounted contingents, and delegates from more distant tribes assured him of their support when once his troops had crossed the Um-er-Rebia. The two powerful tribes, the Tadlas and the Sraghnas, through whose territory he had to pass, were reported on good native authority to be very favorable to him. They were said, indeed, to have promised him their support. Nor was it anticipated (states the Tangier correspondent of The Times) that his return through the Shawia country would involve great danger for him, the quiescence of tribesmen in that country being assured by the vicinity of the French troops, by whom they had been effectively subjugated.

Abd-el-Aziz arrived in the vicinity of Marakesh about a week ago, and immediately gave battle to the enemy. Fortune favored him, but on Saturday the tide turned in an engagement 50 miles from the town, and he was crushingly defeated. Before the second flight many of his soldiers joined the Hafidist mahalla, and when the firing started the Sultan's artillery proved ineffective, owing to the panic among his men, caused by the bursting of several of the guns. The battle ended in the remnants of the Sultan's army taking flight towards the French zone in the Shawai district.

Abd-el-Aziz barely escaped with his life. The scene in his camp during the critical time is described as having been one of the wildest treachery and panic, and he fled when his followers turned on him and pillaged the camp. He has already reached Settal, half-way between Marakesh and Fez. He intends to proceed to Casa Blanca, and thence to Syria, to await a change in circumstances which will enable him to return to Morocco. It is understood that Mulai Hafid has promised to allow him a pension and a place of residence.

So soon as the news of the victory of Mulai Hafid was received in Tangier he was proclaimed Sultan amid great enthusiasm. Similar ceremonies were carried out at several of the coast towns. It is announced that none of the officials will be changed.

The correspondent of The Times at Tangier states that there has been too much tendency in the past to describe the two Sultans as representing reform and reaction respectively. The actual personality of the Sultan is unimportant, because the correspondent considers that Mulai Hafid will probably prove as amenable to "loans" as was his brother.

———

The New Sultan.

Not Yet Recognized by Powers.

———

London, August 25. The trouble in Morocco is by no means settled yet. Not withstanding the fact that Abd-el-Aziz has been defeated and deposed by his brother (Mulai Hafid) the French government announces that it will not recognize the latter as Sultan until he definitely agrees to accept the terms of the Algeciras Convention. In the meanwhile France and Spain will continue to exercise the powers and duties placed upon them by the agreement arrived at by that conference.

The foreign diplomatists at Tangier have communicated with their respective Governments seeking instructions as to the attitude they shall assume respecting the recognition of Mulai Hafid.

The treachery of the Moorish soldiers to the ex-Sultan was beyond parallel, and it has been ascertained that almost the only men who did not desert to defeated Sultan Abd-el-Aziz in his time of need were the members of the French military service and Dr. Verdon and Sgt. Balding. These assisted him to a place of refuge at the French outposts at Settat.

———

Daring Adventure of Young Englishmen.
Backed by a Syndicate.

The London Daily Express for July 24 stated: – "Six enterprising young Englishmen are doing their utmost to establish Mulai Hafid firmly on the throne of Morocco, in the belief that if they succeed the country will be opened up to foreign enterprise, internal troubles will cease, and Morocco will no longer be a constant menace to the peace of Europe. The audacity and enterprise of this little band is astonishing. At a time when the whole country is in a turmoil for the very reason that the Moors resented the influence of foreigners with Abd-el-Aziz, these venturesome men have actually penetrated to the heart of the country, and have even succeeded in attaching themselves to the immediate entourage of Mulai Hafid.

– Voice in Council –

In the middle of last summer, when the internal troubles in Morocco were at their height, it became evident to Mr. Ellis Ashmead-Bartlett, son of the late Sir Ellis Ashmead-Bartlett, M.P., who had just returned from a visit to the country[,] that no settled state of affairs was likely to be brought about without intervention of some kind. Neither Ab-del-Aziz nor Mulai Hafid was likely to gain the mastery, for the simple reason that neither was able to maintain any efficient fighting force in the field. If, however, either of the rival claimants to the throne were furnished with effective foreign assistance the scales would be turned in his favor. Now, officially no Power could intervene in the matter, which was purely a private one, so far as Morocco was concerned. France, it must be borne in mind, sent her troops and warships to the country for the protection of

French interests and of Europeans threatened with danger, but not to meddle with the internal politics of Morocco. Any support which France has given to Ab-del-Aziz appears to have been strictly limited to moral support.

– Concessions Offered –

Nevertheless, Mr. Ashmead-Bartlett was convinced that much benefit would result from the success of Mulai Hafid, and determined that, with the aid of friends, he would furnish that aid. After sundry negotiations it was made clear that Mulai Hafid was prepared to grant sundry concessions, which, given a settled state of the country, would be exceedingly valuable. He offered, in return for English (unofficial) assistance, to give concessions for the building of railways, mining, the reorganization of the finances of the country, various important political posts, and a partial control, at least, of the customs. All these things he would grant in return for efficient military assistance from the little English syndicate which Mr. Ashmead-Bartlett promptly formed. These were prizes worth fighting for. There is considerable mineral wealth in the country, and railway concessions, if granted by one whose authority was genuine, might very well prove to be a source of considerable profit. Indeed, so widely recognized are these facts that the English company were by no means without competitors.

– Eager rivals. –

It is asserted that on one occasion the standard oil company of America offered £200,000 cash down for the right to build a railway in a rich mineral district, the conditions being that they should have mining rights for 30 miles on either side of the line, the property to revert at the end of 80 years to the Moorish government. There were also German and Portuguese competitors in the field. One German company claimed that they had sufficient money, put up by Berlin financiers backed by the German Government, to reclothe and arm Mulai Hafid's entire force. The main point about these gentleman, however, appears to be that they could not leave Tangier and come to close quarters with Mulai Hafid in order to negotiate. With the English party it was different. As soon as their scheme had got well underway, Charles Beadle, one of the party, went out to Morocco to join the agent already there. This latter – Redman by name – had been in the country for a considerable period prior to the inception of the scheme, and from the first was in touch with the chief advisors of Mulai Hafid. Mr. Beadle joined him in March, the expenses having been raised by Mr. Ashmead-Bartlett, who had lost no time in entering into an agreement with a firm of London financiers. By this agreement it was arranged that any profits should be divided in equal parts by the syndicate and the other parties to the agreement. The first emissary of the syndicate had no sooner landed in Tangier than he came into contact with the German party to whom we have already referred. A second man, Belton, was promptly sent out to reinforce him; and the three members of the English party – Beadle, Belton, and Redman – were tentatively approached by the German party, but did not disclose their own plans. Instead, they made every effort to get into personal communication with Mulai Hafid himself. In this they appear to have received valuable assistance from El Glawi, brother of the Vizier, and Mulai's righthand man. Mulai Hafid was at this time in Mequinez, and was hourly gaining adherents from all parts of the country. It was now imperative that the syndicate should strain every nerve if they did not wish success to slip through their fingers. Accordingly Mr. Ashmead-Bartlett sailed for Morocco, leaving affairs in England in the hands of a thoroughly capable member of the party, Mr. Hardwick, with whom he regularly corresponded, and to whom he proposed to send word when the time should be ripe for the rest of the party to follow him. On arriving at Tangier he found that his three friends, unable to wait for him, had started up country. He therefore decided on the very risky plan of making his way direct to Fez, where the Moorish Pretender had by this time taken up his quarters. Luckily for him, his plucky attempt succeeded. Disguised as a native of the country, he reached the Moorish capital, recruiting on the way two more Englishmen from a town near the coast.

– Triumph of Daring –

Before long there were thus six Englishmen in Fez, and they were quickly successful in gaining the approbation and attention of Mulai El Hafid. The whole story is one of enthralling interest, and when the time comes for it to be told in full it will add another page to the vast record of daring private enterprise by Englishmen. With this, however, we are not so much concerned as with the probable results of the action of the party concerned. As a matter of fact, it almost seems as though they may afford the solution of more than one difficult problem. Where national interference in Moroccan affairs was impossible, this private and unofficial intervention may have the result of laying the foundations of a strong, self-governing Morocco. France, it is fairly safe to say, will welcome an easy way out of what is daily becoming a more difficult situation. The less trouble Morocco gives her the better will her people be pleased. Then again, there is the question of the opening up of the country – undoubtedly a rich one if properly developed – to European trade.

"Swindon Doctor in Fez." *Swindon Advertiser and North Wilts Chronicle* (England), 5 May 1911, p. 10.

SWINDON DOCTOR IN FEZ

———

ANXIETY FOR HIS SAFETY.

In view of the alarming disturbances in Morocco and the precarious situation in Fes some anxiety is felt in Swindon for the safety of Dr. Verdun,[275] the private physician to the Sultan. Dr. Verdon, who is the son of the late Sir George Verdon, qualified at St. Thomas' Hospital, London, and came to Swindon some 18 years ago to take up an appointment on the Medical Fund Staff, serving under the late Dr. G. M. Swinhoe, Dr. Rodway Swinhoe's father. He remained in the town about a year, and subsequently proceeded to Morocco, where he became private medical advisor to Abdul Aziz, and later to the new Sultan – Hafid. A portrait of Dr. Verdon, his wife (who is an Irish lady), and two children appeared a few days ago in one of the London illustrated papers.

There are many British subjects in Fez. Mr. McLeod has been a resident in Fes for the past twenty years. With him are his wife, child and sister-in-law. They all live at the British Consulate, one of the finest houses in the capital, with the beautiful walled gardens typical of Morocco.

Another British subject who is almost certain be in Fez at the present juncture is Mr. Wm. Redman, the Sultan's English interpreter. He was born of British parents at Mazagan, and speaks the Moorish dialect as a native. He and Mr. Charles

———

[275] Dr. Egbert Sumner Verdun (c. 1867 – 1931).

Beadle were the only two Europeans in Fez during the 1908 revolution, and were present at the arrival of Muley Hafid.

Reviews of *The City of Shadows*

"Moorish Revolution." *The Guardian Journal* (Nottingham, England), 7 March 1911, p. 15.

"The City of Shadows," by Charles Beadle, is an exciting story of love and adventure, its hero being an Englishman, Paul Towers, who in a reckless mood is induced to join a German adventurer, the Baron de Bouche, anxious to gain profitable concessions from Abd-el-Kaber, who is raising the standard of revolt against Abd-el-Rahman. The reader is consequently given a very stirring and lifelike picture of the way in which Moorish revolutions are engineered, and the wild unaccountable ways that Moorish battles are fought, for he is given a detailed description of that in which Abd-el-Rahman was overthrown. The cunning and brutality of Moorish leaders and their haughty disdain for Nazarenes are clearly brought out, as well as the crude conditions of the life of the people generally. Paul and his colleague are not much better, for they fall out over a dancing girl, who ultimately gives her life for the Englishman, and intrigue against one another unscrupulously. Paul finally comes out top dog, but apparently sacrifices English interests and friends who have trusted him for the sake of a beauty of the harem. Still it makes a good story.

Croydon Chronicle and East Surrey Advertiser (England), 18 March 1911, p. 20.

In "The City of Shadows," which Messrs. Everett have published at 6s. for Mr. Charles Beadle, lovers of exciting and strenuous adventure will find their tastes admirably catered for. Paul Towers is an enterprising young Englishman who enters into a scheme with Baron de Bouche to establish a kind of Eldorado in the Sahara by assisting Abd-el-Kader to displace his half-brother, Abd-el-Rahman, from the Sultanate of Morocco, and, incidentally, to make the predatory Baron Khedive of Sus. After a time, however, Towers, from being the friend and fellow-conspirator of the Baron, becomes his enemy, and much that is exciting and fascinating in the way of adventure is the result. Mr. Beadle reveals a striking knowledge of Eastern manners and customs, and he paints the cruelty and pitilessness of the Eastern character in vivid and graphic colors. The story comes to a very appropriate end when Towers rides away from Fez with his Moorish child wife.

Daily Mirror (London), 7 April 1911, p. 7.

There is a strong thread of narrative, strung pretty thickly with the beads of stirring event; there is effective character-drawing, and there is a perfume of the hot southeast in which its scenes are laid, in "The City of Shadows." It is a story of the sort of thing which is still possible and might at any moment happen in the fierce and fluid politics of North Africa – reversals of fortune as sudden and complete as any in the "Arabian Nights," upsetting of dynasties, amazing *coups* of diplomacy and arms. Mr. Beadle obviously knows the country, and has the gift of imparting the spirit and savor of the queer things he has seen and the yet queerer people he has met.

The Globe (London), 7 April 1911, p. 6.

The sense adventure is so strong in this story of the East that it will probably seize hold of most readers, and forbid them to. question what is unreal and unsatisfactory in the plot. The hero is an Englishman, and the villain a German Baron—which, to begin with, offers the fairest promise! A city is to be built in the Sahara for the benefit the half-brother of the Sultan of Morocco—and the Germans; and Captain Towers agrees help the Baron to this end. But he finds out that wily one's real intentions, and forthwith begins a series of exciting events, full of adventurous exploits that shortly set Europe ringing with the fame of the gallant soldier. Love, too, enters m the story, which, with its Oriental setting, its picturesque background, is well worth reading. The author shows acquaintance with Moorish customs and people and scenery—of all of which he writes in a fascinating way.

The Bookseller (London), 14 April 1911, p. 11.

Those who like the East, more or less colored for pictorial purposes, will find this Moroccan romance very good reading. Local color is plentifully splashed through its pages, and there are abundantly vivid scenes descriptive of Moorish and Arab life that are perhaps none the less alluring in that they seem to be a trifle exaggerated. However, Mr. Beadle can tell a good and thrilling story, and at least his setting is very effective. Paul Towers, newly returned from a dangerous political mission only to find the girl on whom his faith was pinned married to another, comes out to Morocco to heal his wound. He is born for adventures, and meets with one the very first night of his arrival in the queer old Moorish city. He falls in on this occasion with a mysterious Baron de Bouche, subsequently joins forces with him, and plots to dethrone the Sultan. This makes a promising basis for an exciting story, and the reader will find that promise more than amply fulfilled. Paul's adventures are amazing. There is some fresh excitement on almost every page, treachery is rampant, Paul's coolness and courage and resource are limitless, and withal he manages to do a considerable amount of lovemaking. It is a decidedly lively and effective tale of its kind, and a change from the ordinary story of adventure.

"A Story of Morocco." *Evening Express* (Liverpool), 20 April
1911, p. 3.

A Story of Morocco.

The hero of "The City of Shadows," by Charles Beadle, is an
Englishman, and the villain a German Baron. A city is to be
built in the Sahara for the benefit of the half-brother of the
Sultan of Morocco – and the Germans; and Captain Towers
agrees to help the Baron to this end. But he finds out that wily
ones real intentions, and forthwith begins a series of exciting
events, full of adventurous exploits that shortly set Europe
ringing with the fame of the gallant soldier. Love, too, enters
into the story, which, with its Oriental setting, it's picturesque
background, is well worth reading.

The Academy and Literature, 6 May 1911, pp. 555-556.

Mr. Charles Beadle has written a well-constructed and highly readable tale of rebellion and political intrigue in Morocco. The hero, Paul Towers, joins a Baron de Bouche, of uncertain nationality, in a scheme to supply the Pretender with arms and ammunition and money in return for concessions of land in the South, where the Baron dreams of making himself a monarch on his own account. The arms are landed by an American yacht in the charge of some typical novelistic specimens of the "yew"-ing, "guess"-ing, and "anyway"-ing Yankee. The fortunes of the Pretender are neatly woven in with those of the individual characters. There is plenty of vivid description, including a forcible sketch of a Moroccan prison, into which Paul is thrown by the machinations of the Baron, who proves rather a tough customer when Paul has the misfortune to quarrel with him. Paul meanwhile has fallen in love with a Moorish girl, the occasion of several pretty scenes, and in the end he rides off with her, snapping his fingers at ambition. The Moors are all well done, particularly the Pretender, and a certain handyman of Paul's, who talks a weird and slangy English, and is altogether quite amusing. We feel compelled to utter a word of protest against the portrait of the Moorish girl on the cover of the book; despite a properly Oriental background, it contains rather too much suggestion of a prize costume at a servants' fancy-dress ball.

"A Moorish Romance." *Sheffield Daily Telegraph* (Yorkshire, England), 25 May 1911, p. 3.

A Moorish Romance.

Fez is just now the amphitheater of warlike operations in Morocco, and accordingly attracts the attention of the reading public. Those who wish to know more about the "inside life" of the passionate, strife-loving Moors would do well to purchase a copy of "The City of Shadows," by Charles Beadle (Everett, 6s.). This is an absorbing novel, in which a handsome Englishman is the hero of many adventures during a protracted sojourn in Moorish towns. Paul Towers has the most marvelous escapes from fire and sword, not forgetting the dagger of the secret assassin, and more than once owes his life to the infatuation he has inspired in the heart of the sensuous houri of the East. Apart from their passionate love episodes, the book abounds with descriptions and situations which are specially instructive at a moment when the country is in the forefront of international affairs which may have a far-reaching effect.

The Queenslander (Brisbane, Australia), 3 June 1911, p. 20.

A tale of Morocco, in which Paul Towers, who has been a soldier, a diplomat, and a wanderer, takes service under a German secret service agent against the French in Northern Africa. It is a story full of adventure and very cleverly done indeed.

"New Books," *The Age* (Melbourne, Australia), 10 June 1911, p. 3.

A well-woven story, following the course of a successful revolution in Morocco, gives an admirable picture of that strange land. The central figure is a young Englishman, who, in return for promised trading concessions, joins the services of the claimant Sultan, and aids him with military instruction and advice. The story is full of adventure and intrigue, and emphasis is placed on the religious fidelity of the Moors, their stoicism in times of trouble, their inbred barbarity, and their weakness in concerted warfare. Several love incidents occur between the Englishman and native girls, and they afford opportunity for an occasional glimpse into the position of Moorish women. Mr. Beadle has chosen ordinary human characters, with ordinary imperfections, and thus the story is the more artistic. Yet it lacks grip, and is not always consistent.

The Australian Town and Country Journal (Sydney), 14 June 1911, p. 55.

"The City of Shadows," by Charles Beadle, is an absorbing story of an Englishman's adventures among the Moors. Paul Towers has some exciting times, but weathers every storm. One of the cleverest phases of the book is the description of the characters he meets, one Rabbits, otherwise Ana Mohammed Rabat ben Bussulham, being an extraordinary product of the association of the English with the Moors.

"Morocco Bound," by Charles Lowe. *London Daily Chronicle*, 21 July 1911, p. 6.

Morocco Bound

Mr. Charles Beadle's book, "The City of Shadows," transports the reader to another distressful country of Africa – Morocco – and another masterful Englishman, who at the moment when he is on the high road to political fortune, to become, as it were, "the Cromer of Morocco," surrenders all for love, the love of a Moorish maiden with Titian hair. It is a story full of stirring adventure, plot and intrigue, civil warfare, barbarous cruelty, and hairbreadth escapes. Both the dark and the gorgeous sides of Moroccan life are painted in full color. Between scenes of lurid tragedy are idyllic passages of love, and comic relief is supplied in the person of an irrepressible Arab attendant, a sort of Oriental Sam Weller.[276]

---

[276] Sam Weller: a character from Charles Dickens' novel, *The Pickwick Papers*, who becomes the servant of the protagonist, Mr. Pickwick. Weller is known for his witty, unique manner of speech, just like Rabat / Rabbit in *The City of Shadows*.

Reviews of Beadle's Novels

The City of Shadows (1911):

— *The Times* (London).

— *Manchester Courier*.

— *Daily Mirror* (London), 7 April 1911, p. 7.

— "Moorish Revolution." *The Guardian Journal* (Nottingham), 7 March 1911, p. 15.

— *Westminster Gazette* (London), 11 March 1911, p. 1.

— *Croydon Chronicle and East Surrey Advertiser* (London), 18 March 1911, p. 20.

— *The Globe* (London), 7 April 1911, p. 6.

— *The Bookseller* (London), 14 April 1911, p. 11.

— "A Story of Morocco." *Evening Express* (Liverpool), 20 April 1911, p. 3. (Copied verbatim from the *London Globe*.)

— *The Academy and Literature* (London), 6 May 1911, pp. 555-556.

— "A Moorish Romance." *Sheffield Daily Telegraph* (Yorkshire, England), 25 May 1911, p. 3.

— *The Queenslander* (Brisbane, Australia), 3 June 1911, p. 20.

— "New Books," *The Age* (Melbourne, Australia), 10 June 1911, p. 3.

— *The Australian Town and Country Journal* (Sydney), 14 June 1911, p. 55.

— "Morocco Bound," by Charles Lowe. *London Daily Chronicle*, 21 July 1911, p. 6.

A Whiteman's Burden (1912):

— *The Athenaeum: Journal of Literature, Science, the Fine Arts, Music and the Drama* (London), 26 October 1912, p. 477.

— *The Scotsman* (Midlothian, Scotland), 4 November 1912, p. 2.

— *The Review of Reviews* (London), 1912, vol. 46, p. 696.

A Passionate Pilgrimage (1915):

— *Freeman's Journal* (Dublin), 2 October 1915, p. 8.

— *The Devon and Exeter Gazette*, 2 November 1915, p. 6.

— "Echoes from Everywhere: What Men and Women are Talking of." *Liverpool Echo*, 11 November 1915, p. 4. (A list of quotations from various books, including three from *A Passionate Pilgrimage*.)

Witch-Doctors (1922):

— *The Scotsman* (Midlothian, Scotland), 13 July 1922, p. 2.

— *The Times* (London), 28 July 1922, p. 13.

— *Punch* (London), 16 August, 1922, p. 168.

— "An American God." *Westminster Gazette* (London), 29 August 1922, p. 12.

— *The Province* (Vancouver), 30 August 1922, p. 6.

— *The Kingston Whig-Standard* (Kingston, Ontario), 2 September 1922, p. 4.

— *Calgary Herald* (Calgary, Alberta), 2 September 1922, p. 2.

— *The Topeka State Journal* (Topeka, Kansas), 9 September 1922, p. 8.

— *The News Journal* (Wilmington, Delaware), 9 September 1922, p. 8.

— *The Kansas City Star* (Kansas City, Missouri), 9 September 1922, p. 6.

— *Evening Public Ledger* (Philadelphia), 12 September 1922,
   p. 18.

— *Liverpool Post and Mercury*, 13 September 1922, p. 9.

— *New York Herald*, 17 September 1922, p. 19.

— *Buffalo Morning Express and Illustrated Buffalo Express* (Buffalo, New
   York), 17 September 1922, section 7, p. 4.

— "Fiction Snapshots," *New York Times Book Review and Magazine*, 17
   September 1922, p. 7.

— *Buffalo Courier* (Buffalo, New York), 24 September 1922, p. 15.

— *New York Tribune*, 24 September 1922, section 5, p. 7.

— "Charles Beadle Tells Something about Himself." *Deseret News*
   (Salt Lake City), 30 September 1922, section 5, p. 3.

— *Detroit Free Press*, 15 October 1922, p. 12.

— *Daily Arkansas Gazette* (Little Rock, Arkansas), 15 October 1922, p. 4.

— *Hartford Courant*, 15 October 1922, p. 13.

— *Democrat and Chronicle Rochester* (Rochester, New York), 15 October
   1922, unpaginated, section B.

— "The Witch Doctors." *Oakland Tribune* 15 October 1922, section S, p. 8.

— *The Chattanooga News*, 28 October 1922, p. 8.

— *Omaha Daily Bee*, 5 November 1922, p. 8.

— *The Buffalo Times*, 26 November 1922, p. 45.

The Blue Rib: A Romance of the Riviera (1927):

— *Aberdeen Press and Journal*, 21 April 1927, p. 3.

— *Montrose Standard* (Angus, Scotland), 22 April 1927, p. 6.

— *Birmingham Post* (West Midlands, England).

— *The Observer* (London), 15 May 1927, p. 8.

— *Sheffield Daily Telegraph* (Yorkshire, England), 11 June 1927, p. 10.

The Esquimau of Montparnasse (1928):

— *Sheffield Independent* (Yorkshire, England), 12 November 1928, p. 3.

— *Birmingham Daily Gazette* (Warwickshire), 22 November 1928, p. 3.

— *Northern Whig* (Antrim, Northern Ireland), 24 November 1928, p. 11.

Expatriates at Large (1930):

— *Argus-Leader* (Sioux Falls, South Dakota), 9 March 1930, p. 14.

— *Saturday Review of Literature*, April 1930).

— *Buffalo Times* (Buffalo, New York), 6 April 1930, p. 6-B.

— *Buffalo Evening News* (Buffalo, New York), 19 April 1930, p. 4.

— *Kansas City Star*, 19 April 1930, p. 8.

— *San Francisco Examiner*, 20 April 1930, p. 10 E.

— *Boston Globe*, 26 April 1930, p. 13.

— *Sioux City Journal* (Sioux City, Iowa), 18 May 1930, unpaginated. Features a photo of Beadle standing in profile.

— *The Minneapolis Star*, 3 June 1930, p. 15.

— *Birmingham News*, 8 June 1930, p. 4.

— *The Gazette* (Cedar Rapids, Iowa), 22 June 1930, p. 5 A.

— *New York Times Saturday Review of Books and Art*, 22 June 1930, p. 9.

— *St. Louis Post-Dispatch* (St. Louis, Missouri), 2 July 1930, p. 3 C.

— *Atlanta Constitution*, 3 August 1930, p. 8.

— *Detroit Free Press*, 17 August 1930, part four, p. 4.

— *Los Angeles Evening Post-Record*, 19 August 1930, p. 2.

— *Brooklyn Daily Eagle*, 10 September 1930, p. 18.

— *Book Review Digest*, 1931, volume 26, p. 62.

The White Gambit (1933):

— *The Daily Times-News* (Burlington, North Carolina), 10 June 1933, p. 2.

Artist Quarter: Reminiscences of Montmartre and Montparnasse in the First Two Decades of the Twentieth Century (1941):

— *The Observer* (London), 13 July 1941, p. 3.

— *Birmingham Post* (Birmingham, West Midlands, England), 22 July 1941, p. 2.

— *News Chronicle* (London), 1941.

— *Western Mail* (Cardiff, South Glamorgan, Wales), 5 August 1941, p. 2.

— *Time and Tide* magazine (London), 1941.

— *The Gazette* (Montreal), 29 November 1941, p. 21.

Charles Beadle Publications

Literary and genre fiction novels:

— *The City of Shadows: A Romance of Morocco*. London: Everett and Co., 1911.

— *A Whiteman's Burden*. London: Stephen Swift and Co., 1912.

— *A Passionate Pilgrimage*. London: Heath, Cranton and Ouseley: 1915.

— *Witch-Doctors*. London: Jonathan Cape, 1922. Boston: Houghton Mifflin, 1922.

— *The Blue Rib: A Romance of the Riviera*. London: Philip Allan and Co., 1927.

— *The Esquimau of Montparnasse*. London: John Hamilton, 1928. Later republished as *Expatriates at Large*. New York: Macauley Company, 1930.

— *The White Gambit*. Paris: Palais-Royal Press, 1933.

— *Dark Refuge*. Paris, Obelisk Press, 1938.

Nonfiction:

— *Artist Quarter: Reminiscences of Montmartre and Montparnasse in the First Two Decades of the Twentieth Century* (with Douglas Goldring). London: Faber and Faber, 1941. Published under the pseudonym "Charles Douglas." Later republished as *Artist Quarter: Modigliani, Montmartre and Montparnasse*. London: Pallas Athene Arts, 2018.

Short works of fiction and nonfiction in journals and periodicals:

— "Our Trip Down the Zambezi" (nonfiction). *The Wide World Magazine: An Illustrated Monthly of True Narrative, Adventure, Travel, Customs and Sport*, May 1907.

— "A Talk with the New Sultan of Morocco" (nonfiction). *Pall Mall Magazine*, October 1908.

— "What Has Happened to Muley Hafid: The Story of the Inevitable Counter-stroke" (nonfiction). *The Sphere: An Illustrated Newspaper for the Home*, 3 July 1909.

— "Two Close Calls" (nonfiction). *The Captain: A Magazine for Boys and "old Boys,"* June 1910.

— "My Narrow Escape From a Lioness." *The Brooklyn Daily Eagle*, "Junior Eagle" section (nonfiction), 7 August 1910.

— "In the Heart of the Kopje. A Story of the Mashonaland Rebellion." *The Wide World Magazine* (nonfiction), June 1912.

— "The Triumph of Tony." *Windsor Magazine*, July 1912.

— "The Better Man." *The London Magazine*, March 1913.

— "Romance for Sylvia." *Cassell's Magazine of Fiction*, March 1913.

— "A Decade of Christmas Dinners." *The Badminton Magazine of Sports and Pastimes* (nonfiction), December 1914.

— "A Pinch of Fever." *The Badminton Magazine*, June 1915.

— "An African Love Song." *The International*, October 1917. This piece appears to be a translation into English of a traditional African poem. (The same issue of the *International* features a lead story by Aleister Crowley titled "Cocaine.")

— "NQO," *The International*. December 1917.

— "The Palm Tree and the Window." Originally slated to appear in the March 1918 *International*. (In the February issue, under the feature "Jugging the March Hare," Aleister Crowley remarked: "Mr. Charles Beadle brought out his Eastern comedy, "The Palm Tree and the Window.") However the story never made it into print.

— "A Doctor of Men. *The International*. April 1918. (In the March issue, under the title "April Showers of Amusement," Crowley writes: "Charles Beadle contributes a delightful sketch of life in the Latin Quarter of Paris with its curious mixture of religious fervor and debauchery."

— "The Christman." *Adventure*, 18 May 1918.

— "The Autocrat." *Everybody's*, June 1918.

— "The Idol of 'It.'" *Adventure*, 3 July 1918.

— "John O'Damn." *Adventure*, 3 August 1918.

— "The Double Scoop." *Adventure*, 18 August 1918.

— "The Cave." *Adventure*, 3 October 1918.

— "The Winged Avenger." *Adventure*, 18 October 1918.

— "The Black Lure." *Adventure*, 18 November 1918.

— A story in *The International*. December 1918. (In the November issue, in a feature titled "The Editor Boosts the Next Number, Aleister Crowley writes: "A story of African magic by Charles

Beadle is really better than any of Kipling's African tales. That's going some, but it is true."

— "Rabbit: Philosopher" (novelette). *Adventure*, 18 January 1919.

— "Witch-Doctors" (novella). *Adventure*, 18 March 1919 (part one); 3 April 1919 (part two); 18 April 1919 (part three); 3 May 1919 (part four).

— "Uncle." *Ainslee's*, April 1919.

— "The Breaker of Idols." *Ainslee's*, May 1919.

— "Red Infidel" (novelette). *Adventure*, 18 May 1919.

— "Through Rabat's Eyes" (novella). *Argosy*, 2 August (part one); 9 August (part two); 16 August 1919 (part three).

— "The Tree of Life" (novella). *Adventure*, 3 August 1919.

— "The White Frog." *Adventure*, 18 August 1919.

— "Captain Tristtam's Miracle." *Adventure*, 18 October 1919.

— "The Inner Hero." *Romance*, November 1919.

— "The Brothers." *Romance*, December 1919.

— "The Woman Courageous." *Ainslee's*, January 1920.

— "The Alabaster Goddess." *Adventure*, 3 January 1920.

— "Technique." *The Blue Magazine*), February 1920.

— "The Spell." *Adventure*, 18 February 1920.

— Untitled. *The Editor: The Journal of Information for Literary Workers* (nonfiction contribution to the forum "Contemporary Writers and Their Work." A discussion of Beadle's writing process), 25 February 1920.

— "An African Love Song." *Coterie* No. 4, 1920. (Reprinted from *The International*, October 1917.) The *Coterie* journal, a quarterly of art, prose, and poetry, boasted an impressive editorial board, including Conrad Aiken, T. S. Eliot, Richard Aldington, and Aldous Huxley. This particular issue features a poem by Douglas Goldring, who would later coauthor the book *Artist Quarter* with Beadle. It also hosts work by several of these contributing editors, poetry by Amy Lowell, and drawings by Zadkine and André Derain.

— "The Singing Monkey" (novella). *Adventure*, 3 March 1920.

— "The Picture." *The Blue Magazine*, June 1920.

— "The King's Sword." *Adventure*, 3 August 1920.

— "The McIntosh" (novella). *Adventure*, 3 October 1920.

— "The Bowl of Alabaster." *Adventure*, 18 September 1920. (A sequel to "Alabaster Goddess.")

— "The City of Baal." *Adventure*, 18 January 1921.

— "Buried Gods," (novella). *Adventure*, 3 September 1921.

— "The Land of Ophir" (3-part serial). *Adventure*, 10, 20, 30 March 1922.

— "Gifts of Diamonds." *Adventure*, 20 June 1922.

— "The Lost Cure" (novella). *Adventure*, 30 January 1923.

— "Sparklers and the Rascals" (novella). *Top-Notch Magazine*, 1 March 1923.

— "The Ghost of Fat Lung." *Argosy Allstory Weekly*, 4 August 1923.

— "Toll of the Jungle." *Tip Top Stories of Adventure and Mystery*, January 1924.

— "The Alabaster Goddess." *The Regent Magazine*, June 1924. (Reprinted from *Adventure*, 3 January 1920 or 1921.)

— "The Philanthropist" (novella). *Short Stories*. 10 June 1924.

— "White Medicine." *Short Stories*, 10 August 1924.

— "The Blond Spiders" (novella). *Adventure*, 20 December 1924.

— "The Wild Man." *Short Stories*, 25 February 1925.

— "White Magic." *The Frontier*, March 1925.

— "Romance," *Adventure*, 20 April 1925.

— "The Mark of the Leopard." *Short Stories*, 10 May 1926.

— "Hashish," "Voyage," and "Small Body." Bob Brown. *Readies for Bob Brown's Machine*. (Cagnes-sur-Mer: Roving Eye Press, 1931), p. 105.

— "Black Velvet." *This Quarter*. March 1932.

— "The Idol." *Short Stories*, 10 October 1933.

— "Mr. Burnjack's Crime." *The 20-Story Magazine*, January 1935.

— "Magic Head." *Short Stories*, 25 October 1938.

— "The King of Many Voices." *Short Stories*, 10 November 1939.

— "The Explorer's Graveyard." *Short Stories*, 25 April 1941.

— "The Baboon's Paw." *Short Stories*, 10 December 1945.

— "Ant Island." *Short Stories*, 10 October 1946.

— "Lost Heritage." *Short Stories*, 25 December 1946.

— "Nameless Spy." *Short Stories*, 10 June 1947.

Posthumously reprinted stories and collections:

— *The City of Baal*. Introduction by John Locke. Castroville, CA: Off-Trail Publications, 2007.

— *The Land of Ophir*. Introduction by John Locke. Castroville, CA: Off-Trail Publications, 2012.

— *The Blond Spiders* (e-book). Good Press, 2020.

— *The Double Scoop* (e-book). DigiCat, 2022.

Commentary in *Adventure*'s "The Camp-Fire" column:

— 3 July 1918. A detailed five-paragraph autobiographical sketch, from which we can draw various threads from Beadle's early life, including childhood trips into Asia and various titles of employment later in Africa. (The letter was composed circa May 1918. See John Locke's "Introduction" to *The City of Baal*, p. 13.)

— 18 January 1920: A commentary on the walled cities of Zululand (with a passing reference to Sir Richard Burton).

— 3 October 1920. Describes the events that inspired "The McIntosh."

— 18 January 1921. Some remarks about "The City of Baal."

— 20 June 1922. Provides biographical background to "Gifts of Diamonds."

Commentary in *Adventure*'s "Ask Adventure" column:

— "Diseases of East Central Africa." 18 September 1918.

— "The Rhodesian Mounted Police." 18 September 1919.

Letter to *Romance* magazine's "Meeting-Place" forum:

— January 1920. Beadle remarks that "Personally I have a theory that a writer should only use material which he has more or less actually lived. Anyway, I work on that principle." And he adds: "That is all writing is (to me); a mania to tell other folk what I see in my walks abroad."

Posthumous Reviews and Commentaries

"*Dark Refuge* appears in print for the first time since its original publication in 1938, presenting a world traveler's experiences with bohemian life in Paris in a novel that also serves (thanks to Rob Couteau) as a biography of Beadle's life. Extensive annotated references link Beadle's experiences to his fictional representations, offering a literary backdrop for understanding both the atmosphere and progression of his fiction and its roots in reality. Readers should be prepared for a sexual romp that is ribald, explicit, and thoroughly steeped in Beadle's personal experiences of the times….Whether exploring drug experiments and the revelations that follow them or descending into the sordid and colorful world of bohemian Paris, Beadle flavors all of his impressions with the same attention to flowery detail that makes his writing so timeless…. Pair this with the extensive notes and annotated references Couteau injects to not just explain but expand the story, for a sense of the unique literary and historical importance of this reappearance of Beadle's rare classic, which has been out of print for far too long. Libraries seeking literary representations of the marriage between fiction and nonfiction will find *Dark Refuge* a fine example. The 200+ annotated notes come from previously unpublished letters and documents, combining with photos and historical reviews to represent a hallmark of not only literary fiction, but biographical research. *Dark Refuge* deserves a place in any library strong in works of literature that represent the intersection between fictional devices and biographical inspection, whether or not there is prior knowledge of or interest in Beadle's works and importance." – **Diane Donovan, Senior editor,** *Midwest Book Review*, **November 2022.**

"There is no doubt in my mind that *Dark Refuge* deserved to be reprinted, especially in its present form which reinforces the text with numerous annotations, a long afterword which charts Beadle's life and activities, photographs, a bibliography, and additional material. Rob Couteau, who is largely responsible for discovering so much about Beadle and his publications, deserves our thanks for all his hard work." – **"Three Curious Interwar Novels," by Jim Burns,** *The Penniless Press Online*, **October 2023**.

"This new publication of *Dark Refuge* is a helpful addition for all those interested in the adventurous life of bohemian author Charles Beadle ... His book *Artist Quarter* is the source of both fictional and nonfictional stories about Modigliani still prevalent today. In this book expertly edited, annotated, and commented upon by Couteau and Sawyer-Lauçanno, we gain greater insight into Beadle's life and the origins of his novel, *Dark Refuge*, that thankfully is once more available to the public." – **Dr. Henri Colt, Emeritus Professor of Medicine at the University of California and author of** *Becoming Modigliani*, **January 2024**.

"*A Passionate Pilgrimage* was first published in 1915, when it earned the acclaim of being one of ten books blacklisted for years by Britain's Circulating Libraries Association. Modern readers may be puzzled by this fact when they read this novel; but its descriptions of free-ranging sensual encounters between the protagonist and a host of consenting women made it a scandalous piece at the turn of the century. Why reissue *A Passionate Pilgrimage* now? The introductory notes (which are extensive and vital to understanding the novel's continuing importance) state that the novel: 'provides a variety of clues about Beadle's early life.' In so doing, it reveals the essence of social and psychological transformation, toeing the line between autobiography and a fictional discourse containing many topics vital to understanding not just these times, but modern morals and values. Its subjects and considerations make for thoroughly engrossing reading, presented in a way that builds the character's focus, emphasizes his differences, and ultimately creates a captivating tale of transformation and insight. Libraries that choose *A Passionate Pilgrimage* will find it highly recommendable to students of literature; teachers seeking novels that hold lively debates about not just banned literature, but banned ideas; and book clubs that will find *A Passionate Pilgrimage* thoroughly thought provoking." – **Diane Donovan, Senior editor,** *Midwest Book Review*, **March 2025**.

"*A Whiteman's Burden* was first published in 1912, when African sleeping sickness raged through the sites of Charles Beadle's various African expeditions. The fictional representation of this milieu and his experiences in *A Whiteman's Burden* creates a thought-provoking story set in 1904-06, the time frame of Beadle's own journey. It brings to life the contrasts between and dilemmas of the white man's expeditions into deepest, darkest Africa.

Here, a deadly illness has ravaged the native population and is now making headway among colonists who had believed themselves immune to the disease. Issues of survival and racial perceptions of life and death rage alongside the illness, adding existential strength and depth to a tale of adventure, exploration, and angst.

An unexpected focus on points of co-mingling, contrasting viewpoints, shared experiences that bring to light different ways of confronting life and death, and the disparate experiences and insights of men and women are transmitted through characters whose perceptions are oftentimes surprising. Embedded within these encounters are social and political reflections which emerge from privilege and African native encounters alike.... By including the reflections and observations of women as well as men, Beadle expands the potential of understanding this environment in a valuable manner....

Libraries seeking literary works about turn-of-the-century Africa and the colonists and natives whose lives intersected around illness and struggle will find *A Whiteman's Burden* exceptional. This stems from both its setting and its juxtaposition of characters buffeted as much by their own prejudices and perspectives as by an illness which feels unconquerable.

Replete with philosophical, cultural, moral, and historical insights, *A Whiteman's Burden* is highly recommended not just for leisure readers seeking an adventure story of African exploration, but to book clubs interested in thought-provoking existential examinations that can provoke lively debates and discussions about hazardous worlds and equally deadly prejudices." – **Diane Donovan, Senior editor,** *Midwest Book Review*, **August 2025.**

"*The City of Shadows: A Romance of Morocco* returns to print Charles Beadle's first novel (originally published in 1911), which vividly portrays the 1908 Battle of Marrakech that led to the defeat of Morocco's Sultan Aziz. The story is embedded in real history that brings the times, place, and politics to life with characters such as adventurer Paul, who falls in love with Moroccan woman Zahra.

These characters and elements will attract readers who may hold little prior familiarity with the politics of Moroccan culture, but who will find plenty of insights and attractions woven into the Moroccan backdrop and events.

The first thing to note about Charles Beadle's style is the inclusion of local color and dialect. This may prove somewhat challenging to read, but creates atmosphere and authenticity....

Editor Rob Couteau provides numerous footnotes that reference background history. This also is unusual for a novel, but proves perfect as a reference for historical fiction readers interested in the background supporting these events.

Between romance and sharpshooters to urban conflict and confusion, Beadle brings to life the people, purposes, and politics of these times in a way that invites all kinds of readers to appreciate the people and movements of early Morocco.

As Paul risks death for courting Zahra and social and religious rules are broken, the characters must consider the impact of their choices in a moving story that traverses hearts, minds, and political traditions. The result is a historical novel rich in Moroccan culture and revealing in its exploration of a forbidden love against the backdrop of change.

Librarians and readers looking for novels of North African history that bring these times alive through characters that make important decisions that affect the world around them will relish the opportunity to see Morocco through the eyes of a man and woman who risk much to achieve their vision of happiness.

The City of Shadows's blend of high adventure, risk-taking, and immersion in Moroccan affairs is cemented by characters whose lives and concerns are realistic and thoroughly engrossing." – **Diane Donovan, Senior editor,** *Midwest Book Review*, **February 2026.**

ALSO BY ROB COUTEAU

Fiction:

Doctor Pluss
Afterword by Jim Feast

Essays and Interviews:

Collected Couteau

More Collected Couteau
Introduction by James Dempsey

*Portraits from the Revolution: Interviews with the
Protestors from Occupy Wall Street*

Biography:

*A Blind Man Crazy for Color. A Tribute to Leon Angély: Illustrated by
Picasso's Model and Muse, Sylvette David*

Poetry:

The Sleeping Mermaid
Introduction by Christopher Sawyer-Lauçanno

Selected Poems
Introduction by Ed Foster

Memoir:

Intimate Souvenirs
Introduction by Robert Roper